I0761061

SILVER BUCK
AND THE
APACHES

LYNN LUICK

ISBN: 978-1-998784-65-3 (Paperback)
978-1-998784-66-0 (Hardback)

BookSide Press
877-741-8091
www.booksidepress.com
orders@booksidepress.com

Contents

1

It was a nice, warm late-spring day. The leaves had just started to bud. The morning frost had disappeared into the soft green grass of the mountains.

It had been almost three years since I had been up here. Alongside me was my young son Buck Junior. My wife, Red Bird had insisted on that name. We were on a little trip to see our silver mine. His ma had made it clear that we men should get out from underfoot of the women during spring cleaning. She had taken to some of the white man's ways after nine years. She had my ma and little Song Bird—she was five now—to help her in our house and in Ma and Pa's house.

Little Buck said, "Pa, we going to see Uncle Foster, and Uncle Jim and Tim. They make me laugh. They're real funny."

Buck said, "Yeah, they're pretty funny. It's been almost six months since they've been to town. It will be good to see them."

I got off Blacky and Little Buck off his horse, Windy. He said Windy ran as fast as the wind, as we walked up to the mine. It was a ways off, but it was a nice day for walking. The blue skies were above our heads, and the green grass below our feet. What a wonderful time with my son walking beside me. It was surprising how at age eight he was almost four and a half feet tall and smart as a whip.

The mining camp was coming into view. The men are milling around. Then Little Buck spotted him—Foster, big as life itself. Foster's hands were on his hips, and he had a big grin on his face.

"Hi there, boys. What you'se doing up this way? I was wonderin' if you'se forgot about this old buzzard. You'se keepin' your'se old man out of trouble, little Silver?"

"Yes, sir, Grandfather taught me well about the forest and what to watch for to stay out of trouble."

"Never forget what Dancing Bear teach you'se for he is wise in the forest."

"From the bank statements, I thought everything was under control."

"It is, it is, just get tired of laughtin' at those two crazy men you'se hired and then made partners, Tim and Jim."

"Oh, that's it."

Thinking about Tim and Jim took me back to how men and one woman died for this mine, starting with Great-Grandfather Jeb. He discovered it, and Foster and I rediscovered it after his death. How my life had changed since coming from Texas. I had my loving wife and two wonderful children that I would give my life for.

"Where are you'se, Buck?" Foster said.

"Just rememberin' how we got this mine and that hard winter we spent in that cave and nearly starved to death."

"Yeah, those were the days. Nowadays it's downright civilized around here'se."

"Pa, can I go out to the mine and see Uncle Tim and Uncle Jim?"

"Go ahead, but don't get underfoot, you hear?" "Yes, sir."

Little Buck went out the door, and I turned to Foster.

"What's goin' on with the mine? I said everything looked all right with the statement 'cause I didn't want Little Buck tellin' his ma, and then she would worry."

"It's slowed down lots. I'se wanted to talk to you'se about it. The vein of silver is gettin' smaller. I'se goin' to take half the men and start diggin' to the right and the left of the main vein and hopes we'se hit another vein. If we do, it might be smaller than the main vein. I'se was waitin' for you'se to come up here's 'cause I'se didn't want a letter getting' in the wrong hands."

"That sounds reasonable."

"I'se been thinkin', Buck, we'se been friends for now on to ten years." He stopped.

"What is it, Foster?"

"I'se been thinkin', I'se was almost sixty when we'se met, so that makes me nearly seventy. Tim and Jim know'se just about everything about this here mine." He put his hand on his chin, as though he didn't want to say what he was going to say.

"Come out with it, Foster. What is it?"

"Well, I'se think it's about time I'se turn the reins over to those two funny men."

"No, Foster, you're not old to me. You're like my granddad and great-granddad all in one. I don't want to lose all that you know and mean to me."

"You'se want, I'se still be around if any trouble comes up."

"You think they're ready to take over?"

"Sure do'se. They been doin' most of the work, anyways. I'se been just sittin' around here mostly. I'se been thinkin' about a small cabin close to the ranch, where I'se can go to town when I'se want and see Red Bird and the children anytime, and go spend time with Dancing Bear and his village. Me'se and him can go huntin'."

"You sure that's what you want to do?"

"I'se do." I think there was a little tear in his eyes.

"Well then, we'll have to build you a house on the ranch. If you'll stay until Jim and Tim can get men finished with your house and you can tell them your plans for the mine. Then it's done."

"Sure thing, Buck. You'se won't be losing a friend. I'se be around a good long time."

I went up the inside stairs to the door and stepped out onto the platform and looked out over the mining camp and the surrounding forest and mountains— such a beautiful sight. Foster had been up here nearly all his life, and this mining operation was nearly all his doing. I saw Little Buck. I was going to have to think of another name—he was becoming too big to be called little. I spotted him walking around with the men outside the mine.

"Little Buck."

He looked my way. "Yes, sir?"

"Would you go get Tim and Jim."

"They're in the mine."

"I know, go on now."

"Me, in the mine. Sure, Pa."

"Tell them to come soon as they can. Then go check on Blacky and Windy."

A few minutes later, I saw them coming out of the mine. They saw me and came running.

"What's wrong, boss? Little Buck said to hurry."

"That there boy, I tell you. I said as soon as you could. Come on in."

Foster and I sat and told them what Foster wanted to do.

"Foster, you can't leave! You're the backbone of this place," Jim said.

Then Tim said, "Who else will laugh at our jokes?"

"I'se still be around, just at the ranch. You'se know you'se two already nearly run this here mine."

Buck broke in: "Now Foster has a plan for the mine. One of you is goin' to stay here with Foster so he can show you, and the other will be goin' to town on the next wagon to hire some men and build Foster a house."

"Not too fancy," Foster said.

I gathered up Little Buck, and we rode down the mountain on Blacky and Windy.

"I've been thinking, how would you like to go by and see Dancing Bear?"

"Yes, please, Pa. Maybe we can go hunting."

"Not this time, son. We'll bring your mother and sister up here soon so they can visit with your ma's mother. Then we'll go hunting with the men of the village."

He looked disappointed, but that disappeared with the first deer he saw running across our path.

The day went well, with us watching all the small rabbits and the big moose around us. Close to the village, I told Little Buck, "You know, I think we're goin' to hunt a large buck to take to the village."

"Really, Pa?"

"Sure, I think it's time for you to put all that practice you been doing to good use."

"You mean it? It will make me feel great to take a buck to the village."

"Now be quiet, and we'll get off and go out a ways."

We tied the horses and went looking for tracks.

"You lead the way, son. I'll follow."

I followed Little Buck, and he led me through the forest, over the dead falls, and across a creek. Then he spotted some deer tracks. We came to a clearing, and he spotted it.

"Looks like a ten-pointer or more, Pa."

"Sure does. Now take good aim."

He put his rifle to his shoulder and against his cheek. I watched as he took careful aim and squeezed the trigger. The rifle boomed in the peaceful forest, and the bullet was true.

"Look, son, you got your first deer. Let's go gut it and put it cross the rump of Windy."

We got it dressed out and on the back of his horse. Little Buck was grinning from ear to ear.

"You know, that was a clean shot. Good as I could have done."

"Pa, really?"

Within an hour, we were in the village. I saw a brave go in Dancing Bear's tepee, and out he came smiling. He came up to us as we got down, and gave both of us a big hug at the same time.

"Good to see you. Been many moons."

"Good to see you, Dancing Bear. Look what Little Buck shot for you and your people. It's his first deer."

"Not little. Look how big, and now this. Have a big dinner tonight. Women, take the deer and prepare."

"Dancing Bear, can they prepare the head and antlers for travel tomorrow? It's his first deer, and I want to put it in our house next to mine."

He grabbed Little Buck in a bear hug.

"Be honor, for son of daughter. Now come, we talk."

They went off a ways and sat down, and I went and staked out the horses on a big patch of green grass. I got out an apple and cut it in half for each horse. Red Bird's mother, Running Elk, came over.

"Daughter not come."

"No, she too busy cleaning the house with my mother's and Song Bird's help."

"I know daughter, was always cleaning tepee. Little Song Bird, not seen many moons."

"We've been really busy with the ranch. I promise I'll bring them to see you in a few moons."

"Hope so, Buck Taylor, my son."

With that, she went over to see Little Buck. That night, we had a small feast in honor of Little Buck's first deer. Then we went to bed and were up early the next day. We got the horses saddled and tied Little Buck's deer's head on the back of Windy.

Dancing Bear pulled me to the side. "Buck, braves out hunting in mountains. Saw other warriors, had war paint on. Say look like Chiricahua Apache—not friend, longtime enemy. Many winters ago come to village try to kill all braves and take women and children for slaves and take horses. Stopped them—lost many good braves, but stopped them. Only four scouts for bigger party. Known led by Geronimo. Be on lookout going back to ranch."

"Thank you. You know where Foster is at the mine. Would you send one of your braves that saw them and tell Foster to be on lookout and to arm all the men in the mine and post men to watch in case of trouble?"

"Will send. Tell him to send man for us if bad trouble. Do not like Geronimo. His people are way south."

"We will go now, a lot faster, to warn everybody around town and the ranch."

We got a ways out, and then I turned to Little Buck. "Be on the lookout, son. There might be some trouble."

"What kind of trouble?"

"There are some bad Indians out here somewhere. Dancing Bear told me, but we don't know for sure where they are. I think you are old enough to know about trouble. They are not his people."

"Grandfather told me all Indians are not always friends."

We headed southwest toward town. We stopped to let the horses drink out of the cool stream and eat some nice green grass close by. We ate some jerky and then were on the trail again. I knew Blacky and Windy were tired, but I kept pushing them, with an hour break every three or four hours.

"Little Buck, I know you're tired, 'cause I am. We need to keep goin' all night. If you get too sleepy, put your arms around Windy's neck and close your eyes."

"I will, Pa."

On the second day, I took Little Buck off his horse and laid him down and let him sleep for two hours. I even dosed off, but I knew Blacky would warn me if anything got too close, and my gun and my rifle were always by my side when I was out on the trail.

I woke up because Blacky was making some noise. I was up and got Little Buck up and in the saddle. He was awake by now, and I was in the saddle, and we were on our way. I patted Blacky's neck and said, "Thanks, boy." He shook his head and kept running. Dusk was on us, but we kept going. Then off to the right, I saw three figures on horseback coming toward us.

"Little Buck, to the right. We're goin' to keep goin' fast. Keep down low. I don't know who they are."

"Right, Pa, I will."

Just then, a shot rang out in the darkness. Then another, then another. They all missed, and we kept hightailing it toward town. Blacky was fast, and Windy was just as fast. Then I remembered Foster's old cabin.

"Son, keep up. We're headin' to Foster's old cabin. When we get there, we'll take the horses in the barn. Grab your rifle and head for the cabin."

We came up to the barn; I jumped off while Blacky was still trying to stop. I threw open the door and we all went in and Little Buck jumped off and grabbed his rifle, and we headed for the cabin after I found four boxes of shells. Inside, I told Little Buck to be quiet and listen for horse's hooves or men's footsteps.

We were there about half an hour when Little Buck said, "Pa, listen, I hear horses."

"You got good ears, son."

I went to the side window but couldn't see anything in the dark. "Little Buck, you try to get some sleep."

"But, Pa, they're out there."

"I know, but I'll keep watch. They may not attack until morning. I'll wake you if things change."

He lay down with his rifle beside him, and I kept my eyes on the darkness. Every once in a while, I would go to the window on the side of the cabin. I kept on going from window to window, but nothing happened—until about midnight. I heard Blacky whinny; I looked out toward the barn and saw a figure in the little bit of moonlight that was coming through the trees.

I took a shot—not to kill, but to maybe scare away, whoever they might be. If Indians, they might only be after the horses. I wasn't about to let them have ours. Little Buck didn't move, and I was glad for he needed his rest, for I didn't know what tomorrow would bring our way. Nothing happened the rest of the night. I woke Little Buck about four thirty so we could be ready. Just some dry jerky was what was on the breakfast menu.

"Anything, Pa."

"Not much, son. We have to be ready for anything. If nothing happens in an hour or two, we'll mount up and hightail it to Durango. We'll only be two hours away.

I sat watching out the front window, and Little Buck watched out the side. Then I saw two Indians going from tree to tree, trying to hide. I saw the war paint on their faces.

"Look out over there. I see two out front here."

There was an open space between the last of the trees and the cabin.

"Here they come."

I took a shot and hit one. The other hit the ground. I put a bullet next to his head.

"There's one over here."

"Aim and shoot."

The one on my side got up and was shooting as he ran toward the cabin. The bullets came crashing through the window, shattering glass all over me. As I took aim, I heard a shot from the other side of the room, but I didn't have any time to look as another bullet came at me as I shot. His missed as mine hit him square in the chest. He didn't move.

"Pa, I think I hit him. He's not moving."

I walked over and looked and saw he was dead on the ground. "Son, never start trouble, but always be prepared to end it."

It was over in five minutes. We buried them beside the barn and then mounted up and lit out for Durango.

As we came into town, I headed for the sheriff's office. He was sitting on the front porch with his feet up on the hitching rail.

"Can I speak to you inside?"

"Sure, come on in."

"Come on in with me, son."

We got down, tied the horses, and went inside.

"What is it, Silver?" the sheriff asked.

"We were attacked this mornin' at Foster's old cabin. There were three Indians wearing war paint. I think they were scouts for a bigger party. I got two, and B. J. got the other."

The sheriff patted Little Buck on the head.

"Why would they be on the war path? Dancing Bear has always been peaceful."

"No, not Dancing Bear. We were in his village, and his hunting party had seen some Indians west of his village, and they were sure it was Geronimo."

"He's on a reservation southwest of here."

Just then, the man from the telegraph office busted in. "Sheriff, read this. It's from the army."

He took it and read it, and then he handed it to me.

Geronimo escaped,
Headed north,
Be on lookout,
Report anything. Stop.

"Keep this under your hat. Hear me, I don't want people to panic. No one hear me."

"Yes, sir," the man said and then left.

"There are some new farmers out east of here. Then your winter miners have started ranches north of here. I need to warn them."

"Why don't I help you? I'll tell my men on their ranches, and you tell the farmers to be on the lookout."

The sheriff took off east, and we headed north. I was bone tired, and BJ had to be as well.

"Pa, back there you called me BJ. Why?"

"Because you're not Little Buck anymore. You have grown up on this trip. You are becoming a man. You got your first big buck, and you had your first fight to stay alive. You handled them both well. Out here, you have to grow up fast to stay alive."

"But what is BJ?"

"I've been thinking. I'm Buck, and you are Buck Junior. I never liked that *Junior* Part, so I shortened it to BJ."

"You know, I kind of like it. How you think everyone will take to it? I expect ma and grandma want. They think of me as a little boy."

"The men at the ranch and Grandpa will be all right with it when they see the big buck's head and I tell them how you handled the battle. Ma and Grandma, you let me handle them. That might be a small battle, but I think we'll both win that one."

We rode on to the ranches and explained what had happened and to be on the lookout for trouble. I knew just about everyone and BJ showed the kids his deer head and told them of the battle. I think he added to it a little. That's the way stories go. I told them to send word if they saw anything. Then we headed to our ranch to warn them of the would be danger.

We rode hard and fast. I knew the horses and we would soon get a well-deserved rest. As we came up to the entrance to the ranch, I stopped and looked at the front gate with huge stone pillars on each side and a sign overhead that said, "Silver Buck Ranch" on each side was the brand of the ranch made with our branding irons.

"Son, before we get to the house, 'cause there's going to be turmoil, I wanted to say how proud I am of you, how you handled yourself. I heard you telling the other children at the ranches what happened. That's fine, but don't brag about killing anyone no matter how they deserved it. You understand."

"All right, Pa."

It was a short ride to the bunkhouse; Manuel was tossing out a pail of water.

"You seen Pa?"

"No, senor, I was just finishing cooking up supper. The men should be coming soon. Seem like they can smell it out on the prairie. See what I mean, here they come."

I rode out to meet them. I told BJ to go the house and to tell Ma that we were all right. "I'll be there soon."

"Pa, I need to talk to you."

"Boys, go on and eat. I'll be there soon."

Then Buck said to his Pa, "We were attacked by Indians. Geronimo escaped the reservation. We've been up for three days. We need some rest. Let the men eat and then send two out to each line camp with extra ammo and food. I better get to the house. I know BJ has already told Red Bird, and she'll be worried."

Ross said, "You go get some sleep. I know what has to be done."

"I'll tell you the whole story later."

As I walked up to the house, there was Red Bird running down the front porch steps. I got off Blacky, and Red Bird threw her arms around my neck and jumped in my arms; and before I knew it, she was kissing me all over my face. Just then, one of the hands came up and took Blacky and Windy. As he was going to the barn, I managed to tell him, between all her kisses, "Give them both some oats and a good rubdown."

"Sure thing, boss."

He waved his hand up in the air as he headed to the barn. Tired as I was, it felt good to hold Red Bird in my arms. I carried her up the steps and threw the doors open and put her down.

"I fix you something to eat."

"Manuel can do that."

"No, not now. You my man, I fix."

"Yes, ma'am."

"You go up, take a bath. Little Buck already ate and take bath. He already sleeps. Song Bird with mother. Go on, you smell."

I went up the staircase. I looked in to see that BJ was fast asleep. I went into our water closet and saw the bath was ready. I got undressed and got in. The warm water felt so good on my sore body.

"Buck, you all right."

Red Bird was shaking me.

"Yes, just tired. Haven't slept in three days."

"Lean back, I wash."

It felt so good; I just sit there, the warm water and Red Bird's hands all over my body. So good I must have fallen asleep again.

"Buck." Red Bird was shaking me.

I woke up, and there she was. Her dress fell to the floor, nothing as usual under her dress. She got in the tub with me and straddled my lap and sat down.

"I was tired, but not now."

We made love for a long while. Then Red Bird got out and dried her beautiful body. Then she got me out and dried me off. We went down to eat. When we finished eating, she said, "Buck, sleep now. When you wake, we make love again."

As I went out of the kitchen, I heard Manuel laughing. "What's wrong with him?"

"Nothing, honey."

The bed felt so good when I got in that I drifted off to sleep right away when I woke up, there was Red Bird next to me. I could see out of our large window that it was just daybreak. I didn't feel like getting up, so I pulled back the covers. She was naked as usual; the kids weren't up yet, so I felt her body. She awoke and rolled over, and we made love over and over. I loved her so very much.

Just then, there was a commotion outside our door. I jumped out of bed, covered Red Bird, got dressed, and ran to the door.

"What is it, Manuel?"

"Sheriff just left. Want you to come to town fast. There's been an attack. That's all he said."

2

I headed outside, saddled Blacky, and headed to my parents' house. The sun wasn't up yet. I knocked on their door, and Pa came out.

"What is it, son?"

"There's been an attack in town, I'm headin' that way. Make sure every man is armed to the teeth. Have Ma go to our house and stay with Red Bird and the children. Tell BJ I know he would want to go with me but I need him to protect the women and the house. I don't know when I'll be back. Have Ma reassure Red Bird that I'll be all right. I know you would go, but you need to take care of everything on the ranch."

"I will, son. Be careful. If it's Geronimo's bunch, be very careful. They're not Dancing Bear's tribe. You may not be able to reason with them, even if you do get a chance."

I took off toward town. Before I was halfway there, I met Tim.

"Silver, there's been an attack. The stagecoach was attacked. The shotgun rider was killed, and a passenger was wounded—the new schoolteacher. I'll come with you, boss."

"No, Tim, I need you to start on Foster's cabin and keep an eye on Red Bird and the children. Keep your rifle and ammo handy. I don't know what will happen, but go to town later when you need men to help on the cabin."

"Sure, Silver, I will."

I took off to town, and Tim to the ranch. The sun was just coming up. I looked around at the beautiful surroundings and thought of how this could happen in this country.

I rode down Main Street, for the town had grown, and there were streets branching off the main. People were rushing from store to store—gathering food, rifles, and ammo. I saw the stagecoach in front of the sheriff's office. He was there dispatching people in different directions. As I jumped off Blacky, he saw me.

"Good to see you, Silver. Just getting things taken care of so we can leave to check on the ranches and farms to the north and east."

"How's the teacher, was she hurt bad?"

"No, just a flesh wound in the upper part of the arm. Doc Blackburn says she'll be all right in a week or so."

"I'll be right back. I need to talk to Bill. If you need to leave, I'll catch up later. Going north, aren't you?"

"North, then east."

The sheriff had twelve men ready to ride as I went to Bill's office. Crossing the street was difficult because of all the horses, people, buggies, and wagons. They were getting ready for a possible attack on the town. Bill was at the window watching the entire goings-on in the street.

"Good to see you, Buck."

"The men are leavin'. I just needed to talk to you real fast. Tim will be coming in to get some men to build Foster's cabin on the ranch. Then I need to increase Jim and Tim's pay to one hundred dollars a month. They're takin' over operation of the mine when Foster hangs up his shovel. Send a man out to the ranch. Tell my pa to let Red Bird know we're headin' out to the farms and ranches. I don't know when I'll be back, but soon as I can. Also, send a man to the mine. Tell them to be ready for anything. Also, I need Foster here. We're headin' north. He can follow Blacky's tracks. Put Jim in charge of the mine. I'm in a hurry. We'll talk later when things quiet down."

"I understand. I'll take care of everything. I'll ride out to the ranch and check with your dad and Red Bird every few days."

When I mounted Blacky, I could see the sheriff and the men were gone. So I headed out of town to the north. By the time I caught up to them, they were at the first ranch. It was a grizzly sight. John, who was one of my winter men at the mine, was tied to the corral fence, and his body was full of arrows.

"Looks like they used him for target practice. Spread out and look for his wife and kids."

I cut him down and got a shovel off one of the men's horse and started digging a grave. I could see the men looking through all the burned-down buildings. Must have happened a few days ago because I couldn't see any smoke until I was up close.

Someone yelled out, "Silver, better make it big enough for one more. Here's the boy."

As I buried the two, the men looked through all the burned debris. Not a sign of John's wife and their fourteen-year-old daughter.

"We better camp out a ways for the night," the sheriff said.

We build some fires and put some coffee on, but the food might come later. No one had the stomach for it right now. There was talk around the campfire about the women. I could make it out while I tended to the horses and stood watch until someone relieved me at midnight,

"The Indians must have taken them prisoner."

"Maybe they escaped to the next ranch."

"Maybe they went to the fort east of here."

"That's a far piece."

We got an early start, come morning. We rode fast and hard to the next ranch. It was midday when we came into the yard. Everything seemed normal as we dismounted and started looking around. None of the buildings had been burned. The barn was empty. As we started for the house, a man came running out with a rifle.

"Who are you? What do you want?"

"I'm the sheriff of Durango. We're out making sure everyone is all right. There was an attack on the stagecoach yesterday morning, and your neighbor was killed and his boy. The womenfolk are missing."

The man lowered his rifle.

"John's dead? He was a good neighbor. Sorry for the rifle, but I'm new around here, and I haven't been to town yet. I didn't know who you were. I'm Pete. Pete Sutter."

"We're lookin' for the Indians that did both attacks. We think it's a band under Geronimo."

"Well, I guess I's lucky."

"Why's that?"

"Yesterday just before dark, about ten or more Indians attacked us, but we fought them off, me and my boys. Honey, come on out, you and the boys."

A mild looking woman and two tall boys came over to them.

"This is my wife, Jane, and my two boys, Seth and Zack."

The two boys were nearly as big as their father, and both were carrying rifles.

"We would mount up and go with you, but they took all our livestock except for that donkey over yonder."

"You said Lizzie and Carolyn were missing?" Jane said.

"Yes, ma'am."

"Get down and I'll fix you all some dinner."

"Thank you, ma'am, but we need to get after them and rescue the women before they hook up with Geronimo, or we may never see them again. What direction did they ride off?"

"They headed to the northwest. By the way, I didn't see any women with them."

I spoke up as we were riding off. "If an old man comes this way, head him off in our direction. I'm Buck Taylor."

"Sure will. Good luck."

I was thinking the women were probably left with one or two braves a ways out from the ranch. They wouldn't want them around the attack.

We were headed northwest to the next ranch when we saw some dust coming toward us from the east. We stopped to rest and water our horses at a small creek and see who might be in front of that dust.

"Sheriff, you think that might be them?" one of the men said.

"Not unless they circled around and got behind us. What do you think, Silver?"

"No, I don't think Indians would make that much dust. They would be goin' slower, and that looks like a lot more than the ten or twelve that was reported. We'll just have to wait and see."

"We need to eat anyway. By the time we eat, whoever it is should be nearby here. Let's eat, and keep your rifles handy."

We made a small fire, so as not to make a lot of smoke. By the time we had eaten, we could see it was the soldiers from the fort. They rode right up to us.

"Hello, I'm Lieutenant Mayfield. We're out looking for a group of Indians that were reported to have left the reservation last week south of here."

"I'm sheriff of Durango. I think we're looking for the same bunch. They attacked the stagecoach coming to town. They killed the man riding shotgun and wounded the new teacher. Then they attacked a ranch east of town and killed a father and his son and took the wife and daughter. Then they attacked another farm north of there but were fought off. They told us they were heading northwest."

"That sounds about right. It was reported to our commander they were heading north to the mountains in Wyoming. We're trying to catch up to them. You can head back to town now. We can handle them."

I spoke up. "The hell you say. Two of our women were taken, and a woman was wounded, and one man on the stagecoach was killed, and one of my men and his son were killed. I'm not turnin' back until those women are free."

"Who might you be?"

"I'm Buck Taylor, and I'm not hightailin' until my dead man's women are free."

"I understand the way you feel, Mr. Taylor, but we're better equipped to handle them."

With that said, the lieutenant and his men headed off to the north.

"Well, Sheriff, what do you think?"

"I think he might be right. they are better equipped to handle the Indians than we are, and the town is left unprotected as long as I'm out here, so I'm going back and let the army handle it. I can't stop any of you that want to continue."

"You remember Walters, don't you. I think if we don't go after them ourselves, we won't see them again."

"This is different. We know what Red Bird's family is like, and we like their peaceful ways. But Geronimo is bad—really bad."

"Well, boys, I'm stayin' put and wait for Foster. You all know him. He knows more about Indians than any army men do. Foster's been dealin' with them for fifty years or more. If any of you go back, I won't hold it against you. You'll still have your job, but if it was you back in that grave, wouldn't you want us to save your womenfolk?"

The sheriff took off with about five townsmen. All my men stayed put with me. There were seven in all, counting me. I was hoping Foster would catch up to us by the following day.

"You think we can handle them Indians and get the women back?"

"I know so, with Foster's help. We just need to reach it before they hook up with Geronimo. Y'all unsaddle your horses and let them get their fill of grass and water and be ready to go soon as Foster comes. And get some rest."

By the next afternoon, I was getting worried that Foster wasn't coming. Then just at dusk, I saw a small cloud of dust. As the rider got closer, I could see it was Foster, and he was riding Lagger, and he had three men from the mine.

"What kept you? I thought you may not come."

"You'se know me'se, I'se come when you'se need help, and these three wouldn't let me go without them. They'se told me'se they'se told you'se if you'se need help, just call. Then we'se got to town, and Bill told me what the sheriff said, so I'se headed to the ranch to get some fresh horses from your'se dad, and Red Bird made me take Lagger. She said, 'Lagger faster, get Buck back sooner.' I'se told her why that boy can handle anything. She said, 'I know Foster. Buck not boy, he man. Prove it at night.'"

We laughed. "You'se know your wife."

"To more serious matters. I hope you can guide us to help those two women. I want to thank you men for comin' with Foster. You get some rest. I'll get some men to take care of your horses. We'll leave in the mornin'."

I went over and told Blacky we were leaving in the morning, and I cut up two apples for him and Lagger, and they both neighed when I gave them the apples.

We mounted up and headed northwest toward the mountains. We rode all day, and that night, men and horses were tuckered out. Ken, one of the men from the mine, came over.

"You know, Silver, every one of the men wanted to come to help, but Foster picked us three and told the rest they needed to keep the mine rolling. I just thought you should know how every one of the men feels."

"Ken, I sure do thank you for that."

Foster was already in his roll, as were most of the men. I drank some coffee and was in my roll fast asleep. In the morning, I stirred up the fire and got breakfast and coffee going. You could tell everyone was still tired. We ate in the quietness of the early morning. Not many words were spoken as we got on the trail of the cavalry. It was about noon when Foster rode over to me.

"See where the trail leads." He pointed to the entrance to a canyon.

"I see, Foster. What of it?"

"The Indians and then the cavalry went in after them."

"So!"

"I'se know there's no way out except this way. Looks like only the Indians came out. I'se going in and see what happened. You and the men take a rest here while I'se gone. If what I'se think happened, better round up some shovels. Sure looks like they were ambushed. I'se try to be back in an hour."

In about forty-five minutes Foster came back at a slow pace.

"Get the shovels, there's no hurry. They'se not going anywhere."

We all rode into the canyon, and there in front of us were all the bodies lying dead, and not a single horse. We buried all the bodies. I looked around, and everyone looked worried. Somebody said, "If they did this to men that are trained to fight, what will the Indians do to us?"

I heard some of the men agreeing.

Foster spoke up. "This is what you'se get when you send men that don't know the country. I'se been roaming this here mountains for on to sixty years, and I'se know every nook and cranny. They'se will slow down their'se pace. They'se won't expect anyone else to be on their trail for a while. Me'se and Buck here are going ahead and make sure they don't have anybody on their backtrail. You'se come at a fair pace behind us."

"If anyone wants to turn back now, I won't hold it against you."

Young Josh stepped forward; he had worked at the mine this past winter. "I know Carolyn. I'll go through hell for her, so count me in."

All the men agreed, so Foster and I threw our leg over our saddle and headed for the Indian's trail, with the men coming up behind us.

The trail was easy to follow, but Foster took a wide sweep to the left and I to the right. We were trying to make sure they wouldn't see us. It was about nightfall when Foster came over to me.

"I'se see them, about two miles ahead. I'se couldn't get close enough to spot the women. They do have one brave on watch. I'se think if we be real careful, we might sneak up close enough on the east side to see where the women are."

"If we find where they are, we can attack in the mornin'. Me and you can get around and maybe get the women out."

It wasn't too hard to sneak around 'cause there were very large boulders and trees all around. I guess that was why they had only one guard. They didn't expect that anyone would attempt to go up the steep hillside and across this narrow ledge that we were on now. We were on foot; we had left the horses two miles back. We got across the ledge and from up high, like we were, we could see down into the Indian camp. They had fires ablaze, so we could make out where the women were tied up. They had one guard watching them away from the other braves.

"You know, Foster, we don't need to go any farther. We can see right where they are and look over there. There's a trail over yonder that goes down in back of their camp."

"We'se seen enough. Best get back to the men and lay out a plan for an attack in the early morning."

We worked our way back across the ledge and made it to the horses. We got back to camp; they were in a forest area with no fires going. We thought they were already in their bedrolls when we walked up. I started to wake them when out of the trees came the men.

"We heard you coming, boss. Just wanted to make sure it was you."

"You'se surprised me'se. I'se didn't think you'se were that good."

"We found them. They are about four miles from here. We will ride our horses about two miles, then walk. I'm goin' up the hill to the back. I'll need about thirty minutes. Foster will lead you to the front of the camp. Foster will show you where the guard is.

Whoever is good with a knife will need to take out that guard quietly. You'll need all the ammunition you can carry for your rifle and side arm. Then, hopefully, I'll have the women up the hill and across the ledge. If y'all attack while we're on the ledge, I'll try to take a couple out from up there. They're fourteen all together. If y'all take out the guard and I take out guard that is guarding the women, that will leave them with twelve for you to deal with. There are eleven of us, and hopefully, we have the surprise factor on our side. No one rests tonight. You know what to do. Just follow Foster. Let's get goin'."

We left the horses. I started up the hill to the ledge, and they started toward the Indian camp. I was across the ledge and going down the trail to the back of the camp when I heard a noise. I drew my knife and lay down on the ground. There walking toward me was a brave. He was looking around as though he heard something. He looked up the hill that I had just come down, and as he started to turn and go back, I jumped up and put my hand over his mouth and plunged my knife deep into his chest. He fell silent into the undergrowth. He was dead.

The camp was quiet as I worked my way to where the women were tied. I tried to get their attention as I came closer, but they seemed to just stare into the darkness. Their wrist and ankles were bound, and they had gags in their mouths. I crawled on my belly up to them, and they seemed not to notice me at all. I was going to cut the ropes on their wrist and ankles, but I was not going to take out the gag. I didn't want them waking everyone up. I cut their ropes, and they just stared down at me. I looked around and got up and put the daughter's hand in the mother's hand and closed her hand. I grabbed the mother's hand and headed up the trail to the ledge. We were just across the ledge when I heard shooting.

I sat the women down and turned to see the men rushing into the camp. The Indians were getting up fast, so I let off two shots and two went down. It looked as though the men could handle the rest. I took off the women's gags and headed toward the horses. They never said a word. We got back to the horses, and I gave them some water, but they just stared. I had to pour water into their mouths. We sat down and waited for the men to get back.

The men came back in two groups. They looked rugged from no sleep and the shootout.

"Where's Foster?"

"He said to get back and tell you to get everyone moving. We brought all the horses back, the ones stolen and theirs. Foster went after one Brave that got away. He was goin' to try to stop him from gettin' back to Geronimo. He said he would catch up with us as soon as he could."

"We better get goin'. Maybe we can get a little sleep later on. Let's move out."

"What wrong with Carolyn?" Josh said.

"I don't know. They just stare into the dark. I had to force them to drink a little water.

Josh, would you get your and my bedrolls. Their clothes are pretty well torn up. We need to get them back to town, to the doc."

We got them on two of the horses, and then each man had to lead two of the extra horses behind them. We drove ourselves hard for about five hours until we were out of the thick forest and out on the prairie. We took a break and got some much-needed rest. I knew Blacky would wake me if anything came near. We were up and going in three hours. I don't know if the women got any sleep. Josh had Carolyn on a horse behind him, and I had Lizzie on a horse behind me.

I told two men to take Pete Sutter's five horses to him and one of them to go on to the fort east of here and tell the colonel what happened to his men and where to find them. We took off for the town. We had to eat jerky on the run. That night Foster caught up with us.

"Glad to see you, Foster."

"Yeah, that there brave made it back to Geronimo's camp. So, we'se better just get four or five hours' sleep and be on our way. Should make town by tomorrow night."

We were up before sunup and moving toward town. That night we made it to town.

"Foster, go tell the sheriff what happened out there and tell him I sent a man to the fort. You men, I thank you for all your help, and you can divide the ponies between you. If you don't want them, take them to the livery and tell him I'll foot the bill, and if you would, take Blacky and Lagger over to the livery. Then get some well-deserved rest."

Josh and I got the women over to the doc's house, and his wife let us in. The doc came out, and I shook his hand.

"Doc, I don't know what's wrong with them, but they won't talk, and they just have a blank stare."

"June, help me get them into the examining room. You two wait out here."

"Josh, it's goin' to be a while. Would you go to the sheriff's office and tell Foster to go to the ranch and let my father know what happened and keep the men on full alert. Then let my mother and Red Bird know about the women. Then get some rest. If you need a room, I'll pay for it."

"No, sir, Silver, I'll come right back here and wait."

Josh came back and told me Foster would get it done and then get some sleep at the ranch. Five hours went by; I dozed off and on. Then the doc came out.

"Silver, they are both in shock. Lizzie has some cuts and bruises, but nothing bad. I think seeing John and her son brutally killed put her in shock."

"What about Carolyn, Doc?"

"Well, Josh, that's another story. You sure you want to know?"

"Yes, sir. I hope one day when she's older we can get married and start her parent's ranch up again."

"Well, Josh, Carolyn has deeper wounds all over her body. She must have put up a real fight. But they overwhelmed her, and she was brutally violated over and over again. She's not a virgin anymore. I'm sorry, she's torn up bad. That will heal in time. Not much is known about shock. Some come out of it, and some don't. They just need to be taken care of, and in time, maybe, but I don't know. The deep cuts on her body will leave scars. Josh, I just thought you should know. It's not pretty."

Josh sat down and put his head in his hands and said, "I don't know. I love her so much. I don't care what happened to her. I'll still love her. Just let her be all right."

The door burst open, and coming through it was Red Bird and my mother. I gave her a kiss and hugged her and my mother.

"Foster told us about the women. I want to see them."

"Doc, you think it will be all right?"

"They won't know you're there, but it can't hurt."

He took Red Bird into the next room. I said to my mother, "Their clothes are torn nearly off them, and their house was burned down. Would you go over to the dress shop and pick out some new clothes. They are goin' to need everything. Just tell the lady at the shop to collect from Bill at the ranch office."

"I will, son, but Foster told us you haven't slept in days. You need to eat and get some sleep."

I hugged her again.

"I will as soon as Red Bird gets done and we head home."

Mother went out the door. Josh and I sat down and waited. We were dozing off when my mother came in with four bundles of things and two boxes of shoes.

"I had to wake up Pam, but she was glad to do it."

"I forgot how late it is."

That's when Red Bird and the doc came out. Red Bird said, "Buck, we brought the wagon. We take them to ranch. I know what to do. You need some rest. Send someone out to get some plants to heal. Like the ones I put on you when the bear attack you. Bring to ranch."

"That's all right, Doc?"

"Sure, just keep their cuts clean. I can see that she knows what to do. Maybe she can help mend their mind. I can't."

We took them out to the wagon, and Josh offered to look for the plants. Red Bird told Josh what to look for, and he left. I came back from the livery with Blacky, and we headed to the ranch with Mother driving the wagon and Red Bird in back taking care of the two women. I rode up by the wagon.

"I think that young man loves this young woman."

"I think so too, honey. He'll take care of them the rest of their lives. I see his love for her as mine is for you. That kind of love you can't stop. I have to make her well."

3

We drove up to the ranch house. BJ and his little sister, Song Bird, came down the steps of the house.

"Ma, Pa, what is it? What happened?"

"These two women were hurt. BJ, help your ma with Lizzie. Song Bird, help your grandma with Carolyn."

"Buck, you need rest. You go to the bunkhouse. Tell Manuel to fix you something to eat, and then take a bath and get some sleep."

"Don't you need some help?"

"No, this women work, me and Mother can take care of this. BJ, go back to the wagon and get those packages and bring them up to the water closet."

I went to the bunkhouse. No sense arguing with her. I must have slept for ten hours. When I woke up, Foster was staring at me.

"I'se wondering when you'se going to wake up. Never in my life seen anyone sleep that long unless they'se be sick."

"Felt like I been dragged across a field by a runaway horse. Any word from the house?"

"Well, Manuel said Red Bird had him fix some broth. She told him that they got them cleaned up and in their new night clothes, and then put them to bed. Then she told him to burn all their old clothes."

BJ came running in. "Pa, Ma said for you and Foster to come running."

Foster and I ran to the house, up to the bedrooms upstairs. Red Bird came out, kissed me, and said, "Buck, you and Foster look after them. We fed them what we could, and they sleep now. Me and Mother need some rest."

Mother said, "I'll be back in five or six hours after I check on your father and clean up and get some sleep."

"They are going to need a lot of looking after. If they make any noise, come get me."

Foster and I sat in the hall overlooking the downstairs for what seemed like hours. I saw Mother come in the front door and go into the kitchen and, in a while, come up the stairs.

"Any movement from in there?"

"Not a sound."

"You know, that daughter of mine sure knows what she's doing. Josh came back with lots of plants, and Red Bird boiled them and took the leaves and put them over the wounds. Then she poured the liquid from the leaves into a broth, and we got a little down them. Let Red Bird sleep. I'll wake her if I need her. She worked so hard she needs some rest. Now you two get out of here and go find something to do."

"Yes, Ma. Come on, Foster, let's go and look at your new house. See how's it comin' along?"

"Find with me'se."

We went out the front door, and there on the front steps was Josh.

"Any change, Silver?"

"No, Josh, it's goin' to take some time. You come with us. You're goin' to have to busy yourself,"

We went to the barn, got our horses, and rode northwest of the house for about a mile, and there was a house to rival any in St. Louis. Tim saw us and came out.

"Welcome, gents. With all the trouble, I thought you forgot about us way back here."

"I thought it's about time Foster saw his new cabin."

"That's not mine. That's like no cabin I'se ever seen—that's a palace."

Tim said, "A palace for a king of a man and vice president of the largest company in Durango, and maybe in all of Colorado."

"That's too big for me'se. I'se can't keep that clean."

"Why, you old moneybags. You can hire someone to cook and clean for you," I said. "Let me take you on a tour through the house. This is the front door, and just inside is the main room with that huge fireplace. The stone came in on two wagons from the mine. Over here is the kitchen, and in the back of the kitchen is two rooms for the cook to live all year round, with a water closet of their own. Then across the house is three bedrooms. This one is yours, Foster."

We walked into a room that was as big as the main room with an opening in the wall about six feet high and about ten feet wide.

"You have a tremendous view of the Rocky Mountains and a door to the outside. That's going to be the window. Your bed will be across from it so you can wake up every morning and see your beloved Rockies. Your water closet is over here. There is another one out in the hall for your guests to use."

We looked over, and Foster was nearly in tears.

"I can't believe's this here place will be mine."

I said, "Foster you are goin' to have fifty acres, most of which is to the west of here."

"Whose stay in the other two rooms?"

"Anybody you want. Maybe you will get married, or maybe one of your best girls around the saloon." You say you get the urge once in a while."

We all laughed, and Foster turned a little red, which you could hardly see under that beard. We went outside, and I asked Tim, "When will it be done?"

"About a month and a half."

"Foster, why don't you just stay here. I'll send a man to the mine and let Jim know and tell him Tim will be back in a month and a half. He can let us know if he has any problems. We have plenty of room in our house, or you can bunk with the boys in the bunkhouse. Whatever you want."

"Thank you'se, Buck. I'se take you'se up on that. These old bones just can't take another winter in those mountains. I'se enjoy looking at them from that big window."

I saw my dad coming from a ways off.

"Can I talk to you son?"

"Sure."

We walked away a little.

"You know, son, our herd has doubled or more in size. I had the boys take a count, and there are nearly nine thousand or so head. We had some mild winters, and there's no tellin' when we'll get a harsh year. We could lose half the cattle if that happens. The boys have been in town and have heard that the mining in Wyoming and Montana is gettin' huge and miners need beef and at a good price."

"You think so? How about the Indians between here and there?"

"Yes, that will be a risk. I think it will be worth it. I think we should send Sam and another man to go up there and try to get contracts with the mine owners. Bill can make up a lot of contracts, and who better to send than Sam? He's part owner in the mine. He'll look after your investments better, and they can see where the Indians might be and if the army has rounded them up yet."

"I know from what Dancing Bear said about Geronimo that he won't take it easy about us killin' his braves. He'll look for revenge. I think it might be worth it. What do you think about sendin' Josh with Sam? He needs to be away from Carolyn for a while. I know he will not want to go, but I think I can reason with him."

"If you think so, son."

"Would you send Sam up to the house and we'll talk about it? He was raised around here and knows better how to get there and back without a hitch."

Buck said, "Josh, come with me. Foster, you can stay here and supervise Tim. Let him know if you want any changes or add anything."

"I'se think of something."

Tim said, "Now, why did you tell him that? Now it won't be done for six months."

I rode off with Josh laughing at those two. We reached the main house, and Sam was there, and BJ came running down the steps. I explained to Sam and Josh what was going to happen.

Sam spoke up. "That sounds like a good deal. Just have to watch for Indians. There's only two of us, so we'll be a lot less noticeable than most."

Josh spoke up. "No disrespect, Silver, but I can't see leaving Carolyn for a month."

"Josh, she's goin' to be a long time healin', and Red Bird's not goin' to let you see her anyways. When you get back, I want you to work on the ranch so you can rebuild her ranch. You'll know what to do. I'll try to get Red Bird to let you see her before you go. You know she's in good hands."

"I know, but a month."

"It's hard, I know, son. When Foster and me were lookin' for our mine, I was away from Red Bird for a year. It was hard, but I had the thought of her in my mind. That made me keep goin' when times were harsh. Believe me, they got harsh."

"All right, Silver, if I can see her and talk to her."

"Good. I'll talk to Red Bird tonight."

I went up to the rooms, and Mother was coming out of the women's room.

"Red Bird, is she there?"

Molly said, "No, son, she's in your room trying to get some sleep. She's going to look after them later. Their wounds are healing, but their minds have a long way to go."

I gave her a hug.

"Thank you for helpin' Red Bird. She would try to do it all herself if it wasn't for you. Good night."

"Good night, son."

I went to our room, and there she was, in all her beauty, asleep. I took off my clothes and lay down beside her. I knew she would wake me up before she got out of bed.

She woke me up, and we made love; and then she went in the water closet, and I could hear the water running in the tub. She had gotten so used to the tub and now preferred it to the pond where she used to take a bath. So I sat down beside the tub and started washing her back.

I said, "You know, honey, I was goin' to send Josh with Sam to line up some buyers for the cattle up north of here. I think it would do him good to get away, instead of sittin' around here worrin' about Carolyn."

"What this about cattle?"

"Pa thinks we need to sell four or five thousand head of cattle. Our herd has doubled in size, and if we had a harsh winter, we could lose that many, and I agreed."

"That mean you be gone."

"Maybe two months. You may be taking care of the women that long, and I can't help much with that. Josh doesn't want to go unless he can see Carolyn. Maybe you can talk to him and let him see her. They should leave in two or three days."

"I don't know. She looks bad; cuts are healing but looks bad."

"Well, he saw her all the way back on the trail, so he knows, and Doc told him what other things they did to her."

"Send him later today. I talk to him and let him see her. Now hand me a towel to dry. I need to get busy."

"Not on your life. I'll dry you off. Be my pleasure."

"Oh, Buck, you funny."

"No, I just love you. I'll send him up to see her. I'm goin' to take the children to town with me to meet the new teacher today."

"You think teacher could teach me more than you have taught me?"

"I know she could, but with the women to take care of, when would you have time?"

"When Mother comes over to watch the women, I have time. I want to learn more, so I feel more at ease around white people."

"All right, I'll see if she has time."

I lay down to get some sleep. I had a lot to do in the morning. Red Bird was in Carolyn and Lizzie's room. I got Song Bird and BJ up and told them to get ready. We were going to town. That was all they had to hear, and they were up and at it.

"Meet you in the kitchen. I can smell breakfast."

I got to the kitchen and warned Manuel.

"Yes, I am used to them. They always like my cooking. I love people that appreciate my food. Not like those cowboys out in the bunkhouse. I may have to take a meat cutter to them."

"They're just funnin' with you. I know if you left, they would starve, not wantin' to eat their own cookin'."

"Maybe I take a little trip. Teach them a lesson."

"I don't think you have to, 'cause we are goin' on a cattle drive. I'll have to hire a cook to go. I know after they eat someone else's cookin', they will be more appreciative of you. I would take you, but you know Red Bird's likes and dislikes. In the next five weeks, Foster will be movin' into his new house. He's goin' to need someone to cook and clean. If you know of someone, let me know."

"I think of someone, I will ask next time in town for supplies."

"Song Bird, you want to go to school?"

"Yes, Pa, very much."

"We're goin' to meet the teacher and see when school starts."

BJ said, "I don't want to go to school. I heard you talking to Ma last night, and I want to go on the cattle drive."

"Son, you're just too young. A cattle drive is too rough. Ask any cowboy out there. You need your schoolin'. One day you will be taken over this ranch, and you need to know more than I have taught you. We may meet up with some Indians."

"I handled that one out at Uncle Foster's cabin."

"See here, son, I told you not to brag on that. Now go and saddle up the horses."

"Even sister?"

"Yes, son, even Song Birds." Then I turned to Manuel.

"When you see Josh tell him Red Bird wants to talk to him."

"Si, Silver."

I got down to the barn with Song Bird alongside me holding my hand and singing like a little bird.

"Take me away, take me away, I'm going to school, I'm going to school, take me away."

Foster came running out of the bunkhouse. "Where you'se all going?"

"To town. You want to go?"

"Sure thing, wait for me'se. I'se need a drink and maybe some other things."

"Foster, the children."

"I'se didn't say anything."

BJ came out of the barn with our three horses and Foster's old mule. "I heard Uncle Foster and knew he would want to go with us."

"Thank you'se, BJ. That's a fine name. I'se like that handle, it suits you."

"Can I have a handle, Pa?"

"Maybe I'll think of one for you, little one. Now let's get to town."

We rode up the dusty streets of Durango. Foster spoke up. "I'se think I'se stop here. That there dust made me pretty thirsty, if you'se all don't mind."

"Go ahead, Foster. You can find your way back to the ranch."

We three went into Bill's office.

"Hello, Buck and BJ. I like that name. There's Song Bird. I bet you're ready for school."

"Yes, sir. I can't wait."

"How are Lizzie and Carolyn doing?"

"Well, their wounds are healing, but they're still not talkin'. I stopped by to tell you that we are setting up a cattle drive to Wyoming and Montana. Dad said our herd has doubled in size, and he thinks we might have a hard winter and lose quite a few head. So I'm sendin' Sam and Josh to try to set up some deals so we know how many head to take. They will need some simple contracts for the mine owners to sign and about five hundred dollars to take."

"How about the Indians?"

"That's another reason I'm sendin' Sam, to try to see where they might be, and hopefully, the army has rounded them up. Come on, BJ, Song Bird, we have to get along to see the teacher. Got to get you in school."

"I'll have the contracts ready in a couple of days."

"Fine. Say bye to Mr. Gills. By the way, where is the school?"

"Bye, kids. It's in the church right now."

We were heading down to the church when a man came out of the saloon waving a gun and looking at me. "There you are, you dirty Indian lover."

"I don't know what you're talkin' about, mister, but you best go back inside and quit causin' trouble."

"You going to make me."

Foster came up behind him and hit him over the head with the butt of his gun, and two others dragged him back inside.

"Sorry, Buck, he'se a newcomer and heard you were married to Red Bird, and I'se was trying to explain, but he was too drunk to listen."

"That's all right, Foster. Go on back and have some fun. We'll see you later."

"Pa, what did he mean by Indian lover?"

"Song Bird, you know your ma is Indian, right?"

"Yes, Pa."

"We been havin' trouble with some bad Indians, and some people think all Indians are bad. They don't know your mother or her people. They don't know how good Dancing Bear and Running Elk are."

"Why not, Pa?" BJ said.

"They just don't understand. You just have to get used to it. Maybe by the time you two have children, things will change."

We went in the school, and I took off my hat and held it in my hand when I saw the new teacher at her desk. She had blonde hair and wore glasses and looked to be twenty-one or twenty-two. The school was the same as the church we came to on Sundays. Red Bird still had trouble understanding why we had to go in a building when the Great Spirit was all around us. The preacher was still trying to help her understand. The teacher looked up from her papers.

"Hello, I'm the new teacher, Ms. Trumble."

"Hello, I'm Buck Taylor, and this is Buck Taylor Jr. We call him BJ, so as not to get confused with me all the time, and this is Song Bird."

"May I help you?"

"I just wanted to know when school starts. They never have been in school. I taught them some that I know, but I know that's not enough. You're the first teacher in Durango. By the way, how is your wound? Doc said you were doin' fine."

"It's fine. It hurts once in a while, but Doc says that it will pass in time. I'm finding out a lot of children around here haven't had much schooling, so I'll test them to see what they know and then place them from grades one to twelve."

"When does school start?"

"The end of August, on Monday, the twenty-second."

"I won't be here, but I'll make sure someone from the ranch gets them here." I told the kids, "Would you two sit in the back? I need to talk to Ms. Trumble for a minute."

"Yes, Pa."

"I wanted you to know Song Bird wants to go to school, but BJ, thinks what I taught him is enough."

"I understand. Lots of the boys from the ranches and farms feel that way. I'll try to make it interesting for them, especially history."

"There are two other things."

"Yes, sir."

I don't know if you guessed by my daughter's name that their mother is Indian. She comes from a very peaceful tribe northwest of here. I hope there are no hard feelin' about them 'cause of what happened to you."

"Oh, no, I've heard about Silver Buck around town and your wife and her people, what you both have done for this town and its people. No, sir, not from me. I can't promise about the other children—you know they tend to act out what they hear at home. If that happened, I'll try to control it."

"Yes ma'am. The other is that Red Bird would like for you, if you can, to come out to the ranch. I taught her to write a little and read some, but she wants to learn more. She would like to discuss if maybe you can help her learn more. She is a fast learner, and she wants to blend into our world. If I judge your age, she might be just a little older than you. You two might become good friends."

"I don't know. I'm pretty busy."

"I realized that you might be, with school startin' up and all. I told her you probably would be. But I told her I would ask. She insisted that I tell you that we would pay you and it would be only when you had the time."

"It's not the pay, it is the time, but if it can be whenever I can make it, then I say yes. The pay will be a blessing. You know teachers don't make too much, and things cost a little more than I thought they would. Anyway, your wife sounds delightful."

Song Bird said, "Pa, can we go? I'm hungry."

"Just a minute. Song Bird. Then Miss Trumble I'll tell her that you'll be out when you can. I better warn you, she's very open and honest. She says what she means. So don't get upset if she says something embarrassing."

"What do you mean?"

"Well, here goes. We will be eating in the hotel, and Doc or Bill will come over and pat me on the back and say, 'How are you, boy?' And she'll interrupt and say, 'Not a boy. He is my man and prove it at night.' They just laugh 'cause they know Red Bird and care about her."

"Now I have to meet her. She sounds to be a delight."

"I better go. The children are impatient."

We went back to the ranch; Manuel had supper ready for us. The kids went out to play. I went up to talk to Red Bird. She was sitting outside the room. I went over and gave her a kiss.

"Shh, shh, Josh is in there."

I sat down and held her beautiful hand. Josh came out and had a big smile on his face.

"Silver, I'm ready to go now."

Red Bird said, "What, Josh? What is it?"

"I sat on the bed next to her and held her hand and told her everything that is in my heart. When I got done—"

"What!"

Josh said with a tear in his eye, "She squeezed my hand."

"You brought a ray of sunshine into her world. There's hope, Josh—real hope."

"Thank you, Red Bird, for all you do for her and her mother. Maybe you could talk to her about what's going on around town and the like. I'm ready, Silver, anytime. I need to build a ranch."

"I'm glad to hear you talk like that. You're on the payroll. Tell Sam you two leave in two days."

"Yes, sir."

He nearly flew down the staircase.

"I'm glad you talked me into letting him see her. There is hope. I start talking to her, maybe she responds soon."

Red Bird kissed me and ran off to tell Mother. I waited there, keeping an eye inside until she got back. Mother was with her.

"Sorry, honey, did not mean to leave you alone. I was just excited."

"It's all right, they're still there. I looked in once in a while. Now if you two will excuse me, I need to talk to Pa. We need to start plannin' this cattle drive." I kissed Red Bird and hugged Ma and then headed out of the house.

"Pa, in two days, Sam and Josh will be headin' out. I been thinkin' we can get two or three thousand head rounded up and get them branded and keep them in one area on good grass, to fatten them up. I'm goin' to have Sam get signed contracts. If he can find a telegraph and let us know how many are under contract, we can head up there sooner and meet them along the way, and he will know which contract belongs to what mine. And what price to start?"

"I've been thinkin' along those same lines. 'Cause we don't want to get caught up there in an early snowfall. I think we should start at fifty dollars a head. You know they are goin' to try to get Sam down. I say we tell Sam to begin with fifty, but not under twenty-five at the last resort. Don't go down all at once. Just haggle slow with them."

"Sounds good. I'm hungry."

"Son, you think Manuel has enough for me? Red Bird got your ma so worked up she forgot to make dinner."

"Sure, Pa. Let's go and get the kids and go eat. I think it will be good to be on the trail with you. My first drive."

Two days later, we were at Bill's office. Sam and Josh had the contracts in their saddlebags, and the money in their wallet with my instructions.

"Sam, when you think you have all the contracts you can get signed, find a telegraph office and wire to Bill here the total number of head sold. Start at fifty dollars. They may want to bargain, but don't go down too fast. Don't go under twenty-five dollars a head. Try to get as much as you can. The higher you get, the more bonus you both will get."

"You said bonus—the higher we get, the more we'll get."

"Yes, that's what I said. Also, on the way up, scout for a good trail for the cattle. Put that in the telegram. We'll be getting the herd rounded up and branded so we can leave as soon as we hear from you. We'll meet you somewhere on that trail, and you two can show us back and which contract goes with which mine. If you do a good job, I'll be sendin' you on other trips to the east. That's later. Also, keep a lookout for Indians, and maybe outlaws, in the towns you stop in. Last thing: if you see an army patrol, find out about Geronimo and his band. Well, good luck, boys. We'll be waitin' to hear from you."

"Yes, sir, we'll do our best."

"Silver, I'll make sure he gets the most we can. I have a ranch to build."

They mounted up and rode out of town, yelling and waving their hats in the air.

"Bill, I hope they do all right. We'll see how much this ranch will pay off."

"I think it will. Where there's men, they will need beef."

"I'm headin' for the ranch. We are goin' to be busy, so let me know as soon as you hear from them."

"Will do. By the way, here's your bank statement and a letter from Jim at the mine."

I headed back to the ranch. By the time I got there, Pa had the men out on the range getting the cattle and horses rounded up. We had fenced off about three hundred acres and planted in grass. They also had three water tanks in this area. I rode out to where the men and Pa were branding the cattle. I sat there atop Blacky and watched Pa directing the men. He was in his element. The men showed nothing but respect for him. I walked over to where the branding was going on.

"How's it goin', Slim. Need anything?"

"I sure could use a rocker. These boys are slow enough I could sit and watch the grass grow."

Pa came over and said, "Why, Slim, you wouldn't know what to do if they were any faster. You better get ready. Here comes ten more head."

Slim got the four branding irons in the fire that was going during branding season. They were red-hot by the time the cattle were near. They brought them in one at a time, and Slim put the red-hot iron to their hindquarters and then turned them loose into the fenced pasture. I took out the letter from Jim.

> Everything is going good. The ore that we're finding in the new vein, yes, I said new vein, in fact, two. Tell Foster that he was right. About a hundred feet from the main vein to the north, we hit another, looks to be ninety percent pure. Then to the south another smaller vein about fifty feet. Every day we are digging deeper. I ordered more rails. John should be back in a couple of days. Tell Foster he is missed. When is Tim going to be through with Foster's palace? I seem to have it harder now. Ha-ha. We got your letter about the Indian trouble. We haven't seen any except Dancing Bear's braves. That all for now. I know you're busy but it would be nice to see you and the family.

I watched for a while, and then rode back to the bunkhouse. Foster wasn't in there, so I went to his house, and there he was, trying to tell everyone what he wanted. Tim came over.

"Silver, that man is driving us nuts. You think you could get him out of our hair for about two weeks, and we'll be done."

"I don't know, I'll try. Foster, come over here. I got a letter from the mine. Tim, you read it too."

"That sounds great. We will be in business, looks like, for a long time."

"They could use your help, I'm sure, but I'm sure they will make it on their own. Foster, if you leave these men alone, Tim can get up to the mine faster."

"I'se just trying to help."

"I know. Read this bank statement."

Tim looked, and Foster looked, and Tim said, "Looks like with these two new veins, I'll be able to retire soon and build myself a fine house and find me a wife."

"See, Foster, you can afford a woman to cook and clean for you. Let's head to town. We need to find someone to start in a couple of weeks before we start the cattle drive."

We headed for town. As we were coming down Main Street, Foster said, Why don't we'se stop and get a beer."

"I don't think that's a good idea after the last time we were here."

"That man is at his farm by now. Come on, I'se don't like drinking alone."

"All right, but remember, you talked me into this."

We pulled up and tied our horses and went through the bat-winged doors and walked up to the bar. We ordered two beers. I was telling Foster about the cattle drive and how we hoped to get back before the first snowfall when the bat-winged doors flew open and a big voice said, "I see that Indian lover's horse outside."

I said to Foster, "I told you this wasn't a good idea." I set my drink down and turned around, taking my tie down off the hammer of my gun. "Look, mister, I don't want any trouble. We're just in here havin' a few drinks."

I had to be careful this time. He wasn't drunk, and he walked right up to me. I'm six foot two inches, and he stood over me a good three inches. His confidence was in his size.

"I don't like the stink of no Indian lover." He bent down as though he was smelling my hair, and at the same time, he reached for my gun. But to his surprise, the holster was empty. He looked up, and the butt of my gun was coming down on his head. He fell back from the blow, but regained his footing and came at me. I had my gun holstered and doubled up my fist and caught him right under the chin. I went after him, and he got me in a bear hug and was squeezing me. My arms were free, so I kept hitting him in the face and finally caught him a good one under the chin. He let go of me, and I threw a fist full into his belly. He bent over, holding his belly, and I got him right full on the chin again. He flew back and landed on his back and didn't move. I shook my hands 'cause they hurt like the devil.

I picked up my hat and told Foster, "I told you this wasn't a good idea. Let's get out of here."

We walked our horses down the street to the diner. "You hungry? I want to talk to Juan."

"Sure, I'se am always hungry."

Juan came out. "Hello, senor."

"Hello, Juan. You're not in the kitchen?"

"No, not today. My cousin is back there. What happened to you? Looks like you got run over by a wagon. There's a washbowl in the back room if you want to clean up. I'm out here teaching my other cousin to wait on tables."

"Thanks. I think I got hit by a bear again." I went to the back to wash up. When I returned to the table, Juan's cousin was taking Foster's order. He must have said something funny because she was laughing. She looked to be around twenty.

"I'se was telling Juanita about you'se fight in the saloon."

"That's not very funny."

"I'm sorry, Mr. Silver, but the way he tells it, it sounds pretty funny."

"I bet it does. I know the way he tells things. I'll have the same thing he's havin'."

She left, and we watched her move from table to table, taking orders and bringing food to the tables.

"She's a nice girl, and she likes the way I'se tell stories."

"Are you thinkin' what I'm thinkin'?"

"What's that?"

She brought the food to our table. We were sitting enjoying our dinner. I called Juan over.

"Juan, your cousin Juanita, does she work here a lot?"

"No, her and her brother just moved here from El Paso. Mr. Russell just gave them a few hours a week during our busy times until they can find permanent work."

I called out to the owner, "Mr. Russell, over here."

"Yes, Buck, how are you doing? I hear you're setting up a cattle drive."

"You can't seem to keep any secrets around this town."

"Well, you know most everyone around here eats here once or twice a day. I listen to what's going on around town."

"Your cook Juan said his cousins are only here until they find a permanent job. I know Juanita's brother can cook breakfast. I just tasted his, but can she cook like Jose'."

"She sure can. I just don't need three cooks, and anyway, she's prettier for the customers to look at."

"Always lookin' after business."

"I sure am. Why you ask about her cooking?"

"I think Foster here may have a job for her, and I might have one for him. I just wanted to ask you before I ask them."

"Always taking my good help. I thought Manuel is out at your place. Why would you need Jose and Juanita?"

"Tell him, Foster."

"Buck here built me's a fine big house. He thinks I'll need a cook and a housekeeper. I like her, she laughs at my stories."

"Well then, ask them. I'll send them over."

We ate our dinner and were talking when Jose' and Juanita came to the table.

"Sit down, you two. I want to discuss something with you."

"Was anything wrong with the food? Or maybe I shouldn't laugh at Mr. Foster's story."

"No, no, the food was great. Well, everything was great. Foster liked the way you laughed at his story. I want to ask you two if you want a permanent job."

"A job."

"Yes, let me tell you about it. Foster isn't much of a cook."

"I'se dare you'se, Buck. You'se hurt my feelings."

"You forgot I ate your cooking. He's not much of a housekeeper, either."

"Now, Buck, I'se leaving."

Juanita was laughing.

"Foster, you ask her."

"I'se guess he'se right. I'se not much good at either one of those things. Anyway, Buck built me a big house 'cause I'se hanging up my mining boots. I'se guess I'se do need someone to cook and clean. You'se would have you'se own bedroom by the kitchen, and you'se own indoor plumbing in you'se room, and a door leading to the outside, and you'se can use the wagon anytime to come to town. I'se leave out anything, Buck?"

"How much you goin' to pay her?"

"Oh, I'se forgot. Never had much money before. What you'se think, Buck? You'se the money man."

"To put up with you, and you don't like to take a bath, I'd say at least fifty dollars a month."

We could hear "Aha" from both of them.

Jose spoke. "I look after my little sister. That is a lot of money. What else is expected from her?"

"Jose, how could you? I'm embarrassed."

"I'se assure you'se, just cook and clean and laugh at my stories. It won't be for two weeks or so. I'se let you know."

"Then me, what you want me for?"

"I'm the one that wants you," I told him. "I'm goin' to start a cattle drive. I need a cook. We're goin' to Wyoming and Montana. We are takin' ten to fifteen men. Then when we get back, you can help Manuel at the ranch. Right now he does the cookin' for the ranch hands and for my family and me. He doesn't complain, but I think it's too much for one man. You both will be on the same ranch. I would pay you forty dollars a month. You don't have to put up with Foster."

We all laughed.

"Soon as I hear from my men up north, I'll come let you know. You may not have much warnin'. You can go order everything you might need. We'll have a chuck wagon ready. And you'll get a bonus, like the other men. It depends on how much we get for the cattle."

"How long would we be gone? We are new here. I hate to leave my little sister for a long time."

"Hopefully, there and back, two or three months. My wife and children will be at the ranch. My mother and Foster and about five ranch hands to look after the cattle, and of course, Manuel will be there also. Isn't Manuel kin to you?"

"He is, somehow. Sounds like she'll be safe."

"I'm sure she will be."

"Well, little sister, looks like we will have a job."

"Thank you, Jose'."

She hugged him around the neck.

Jose said, "Thanks to you both, Mr. Foster and Mr. Silver."

"Call him just Foster. Everyone does, and me, Silver or Buck, or both. We'll let you know. So long. We better get back to the ranch." We were halfway there when Blacky started acting up. He reared up on his hind legs and just about threw me. That's when we heard a shot that came out of nowhere.

4

Foster and the mule were on the ground. I drew my .45 and jumped off Blacky.

"You all right, Foster?"

"I'se all right, but I'se be pinned under my old mule. Where that shot come from?"

"I don't know. Maybe those boulders over yonder. Don't move. I'll help you soon as I can."

"My mule's not moving much. I'se think it hit him."

"Hold on, he's still out there. He might try to finish the job."

I heard horses coming from the ranch. My dad and five men were coming. I motioned toward the boulders, yelling, "If he's gone, track him down and take him to the sheriff. Dad, over here, the mule's on Foster. We think the bullet caught him."

We got Foster from under the mule.

"You all right?"

"I'se am now." He was looking over at the mule.

"I'se don't see any place where he got hit."

My dad said, "Here, let me look." He looked all over, and then said, "Look here, right behind his left ear. It doesn't look bad, just a crease. I think he's just unconscious."

I got my canteen and poured some water over the mule's head and the wound and rubbed it in his hair. After five minutes, I did the same. This time he shook his head and tried to get up. He made it onto his legs and kept shaking his head. Foster hugged him around the neck.

"Let's walk him back to the barn. We can take care of his wound better."

"Buck, I sent three men to your house and two to mine just to be on the safe side. I'm going to help the boys round up the hombre. You all take care of that old mule. I know how you feel about him after that ordeal on the mountain and bringin' all the silver in."

"Thanks, Dad."

We made it to the barn and were taking care of the mule when the barn door opened and in ran Red Bird. She threw her arms around my neck and was kissing me when the kids showed up. They were laughing at the way their mother was acting.

"It's all right. They hit the mule, but they didn't get me yet."

"Not funny, Buck. What we do without you? What happened to your face?"

"I know, honey. I was just tryin' not to scare the kids. I must have fell off Blacky too hard and hit the ground."

My dad came in and unsaddled his horse. "Well, we got him. He was already on the other side of town. I told the boys to take him to town and tell the sheriff what happened. It was a fat, bearded man with a mean temper and a beat-up face."

"Pa, that's the man in town that was calling you names."

"All right, kids, that's enough."

"What names was he calling you, Buck Taylor?"

"Never mind. There will always be some people like him. It's over, everyone's fine."

"That's the man in town that called you an Indian lover. Pa said some people don't understand and say things to hurt people, but not to let it hurt us because we love you, Ma."

"All right, Song Bird. I understand."

Foster stayed and took care of the mule with Dad, and we headed for the house.

"How are Carolyn and Lizzie?"

Carolyn is eating more broth now. She is healing slowly."

The next morning, Ms. Trumble came up to the ranch. I went and helped her down from her buggy.

"Good mornin', Ms. Trumble. Good to see you."

"Good morning, Mr. Taylor."

"Just call me Buck."

"Well then, when we're not around the children, call me Jenny. It will be nice to have someone call me by my first name. I haven't heard too much since I left home. Is Mrs. Taylor home? I thought we could make arrangements for me to teach her."

"She's in the house, I think she's done feedin' Carolyn and Lizzie. I'll go get her. Come on in the house and make yourself at home."

We went in the house, and I went upstairs to get Red Bird. I introduced the two women.

"Red Bird, this is Miss Trumble. Miss Trumble this is my wife, Red Bird."

"Red Bird, as I told Mr. Taylor, you can call me Jenny, except around the children. Mr. Taylor has told me so much about you, but he failed to mention how beautiful you are."

"Buck says I am, but I know I am not. Did not know anyone else thought I was."

"You are, let me assure you. Anyway, Buck told me you wanted to learn more of how to read and write, and maybe about the history of our people and your people, and to add numbers."

"Buck, what is history?"

"That's like Dancing Bear tellin' me how he got his name. Things many moons ago."

"What is add numbers?"

"Like you and me are two, and the children are two more. That makes four of us in our family."

Ms. Trumble said, "I just came out to meet you and make arrangements for me to come out. I think we will get along well. Do you have anything to ask me, Red Bird? That's a lovely name?"

"Do you have a man? How many moons are you?"

"No, Red Bird, I don't have a man. But I have met one in town that I like. I think he's a good man. I'm twenty-six years old. I'll start your first lesson right now. Twelve moons is one year. So 26 years equal 312 moons. I am thinking I could come out three times a week after school, maybe for one and a half hours."

Manuel brought out a tray of coffee and some of his Mexican bread, and I introduced him.

"Jenny, this is Manuel. He's our cook around here. Taste one of his sweet breads."

"How delicious. Thank you very much. Can I take one home?"

"Si, senorita. I make a small amount for you to take."

Red Bird asked, "Who man you like in town? I know some Buck's friends."

"I told you, Jenny, about her honesty."

"Yes, Red Bird, I'll tell you, but, Buck, not a word to him. Hear me, I'll tell him about that in time."

"I won't say a word."

"Why not you tell him? Tell Buck I like soon I see his harness when he come out of pond."

"Red Bird, you don't have to tell everyone about that."

"That's all right, Buck. You warned me. Red Bird, it's Mr. Gills, who works for Buck. I don't know why, but white women let the man ask her first."

"He doesn't work for me. He just takes care of my business. I'm sure he has other people he helps."

"Yes, he told me how you did so much for him."

"I just gave him a chance, and he took it. Anyway, he's a fine man. All the luck to you, and I won't say a word."

"I better get back to town now. I'll come out Monday, and then after school when it starts."

"That's good. Hope we become friends."

"I'm sure we will. Oh, Buck, Mr. Gills gave me this for you when he found I was coming out here." She handed me a telegram as I was helping her into the buggy.

Manuel came running up. "Here is your bread."

"Thank you, Manuel. I will sure enjoy it. Bye now. See you Monday, Red Bird."

My mother came up from her house. "Who was that?"

"My new teacher. She help me learn more reading, writing, and adding and history. You seen Little Buck and Song Bird?"

"They're down with their grandpa and Foster at the corral. I think the men are breaking some broncos for the cattle drive."

"Buck ... Buck, where are you?"

"Yes?"

"We are going to check on the women."

"Fine, I have to go find Pa. This is from Sam."

I walked down to the corral with a happy feeling. At the same time, there was a sad feeling in my heart, for I was going to have to leave Red Bird again. It had to be done.

My dad was getting to old to take this on by himself. I wouldn't ever let him know that. He had always been a proud man. And proud men don't like to admit that they couldn't do anything on their own. I handed him the telegram, and he read it.

"He said 4,860 heads have been bought under contract."

"Look at the price."

"Two thousand at $50 a head. Two thousand at $40 a head. The rest of the cattle at $35 a head. Have you figured the full amount?"

"Not yet. But that's a great deal. You have that many ready to go. How long till we can leave? Why don't we take five thousand even in case of trouble with Geronimo or rustlers?"

"I have four thousand penned up in that area by the river. That's one thousand we have to bring in from the range and brand the ones not branded yet. I'd say, if we work hard, about a week."

"I been thinking, to leave maybe eight men we trust the most here to take care of the ranch and watch after the women and children and Foster here."

"No one has to watch over me'se. I'se got my house to set up with Juanita's help. I'se going in tomorrow to buy things for the kitchen and bring her out here."

I laughed. "See, Pa, he's already takin' to that house in his old age."

Everybody laughed, and Foster started chasing me around the corral. Even the kids were laughing at Uncle Foster. He got tuckered out and stopped and sat down on the edge of the water trough. The kids went over and hugged him, for they loved him as much as I did.

"Pa, tomorrow I'll take the chuck wagon to town and get Jose and stock it up. Do you think we need to hire any more men for the drive? Did you read about the trail goin' up there?"

"I read that. It was good to hear about the amount of grass and water. I think we can follow that. I think we might want to take about ten more men with leaving eight here. If some can be had that know cattle. If not, they can learn fast."

"I'll have everyone take their rifle and side arm. Maybe buy some more rifles and lots of ammunition. Don't want to get caught short."

"That's for sure. Be sure to brin' that map. We might need it."

"Well, I have to go deal with Red Bird. She looked sad when I told her this was from Sam."

"I know. I'll have your mother to deal with tonight. She thinks I'm gettin' too old for these cattle drives. You know, she might be right. This might be my last one. But don't tell her I said that."

"No, Pa, I won't. Kids, stay out from underfoot. Take care of Uncle Foster."

"Look, kids, you'se want to help me'se take care of my old mule?"

"Sure thing."

"Well then, let's goes."

On the way to the house, I was trying to think of what to say to Red Bird. An idea just popped in my head. I wasn't going to say anything until she did. Then I knew exactly what to say.

We had supper, and we were on the couch with my arm around Red Bird. The kids were outside on the porch, running up and down the steps. I knew BJ thought he was grown up since that trouble with the Indians at Foster's old cabin, but he still liked to play like a kid.

"Buck Taylor, don't want you to go."

"Go where?"

"Don't be funny. You know what I mean. The cattle drive, get hurt, Geronimo still out there. Be gone too long."

"Now, Red Bird, we have to sell the cattle so we can pay everyone. Anyway, my dad is gettin' older, and he needs help. We'll be all right. We won't be gone as long as before we got married. We'll only be two or three moons."

"You mean months. I learned that much. All right, but I will miss you."

"You have the kids. BJ is a fine shot. Mother will be here. She can stay up here with you. Manuel, and maybe seven cowboys in case of big trouble, and you can send for Dancing Bear. And Foster will be here. You have the two women to care for."

"Buck, I say all right."

I got the kids in and ran them off to bed, and then we headed to our bedroom.

The next morning, I went to the bunkhouse and got Foster going. Pa was there eating with the men.

"Foster, I got the wagon and chuck wagon ready to go to town when you're ready. I'm goin' to leave the chuck wagon in town for Jose to get stocked up."

"Fine, I'se be ready to go when I'se get this down. I'se went over to my house yesterday, and Tim said he was done and it is ready for me'se to move in today. You'se know that he put a big sign hanging from the front porch that says 'Here lives the VICE PRESIDENT OF SILVER BUCK MINES.'"

"Anything wrong with that?"

"No, I'se like it."

"Pa, I'm goin' to try to hire ten men, and I'll be sendin' them out to work with you and the men."

"Sooner the better. You know how I like things to run smooth."

"I figured up the total. If we fill all the contracts, it will be $210,100. Plus we are takin' extra in case we lose some."

"We still have that many of the younger cattle left here on the ranch. We better get after it. Come on, boys, let's get to goin'. They won't brand their selves."

Foster and I headed for town. He drove up beside me and was smiling from ear to ear.

"What is it, Foster?"

"I'se was thinking I'se don't have to live in that bunkhouse anymore, and I'se have a pretty woman cooking for me. That's fine living."

"You know, with a woman in the house, you are goin' to have to be cleaner and mind your manners. You treat her well so she won't quit. And don't walk around in your drawers like in the bunkhouse."

"Sounds like I'se getting married."

"It doesn't matter if you're married or not. A woman still likes to be good."

We drove the wagons to the back of the store, and I walked Blacky to the front of the store and tied him to the hitching rail. And we went inside.

Buck said, "Hello, Ed. I hope you're stocked up. We're leavin' in six days."

Foster said, "I'se moving in my new house today."

Ed said, "I think I am, but I'll tell you, if I don't have much of something, I'll send it with the cattle drive. I'll be getting another shipment next week, and old Foster can wait on it. You boys will be gone a lot longer."

"Me'se wait. Well, that's how you treat a vice president."

"Don't pay him a mind He's been that way ever since I gave him that title. He thinks he's royalty. I'm goin' to send Juanita and Jose over from the diner. Just put everything on my bill. I'll pay for Foster's as a company present."

"That's mighty fine of you'se, Buck."

"Well, if I didn't, I might not hear the end of it. Now let's get to the diner and get our cooks. So long, Ed."

"Good luck, boys."

We walked into the diner, and Juanita came over.

"What you have today, Mr. Silver and Mr. Foster?"

"Juanita, you ready to go to work for this old goat today? And Jose too? We'll both have a cup of coffee."

"Si. You see that girl over there? I teach her to take my place. She does really well. I teach well. I go get Mr. Russell. You talk to him. He says yes, I go."

"Hello, Silver. Juanita says you're here to take my help."

"If you don't mind."

"Nope. See that little gal over there? She's doing a real fine job."

"Then I'll have them go to the general store. Thank you, John."

"I hope that's all the cooks you'll be needing. I don't know how many cousins Carlos, your cook at the mine has." He went away laughing. Juanita and Jose came over with our coffee.

"Sit down, you two. Startin' today, y'all are workin' for us. Mr. Russell said it is all right."

"That is good, Senor Silver."

"Listen, first thing, just call me Buck or Silver."

"Call me'se Foster."

"Yes, Buck. Yes, Foster. We try to learn English better."

"That's real fine. Now we need you two to go over to the general store. Ed knows to expect you. Jose, we need everything for the cattle drive. Pots and pans and food and spices, as much as you think you need for twenty men for two months there and maybe two back. Tell Ed to put ten rifles and as much ammunition as he can spare. Both wagons are in the back. Juanita, Foster needs everything. He has all the furniture. He needs food and towels, sheets, and I know you will want to put curtains.

"Foster, we talked about this. You have to keep her happy, or she might quit. Where was I? You can have what you like in your room and the kitchen, but for his room, something a man would like. I'm sure you know how to sew. Get all the goods for curtains and the like. Put his house together well."

"Yes, I know how to sew, and I know what a smart man like Foster likes."

I whispered to Juanita, "Keep that up. He like's praise, and you can have nearly anything you want. Just make his end years good and get him some things he likes, even if you don't."

"Si, I understand. Thank you."

"Jose, if you get everything today, head out to the ranch. And if you can't get it done today, stay over in town until tomorrow, and then head to the ranch. Then you can help Manuel cook and see what the men like. We leave in six days. Foster, now you listen to what Juanita has to say. She knows more about how a house should be run than you do. I'll leave you now. I have to go to the office and have Mr. Gills put y'all on the payroll. I'll have him open both of you an account at the bank. Jose, if you need any money on the trail, I'll advance it to you."

"I don't know what to say, Buck. As a woman, I never had a bank account." Buck said, "Now, that's just for you. If you buy something for Foster later on, have Ed take it out of Foster's account, not yours. That's just for you." Then Juanita said, "Now, Foster, I think we'll pick out some new clothes for you."

Buck said, "Yes, Juanita, he's a rich man. He needs to look like it. See you later."

"Now, Buck. Now see what you'se do."

"Oh, Foster, just do what she says."

I walked over to Bill's office.

"Hello, Buck, been expecting you since I sent that telegram to you."

"Yes, Bill, your delivery woman was real nice. If I was you, I'd get to know her better."

"Buck, we just talk a little. She wouldn't give me a second look. She's too pretty."

"Look at Red Bird, and look at me."

"Now you have a point." He laughed.

"I came in to have Juanita put on Foster's books at fifty dollars a month, and Jose on the ranch books at forty dollars a month. Open a separate account for each. Now I'm goin' to try to hire ten cowboys today. If I do, I'll send them your way. Look at this telegram from Sam."

"You may have this ranch paying for itself after this drive, and making money next year or two. Make sure to have them wire you by next spring if they need more cattle."

"I'll be goin'. Pay Ed at the general store. Foster, things come out of the mining account this time. It's a present from Red Bird and me. You take Jenny to dinner at the hotel. You're a rich man now."

"I'll try, but she'll say no."

I went over to the sheriff's office.

"Hello, Buck, what can I do for you?"

"I'm just wandin' what happened to that man that tried to bushwhack me and Foster."

"He was sent to prison for three years."

"Did he have any family around here?"

"He had a wife and two boys. Why?"

"Can you have someone take this out to them? And don't let her know where it came from. No since they suffer cause of what he did. Just say it's from all the townspeople."

"Three hundred. You beat all a man tries to kill you and you take care of his family. I'll do it."

"Maybe she can have Bill get her a divorce and give her and her boys a new start. We're headin' out in six days. Let everyone know if they want to see a big cattle drive, we'll be comin' east of town in six days from this mornin'. I'm headin' to the saloon. I'm tryin' to hire ten more men for the drive. If you know anyone, let them know."

"Will do."

I headed to the saloon. I stopped by the general store. They were piling things on the counter. Ed was writing things down and putting them in boxes, some for Foster and some for the drive.

"Ed, make sure we have plenty of ammunition and at least ten rifles. Between the mine, ranch, and now the drive, you're goin' to be a rich man, Ed."

"Oh, Buck, I got them right by the back door. You know, if you keep buying like this, I might be the second richest man in town." He laughed and started writing again.

"Foster, how's it goin'?"

"Oh, she got all these fancy doodads. I'se don't know."

"This is what we need. Buck, he does not know."

"Foster, I'm goin' to the saloon to try to hire some cowboys."

"Buck, I'se think I'se go with you."

"No, you help Juanita."

"Take him, he is in my way. When we are done, I will send Jose to get him."

"Fine, come on, Foster. You look like you need a drink." I took Blacky and walked to the saloon.

"Wait for me'se, Buck. I'se glad you'se got me out of there. I'se don't know if I'se can take that. Too much like being married."

We walked into the saloon and ordered two beers. I turned around and yelled, "Could I have your attention."

It became quiet in a minute.

"I'm lookin' for ten cowboys that want to work. We can teach you about cows, but I need men that can shoot straight and ride a horse. We're headin' on a cattle drive to Wyoming and Montana. We'll be gone from two to four months."

"How much you payin'?"

"If you know about cattle and horses and can shoot, well I'll pay fifty dollars a month. If you don't, forty a month. We might have a run-in with Geronimo and his braves. There is always a chance of cattle rustlers. If you're interested go to my office, sign up with Mr. Gills, and he'll give you a note to brin' to the ranch. You can start tomorrow. We leave in six days. You will get paid at the end of the drive, or let Mr. Gills know, and he'll put your pay in the bank in case something happens to you, your family can get your wages."

"Some of us have small ranches east of here. Can we bring some of our cattle to sell?"

"We already have contracts for our herd. How many have ranches that want to bring cattle? And how many cattle?"

Four men raised their hands. All four agreed on twenty apiece.

"That's eighty total. I tell you, I'll fill my contracts, and if anyone wants more or if someone that didn't sign a contract wants some, we'll sell yours to them. But if your cattle die on the way, that's your loss, and I'll try to get top dollar for them. You need to have them branded with your brand so we can tell."

"How much you getting on your contracts? So we know if it's worth our trouble."

"I'm gettin' between $35 and $50 a head. If we fill all our contracts, there will be a bonus for everyone."

"That's a lot. That would be helpful this winter and pay our loan at the bank."

"In six days early, have them on the trail east of town headin' north, and my dad will count your cattle and write your name and number of head in his tally book. You will need to come with the drive. I'm headin' back to the ranch. If you want, you might sign up today if Mr. Gills is still in his office. We only need ten men. First come, first hired. So you men with the cattle, if I was you, I'd get down there fast and sign up. So long. Hope to see you at the ranch, or you four when we head north."

I went by the general store. I saw wagon tracks heading out toward the ranch from behind the store. So I headed Blacky home. I saw Bill's horse still in front of the office. I turned around, and sure enough, the four cattlemen were heading to the office. They knew a good deal when they heard it. I rode up to the barn just before sunset, and I could barely see the wagon at Foster's house. When I entered the barn, there was the chuck wagon, ready to go.

I got a lot done today. I was going to try not to leave the ranch until we left. I wanted to spend more time with the kids and Red Bird. Also, I wanted to see Foster's house after Juanita was through with it. As I went up the steps, I wondered how my dad kept going. I was just thirty-one, and today tuckered me out. The kids came running out on the porch and grabbed my hands and pulled me.

"Pa, supper's ready. Ma said hurry, it's getting cold."

"Sorry, I had a lot to do in town."

"Hello, hon, sorry I'm late. Had a lot to do in town, but I'm spendin' the rest of my time before the cattle drive with you and the kids."

"That is good. Me ready for that."

"Tomorrow afternoon, we can go down and see what Juanita has done to Foster's house."

"Is she pretty?"

"I would say so—but not as pretty as you."

"Then we become friends."

"Oh, Ma," the kids said at the same time.

"Come on, let's all sit on the porch. It's a nice night. Manuel, come on and sit with us. Leave the dishes for later."

Red Bird and I sat in the porch swing. The kids were jumping up and down the steps after fireflies. Manuel was sitting on the wide railing of the porch.

"Manuel, have you seen Jose yet?"

"Si, he help me fix supper for the boys. He is a good cook. I watch him."

"I have a surprise for you. I think you have too much to do. I know you never complain."

"Not too much. I don't mind."

"When we get back from the drive, Jose is goin' to stay here at the ranch and help you. You can cook for us, and Jose will cook for the hands. Any way you like it. You will get a ten-dollar raise a month."

"You are very kind, Senor Buck."

Red Bird said, "Buck, he will cook for us. I like his cooking, and he helps me clean good He helps with Carolyn and Lizzie also. I hope they will be healed soon."

"You heard the woman of the house. You stay and help Red Bird."

"Thank you, senorita, for the kind words. I better get to the dishes. They will not wash themselves. Good night."

"Good night, Manuel." After Manuel had left, B. J. came up to us.

"Pa!"

"Yes, BJ."

"I know you said I can't go, but I want to so much."

"Little Buck, you can't."

"Ma, BJ."

"I forgot. BJ, you mine boy. You know you have school in ten days. School important."

"When you're bigger," I said.

"I'm tall as Ma."

"I mean older. When you are older, your grandpa and me can teach you about the ranch, and you can work at the mine. Tim and Jim will teach you. Dancing Bear will show you more about the forest and animals."

"You own the ranch and mine, why he have to work?"

"To learn all he can. Dancing Bear would not make him a brave if he did not know how to hunt and know about the forest and to fight enemies."

"You are right. He is growing up so fast. I miss my mother and my father and my sister."

"I know. We'll ask Foster tomorrow. I know he would like to see Dancing Bear. Maybe he can take you and the kids up there for a week or two. Maybe Ma can go with you."

"Oh, Buck, that would be good. Children, it's time for bed. Your pa and me are going to sit out here for a while."

"Oh, Ma, do we have to?"

"Go on now. Tomorrow we'll go see Uncle Foster's new house."

"Good night, Ma and Pa."

Red Bird got in my arms, and we did a little kissing and just held each other and watched as the stars and the full moon came up over the tree line in the east.

"Better go check on women," she said.

"I'll come up with you."

We went on up and were in Carolyn and Lizzie's room.

"Buck, I no want you to go on the cattle drive. I miss you."

"I know. I will miss you too, but Sam and Josh will be waiting for us somewhere up the trail."

"Women all right, let's go to bed. At least I want you in me a few more times. We can bathe before we go to bed."

"Oh, honey, you just want me to wash your body."

"You no like."

"I like a whole lot. But they might hear."

"They no hear. Let's go."

The next morning, we got the children up and ate breakfast together. While Red Bird fed the women what Manuel had fixed, the children and I went to the barn, and I cut up five apples and let them feed the horses and Foster's mule. Dad came into the barn, and the kids ran to him, and he hugged them.

"What are you two doin'?"

"Feeding the horses apples."

Song Bird said, "They enjoy them very much."

"As much as you do, I bet."

"Yes, but I like oranges better."

"What you up to, Dad?"

"Your mother just headed up to your house to help Red Bird. I'm about to head out and make sure the boys are roundin' up and brandin' the rest of the cattle we need. The cattle are lookin' pretty good after bein' on that nice, tall grass these last few weeks."

"There might be some more hands show up in the next few days. They should have a note from Bill for you. Some might be new, but I hope they can learn from the old hands. There were four small ranchers there, and I agreed to take twenty head each with us if they came along and are branded. They'll meet us on the trail east of town. I didn't promise any set price. When they show up, you can count and write down how many in your little book I know you keep."

Riding away, he said, "Yes, sir, have to keep track of everything."

"Well, kids, let's go get your Ma and go see Uncle Foster's house."

We picked up Red Bird and walked to Foster's house. It was a far piece, but it was a nice summer day. Only a few clouds in the skies, and the flowers were out in force. We knocked on the door, and Juanita answered.

"It's Mr. Buck and a beautiful young lady and two children. She called out to Foster. Then to me, she said, "Come on in. It's still a little messy. I can't get him to do much."

"I told you."

"I know. I just like giving him trouble."

"Juanita, this is my wife, Red Bird, and BJ and Song Bird." They said hello. "Foster talks about you all the time but he didn't say how beautiful you were."

"You embarrass me. You are pretty one."

Foster came into the room smiling from ear to ear as he shook my hand and gave the children and Red Bird a hug.

"Juanita, show them around our big cabin."

"Foster, how many times I tell you it's a house."

"All right, all right."

They went off looking at the house, and Juanita was showing them everything. She showed them her room and the cloths to make the curtains. I heard Red Bird tell her, "Now, if you can get him to take bath, that would be a miracle. The women in my father's village never got him to take a bath since I was little girl. The men threw him in the pond when me and Buck got married."

"Foster, we're leaving in five days. If you could look after Red Bird and the children while we're gone. I told them you would probably be able to take them to Dancing Bear. Maybe Juanita could help my mother with the women. Red Bird will be lonely, and she would like to see her parents and her sister. We are leaving some men to watch over the ranch. Take two or three for protection."

"I'se could do that for you'se. Look at what you'se give me'se. It would be nice to see the old chief. Maybe go hunting with BJ and Dancing Bear. I need a deer head for over the fireplace."

"Thank you. I'll feel better about leaving them."

We left Foster's and were headed home when Red Bird said, "Think she good for him. He looks happy. Tomorrow Jenny be out given me first lesson. Would you take the children riding while she here?"

"Yes, I'll take them out to see the cattle we're takin'"

After breakfast, Jenny came up in her buggy. I helped her down.

"Excuse me, Ms. Trumble, I'm takin' the children for a ride. Come on, BJ, Song Bird, we're goin' ridin'. Call your ma, Ms. Trumble is here."

Red Bird came out with the children. Song Bird ran up and hugged her.

"Hello, Ms. Trumble. I'm glad to see you."

"You too, Song Bird."

I took her by the hand. "Come on, Song Bird, your ma is goin' to take her first lesson,"

We went to the barn and saddled up and headed out to see the cattle. The men were trying to finish up the branding before we left. Four men rode up to me, and Dad rode over. They started to hand me the notes. I pointed to Dad. ""He's the boss of the men."

They handed him the notes, and he read them.

"We leave in five days. Just blend in with the men and help them where you can. I'm not hard to work for if you do your job. We work hard and have a little fun when we can. Get to know the men 'cause y'all are goin' to depend on each other for the next two to three months. If you do good and learn fast, there might be a job for you after the end of trail. Now get out there and learn all you can. Buck, here's a note from Bill."

Four ranchers came in and signed up. They said that they would meet you east of town when you head north.

Bill Gills

"Well, Pa, we have eight. All we need is two more. This is about the four men with the cattle. We know they know about cattle, so that's good."

"I've been sittin' here watchin' those four. If the others are like them, we won't have any trouble. They know what they're doin'."

"Now, if the army has rounded up Geronimo and no rustlers get wind of us, we'll be all right."

We rode past the bunkhouse to the barn. We were unsaddling the horses when Jose came in.

"Buck, I've been busy. I want to show you what I did to the chuck wagon." I went over to the wagon.

Jose said, "Look inside."

I looked inside. "I don't see anything different."

"Now, you watch. Only me, you, and you tell your dad."

He started moving things around. I would say two minutes. He opened up a double door, and there were the rifles and ammunition.

"Well, I'll be. It only took you about two minutes to uncover it, if we need them real fast."

"Yes, and look here. The mines might pay you in gold and silver. There is enough room for lots of bags over here. I thought if we were attacked, they wouldn't think to look under the food. If they did, they would see only the bottom of the wagon."

"What a great idea. I'm glad I hired you. You're right, not many would take the time to look that far down. Thanks, Jose. I'll show my dad. We'll see you later, Jose. Let's get up to the house, kids, and get some supper."

Red Bird was standing in the door. She was smiling. "Oh, Buck, I enjoyed it so much. She said that I learned so fast that it would not take long."

BJ said, Ma, you enjoyed school."

"Yes, young man, and you should learn all you can. She is a good teacher. Now you two eat and get to bed."

"Ma, I like school and Ms. Trumble," Song Bird said.

"I know you do, Song Bird."

The days went by with normal duties. Foster was taking Juanita into town to buy some more things. I asked him to stop by the bank. "Withdraw two thousand dollars in small bills to take with us, and ask Ed to add two money belts to the order."

Red Bird came to me the morning before we were to leave. "Buck Taylor, too many people in and out of house. You take me riding this afternoon to our spot down by the river. I bathe in river for you. I will not see you in two or three moons."

"I know what you mean. I'll be glad to take you. Be my pleasure."

After dinner, we told the children to go down to Grandma's and tell her we went to the river. She would understand. We enjoyed our spot as much as ever. By the time we got back, it was dark. The children were asleep. Red Bird headed to our room. I went to check on Carolyn and Lizzie. I shut the door and was on my way to our room when I heard someone calling.

"Buck! Buck!"

I turned around, and there in the center of the hall in her nightgown was Carolyn.

"Carolyn, what are you doing up? Red Bird! Red Bird! Come here quick."

Red Bird came running out half dressed. "What is it?"

"Look who joined us!"

"What are you doing, Carolyn?"

"I had to talk to you. I heard you saying you were leaving on a cattle drive and you would see Josh. I could hear but couldn't speak. I forced myself to get up tonight. You tell Josh, if he still wants me, I'll be here waiting for him. I'll try to be well and help Red Bird with Mother."

"How you know our names?"

"I hear you two talking. I hope Josh's and my love is as strong as yours."

She collapsed, and I carried her back to her room, and Red Bird got her back in bed and covered her up. "Sleep well. I know that took all your strength."

"Well, Josh is in for a big surprise. I'm gettin' up at five. If you want, you can get the children up and I'll saddle your horses and y'all can see us off."

"You know we'll be there. I would not miss it. I know the children will want to be there."

I took her in my arms, and we made love again.

5

I got up at five and went out on the porch, out in front of our room, and walked around. There was light in my parents' house. The bunkhouse had smoke coming out of the smokestack and light throughout. Even at Foster's house, I could see light in the far distance. The chuck wagon was out front with the team all hooked up. The hands' horses were all lined up in front of the bunkhouse; even Blacky was there. He looked ready to go.

I got dressed and put on my hat and holster with my .45 in it. There was a note from Manuel outside our door. I lit the lantern to read it.

> "Sorry boss, I had to get up so early to get things started at the bunkhouse. Y'all come there to eat."

I got Red Bird up, and she got dressed. "I'll be at the bunkhouse, hon. You hurry. Manuel has eats at the bunkhouse."

"I get children ready. Know they don't want to miss this."

Jose was already in the chuck wagon when I got out to the front of the bunkhouse.

"Ready to go, Jose?"

"Si, I just make sure everything is here. The rifles are under here."

"You stay to one side of the herd until it's time to fix supper or dinner. Then rush ahead to get started early. When you go ahead, keep a sharp lookout for trouble and keep your firearms handy. Hide this somewhere in case of accidents." I handed him two liquor bottles.

"Si, you better go eat before they eat it all."

I went inside. The boys were leaving to get the cattle out of the area we'd been keeping them.

"I hope y'all left me something to eat."

"No, boss, you have to wait until we get to Montana." They laughed as they went out the door. I spotted Pa, Mother, Foster, and Juanita. They were already eating. I got my breakfast and went to sit down.

"Where are Red Bird and the children?" Ma said.

"She had to get the children up and ready. She'll be along. I wanted to make sure everything was goin' well."

"Just like your father. He's been up for two hours."

"Mother, something happened last night. I'll let Red Bird tell you about it."

Ross said, "Everything's fine, son. The boys are out getting the herd started this way. I got the wagon ready to go for everyone that's goin' to be taggin' along for a while."

Buck said, "I didn't expect you and Foster to get out of your nice, cozy house just to see a bunch of cows head north."

"Wouldn't miss it for the world. I'se help start all this and got you'se and Red Bird together, you'se know."

Juanita said, "You gave my brother a job. And help me get mine. I'll pray for you every day."

Red Bird came in with the children. She sat down by me. Manuel brought three plates of breakfast.

"I cannot eat. I worry for you and Father. Geronimo out there, and I know he is bad. What he did to our people when I was little girl."

"Ma will be here, and Foster and some of the men you know, and Manuel."

"I not worry for me. I worry only for you, Father, and men. You good men, you cannot think what Geronimo can do."

"Red Bird, I know you worry. Molly worries for me too. I know my son, and when he left Texas, I know he was a boy. I also know when we got here, he was no longer a boy, he was a man. We have talked about Geronimo, and we have some plans of our own. We'll be all right."

"Red Bird, I'se knows Buck and me'se and Dancing Bear have taught him lots about the wilderness, and he knows. He's a strong man, and strong men have to do. You wouldn't want him to turn his back on his men. This is what he is."

"Know what you two say is true. Buck, you go do what you have to. I understand but still worry."

"Now you eat. You have to see us off. Foster, would you drive the wagon until we're by town, and watch over our families."

"Sure will, Buck."

My mother said, "Buck said you have something to tell me about last night."

"Mother, I forgot. Carolyn walked and talked to Buck and me. I know she will be all right."

"Praise be."

"Senor Buck, may I go too?" Manuel said.

"Yes, you're one of the family."

"Mother can come stay in our house if she wants to. I would like," Red Bird said.

Buck said, "Let's get out there, Pa. Those mangy critters won't go to Montana on their own."

We rode out a ways, and there they were, all strung out heading north. Jose had the chuck wagon heading in the same direction. Pedro, the horse wrangler, had the horses coming up on drag. I looked back and saw my lovely Red Bird and children and all the others coming up behind in the wagon. I hated to leave them all, but Foster was right. It was what I had to do. I was determined to do it. Pa was already up on the point. That was a good mile ahead of me. I saw him racing back, pointing to the west.

When I looked, I saw wagon after wagon and buggy after buggy and horse after horse. It looked as though the whole town had come out. There was even Mr. Windslow, of the bank, and Tom who owned the Silver Nugget saloon. Miss Jenny was in a buggy with Bill.

I yelled to him. "See, you took my advice, Bill."

He turned to Miss Jenny, and she put her hand on his. I just smiled and tipped my hat and rode on. I saw Dad ride over to the east where the four cattlemen were bringing their cattle from the east. I saw him get his tally book out. I spotted John riding up.

"Buck, I just wanted to warn you. That bushwhacker got away from my deputy on the way to jail in Denver. Heard tell he joined up with some outlaws up north a ways. The colonel from the fort said Geronimo is still out there. Thought you should know."

"Thanks, John. Do me a favor, don't say anything about this in front of Red Bird. She's worried enough about us. We'll keep a look out. See you in two or three months."

I rode over to the wagon and whispered to Foster, "Tell the men to keep a sharp eye out. That hombre that tried to gun us got loose. John thinks he's up north of here, but keep an eye peeled. So long. I'll miss you, you old buzzard."

"Same goes here. I'se keep an eye opened."

I rode back to Red Bird and kissed her and the children good-bye.

"When Miss Jenny teaches you your letters, I want a letter from you. Foster will know where to mail it. I love you."

I rode up toward the front of the herd. When I glanced back, I saw that the wagon had stopped and was turning back to the ranch. I rode up beside Pa. He turned and looked at the wagon going the other way.

"Son, I'll be right back."

I turned and watched him. He took off for the wagon. He stopped Foster and grabbed Mother and gave her a big hug and kissed her. Then he picked up Red Bird and hugged and kissed her on the cheek. Then he pulled the children up and hugged them, and they hugged him back. He kissed Mother again and then shook Foster's hand and tipped his hat to Manuel and Juanita. Then he came back to the front of the herd.

"What was that all about?"

"Well, son, I told your mother this was my last cattle drive. That I needed to show you the ropes of a cattle drive, and I loved her very much. I told Red Bird I loved having her for a daughter and I loved her. The children, I told them I loved them to pieces. I thanked Foster for taking care of you that first winter. Now let's go north. We have a big job to do,"

We headed north just east of the Rockies. It was sometimes grueling. The men had to get some steers among the boulders as we stayed in as close as we could for protection from the bandits or Indians. We made only five miles the first day. I hoped as we got used to the trail that we could make ten to twelve miles a day.

That first night, the boys were complaining about the aches and pains of staying in the saddle all day. I was feeling the same, but Jose was a great cook, and the boys looked content. Then Jose brought out two big apple pies.

"Where did you get those?" My pa said.

"Senor, these I did not bake. Molly and Red Bird made these. They said this would take the bad feelings about leaving home away a little."

They were right; the pies were gone in no time, and the complaining stopped as I got my second piece of pie.

I told the nightriders to keep a sharp look out and come running back if they saw anything.

Pa came over to me. He had the map out. "Look here, we should come to the first river tomorrow. In the mornin', I'm goin' to send Carlos ahead to find a crossin' for us. I wish Sam were here. It might make it easier."

"The first delivery should be a day or two pass that river. He might be here by then. I hope he has the contracts. If not, we'll deliver them anyway. We don't want any trouble with the mine owners. I'm goin' to get in my bedroll. I'm tuckered again."

"Me too, son. See you in the mornin'."

I woke up and listened, but heard nothing, and then I thought it was the cold that woke me. It was the middle of summer, but the nights were still cold. I was just to use to a roof over my head and Red Bird's warmth next to me.

I awoke to the smell of coffee and bacon and eggs. Not just plain eggs, but Mexican-style eggs. Pa and I sat eating while the boys got the herd going.

"Carlos, would you come over here."

"Si, senor. What can I do for you?"

"We want you to go ahead and scout the river. Should be six or seven hours. Get some grub and shells in case of trouble. Find a way for us to cross easily. Be careful, don't trust anyone. You know Sam and Josh. If you see them, send them our way."

"Si. If I can make it back by dark, I will."

Jose stayed east of the herd to stay away from the boulders. We couldn't afford to have a broken wheel. He had to move a little faster than the herd to be able to get supper ready for the men, and then dinner after that. It was hard, but he kept going. He had to get up an hour before anyone then, and after dinner, he had to clean up, and then he kept a hot pot of coffee after that.

The night riders had it hard too. We rotated them so the same riders would not be out every night. Pa and I took our turns. Carlos didn't get back before nightfall, but this didn't worry me too much, for we didn't know how accurate the map was. We woke up to Carlos sitting by the fire drinking coffee. I walked over to him.

"Find the river."

"Si, is good. I find a spot to cross. I left stones to mark the spot. We need to head the cattle a little to the northeast. I did not see Sam, but I did see a lot of shod horse tracks heading north past the river. On the other side of the river, there is plenty of grass for the cattle before we deliver the first bunch. We might make it by nightfall if we're lucky."

"Thanks, Carlos. Would you tell the men to take extra ammo for their weapons for me and to keep a look out? Would you want the job of scouting an hour or two ahead of us until we meet up with Sam and Josh? They'll know the way. Get some sleep."

"I slept last night. I had a dry camp last night. I'll eat and then head out."

"Fine. If you spot any trouble, head back fast. Try not to be seen."

"Si."

"You hungry, Senor Silver? I'll bring you a plate," Jose said.

"You brin' me a plate and then turn around, then turn back around, and if my plate is full, then I ain't hungry."

Everyone around the fire laughed. We ate and then got moving. We moved them a little faster than we had been. We needed to cross that river, even if it was dark.

Pa came over. "Son, why are you pushin' the cattle so hard? They'll lose weight."

"We need to get across that river before we bed them down. We can give them a day to fill their bellies after we're across that river."

"Why not camp on this side and move them across in the mornin'?"

"See, Pa, it could rain on top of the mountain durin' the night, and we might not get a drop down here. But the water comin' down that mountain would swell the river so much we might be caught on this side for a week, or even two. We need to get across."

"I see. I told your mother that I needed to teach you the ropes. I think you're teachin' me."

We kept driving them hard to the northeast. We kept them moving past dinner. We let five or six men come in and eat at a time. The last bunch was fed.

"Jose, take the wagon ahead. I'm sendin' two men with you to help you cross the river. Get the camp set up about half a mile from the river. We're goin' to get the cattle across that river tonight."

"Si."

"Carlos, you pick a man, and you two help Jose cross that river. Then hightail it back here to show us where the crossin' is."

"Si, senor."

We moved them ahead all afternoon. Then about midafternoon, Carlos came back.

"Are we close, Carlos?"

"About three miles. I left Scotty there in case of trouble and helped Jose set up camp. I told them to keep a sharp eye out."

"I know you're tired. We can all rest tomorrow. So you get out in front and head us the right direction."

I saw Carlos talking to Pa. He was pointing straight ahead. I knew with Pa and Carlos in the lead, the job would get done. I went to the rear and ate some dust on drag. Behind us were Pete and two others with our horses about thirty. If we didn't have any accidents, we could sell them to the miners at top dollar. About five in the afternoon, the lead cattle came to the river. Four cowboys were in the river on one side of the herd and four on the other side. The cattle were going in between the eight men. Two others were on the outside of those eight, in case some cattle strayed to the outside. I saw some cattle knock one cowboy off his horse into the river. I threw him a rope, and he got back on his horse and waved thanks to me. It was dark now, and we were about three-fourths across. Thankfully, the full moon was out bright. I saw the fire of our camp. The last were going in the river, and then the horses came in. As I rode into camp, some of the men were done eating and heading out on night watch.

"Men, some of the boys and me will relieve you in five hours. I know you're tired. We are goin' to rest the cattle tomorrow. Let them eat their fill of grass. We'll rotate men all day."

"Thanks, Silver."

"Carlos, tomorrow you rest till noon and head north. Look for Sam and be on the lookout for those hombres and Indians."

"Si, Silver."

"Pa would you come over here. I haven't had time since we left."

We went to the wagon and got inside.

"What is it, Buck?"

"Watch this."

I moved the sacks of food around. "See?"

"See what? I only see the bottom of the wagon."

"Now watch. It was Jose's idea." I opened the door, and my father looked surprised. There were the rifles and ammunition. "Look, over here is a place for gold and silver. I never thought of the mines paying us in gold and silver. We have our money belts for the paper money, and this for our hard money. No one knows about this except Jose, you, and me."

"You know, son, I think he should have an extra bonus for this. If we're held up, no one would think to look under here."

"I just hope Sam comes in soon. The first mine looks to be across the next river, ten miles or so. We need the contracts."

"You think we could have missed each other?"

"Maybe. I just don't know."

"Why don't we send Ben back a couple of days. He can crisscross and keep an eye on our back trail."

I called one of the cowhands, "Ben, would you come here? Bring your food. Tomorrow, we want you to check on our back trail for Sam and Josh. Maybe two days. Keep an eye out for trouble. Tell Jose' tonight to fix up a bag of food for you."

"Will do, Silver. I'm hitting the sack. That river 'bout did me in."

"I feel the same. Good night."

Everyone hit their bedrolls early except the night riders. We were plum tuckered out. I woke up to see the men come in and wake up their reliefs. Then they went to sleep for the night. I saw the men get up and get some coffee and breakfast that Jose had left on the hot coals. Everything was fine, so I rolled over, and I saw that my pa was stirring. I went back to sleep.

I rolled out of my bedroll in the morning. Pa was already up eating. Ben and Carlos were saddling up and moving out, and then Ben was heading to the south and Carlos to the north. I got my boots on and went to sit down by Pa.

"What you doin' today?"

"I think I'm goin' to see how much grass the cattle have eaten. Then move them a ways north to more grass. I'm sure they have eaten it down a ways."

"Pa, I'm a little concerned about Sam. I'm saddlin' up and headin' northwest into the foothills. I told Sam to try to stay out of sight as much as he could. I'll try to be back before nightfall."

"Don't worry, son, we'll take care of the cattle. I'm sure one of you will find Sam."

I headed northwest, and Blacky seemed glad to be out by ourselves. I was about two hours out of camp. I was among the boulders and back in the canyons. I was looking for any sign of a small fire or the tracks of two riders. Another hour, and I saw many unshod horses' tracks, which meant Indians. I looked among the tracks for shod horse tracks but didn't find any. These tracks were about a week old, and they were heading north. I rode on and went into two more crayons, but nothing. I was about ten miles out of camp when I came to a creek. I thought this would be easy to cross and water the cattle. Then I heard a noise that sounded familiar. It was coming from the northwest from where I was. The sound got louder and got clearer. Then from nowhere, Carlos was by me.

"I heard that too from where I was. Then I saw you. What you think it is?"

As we got closer, I knew I heard it before.

"You know, Carlos, I know I've heard this before. It was when I sent Sam to pick up some rails for the mine. Let's go in slow, but I think that's old Sam."

We went around the next bend with our guns drawn. There atop the biggest boulder in the area sat Sam playing his guitar. There at the bottom was Josh dancing up a storm, all alone, clapping his hands. We put our guns away, and I stepped down off Blacky, and Carlos did the same. Josh turned and stopped dancing and shook my and Carlos's hands.

"Good to see you, boys. Sam said his music would bring you a-running."

"What you doin' up there Sam?"

"Best view in the whole country. I saw you a-coming a mile away. I thought I'd let you find me. Didn't want to scare you by firing a shot."

"Now come on down. We have work to do."

"See, Josh, I told you he'd find us and put us to work right away."

Sam came down and shook my and Carlos's hands.

"Good to see you both, even if I have to go back to work. Where's the cows, you leave them back at the ranch?"

Josh and Carlos burst out laughing. I tried to look serious, but that didn't work. Then I started laughing. "Just funning with you. I brought a money belt. The contracts are all nice and complete, next to my warm belly. Now, where are those damn cows?" I stopped laughing.

"We were worried about you two, and then you come out crackin' jokes. The cattle are about three hours behind us. You see any Indians?"

"No, but two of the mining camps were attacked. They fought them off with two or three men killed. Those are the first two we'll come to. I tell you, these camps need the beef. Some haven't seen meat in a year. All the working mines have scared most of the big game away with the noise. The first one about two days away is Job's Crossing. There's a diner in town. They talked me into twenty heads. I figured, what the hell, money is money. They all said they would make arrangements for the cattle to have a place to graze."

"Let's head back and get them movin' in the mornin'."

We mounted up and were gone. On the way, Josh asked about Carolyn and Lizzie.

"When we get back, I'll talk to you. It's good, if you can wait. We can talk alone."

"All right, Silver."

Sam said, "You know, I'm glad it's good news 'cause all that boy talks about is that gal."

"I'm glad too," Josh said.

We got back to camp about an hour before dark. We got our eats and then called Pa over. Sam took his money belt off and handed it to me.

"Here, Pa, is the contracts. You can go over them while me and Sam are eatin'."

"I'll be back. I better go talk to Josh." I called out.

"Josh, come eat over here with me. I want to talk to you."

"How is she?"

"Well, Josh, she's better, but she has a long ways to go. We didn't know it, but she heard everything that has been said to her."

"You mean she told you this?"

"Yes, and more. The night before we left, I went to their room. They seemed to be the same, but as I went out of the room, I heard a noise behind me, and someone called me Silver. I turned around, and Carolyn was walkin' toward me. I called Red Bird and rushed to Carolyn and caught her before she fell. Red Bird came, and we sat her on the bench. She told us that she could hear everything bein' said but could not respond. That's how she knew to call me Silver, and she knew Red Bird's name. She heard what you told her and about the cattle drive, and that I would be seein' you. She told me to tell you if you still wanted her, she would be waitin' for you."

He jumped up and yelled and threw his hat in the air. I heard Sam ask Pa, "What is it, Fourth of July or what?"

"You mean she walked?"

"Calm down. Yes, she walked. But she's still very weak. I had to carry her back to bed. I told her to rest and eat all she could. It's been a week since we left. Red Bird thinks she'll be eatin' at the table before long and helpin' take care of her mother."

I walked over to Sam and Pa. "What you say to that boy?"

"Just that Carolyn talked to us a little and walked some. How was he on the trail?"

"Besides talk about that gal and what he wants to do with that ranch, he was fine. He liked my guitar playing and laughed at my jokes. He wasn't much fun in the saloon. Wouldn't touch the gals. He just sat there and nursed one beer all night. Reminded me of you before you married Red Bird."

"I know how he feels. But I mean work, Sam. Should have known you would be in the saloon all night and a gal in your room. Did you get any work done?"

"He sure did, son. These contracts are all filled out and signed. Our first delivery is Job's Crossing, five hundred head, and Ann's diner, twenty head. Sam wrote something at the bottom. It says, 'Upon delivery of the cattle, the new owners would be responsible for having a place to keep the cattle upon arrival.'"

"Sam, you're a lawyer now?"

"Made sense that we didn't want to stay around keeping cows from roaming all over the countryside."

"Wait till Bill reads that. He'll want to make you his partner. Just kiddin', that's great. You have something in that head besides drinkin' and saloon gals."

"But that's not too bad to think about."

We all laughed, even Pa.

"Pa, did you laugh?"

"I was a little worried. But now one worry is gone. We have the contracts. The second delivery is Sutter's Mine. Another five hundred head."

"There's no town near. It's back in the mountains a little ways.

But I found a way in there with the cattle. Might have to bring more men to keep the cattle out of the draws and canyons. There's only one little creek that we went by and a river after the first town. We can get by the town with no problem."

"We still have the Indians out there, and Ben saw some shod tracks on our back trail."

"The night riders are out. I'm hittin' the sack. Tomorrow's goin' to be the start of some rough country. Night."

The next morning, we were up early. The men were done eating and were heading out to get the herd moving. Josh was in the lead. I heard him saying, "Come on, boys, we have to get this beef to market. I want to be home before winter."

I knew why Josh was in a hurry. I felt a little of that myself. Pa, Sam, and I were finishing our coffee when Ben came riding in. He grabbed some breakfast and came to sit with us.

"Silver, there are about twenty-five men on our back trail. They're about five hours behind us. They didn't see me, but I followed them for a day. They stopped all day yesterday. How long have you been here?"

"We stopped here after we crossed the river back yonder to let the cattle feed on this good grass day before yesterday."

"Then they must have someone watchin' us 'cause that's about when they stopped. They could have overtakin' us anytime."

"Makes sense. They must know we're takin' the cattle somewhere to sell. After the first two deliveries, we'll have over $50,000. We better have a plan ready in case they hit us after that. Ben, you get some rest in the chuck wagon. Sam, you go back and keep an eye on them. Get some food and keep out of sight. Come our way if anything happens. I'll have Josh head us in the direction of Job's Crossing."

"I'll get with Ben. He can tell me where they are. I'll be careful. I like to think about what happens in Job's crossing, Silver. But when it comes to business, I'll take care of it."

"I know you will, Sam."

Sam got going getting things together and then took off. "Don't save any hard work for me, boys." He waved his hat and hit his horse on the rump.

I said to my dad, "I have a plan, Pa. We're goin' to need Jose's help." I went and brought Jose over.

"Have a seat, Jose."

He had a worried look on his face. "I do something wrong, senor?"

"No, sir, we need your help again. We have twenty-five men on our back trail. You think you can make room in that wagon for five or six men?"

"Si, can be done."

"I want you to follow behind a little ways when Sam comes runnin' in hard shoot off one shot, and I'll tell the men close to the back of the herd to be ready. We'll come runnin'. It may not happen for six or seven days, but be ready. Get five rifles and ammunition out and have the rifles loaded. The men can come back to eat and sleep. If Sam comes in ridin' slow, he probably just needs food and to make a report. Make sure when you set up camp to have the side of the wagon facin' our back trail. Make sure the canvas can be rolled up easy. We want to surprise them. If they can't be reasoned with, we'll let the lead fly."

"That sounds like a plan. I'll get things ready."

We caught up with the herd, Pa on the left and me on the right. We told the closest six men if they heard one shot to head back to the chuck wagon, to have their rifles and pistols full at all times." I rode on to the point, and there was Josh. "I had to send Sam to check on our back trail. There are twenty-five men back there. You think you can lead us to Job's Crossing?"

"Sure can, boss. There's a creek up ahead about a mile or two. Then by tomorrow, we should be there."

"We'll camp about one mile on the other side of that creek. Then tomorrow, I'll get about six men and you. You'll point Pa in the right direction to Sutter's Mine, and he'll keep them headin' that way. Us eight will cut out 520 head, and you can show us the way into Job's Crossing and to the mine and that diner.

"They said to bring them right down Main Street. It's not much of a street. The diner is right on Main Street next to the saloon. The woman's name is Ann. It should be on the contract. The mining office is on the other side of town, and the pasture should be right past that. They said that was where they were going to fence. The owner of the mine is Mr. Johnson.

I have to talk to some of the ranches that came along. Remember, bed them down one mile from the other side of the creek. Let them water at the creek. I'm sure Pa will see to that."

"I'll take care of it, Silver."

"Mat, Dru, Tom, and Will, over here," I called out to the others, and they came riding over.

"What's up, Silver?"

"Tomorrow we are goin' to make our first delivery. There's a diner in town that needs twenty head, and if you can find five head of each of yours, that will be a start. If you can't find yours, we'll take them out of ours, and my pa will subtract five off your tally,"

"That sounds good."

"If you don't mind, I'll settle up with y'all at the end. Pa and me have money belts. I like to have the money in one place. There are some men on our back trail. Sam is keepin' an eye on them. We don't think they'll hit us till we make these first two deliveries. If Pa or me are shot, get our money belts off us. Keep an eye out for anyone far off 'cause someone is lettin' them know what we're doin'. Oh, the camp will be a ways behind us for a while. Let the men around you know."

"Will do."

We made it across the creek without any mishaps. One cowboy fell in the creek, but he needed a bath anyways. I thought I was going to be in town the next day, so I stepped down off Blacky and took my clothes off and jumped in the creek. Ten of the men jumped in too. I washed my clothes and let them dry. That night I told Pa what my plans were for the following day. Sam didn't come in, but I wasn't worried.

"Jose, if you need anything from town, make me a list."

"Si."

That morning, Sam came riding in before breakfast.

"Just in time. I ran out of food last night. I thought I'd come in this morning and take you into town. Josh can lead Ross and the cattle toward Sutter's Mine. The gang is still on our trail, and they're still hanging back about the same distance. Bob knows them and can get back there and keep an eye on them."

"That sounds good."

We hit the trail early as usual; and by noon, Sam came to me while I was eating. "Silver, I think we should get those beef together. See that next rise maybe two miles? Just over that is where she'll be."

"Eat and pick six men and round them up. I'll help when I'm done."

The ranchers came over. "We got our twenty round up."

"See that ridge? Drive them toward that. When we get there with our five hundred, we'll take over. If one of you wants to come with us, you can look after your interest."

"No, sir Silver, we already decided we trust you."

"All right, then. I'll meet you on top of that ridge. If you care to write a few words to your families, I'll put them with mine, and if there's a place to mail them, I will. Put your name on the front, and I'll send the bunch to Mr. Gills. He'll see that your families get them."

"Our families may need some money. Could you send our $250 apiece in the same package?"

"I'll tell you what, so we won't take a chance losing money in the mail, I'll write Mr. Gills a note to deposit money in the bank in your names out of my account. He'll let your wives know that they can get it out when they need it. I'll do that every time we sell your cattle."

6

We got the cattle rounded up. It took three hours. We were now up to the ridge and headin' for town. I had the contracts in my saddlebags.

"I see what you mean. It's not much of a town. I see four or five buildings."

"That center one next to the saloon. That's the diner."

"Come on, boys, let's head them through town."

"The pasture should be at the other side of town past the mining office."

The street was lined with people coming out of the buildings. They were yelling and chapping as we went down the street—more like a trail, but they called it a street.

Sam said, "There is Ann. She lives in back of the diner. Has a nice bedroom, and she's a mighty good cook too."

"Took your breakfast in bed?"

"Well, got to have some fun. Let's stop by and say hello."

We let the boys move the cattle on down the street. They weren't even one-fourth through town. She was a pretty woman with blonde hair and dark brown eyes. She was shading her eyes from the sun. We rode over to her, and after dodging the cattle, we made it to the diner.

"Ann, this is my partner, Silver. Well, I'm the little partner. He's the big partner."

"Sam, you're just as funny as the last time you were here."

"Hello, Miss Ann. I'm Buck, and he is my partner."

I shook her hand. Nice and soft for all the kitchen work she must do.

"Nice to meet you, Buck. We sure are glad to see this beef before winter. With outlaws and Indians out there, we just didn't know if you would make it."

"We better get. We need to get these cows home. We'll be back when we get done at the minin' office."

"The pasture is just past the mining office. When you get done, come back. You and your boys have dinner on me. Ask Sam, I'm a damn good cook."

"Thanks. We'll be back." As I turned Blacky, I said to Sam, "Look over there. Those two just tied up in front of the saloon. Let's go, Sam. We don't want any trouble."

The cattle were through town and in the pasture. Sam and I stopped in front of the mining office. Mr. Johnson was out in front watching the boys close the gate. The boys came over.

Buck said, "Here's twenty dollars. Have a couple of drinks on me. When we're done here, meet us in the diner. We'll eat and catch up with the herd tonight."

They grabbed the twenty and said thanks and went to the saloon.

"You must be Mr. Johnson. I'm Buck Taylor." I shook his hand.

"Glad to see you. I'm glad my men well have beef up at the mine this winter. It's a small operation, but I hope we will find more gold. Sam here was telling me about your mine."

"He was. Well, we've been at it for ten years. It's been good, but my heart was in ranchin'. I let two of my other partners run the mine. Foster retired and lives on the ranch now. He's vice president of the mine. We found it together."

"Let's go inside. I'll get the money together. I've been keeping this in the office. I was afraid I would get robbed. We don't have a bank in town yet. Will it be all right if I pay you in gold?"

"Sure thing. I have the contract right here. That's $25,000."

He brought out two large bags and a scale. He set both bags on the scale.

"Thirty-two pounds of gold is twenty dollars an ounce. That's all right, Buck."

"Sure is. Hope we can do business again. By the way, there were twenty-five men followin' our drive. They looked up to no good. I think two just rode into town to keep an eye on us. So be careful. If you need more cattle, write to Silver Buck Ranch, Durango, Colorado. By the way, do you have some place to mail a letter in this town?"

"Sure, we have one right here. We have wagons going out all the time."

"Thanks."

I told Sam to go join the boys because I had to go to the general store. I got what Jose wanted and put the things in my saddlebags. Then I went to the saloon. I was carrying the bags of gold as I went into the saloon. I sat down at a table and looked around. This place wasn't much—five tables and nonmatching chairs, and the bar was just four barrels with wood planks on top of them with a little mirror behind the bar and two shelves with no more than eight bottles of whiskey, and I saw one barrel of beer.

"Sam, would you bring me a beer?"

"Silver, what you bring that in here for?"

"Where you want me to put it, in my saddlebags? Maybe it will make those two over there show their hand. If so, we would have two less to deal with later. Tell the boys to come over to the diner. Then we'll leave."

I finished my beer and was fixing to leave when Sam and the boys came over and helped me with the gold. We walked into the diner, which wasn't much bigger than the saloon. It had about ten tables but was decorated much nicer. She had curtains on the two windows and tablecloths on each table. You could tell a woman owned this place.

Ann came over. "Have a seat, boys. What would you have to eat? I have a new item on the menu tonight."

We all ordered the same. Ann brought the food out.

"Have a seat, Miss Ann. I see you got some of your beef. Here's your contract."

"I'll go get the gold."

"No, sit awhile. I think the boys think you are mighty pretty to look at. They been on the trail for two weeks."

"Thank you, boys. Sam, go get the apple pie back there."

The men said their thank-you's. We talked awhile, and then she went to the back and brought out three pounds of gold. I told her about the men following us and told her to be careful.

She pulled out a .12-gauge shotgun. "When I'm alone, this is by me."

We left carrying all the gold after Sam took her into the kitchen and said his good-byes. We put the gold in my and Sam's saddlebags.

"Sam, you think she would use that?"

"She sure would. I went out with her, and she blew everything out of the water."

"You know, Sam, when we get around this corner, you and Pete hide and see if those fellas follow us. If they do, follow them till we're a ways out of town. Then jump them, and we'll take them back to camp to get some information out of them."

"Will do. Come on, Pete. We're going to have some fun."

We were out a ways when a slug whizzed by my head and hit a tree beside me. Then another and another, and then everything stopped.

"Hit the ground, boys. Don't shoot yet. Sam and Pete are out there in the dark. We'll wait awhile."

Sam and Pete came riding in with one man all tied up."

"The other one is back there in the dirt. They started shooting before we knew it."

"Pete, go back and throw the body over his horse and bring him with us."

Buck asked the man that was alive. "What's your name? What were you doin' jumpin' us? Is there any more men out there?"

"No, we saw you have all those cattle. I knew you had to get paid. We were going to get the money and get away in the dark and leave the country."

"What's your partner's name?'

"Tom. I'm Dan."

"Sam, is there a sheriff in the next town?"

"There's no town, just a mine, but there is one in Oak Creek. It's about five days away."

"We'll just have to hold him till then. We can't spare a man to take him now."

"You could let me go, and I'll light out of the country."

"No, sir, let's head back and find a camp. It's late. We can bury the other one when we hit camp."

We were on the move again. Dan kept saying to let him go and he'd never bother us again.

"You better be quiet, or I'll have to gag you."

I knew the outlaws would be out there somewhere. We saw a small fire up ahead. I was leading the men toward the fire when someone came from in front of us. I drew my gun.

"It's me, Silver. It's Josh."

"I nearly shot you. We already have been ambushed once tonight."

"That's who's laying across that horse?"

"Yes, and the other one is tied up over yonder by Pete."

"That fire's not the cattle drive, it's the outlaws. The drive is up ahead about a mile. You need to go west of here over that ridge. Be careful. There's a ravine up there."

"You comin' in with us?"

"No, I better stay. You know, keep an eye."

"Boys, give Josh your food and some water. Josh, you come in tomorrow and come with us, and Pete will watch them tomorrow. We'll be at Sutter's Mine in two days or so. Be very careful with this one. He nearly took off my head. I'll get some sleep tonight. They're probably waiting for a report from these two. I'll keep Blacky tied close by. He'll let me know if someone is around."

We headed out again and came to the ravine. Good thing it was moonlight, or we might have fallen over the side. Then we saw a much bigger fire. We rode into camp after yelling it was us so we wouldn't get shot.

"Sam, Pa, and Jose, would y'all come over here. Jose, I'm glad you made that false bottom in the wagon."

Sam and I pulled out two large and one small bag of gold.

"Pa, seems Jose was right. There's not many banks up this way yet. Jose, show Sam where it is. He's our partner."

"Come on up, Sam."

Jose moved all the boxes and opened two doors.

"All the rifles and ammunition and see, over here is a place for the gold or silver."

I handed the gold sacks up to Jose, and he put them up and closed it up. "Pa, you can write down $25,960.

"What these rifles over here?"

"I'm goin' to have a little surprise for our attackers."

Pa said, "Who's that man all tied up, and the dead one?"

"They tried to ambush us outside of Job's Crossing. They didn't make it. We better get that one buried and hit the sack. I'm tuckered out."

I got up to Jose's cooking. I heard the men joshing Sam about Ann in Job's Crossing.

Silver, Sam said he's heading back to Job's Crossing at the end of trail to see that gal Ann. They get along."

"They seemed to get along fine. I've seen him kiss her when they went to get those apple pies."

"Apple pies!"

"Yes, boys, that woman sure can cook, and pretty as can be."

Pa spoke up. "Well, Sam maybe in love, but we have some cows to move. Let's get out there and move them out."

"Oh, boss, we just funning him."

"Jose', keep an eye on this bandit and when you stop to cook tie him to the wheel. Give him food and water."

"Si, senor Silver."

We headed north. Everything went find for two days. Josh came in and ate. I told him.

"You want Ben or Pete to take your place for a couple of days?"

"No, sir. You gave me an important job, and I'm going to see it to the end, or you tell me otherwise."

"All right, but if you see them movin' fast, you come a-runnin' as fast as that horse will carry you. Come straight to Jose here. He knows what to do. Then come get Pa and me, and you hear me, be very careful. They may have a lookout as we deliver these next cattle tomorrow."

"Yes, sir, I will. Have to make it back to Durango in one piece."

"Pa, you as fast with that gun as you were in Texas?"

"I may have slowed down a little, but I can still beat you."

"Ross, I've seen Silver, and he's right fast."

"Sam, I know how fast my son is. I taught him."

"Yes, Sam and he would beat me by three seconds. If they come at us, I want you beside me."

"Wouldn't have it any other way. They're not goin' to get our cattle without war."

"Then tomorrow, Sam, you led us to the mine with the same six boys. And, Pa, you keep headin' northwest to Oak Creek. We'll try to get back before night. Oak Creek has a sheriff, so I really think they will hit us before we get there."

The next day, we rounded up five hundred head tighter and went toward the mountains.

"Silver, let's get in and out of this place fast as we can."

"Why, Sam, something you not tellin' me?"

"It's just I think you'll get mad."

"Why?"

"Their operations not like ours. The whole area around the mine is bare of tress or plants. Nothing. Every time it rains, it's a foot or two feet in mud from the mountain. The fence pasture should be a ways from the mine. I hope there is some grass for the cattle."

"Glad you warned me."

"There was a lot of ore piled up, but he had a large safe in the office. I think there's refined ore in the safe. He might try to pay you with the raw ore. He might have paper money in there. I wouldn't have dealt with him, but he ordered five hundred head."

"Thanks, Sam. I'll deal with it when we get there."

"Now I know why you didn't want to clear everything from around our mine."

As we headed into the foothill, I could spot the mine from a mile off. It was bare of all vegetation for as far as I could see. I'm glad it hadn't rained lately. As we came toward the mine, I could see a man spot us and run into the mine, and then out poured ten men to watch us. One ran up and asked, "Them for us, mister?"

"The mine owner brought them. They must be for you. I don't know how big he is, but I don't think he can eat five hundred head of cattle."

"We're tired of no meat. You have any trouble with Mr. Sutter, you send for Big John. Hear me? He has refined silver in his safe."

"I will. I have seven cowboys to back me up if need be."

"The pasture is a ways down toward the valley, but it's there. Good luck."

The cattle were heading down the other side of the mountain. The men yelled, "We see it. We'll be back soon. Take it easy."

Sam and I stepped down off our horses and went in the office. I saw the pile of ore as we went in.

"Mr. Sutter, I'm Buck Taylor. I have the beef you contracted to buy."

"Hello, Mr. Taylor. Hi, Sam. I see you made it back."

I handed him the contract just as our six men rode up.

"I have that stockpile of silver ore. I didn't think you would be here this soon."

"You know, I don't have a wagon. What's in that safe behind you? Mind if we have a look?"

"Why, nothing's in there."

"I gave you a contract. Now you open that safe."

"Or what?'

"Well, our next stop is Oak Creek, and they have a sheriff. We already have one outlaw ready for him. We can make room in the chuck wagon for another, and I have six more cowboys outside that will see to that. But I don't think I'll need their help."

"I'm just funning with you. You tell him, Sam, how we were always funning around."

"Sutter, there's nothing funny about trying to cheat us out of $25,000."

"I'll get it out right now. Here it is, all in silver."

"You have a scale to weigh it?"

"Right here."

I opened up every bag and weighed it. It came out fifty dollars over. I threw fifty dollars on the desk.

"You were fifty dollars over."

"Thank you."

"Sam, your next trip up here, don't stop here."

"Yes, Silver."

We got the silver and backed out and put it in our saddlebags. I stopped by the mine. "Is Big John there?"

Big John came out. "Any trouble?"

"Not much. If you want a better job, I'd go to Job's Crossing. They just had their men killed by Indians. They might need someone, and there's a real good cook there. Oh, I would get all the beef I could. He was mad as a wet hen. Don't know what he'll do with them."

"Don't worry, I'll put a twenty-four-hour guard on them."

"So long."

We took off down the trail. The herd would be about two hours ahead of us. We should reach Oak Creek in a couple of days. All of us were keeping an eye open for the outlaws. It didn't look as if they sent anyone to follow us this time. Josh rode in from the east.

"Silver, the outlaws are east of here. I saw you moving the cattle into Sutter's Mine, so I kept an eye on your back trail. I didn't see anyone leave their ranks. I came in to see if you have food and water again."

"Boys, let's stock Josh up again."

I guess they didn't send anyone after the last time they lost two men. We made it back to the drive without any trouble. They were still moving, so we got Jose stopped and he put the silver in its place and started dinner. Pa rode in.

"They're beddin' them down for the night."

"Pa, could I have the contract for the next stop?"

He got it out of his saddlebags. I looked it over and then called Sam over.

"Sam, I don't want any surprises like we had today."

"You had trouble, son?"

"Just a little, no fightin', but this Sutter, the way he runs that operation is bad. You've seen our mine. If it wasn't for the buildin' and the road, you wouldn't know we were there. This Sutter mine has no vegetation or trees for a half-mile circle. When it rains, the mud comes off the mountain and covers everything. He has his men in tents. I can just guess what happens in the winter. Then he tried to pay us in raw ore, which would have taken two wagons to move it. I told Sam not to stop there next time. I told the head miner to try Job's Crossing; it looked to be a better-run operation. We got paid. I guess that's what counts."

Sam said. "I'm sorry about that, Silver, but Oak Creek is a whole lot better. They have a town nearby. A little like Durango. Mr. Jones at the mine was real cooperative. In town, there is a diner and a restaurant at the hotel. Jones is going to pay for the cattle and sell the beef to the two eating places in town. We checked in with the sheriff—his name is Jack. By the time we got to the mine, it had already reached Mr. Jones why we were there. They wouldn't even let us pay for the hotel or drinks or food. They said Mr. Jones already took care of it. The pasture to leave the cattle is halfway between the town and the mine. They said to come through town. This would be a major event."

"I'll have to thank Mr. Jones, and we can drop Dan at the sheriff's office on the way through. Let's not let down our guard. Those outlaws are still on our back trail."

The next two days went better than I expected. I was sure they would try to come at us by now. After Oak Creek, it would be a week before the next delivery. That could be what they were waiting for. Sam said there was some pretty rough country we had to go through. One river and two mountains passes which would be just right for an ambush. We had to do it because the mines were back in the mountains with small mining towns.

I took three extra cowhands this time for the eight hundred head. By the time we got back to camp, we would have $85,000 total. That was more than most banks. Far as I've seen, this will be the only law within hundreds of miles. We herded them into Main Street. Sam and me were at the back of the herd with Dan in tow on his horse. We stopped at the sheriff's office. Lots of people were lining the street; there were maybe a hundred of them.

"The pasture is outside of town a mile or two west. We'll be along. We have to drop off our guest."

The sheriff looked at us and then at Dan as we got him off his horse.

"Looks more like a package than a guest. Come on in, I'll make room in my hotel. I take it you had some trouble."

We got him locked up and untied. Then we went to talk to the sheriff.

"I'm Buck Taylor. This is Sam Ganger. Yes, we had trouble, and there is another twenty or so more out there followin' us."

He was looking at the Wanted posters. "What did he say his name was?"

"He is Dan, and his partner was Tom. No last name."

"Here's is Dan Janson. This is him, wanted for bank robbery and murder.

Here's a Tom Benson. This looks like the other one and wanted for the same thing."

"That's him, all right."

"There's a $500 reward on each one, dead or alive. That's $1,000, and they run with a bunch called the Delta Gang. Now, who gets the reward? I know you're passing through with the cattle. I'm going out to the mine with you. They put up the reward."

"Sam, who got them two?"

"Pete did. He shot that other one before he shot me. Then he saw where the other one went. We crept up on him. So yes, Pete got them both."

The men were waiting by the gate. The cattle were in the pasture.

"Boys, here is forty dollars. Have some fun at the saloon. I said fun, not trouble. Hear me, Pete come with us to the mining office. The sheriff wants you there."

"Yes, Silver."

We walked into the office. There was a bald man behind the desk. He turned around and shook hands with all of us.

"Hello, Jack, what brings you up this way? Well, hello, Sam."

"This here is Buck Taylor, and his men just put eight hundred head of cattle in your pasture. They also brought in one of the men you put the reward on, and another back on the trail is dead. Here are the posters, and I thought you could go ahead and pay them the reward at the same time you pay them for the cattle. You two may have another thing in common. I heard his men call him Silver."

Mr. Jones said, "Are you Silver Buck?"

"Yes, that's the name my good friends called me, and it stuck after Foster and me found the silver mine that my great-grandfather Jeb found before he was murdered."

"I knew them both. They used to come up this way, and we would talk around the campfire at night. How's Foster?"

"He's fine. He retired and lives on my wife's ranch and mine. I wanted to thank you for treatin' Sam and Josh, when they were here before, the way you did."

"It's nothing, but I know you need to get going. Here's your $40,000, and who gets the $1,000 reward?"

"Pete here, he got the one that's dead and led Sam to the other."

"Me, no, not me."

"Is that right, Sam?"

"That's right, Mr. Jones."

"Here you go, Pete. Thank you, glad to get rid of them."

"Thanks, Mr. Jones. Never had this much money. Silver, can you keep this for me? I might lose it at the saloon. I better chase the boys before they drink your forty dollars. Thanks again."

Pete was on his horse and flying into town. I put all the money and Pete's in my money belt.

"I was goin' to ask you, Mr. Jones—there are twenty or so of the outlaws on our trail. Is there a reward on them?"

"Yes. Sheriff, tell them about the leader."

"Well, he has brown hair and bad teeth and a funny-looking scar on his left cheek right below his eye. He's worth $2,000. The others are worth less. If they attack you and you get them, have one of your men bring in that one. His name is Bart Scott. You bury the rest, and Mr. Jones will pay you for the rest."

"I sure will. Be good to get rid of them. Just have your men look at them and pick out the posters with. Bring the posters to me, and I'll pay. They robbed my shipment several times."

"I didn't know my great-grandfather Jeb at all. I sure would like to come back and hear some stories about him, but we have to get going on down the trail. We have a herd to deliver. Just write to me when you need more. I'm in Durango. Good doin' business with an honest man."

"Come back and I'll tell you some humdinger of stories about Jeb. So long."

Sam and I headed for the saloon. I looked around and saw this had the makings of a real town, not just a mining town. Mr. Jones seemed to run a smooth operation. The buildings looked strong and well built. We walked through the bat-winged doors of the saloon. The boys were sitting at two tables in the corner. They called Sam over.

"We have two bottles, Sam, and a glass for you. Silver, get your beer and join us,"

They knew I only drink one beer. They were used to that and didn't try to get me to drink more. I walked up to the bar and ordered a beer. The bartender said,

"He called you Silver. You that one that struck that big silver mine in the mountains north of Durango?"

"That's me."

"What you doing pushing cattle? I'd be with my wife enjoying life."

"Well, I enjoy the cattle business, but I have eighteen more men along with my father out there pushin' the rest of the cattle north. When we're at home, my father and the men run the ranch, and I do enjoy life and my wife and kids."

"That's good, Silver. That's what life's all about."

"Since we both seem to get along and both enjoy our families, could you tell me if any strangers besides my men and me have been around? We had some trouble south of here. I'm sure they would come in here."

"I just saw that man you brought in all tied up. I haven't seen anyone yet."

I paid him with a twenty-dollar gold piece.

"Your men already paid for their bottles."

"I know. Take that and enjoy family for me. I miss my wife and kids."

"Thanks, Silver."

I tipped my hat and took my beer to sit with the boys. We were there about twenty minutes when three men came through the doors; they were hitting their claps with their hats, getting the dust off. They looked over our way and walked to the bar. The bartender brought a beer over to me.

"I know you didn't order this, but I had to have a reason to come over here. Those three at the bar I haven't seen before. They look to be bad news. Thought I'd let you know."

"Thanks."

"You heard that, Sam. I don't want any trouble goin' back to the drive. Get a good look at them and mosey over to the sheriff's office and look at his Wanted posters. If they're wanted, bring the sheriff with you. Maybe we can rid ourselves of three more. If they're not wanted, we'll have to deal with them later."

Sam headed out the door.

"Be ready to back up the sheriff if Sam brings him back."

"Sure, boss. We haven't had that much. We're ready."

I unhooked my tie down on the hammer of my gun.

Sam came through the doors. The three looked briefly and then turned back to the bar. They turned too soon because the sheriff and two deputies were beside him with shotguns. Sam came over to the table. The lawmen stood right behind the three at the bar. We were all on our feet with guns drawn.

"Put your hands up, boys. We got you covered. Don't go for your guns, or you will be dead where you stand."

Sam said, "Two are wanted."

They turned around with their hands up. The deputies took their guns and took two to jail. To the other one, the sheriff said, "You're not wanted yet, boy. If I be, you I'd light out of here and don't hook up with the likes of those two again."

He gave him back his gun, and he lit out of town as though his pants were on fire. The sheriff came over.

"I sure hope that youngster listens. The judge will be here next week on his rounds. We'll have a trial then. Be a big thing around here. Thanks. You have some more reward coming,"

"Forget it, you got them. Just two more off our backs. You could give the reward to the bartender. He spotted them and told me. Sam, how much were they worth?"

"Four hundred apiece."

"Give it to him. I understand he's a real family man."

He walked up to the bar.

"Boys, drink up. We got to get back to the drive."

As we headed out of town, I looked back and saw the bartender was in the middle of the street waving his hands and saying, "Thank you, Silver Buck. You are a real man."

I was hoping not to run into any trouble. Sam came over.

"Silver, when we get back, I want to talk to you and your dad. I want to draw a better map. More detail. It's rough country up ahead."

"All right, but right now, I'm worried about the outlaws, and if they hit them while we were gone. That third man might have rode back and reported what happened."

We rode on faster, and as we rode up, Jose stopped to fix dinner. The cowboys were coming in a few at a time.

"Silver, glad to see you. Your dad was getting worried. I could tell by the way he kept watching our back trail."

Here came my pa riding in. He got his meal and coffee.

"Good to see you, son. Have any trouble back there?"

"Not really, but we got rid of two more outlaws, and maybe three. Two were wanted. The sheriff locked them up. The other one was young but was not wanted. The sheriff told him to light out and not hang with men like those. I hope he takes his advice. Sam wants to talk to us and make a more detailed map."

Josh came riding in.

"Silver, those men are moving up closer. I would be prepared for an attack soon. I would put a couple of guards out there south of here tonight. I'll stay up all night back where they are and come a-running if they start for you."

"You may be right. We got two more in town. He's getting' tired of us pickin' his men off little by little."

"I'm going to eat and get a couple of hours' sleep. If you put those guards out about one-fourth of a mile."

"I'll set the guards out there. When you get some rest, get back out there. When we deal with these outlaws, maybe we can send somebody else out to watch our back trail for Geronimo."

We were all done eating, so I said to Sam.

"You wanted to talk to us, Sam?"

"Sure do, Ross. Can I have a piece of paper out of your book and a pencil."

"Here goes."

"Our next stop is Rawlins in Wyoming. Before we get there, there is some rough country. You can see some north from here. Those may be two thousand feet above us. There are two big rivers and a lot of creeks. Some will be dry, but the cattle won't lack for water or grass. First, there's the Elk River. It goes in between the Sand Mountains and the Ethel Mountains. The gorge is full with water from the snowmelt in the spring. When we came through, there was plenty of room for us. It will be down lower now. If we keep the men on the side of the river, we should keep them moving through there fast. It's two miles long. On the other side from the river is a sheer rock going up six or seven hundred feet above. Then is the Little Snake River. We may have to swim them across there. After that, we come to lots of creeks, and then into the Sweet Water Basin. We'll have our work cut out for us. We get to that basin, we should be fine into Rawlins. Here's the map. I'll do another one on the other side of Rawlins. It gets tougher going on up north."

"This will help. I just hope the cattle can make it."

"Me also, Pa. I trust him."

I told Jose to get to bed early and get up early.

"Josh seems to think they will try to surprise us early. Have the rifles and ammunition ready. Get the men up and fed."

"Si, Silver, I will."

"Sam, pick five men to sleep under the wagon. When Jose gets y'all up, eat fast and get them in the wagon with their rifles and pistols. There are five more rifles in the wagon. Five more men will be under the wagon. The rest will be on each side of the wagon. Pa and me and you will be out in front in case they want to talk. If not, we'll get in line with the others. Pa, we'll get the leaders in the front, then move to the sides of the wagon so the boys inside and under the wagon can open up on them. If it comes off right, it shouldn't last five or ten minutes. Sam, make sure the men know to shoot to kill."

"Understood, Silver. Hopefully, this want stampede the cattle."

"Go out and tell the night riders what's goin' to happen. In the mornin', send four more men to help with the cattle and horses. I think we're far enough back that they'll be fine."

It took me a long while to get to sleep. Before I knew it, Jose was shaking me. I looked around and saw Pa was up eating with Sam. They had their gun belts on. The men were all around eating and checking their weapons.

"Looks like we're ready for a war."

I saw Jose hand every man three boxes of shells.

"Jose, you stay under the wagon."

"Si, and I will have my rifle and shells beside me."

I could see daybreak over to the east. Then we saw Josh and the two guards riding in as fast as their horses would go. They ran their horses behind the wagon.

"Silver, they're coming right behind us."

I could see the top of the sun coming up. I saw them stop about a hundred yards away and look at us.

"Boys, don't shoot until my Pa or I shoot. Then let them have it with all you got."

7

They all rode up slowly behind their five leaders. Then they stopped about a hundred feet from us. The leaders came on up within twenty feet of us.

I said, "What you need, boys?"

The one in the lead with a scar under his eye said, "It looks like we have you outgunned. So I was thinking you should give us all that gold and silver you been collecting. You can keep those cows."

"I'm downright sorry you rode all this way."

"That's all right. My man from Durango said you were a wisecracker."

I looked over to his left, and there was the ambusher that shot Foster's mule.

"I'm sorry again. He didn't tell you how fast I was, and my dad here is even faster. You are in front, and I'm sorry all we have to give you is lead."

They pulled their guns, but they all five were dead and on the ground before their guns were halfway out. The others came rushing in. We stepped aside, and Jose pulled up the flap of the wagon and jumped under. All the men cut loose with their rifles, and we could see one after another fall out of their saddles. This went on for five or ten minutes. Finally, they were all down except four. As the smoke cleared from the air, they dropped their guns and raised their hands.

"Sam, get two men and tie them up. You four, go round up all their horses. We'll sell them with the saddles and rifles. You two make sure they're all dead. Anyone hurt?"

"Over here."

"And over here."

"Jose, go see to them. Carlos, help Jose. Pa, you all right?"

"Sure thing, son. They didn't seem to have a chance."

"They could have left, but I'm glad they didn't, cause no tellin' how many they killed and would had killed."

I went over to see about the wounded.

"How are they, Jose?"

"One has a leg wound, one in the shoulder. The bullet went all the way through. One is creased in his side, and the last one creased his head."

"Any need a doc?"

"No, I think I can take care of them. It might take a week or so."

Pete said, "One's still alive. Come quick, I don't know how long he'll last."

I went over to his body and bent down.

The outlaw said, "Only wish he'd known how fast you were."

"He did. We had a run-in back in Durango. He knew you wouldn't come after me if you knew. You and your men aren't much a loss to the world."

He turned over and died.

"Sam, get two men and take the live ones back to Jack in Oak Creek. Tie this one to his horse. He's worth $2,000. You take a good look at the dead ones and look at the posters in Jack's office. If he wants to see the graves, tell him where they are. You three go relieve the nightriders. Let the cattle graze. We'll leave tomorrow. After we bury the dead, we can take turns with the cattle."

Sam left as we were burying the dead. It was hard, but I wouldn't leave them even if they were bad. To me it didn't matter; it was the right thing to do.

That night, not much was said. That seems to be the way with good men when killing has to be done to protect what's theirs. Jose had coffee on the fire and some food, but not much was eaten. I wished Sam was there to sing a little tune. It might make it a little easier. Tomorrow we would be down the trail a little way. We might be able to put the day behind us.

The next morning, everyone ate a big breakfast and was eager to hit the trail again.

"Josh, you go with Pa on point. Sam made a map, but you might know something that he might have left out. When Sam gets back, you can take a man and cut east to west. Look out for Indians or something else."

The cattle were up, and we were on the trail again. At supper, Josh came to me.

"Silver, Ross showed me the map Sam made. Sam forgot the Yampa River. It meets with the Elk River. It's big and deep where they meet, but we found a spot at a town called Miner. I guess he forgot 'cause of the trouble we had yesterday, and they didn't want any cattle. They talked about horses. We can cross east of town. We found a good spot there. You might want to ride in and see about horses."

"Thanks, Josh. That's a big help."

The next town, I think I'll take a different group of men and give them a chance at the saloon. The night went by peacefully. Everyone was up and at it early. The days were getting hot. We passed over a number of creeks; some had a little water. Some had lots of water, and a couple were dry. That night, Sam came in with the two men.

"Silver, Tom, Jay and me looked at the posters at the sheriff's office, and besides the leader, there were twelve others that were wanted dead or alive. The bounty on five was $1,000 and five for $500 and two for $250. The leader was $2,000, for a total of $10,000. Mr. Jones paid it gladly to have them off his back."

He handed me the money. I called everyone together.

"What I'm about to say, the hands that relieve the ones out with the cattle can tell them."

"What, Silver?"

"Well, Sam here brought back $10,000 for those outlaws that tried to take our money. I tell you I'm goin' to split it among all of you. That's $400 for each man."

Everyone yelled and threw their hats in the air.

"Silver, they tried to rob us, and we robbed them." The men laughed.

"But if you don't mind, I'll keep it and pay it to you with your pay and bonus at the end of trail. If you are goin' back to Durango, I can keep it till we get back. You know, we still might have some Indian problems. I want you to know if anything happens to any of you, me, my dad, or Sam will make sure your families will get all that is owed to you."

That set them off again. They went off talking to each other. Then Jose made it even better. He came out with five apple pies. That was what a cowboy liked most on a drive—sugar.

The next morning, the boys were up with Pa and got the cattle moseying. I told Sam and Josh to come over and talk. I had already sent Carlos and Pete on our back trail, just in case.

"Sit, boys. I was thinkin' we go have a look-see at Miner, where to cross the cattle and see about sellin' some horses."

"You know, I plum forgot about that crossing."

"Josh told us about it."

"He's right where the two rivers meet. It's too deep. It may be twenty feet deep and very rough water. We might lose cattle and men there."

"I told Silver with all the trouble the other day, it probably just skipped you mind. There were men at the stable talking about needing horses."

"He's right. I'm sorry I forgot about it."

"That's all right, Sam. That's why it's good to have two go. Get some food from Jose, and I'll go let Pa know and we'll head out. Meet me on point."

I talked to Pa awhile, just moseying along. Sam and Josh came up, and we took off due north. I could tell Blacky was glad to be out where he could get up some speed.

Sam said, "I think he misses Lagger."

"I should have brought him, but you know Red Bird. She has to take her ride on Lagger. No other horse will do."

"Sam, I got Red Bird. Josh here has Carolyn. Bill has Jenny. When you goin' to get hooked up with someone?"

"Bill and Jenny the schoolteacher?"

"Sure. didn't you see them when we left? That's right, you two were out on the trail. She was holdin' his hand."

"Well, I'll be."

"Now you're avoidin' the question."

"Now that I think on it, if I found someone like you three have, I'd say tomorrow. You know, that Ann back at Job's Crossing is a looker, and sure can cook. But I doubt if she'd give up what she has for this old cowboy and move back to Durango. You say I'm a well-off man now. When we come to the end of trail, I think I'll go back there and spend some time with her."

We rode at a good pace. We came to two or three small creeks. There was nothing out here but big mountains, big trees, flowers, and this time of year lots of animals and hot down in the valleys and cool in the foothills. We were experiencing it all in the big sky country. We came up over a ridge, and there was where the Yampa and Elk Rivers met. The water was rolling so much it looked as though it was boiling and muddy as all get out.

"No wonder you said we might lose cattle and men."

"Look over there, not three miles away. See how smooth the water is. They may have to swim a little, but not much. See a little farther, that's Miner. Now look north of the rough water. That's the Elk River, and those two peaks is where we're going. The Elk goes right between them."

"I can't tell from this distance, but it might be lower."

"Let's get to town and try to sell some horses."

"The men we heard were talking about $350 or $400 for one horse. I would try to start at $400 and not go below $250 at the stable. That way, we won't have to go all over creation to sell them. Just one place to sell them, and that will give him some profit."

We rode on down by the river. Sam went across, and when he came back, he said, "You see that, Josh. Didn't have to swim at all. The river is down about half a foot."

"Looks like it will be easy."

We rode on into town. Not much of a town—just a saloon, a diner, the stables, and a general store. We stopped in front of the stables and walked in. There was only one man inside.

"Can I help you? Sam, Josh, how are you two? Didn't expect to see you back."

"Mr. Timas, this is Silver Buck. He's the one with the cattle. He wants to talk to you."

"I'm Buck Taylor. Sam and Josh heard some men here saying they might need some horses. At the time, they didn't know we were bringin' horses to sell with the cattle. I was wonderin' if you might be interested in some horses to sell to people around here. Your corral looks to be bare."

"Sure is. Hard to find horses, good horses around here."

"These are fine horses, only half broke. They tend to go back to their old ways when not ridin' every day."

"Know what you mean. I did have some farmers ask about horses sometime back. How much you asking?"

"I'd say $550. I hear tell up here that's a bargain."

"I see. Well, I don't know if I can sell them. I will have to feed them till they're sold. I can't see paying any more than $300"

Your corral is bare. How many you think you might want? We came all the way from Durango and won't be up this way for a long while."

"If the price is right. I would say ten."

"How about $500 if you buy ten?"

"I can't do that. I have to make a little profit. I'd come up to $375, 'cause you're a friend of Sam's."

"If you pay cash or gold or silver, I'll take $475."

"If you take silver and you'll deliver them here, I'll pay $425. That's my last offer."

"That's a deal."

I stuck out my hand, and he took it and we shook on the deal.

"Buck, now we made a deal, I can tell you I would have paid $450 for them. I'll get $600 or $650 for them."

"I know, I thought I'd let you make a little more profit. You have time, I'll buy you supper. Looks to be a nice diner."

"I sure do. It's a fine place to eat. Let me close up. I'll be right along."

We went over to the diner.

"What can I get for you, gents?"

"Sally, I'm with them. Sally, let it be known by tomorrow I'll have horses for sale. Half broke for $700."

Sam says, "Mr. Timas, $700?"

"You know everyone will try to get me down. That price, I can come down little."

We all laughed.

I said, "Watch Sam."

Sally said, "Now what you cowboys have?"

"We'll all have steak and potatoes and a round of coffee. Sound good, boys?"

"Sure does, Buck."

"Well, I can get you the potatoes and coffee, but you can go to Texas for the beef. I have potato soup and some good biscuits."

"You the owner, Sally? You know, that sounds real good. Right, Mr. Timas? Boys?"

"It sure does."

"I am the owner. I'll bring you supper right away."

Sally brought the soup and biscuits, and they were good, really good.

"Sally, have a seat a minute and rest awhile. I don't see many people in here."

"Tell you the truth, they get tired of the same thing. They say, 'We can get this at home.'"

"I bet if you had some beef, you could double your money."

"Where am I going to get beef?"

"By tomorrow, we'll have two thousand head of well-fed steers about a mile from here crossin' the river goin' to Wyoming. If you had beef, the men would want to bring their wives to eat here at night. You could double, or even triple, your money. I bet to get a free dinner once in a while. Mr. Timas would keep them in his corral."

"To eat beef, sure, I would just charge for hay. That's fair."

"It is, but how much you charging for these steers?"

"Sixty, if you buy five. Double or triple your money. More business, more money."

"I see what you mean. But I could only pay forty. You know, I'll have to hire some people."

"Why don't we split it down the middle at fifty if you pay cash?"

"You know, I'll do it."

She shook my hand. And she was smiling from ear to ear. Even Mr. Timas was smiling.

"That's a deal. You know, that's the best soup I've ever had. And I bet there's some apple pie back there. We'll all have some. And I thank you. My men here will bring them in tomorrow and collect."

We had our delicious apple pie. I paid, and we walked out.

"Well, I'll be. I was just in here a month ago, and she wouldn't buy."

"Sam, your boss is a smooth talker. That woman won't buy anything. But I get beef for a while. I thank you for that, Buck."

"Thank you, Mr. Timas. Sam and Josh will deliver the horses and cattle tomorrow. We better get back. We'll bed them down tomorrow night and cross the river the next morning. Sam says that river pass is tight, but he thinks we can make it."

"This time of year, I think so. You'll have to take it pretty slow. See you later in the day, Sam. You too, Josh."

I wanted to get back before nightfall. We were moving at a pretty good pace when Sam and Josh came up beside me.

"You know, Silver, you just made more work for us, and I didn't even get to go in the saloon."

"Wait till we hit that river pass. We'll all have plenty of work."

"You had to mention that. That pass is going to be mean. But it's better than losing two weeks to the next pass."

We pulled into camp just after the sunset. It was a good day. I saw the lay of the land, and we sold some stock and met some real nice people.

"What took you? I thought it was a short ride on horseback."

"It is a short ride. I had to look things over. We won't have to swim the stock over. It went down a little since Sam was through. I sold some horses and five steers. Every little bit helps. I met some nice folks. You got closer than I thought you would. We might get over that river tomorrow and head for that pass the next day when we're fresh."

"How's that pass and grass?"

"The pass is very loomin'. But Mr. Timas at the livery thinks we can make it if we're careful. It beats goin' around. It would take two weeks. It may take a day to get to the pass after the Yampa River. Then we follow the Elk River through the pass. It may take a day to get through the pass. Between the Yampa and the pass, there's plenty of grass."

Pa said, "You know, Sam, I thought Texas was big. It is mostly flat. Up here, the mountains are so huge. I heard about this country, but you have to see it to believe it. This is a fine place for a cattle ranch, plenty of water and grass. The only bad thing is the harsh winters."

"You wait till we get to Wyoming and Montana. You ain't seen nothing yet. The mountains are bigger. The valleys are too beautiful to put into words. But it is dangerous. You misstep or look away at the wrong time, and you could be dead. I'm glad we're getting rid of the cattle. There will be less to herd later when it gets worse."

"I'm goin' to hit the sack. The next two or three days look to be rough."

"You mind me playing my guitar?"

"Not at all. Be like a lullaby."

So Sam got his guitar out of the chuck wagon. He played some lively tunes, and then some slow and relaxing tunes. That's when the men started drifting off to their bedrolls. Pa was right. It was going to be three or four hard days. He hadn't seen the pass up close yet. I just hope we don't lose any men or animals through that river pass. Pete and Carlos were out on our back trail. We would need them when we went through that pass.

We were all up early, and even I was out on drag all day hopin' Pete and Carlos would come in. They did at dinner.

"Nothing to report. Everything's calm back there."

"Why don't you two stay in camp a few nights? Tomorrow we're goin' through the river pass. I don't think anything will happen in the pass. Sam says it's sheer rock straight up on both sides for six or seven hundred feet."

That afternoon, we pulled up to the river.

"Sam, you and Josh take two men and cut out ten of the best horses and five of the best steers and take them into town and collect. That's $4500 for the horses and $250 for the cattle, and make sure you stop and let Sally see them." I tossed him a ten-dollar gold piece.

"I wouldn't want you to think I'm too mean. Have a couple of drinks on me. Just a couple, hear me, Sam? We need you alert when we go through that pass. Don't want anyone killed. We got to get these cattle into the river, with no trouble."

"Sure do, Silver. Only two."

"Sam!"

By the time Sam and the men rounded up the steers and horses, the rest of the cattle were in the water, along with the men; and some were already coming out on the other side of the river. I looked toward town, and I could see buggies, wagons, and men on horseback and some down by the river looking our way. One man rode up.

"Where you goin'?"

"Up Montana way."

"Wish we had some beef like that here."

"Go to Sally's. She just bought five head, and Mr. Timas bought ten horses."

"Thanks, mister. I will."

It was dark by the time we got them all across the river. Jose had a great supper for everyone. It had been somewhat an ordeal getting the chuck wagon across. We had to get some old fallen trees and tie them to the wagon with our ropes. We made it like a raft; we didn't want to get the ammunition or rifles wet. It worked great, with the horses pulling and the men with their ropes tied to the wagon helping pull the wagon across.

"Pa, I'm goin' to do something you may not approve of, but these men have worked hard, fought outlaws, and Sam tells me the next town we have business in is a hundred miles over some rough country. I'm goin' to let them go to town."

"Men, if you want to cross the river again, you can go to town. But just a couple of drinks and back again. No trouble. If anyone causes trouble, tomorrow you can light out for Durango with no bonus and no reward money. No complaints about bein' sick. We have a long, tough trail. That's the only reason I'm doin' this."

"Yes, boss."

Pa and I, along with some of the older men, stayed in camp. Some dried their boots and socks and clothes over the fire. One of the men said, "Sure do miss old Sam and his guitar."

"Don't worry, boy's. I'm here. No more town for me."

Sam cut loose on his guitar for an hour.

"That's it. I'm tuckered out."

Sam came over to us.

"Silver, here's the money. Mr. Timas told me that two men came in this morning. They told him they barely missed a large group of Indians in Wyoming down in the Sweet Water Basin. That's where we have to cross part of it."

"We'll worry about that if this pass doesn't chew us up and spit us out after the next two days."

We all went to bed. I kept waking up, and the men were coming in little by little. We woke up very early to some horses coming in. It was two riders.

"It's me, Buck. Sally and Mr. Timas."

"What is it? My men cause any trouble?"

"Oh no, the town liked having them in."

"We just came early. We thought we'd miss you."

Jose beat on his pan to wake everyone out of their sleep and said, "Get up, boys. We have a lady in camp."

They were running trying to get their pants and boots on, and Sally covered her mouth because she was laughing so hard. Then everything calmed down.

I spoke up, "What can I do for you?"

"We know you're across the river. But we were wondering if you could sell us some more stock."

Sally said, "You were right. There is only two head left, and if the price is the same, I would like five more."

"I'll take five more horses 'cause I sold five yesterday. Here's the money."

"I told you, didn't I? Sam, Josh, get two men and round up what they need and take them into town. Get back fast. You two are the only ones that know that pass."

"Thank you, Buck. If you'er back this way again, stop by."

"Sure thing, Mr. Timas. I bet you made more than you thought you would."

"Well ..." I laughed and slapped him on the back.

"That's what we're in business for. Good luck. Now, boys, eat and then let's get goin'."

We stayed on the west side of the Elk River. I told the men to get them moving at a good speed. Let them water so their bellies would be full when we hit the pass. Sam and Josh came riding in. I told them both to go ride point with Pa. The majestic beauty of this place, with the mountains in front of us that just got bigger as we approached. It looked to be solid rock straight up to the sky. The wall went up several hundred feet. I could see the cattle drifting down to the water, and the men would hurry them along. The river must have cut this path through the mountains millions of years ago. We were going slower now, and there was a ledge so the cattle couldn't get to the water without falling off. Sam came back and snapped me out of my reverie.

"Silver, think we should take a ride up ahead? We're coming to the narrowest part. We better get the men on the river side all up and down the herd."

We went along and told all the men to ride on the river side and not let the cattle crowd them off the edge. It was a good ten-foot drop to the river. Later, it would be fifteen feet to the river below. We went past Pa and Josh.

"Be back in a little while. We got about half a mile ahead."

"Here it is, Silver. After this, it gets wider and wider till they can spread out again."

"We might get four wide with a man and his horse. We'll have to take it real slow and just kind of mosey through. Let's get back."

"Silver, look up ahead."

"Oh my God. Sam, what you got us into?"

The river must fall fifty feet, and below the falls, it was like boiling water. It was all churned up. If a man or horse or some cattle fell off the ledge, there would be no way of saving them. We went back, and I looked at Pa. He didn't look too happy. I went down the line, telling them not to let them bunch and slow them and only three or four wide.

"Watch your horse's hooves. Make sure they don't let the cattle crowd them over the edge."

I was worried the cattle and horses would get nervous in this narrow spot and want to run, but the cowboys were experienced enough to know how to handle them. The newer men I put on drag, so all they had to do was keep them moving forward and not let them go back. They moved along slowly. The minutes seemed like hours. The hours seemed like days. This reminded me of when Foster and me were caught on that mountain in the blizzard and couldn't see our hand in front of our face. It was like being in a box. At least this we could see what was coming, and that wasn't good.

The falls were coming up, and the noise might make the animals want to run. The noise was so tremendous. I could see the horses, and even the men, were shaken by the noise. There were a few horses that started to lose their footing but made it back upon solid ground. We could not talk to each other because we could not hear anything except the roar of the falls. I could tell even Blacky didn't like this very much, but we had been together all these many years, and he trusted me, and I him. When we were past the falls, the tension left my body.

I couldn't see Pa or Josh for we were strung out for a good two miles. They must be coming to the end, or out of the pass. We were past the falls. Sam came over.

"Should be all right now. It should be widening up. Your dad should be out by now. I'm glad we sent Jose first. Maybe he'll have dinner ready."

"I didn't know if we would make it or not, and all you think about is food."

"Not to worry, Silver. I knew we would make it. You really think I would do that?"

"I just hope there's not more like that."

"No, just a lot of rivers and creeks."

We came out of the pass, with the horses and the rest of the men on drag. There were all the cattle spread out. There was the chuck wagon with a fire going, and a lot of the men were around Pa. We got off our horses, and the men moved to one side.

"What's goin' on, Pa?"

He pulled out a rope with a noose on it. "The boys here and me think we should hang old Sam from that tree over there for bringin' us through that."

"Wait a minute, boys. We might get home a month sooner 'cause of that pass."

They all started laughing.

"Now it's over, we can laugh. But, Sam, there better not be any more places like that 'cause this noose is easy to put together, and there are plenty of trees."

"No, no, just rivers and creeks and Indians. I'll make you feel better. I'll get my guitar and play some music."

The nightriders were out with the cattle. The men had settled down along with the cattle and horses. We seemed to be back to normal with the help of Sam's music. The one that took us through that hair-raising experience was the one that calmed everything down with his music and singing. The next morning, everyone saddled up and got the herd moving north again.

"Where we goin', Sam?"

"I'll ride ahead and find the place that I found to cross the Elk. Then we head northwest into Rawlins, Wyoming. They bought five hundred head at $40. See that peak up ahead to the right, that's Mt. Zirkel. We have to go this side of it. About a half a day we'll be in Wyoming. Some old timers told me that mountain is better than 12,000 feet high. Silver, I better get going. That crossing is going to be coming up before twelve o'clock."

Sam left and I headed to the point. I was riding beside my pa.

"You know, son, I don't worry about much. I think the good Lord will take care of most, but I tell you, that pass back there had me worried."

"I know what you mean. It had me a lot worried. Sam should be back soon. The crossin' for the Elk should be comin' up and into Wyoming. See that peak over there?"

"The one with the snow on top?"

"Yes, he said that's over twelve thousand feet. That snow stays on top all year long."

"I know if he took us over that, there would be a hangin'."

We both were laughing when Sam came riding up.

"What's so funny?"

"Nothin', Sam. Just a little joke."

"The crossing is about half a mile up a ways. We might have to get some men and tie ropes to the chuck wagon to get her across. But I think she'll go across just fine."

We came to the crossing. Five men came up and tied their ropes on to the wagon, and we were in the water. It took an hour to get the wagon across. Then the cattle got wet. I told Jose to head west of the peak up ahead. The trees were thick, but I thought he could make it through. The cattle just wound around the trees after they came out of the water. It had been much like this most of the time, but these were much thicker than before. They were thick enough to keep the sunlight mostly out, so there wasn't much undergrowth, so they had it pretty easy, not like in Texas with all the mesquite brush.

That night in camp, Sam and Josh came over and sat down to eat.

"Josh and me been talking. If it's all right with you and Ross, Josh can lead you toward Rawlins. I can go and look out for trouble, and we're coming soon to some big creeks and some small ones that come off the North Plate River. Some may be drying up from the lack of snowmelt. I can see where to cross, and it's about sixty miles to Rawlins. I can go halfway there and back in three days, if everything goes right. Josh knows the general direction. When we came this way, we didn't look around for details much, just the size of mountains and rivers and the direction."

"That sounds good. We need someone to scout ahead. But get back as soon as you can. Take enough grub. How's that sound to you, Pa?"

"Sounds good, if Josh knows the way, 'cause in three days, we should be over halfway there."

"Yes, sir. I kept my eyes peeled up and back this way. Tomorrow we should pass through two or three of those creeks off the Plate River. They should be easy. We head north and a little west."

"Take off in the morning. If you run into anyone, find out if they heard anything about Geronimo."

In the morning, Jose got some grub for Sam, and then he took off. The herd got moving with Pa and Josh on point. As Josh had said, we came to two creeks. The first one was almost dry, and the next had enough water for the cattle to get their bellies full of water. The mountains were smaller as we moved north. Josh said the peak to our west was Bridger Peak. It was said to be ten thousand feet. We were three days into Wyoming when Sam came in to report. We stopped for the night. The cattle were feeding better as there were less trees and more grass.

"How's it up ahead, Sam?"

"About the same as here. Plenty of grass and four or five more creeks before Rawlins. There were some cowhands that were on the trail. They were coming from Riverton going back to their ranch over east of here. They said there are small ranches starting up. There's plenty of grass out on the plains. They said they went through Rawlins, and both towns were waiting on cattle to be delivered. I guess they got a late start. Those ranches are just getting started, and they didn't have enough yet for what they needed. They were going to wait two more years. They said their herd might be big enough by then."

"Looks like I sent you at the right time. The ranches will grow up here. This might be our last trip up this far. We might have to go west to Utah."

"I also ran into a cavalry unit from Fort Laramie. The colonel said that the Sioux and the Crow were gathering tribes together to fight the army. They didn't like the Apache being north this far. They were in the Sweetwater Basin, but Geronimo and his band of Apache were reported north of there in the Great Divide Basin. We need to be careful in both areas."

"Are we goin' through those areas?"

"We leave Rawlins, we are in the north Sweetwater Basin. But we go right through the middle of the Great Divide Basin. They didn't know where Geronimo was in that area. It's big. Riverton is ninety miles from Rawlins. That's about eight to ten days with the cattle. There is a certain area that may not have much water for twenty miles. But it's not as hot as it was in New Mexico. I think the cattle won't be as dry. I'll ride ahead when we get to that point."

"Is it like that all the way?"

"No. Once we hit Riverton, the Bighorn River goes all the way to Montana. We're going to be along that river all the way. The Bighorn River will keep us away from the large mountain peaks."

"Pa, you think we can move them along any faster than we have been? It looks like some dangerous times up ahead. Even a mile or two a day would help."

"We can speed them up some. We don't want them to lose too much weight. The people won't like skin-and-bones cows." Sam said. "Most of the remaining contracts are north of Riverton. There's lots of grass north of there."

That night, everyone went to sleep, and the night riders went out. Jose was done. Everything was quiet until around midnight. A rider came in so fast and yelling that everyone was up.

"Silver, something is out there. The cattle are up and spooked. I don't know, even the horses are spooked. The others are trying to keep them calm."

"Make sure everyone have your rifles. Don't shoot unless you have a clear shot and know what you're shooting at. They're already spooked. We don't want a stampede. Whatever it is, try to run it off."

In five minutes, we were mounted and out among the cattle and trying to calm them down and at the same time looking for what was causing the trouble. I sent four men to go out and circle the herd to see if they could find anything. It was slow for the moon wasn't out yet and it was pitch black. I could even feel Blacky under me. I could tell he was nervous.

"Sam, sing to them. It might help."

Sam started singing. They were still milling around pretty good. Someone over to the west side of the herd had relayed to me from cowboy to cowboy. We didn't want to start a stampede with a yell.

"Silver, to the west. Over to the west."

I rode Blacky, with Sam beside me singing gently to the cattle.

"We have two steers down and dead."

I got down and had a look. I could see it was wolves.

"Sam, ride through and around the cattle. It seems to be helping. Men, spread out. We need to find them. If we don't, they will follow us to Montana. That's money out of all our pockets. If you have a clean shot, take it. We have to take a chance it won't spook the cattle. You two stay, they only took some meat. They might be back for more. Hide close downwind so they won't see or smell you. The moon is comin' up. That will help us. There are probably packs of four or five."

I went out a ways. I knew Blacky would let me know if they were close. Two hours had already gone by since the first alarm, and nothing yet. It was only three hours until daylight, and we would lose our chance until they would make a flesh kill tomorrow night. About another hour went by. Then I heard a shot, then another, and another. I rode in the direction of the shots. Then I heard a fourth. It was closer now.

It was toward the carcasses. I jumped down, and there on the ground, were three dead wolves.

"Over here, Silver."

There was another one behind a boulder.

Sam came riding in. "It didn't seem to bother the cattle. They're just milling around."

"Thank you, men. I know it's been a short night of sleep, but get back to camp and have a bit to eat and let's get them moving north," Pa said.

Everyone was tired, even Pa and me. I looked at Pa and knew he was worn out. His age was showing, but he kept going and was up on point with Josh and Sam. I hated losing two steers, but that was the first we'd lost. We expected to lose more than two. We had a good day. We crossed three creeks; one was about dry. The other two had water enough to satisfy the stock and get them moving faster. I missed Red Bird and the children. I knew she would be learning the words to write me. I just hopped it would find me. I would check in Rawlins. I had told everyone that wanted to write home that I would see if Rawlins had a place to send mail.

All the day we drove the cattle harder than usual. Over foothills and through trees, and some so close together that Sam had to find a way around. There were trees like I had never seen, but the cattle and horses could get through. It was a long day a very long day. We got into camp after dark. The food was good, but everyone was worn out and just ate a little.

"I know we're all tired, so Sam, Josh, and me are goin' to take the first watch. So roll up and get to sleep 'cause at midnight, we're goin' to wake up four of you to take the second watch till we move out in the mornin' early. When we get to Rawlins, you can go to town for a little fun."

They didn't say a word. They just drifted off to their bedrolls. Sam, Josh, and I were on watch. I had taken one of our stock horses, which gave me a little trouble when I got on. But he settled down. I knew Blacky was getting up there in age for a horse, and I knew he would have gone on 'cause he had never failed me in all the years we'd been a team. It was quiet till midnight when we woke up the men to take our place. There was a little complaining. Jose had left a little grub on the fire. We all ate, and then they went out to the herd and we went to get in our bedrolls. Jose was great on this drive. He not only kept us full, but he picked up our bedrolls in the morning and put them in the chuck wagon and had them laid out for us at night. He didn't know it, but he was getting a bigger bonus.

In the morning, the men were a little livelier. As they finished eating, they began drifting out to get the cattle moving along with Pa and Josh. The men had given all their letters for home to Jose. I was eating with Sam.

"You know, Sam, I think you and me are goin' to Rawlins and meet some folks. By what you told me, we should be there tomorrow. I'll go gather up those letters and we'll get goin'."

"Sounds good to me. There's not a mine. I didn't tell you, but the contract is with Tom Jeffery. He owns a lumber mill, and he's smart. He made a deal with Sid, owner of the diner, to buy from him."

We gathered up things we needed. Blacky was rested up and ready to go. We headed to the point. I told Pa and Josh we were going to Rawlins, and then we were gone.

It was nice traveling at a faster pace than the cattle were going. We stopped at noon to eat a bit and rest the horses. We didn't bother to start a fire; we had a dry camp. We had jerky. We would eat a good supper in town and head back to the drive.

"Silver, the mill is on this side of town. The pasture should be around the mill. He has twenty men that have a camp on the mountain on the other side of town. It looks like a smooth operation. They may need horses. They have wagons that bring trees down from the mountain and other wagons that take the finished lumber to deliver to customers."

We rode up to the milling office and went in. I saw the new fenced pasture as we came in. A middle-aged man was sitting behind the largest desk I'd ever seen. He was wearing glasses and doing paperwork. He had the appearance of a businessman that was doing well. There was another man behind a counter.

"Can I help you? Oh, Sam, it's you."

"This is my boss, Silver Buck Taylor."

Mr. Jeffery looked up from his paperwork. He put down his glasses and came over and shook hands.

"Hello, Mr. Taylor. Good to see you, Sam. I've been looking for you, but not this soon. And call me Tom."

"Just call me Buck. We came in to let you know the cattle will be here tomorrow."

"Let me get my hat, and let's go eat at the diner. We can talk there."

We walked down the street. I could see it was a growing town. There were new buildings going up. They even had a bank and a sheriff's office. We walked in to the diner and were seated by a pretty redheaded woman. I looked at Sam, and he shook his head no. I understood. We ordered our supper.

"Tom, Sam told me that you have wagons that do different jobs around here. He didn't know that we were bringin' a good bunch of horses with us. So if you need any horses, they're yours at a good price."

A man came over from the back counter.

"I saw you, Tom, with these gentlemen. I know, Sam."

"Sid, this is Buck Taylor. He's got our cattle about a day out."

He shook my hand.

"My wife told me there was a man with Sam. I'm so glad you're here. We can use some beef on our menu. I better go back to work. Good to meet you."

"Same here, Sid."

"Buck, I been thinking. I have three horses about four years old. I have four wagons and eight horses. It would make sense to have more in case some get hurt. It's hard to get good horses up here."

"Let me warn you. They're a little bit wild. They're broke to saddle. But I think they could be broke to harness. If not, you could sell them at a profit."

"You know, I think I'll take ten if the price is right."

"You got the cattle for $45 a head. Everyone else has been payin' $50 a head, so the horses would be $600 a head."

"I'm a businessman, and I try to get the seller's best price. I'd say $450."

"I'm a businessman, and I try to get the most I can. How about $550?"

"Tell you what, if they're good as your two horses look, I'll pay $500."

"They are good as ours, and younger. It's a deal. That's $22,500 for the cattle and $5,000 for the horse. I'll collect tomorrow when we deliver them. I don't know who got the better deal. I see you have a bank. You're the first town with a bank."

"We're up and coming. Hope to be as big as Laramie one day. Be nice to get that beef on the table in here. It will be worth the price. And I think I got the better deal."

I laughed. "You know the customer is always right."

He laughed. "You are a businessman, all right."

I saw a man walk in the door. He had a star on. I said, "Can you introduce me to your sheriff?"

"Sure can. Toby, can you come over here a minute. This is Buck Taylor. He's bringing some cattle in, and horses."

The sheriff and I shook hands, and then he pulled up a chair. He ordered, and we talked a few minutes. Then I asked, "I'd like to know the sheriff, if the towns have one, 'cause I have twenty-five cowboys. Some don't come in but the younger ones do. I just like to make sure of your rules. They know not to cause any trouble or they'll be sent back home without their bonus at the end of the drive. On other hand, if someone gives them trouble, they can handle that. I just want you to be fair. We have a long ways to go, and we're not lookin' for any trouble."

"You can ask Tom. I'm fair to everyone."

"They should only have a few drinks 'cause we move on early the next mornin'. The last town they stayed too late and drank too much. I showed them no mercy, and they paid for it the next day. We don't wait for them to sober up."

Sam said, "I should know. I was the one with the biggest headache."

We all laughed.

"Serve you right, Sam."

"I know. I'll be sure to get back early."

"Buck, are you the bunch that killed all the outlaws down in Oak Creek? It's been all over up here. Those were a bad bunch. They robbed our bank once, and the mill. Tom can tell you about that one. Glad to be rid of them, so I better get back to the office so my deputy can come to supper. I'll let Homer know about men comin' in to have a few drinks."

"Thanks, Sheriff. I'll see you tomorrow. By the way, Tom, do you have a place to mail some letters?"

"Over at the General Store, I better get back to the office so Jim can come eat. See you tomorrow. I'll have the money in the office ready for you. Just put them in the pasture. I'll have Jim count them."

Sam and I headed up the street to the general store.

"Can I mail these here for Durango, Colorado?"

"Sure can. It will go out tomorrow. Let's see twenty letters. That will be fifty cents."

"Add two apples to that. My horse just loves apples."

"That's seventy cents."

"Buck, can I get some candy?"

"Sure, Sam. Tell him what you want."

"That red one there."

"That's a gumball. You chew it, and it lasts a long time. He called you Buck—are you by chance Buck Taylor? And I have one for a Ross Taylor."

"Yes, that's me, and my dad. He's out on the trail with the cattle comin' this way."

"Here they are. Been here a week. I didn't know anyone by that name here."

"Thanks, mister. Here's a dollar for everything."

I put the letters in my pocket to read later.

"Sam let's get back to the drive."

We left town going south; we would be back in the morning.

Camp was no more than three hours from the town. The food was hot, and the coffee was even hotter. Dad and Sam sat down beside me.

"Dad, here's a letter from Ma."

Then I looked at my letter. I had thought it was from Bill, but it didn't look like his writing. It was printing. I tore it open and saw it was from Red Bird.

Buck, I know this is not very good, but Miss Jenny is helping me. She is good teacher. Says I learn fast. Children are good. She says they do good in school. Mother is well. Foster took me and children to see Dancing Bear and all my people. I got your letter. Miss Jenny help me read it. Am learning about history too. Hope to do better next time. I wrote this myself. Miss Jenny help me say this. I love you very much and I can't wait to have you in our big bed again. Tell Josh that Carolyn is up and around and waiting for him.

Love, Red Bird

I put the letter away in my shirt close to my heart.

"What is it, son?"

"It's a letter written to me by Red Bird. What did Mother have to say?"

"She knows me. The ranch is all right. The men are doing the everyday chores around the ranch. No trouble. Foster, Red Bird, and the children are all well. There is a new hat shop in town. Oh, she said Red Bird bought some New Mexican dresses at a new shop in town also. Miss Jenny helped her, and that's about it."

"You know, Dad, you are going to have to take Ma somewhere nice when we get back. Sam can run the ranch with my help."

Sam nearly choked.

"Me run the ranch? I don't know about that."

"I don't know. I still remember that pass back there. I think I aged five years."

"But we made it, didn't we? Besides, it saved us two weeks. I know you both need to take your wives somewhere fancy, like Denver or St. Louis, and stay in a fancy hotel."

"Sam, you need to play your guitar and get those notions out of that head of yours."

"But it's a good thought."

"Sam, yes, sir."

Sam played for a little while, and everyone drifted off to sleep. The next morning, we started earlier than usual. Sam got six men about two hours outside of town, but by the time they had the cattle and horses out, we were almost there. I told Dad that I would send these six back out and send twelve back in. The herd was smaller now and could be driven by fewer men. Josh said we were turning to the northwest out into the Great Divide Basin. We left, and in about an hour, we were running the cattle into the pasture.

Jim was out there counting every head when the gate was closed. I gave the men fifty dollars. "Don't spend it all. Give it to the bartender. This is for all the men. Drink a few drinks, then get back to the drive. They're headin' northwest. Don't get drunk and get lost."

They laughed.

I went in to collect. "Hello, Tom."

"Jim said the count is right." I was looking out the window. "They look to be in fine shape, and the horse looks just great."

He paid me, and I said, "Thanks! Good doing business with you."

"Sam, if you come back looking for orders, stop. We're ready."

"Yes, sir, I will."

"I can't tell you, Buck, how good it is to find someone I can trust in business. I may have a bigger order next year. I didn't know if I could trust you, but now I know I can. When I signed that contract and Sam didn't want any money, I thought this might be all right."

"So long, Tom. We better get to the saloon before my boy can get in trouble. I'm goin' to have a beer myself."

We were walkin' to the saloon when a man came out. Drunk, he stopped us.

I saw the sheriff over behind him a ways.

"Your boys in there said you the one found all that silver down in Colorado, that right?"

"Yes, sir."

"I hate rich people."

I saw the sheriff come up behind him and hit him over the head. He fell in a clump in the dirt on the street.

"I'm sorry, Buck. It's early for him to be drunk. He seems to stay like that ever since Tom fired him for drinking on the job. May have hurt someone up with those saws. I'll keep him in jail until tomorrow. You'll be long gone."

"Thank you. I didn't want a gunfight. Sam, help the sheriff take him to jail."

"I will, but you tell the boys not to drink it all up and save that pretty gal for me."

"Yes, Sam, I will."

I walked into the saloon and saw the boys were at a table in the middle of the room. They had three bottles on the table half full. They also had two girls in their laps. I walked up to the bar and ordered a beer. The bartender brought me my beer.

"Let me ask you, those men over there, are they causing any trouble?"

"No, they're from a cattle drive goin' north. There're twelve more coming in tonight. They should be leaving early."

"They give you fifty dollars, right?"

"Yes, sir."

"Here's another hundred dollars for the men tonight. If any is left, keep it."

Sam came in and grabbed another girl and sat down with the girl on his lap. He grabbed a bottle and started pouring drinks.

"Thank you," the bartender said.

"If they start making any trouble, run them out. They've had their warning about trouble."

I went over to the table and sat down with the men. One of them said, "You want a girl, Silver?"

Sam said, "You know he's happily married."

"Sam, they leave in an hour. The other boys want to come in. You stay in and make sure they get back. Remember last time, boys, how sick you were the next day. I'm leaving for the drive."

Three came with me, and we left out of town. We found the herd two hours away. They were stopped for the night. It was still daylight.

"The rest can go in. If the others are still there, tell them to get back now. Your dinking is already paid for. Just tell the bartender you're with the cattle drive. Dad, you stopped so early."

"I didn't want to get too far away. The men would get back too late."

"You goin' in, Josh?"

"No, sir, I don't enjoy that anymore. I just think about Carolyn and her mother."

"You wrote a letter, right? I'm sure Red Bird or my mother will read it to her if she can't. That letter I got said that she was up and around waitin' for you. I thought I told you already."

"Really, she said that? I hope she gets my letter."

"I'm sure she will, Josh. I been thinking, you know Carolyn's ranch?"

"Yes."

"You know, I been selling horses. Down in Durango, I'd be lucky to get three hundred for a horse. Up here we've been getting $450 to $600 for a horse. This country up here don't have many good horses. I think you should start a horse ranch."

"You know, I'll get you started by having Jim build you a house for the three of you. I'll start you out with fifty head and two stallions. You can pay me later when you bring herds up here to sell."

"You think I can make a go of it?"

"I know you can! Your first drive, I'll help you and Sam. You'll know who to contact. You can pay me out of that first herd."

"Why would you do that for me?"

"I see a young man that wants to work hard and better himself. I see the love you have for Carolyn after all she has gone through. Just don't ever bring that ordeal up to her, or you two will be always fightin'."

"I know, sir."

"You don't look too happy."

"It's not that. I thank you. I have to think about it and let it sink into my brain."

"Why don't you think about it while you ride out and keep an eye on the cattle until the others get back? You have lots of time."

"Yes, sir. It's a big thought you gave me."

The men started coming in. Not too late. I told them to eat and get to sleep. "Four of you are going to be woken up about midnight. I told you not to drink too much. I could hear all the 'Ahas.' Where's Sam?"

"He was saying good night to one of the gals. You know Sam. He'll be along."

"I sure hope so. I need him, and I know his good nights. Him and Foster are the same."

"You mean old Foster is like that?"

"Not with Juanita. He has more respect for her. That's when we were lookin' for the mine and were stranded in Telluride for the winter. That was old times."

Jose said, "It better be, or he might find himself in the pot for supper."

"I think he means it." Ross said.

"Boys, I know he does."

Everyone laughed; even Jose had a smile on his face. They went to bed. Sam came in about midnight. I saw the men come in and wake up four others. Sam got them going despite all the moaning. But they went out to do their job. I saw Sam get into bed, and then I was asleep.

The next morning, things were nearly back to normal, except Sam didn't want to get up. After calling him for ten minutes while I ate, Pa, Josh, and the men were all out getting the herd moving. I told Jose to pour a pan of dishwater on him. Sam came out of his wet bedroll as though the house was on fire.

"What you mean doing that?"

"The boss told me to."

"Silver, what you mean telling him to do that?"

"The herd is on the move. We have work to do. That's what you get when you say good night too long. I thought you were stuck on Ann back in Oak Creek?"

He got his breakfast, and Jose packed up and moved out.

"You know, I like her a lot. She's different than these others. I don't even know if she would have me."

"There's only one way to find out. Go spend some time with her. Get to know her. You know, when Pa retires, which probably be when we get back, you know, Pa has agreed to make you the foreman. The foreman needs a house. You know you're a rich man. You haven't spent much of the money. If you had a new bride, you have money to take her on a two-week honeymoon. You can buy her the things she wants and deserves if you love her. Don't do it if you don't love her, and not just to have someone in your bed. You can have that anytime."

"I just don't know."

"Let's get goin' and get these cows delivered."

As we rode out, Sam told me what was ahead. "We go northwest about sixty miles. There's a few rivers and creeks, then we come to the South Pass through the mountain, and Sweetwater River goes through the pass."

"Sam, again?"

"Yes, but I assure you, it is wide, not like Miner's Pass. There are lots of boulders. I mean to tell you big, big boulders. It should be easy. We have less cattle and horses. It should be easy. We have four more deliveries, and there are 400 each. That's 1,600 all together. You can sell the horses and the extra cattle at the diners at each town. Each town, the diner said they didn't want any. But I seen you sell. I know we can get rid of the others."

"I sure hope so. We don't want to herd them back with us."

We kept pushing them. The men seemed to have worked out their night before. After they ate at noon, things were back to normal. They were eating hardy and joshing among themselves. We moved ten miles the first day out of Rawlins. I rode out to Pa.

"Pa, there's not much out there, and we have a lot less cattle, only around 1,700 head and 50 horses. You think you can spare six men?"

"Sure, what's goin' on?"

"Just precaution. I want two out to our east and two to our west and two on our back trail. I want them to go out about two miles and keep comin' in and goin' out all day. Then Sam and me will go north and scout out the South Pass. There is the Sweetwater River through there. He said there is plenty of room for us and the cattle with room to spare."

"There better be 'cause there's plenty of trees for a good hangin'."

I laughed. At dinner, I picked out six men, and we went to the side and sat down to eat.

"We have less cattle and less horses now. I want two of you to ride east and two west and two on our back trail. Go out about two miles and make a circle back in toward the cattle. Come in at supper and at night at dinner. If you see anything that might mean danger, one of you come ridin' in and the other keep watchin'. If it looks for sure it's comin' our way, you come a-ridin'. Be sure to take enough ammunition."

The men rode out. They came in and reported having seen nothing. We made another ten miles. The third and fourth days were about the same.

At breakfast the next day, I said to Sam, "That pass should be gettin' close."

"About two days or so."

"Get some grub and ammunition, and we'll go see that pass. I want to see it firsthand. If any trouble is comin' our way, that may be the place for it."

I told Pa, "We will get back before you head into the pass. If not, just hold the cattle on this side until we get back. Josh would know. I want to scout that pass. If we're goin' to have an ambush, that will be there."

"Be careful."

8

We headed out and made it to the pass in less than a day.

"Silver, let's cross the river and go a ways up in the foothills. The river is close to this side of the mountains."

We went up and up until we could go from the beginning of the pass to the end of the other side. There was lots of room for the cattle to pass through, but not much room for anything more. We left Blacky and Sam's horse behind a huge boulder and placed a heavy rock on the reins so they wouldn't pull away.

"Look over there, Silver. There are seven Indiana chiefs up on the boulder right out in the open."

"Sam, that one that's higher up than the rest."

"I see."

"I bet that's Geronimo. I've learned from Dancing Bear that the highest in rank is the one higher than the rest. The others are chiefs, but of their own tribes. Geronimo is chief of all the tribes."

"Look how many there are, maybe two hundred."

"We need to get back and make sure the cattle don't come in the pass. I have a plan that I'll tell everyone tonight."

We eased out and went down, slowly walking the horses. When we were out of the foothills, we mounted and headed to camp. When we rode in, it was still daylight.

"Everyone, gather around, if you please. Geronimo and six other chiefs and about two hundred Indians are in the foothills overlooking the pass."

"Son, what are we goin' to do?'

"We're not turnin' back. We've come too far. I have a plan. I hope it works. We're goin' through the pass like nothin' is wrong. Jose in the chuck wagon will go in first next to the river."

"That's right, Silver. Make me a target."

"Let me finish, Jose. I'm goin' to put four men in the back with two rifles each. That's why I want the wagon to be a target. When the Indians go after you, the men will raise the flaps and start firin' and shoot to kill. Try not to turn the wagon over. Hopefully, this will draw most of the Indians out in front of the cattle. They don't know cattle like we do. When they are in front, we are goin' to stampede the cattle right up the pass into the Indians."

"Stampede our own cattle?"

"Yes, they have maybe two hundred, and we have twenty-seven men. We will have 1,750 animals runnin' right over them. We will be on the outside of the cattle firin' all we can. You see the chief with the big headdress, shoot to kill. There are six chiefs. The more we kill, the more they'll want to light out. I hope we can avoid anyone gettin' killed, but if that happens, I'll make sure your family will get your full pay and bonus. We have about one hundred cattle we can lose, but I hope we'll lose less. Run them right over the Indians and keep firin'. Let's get to sleep and up early. Jose, I need to talk to you."

"Si, Silver. I feel better you put men in my wagon."

"All right, Jose. I want you to get all the rifles and ammunition out from below the floor and pack your pots and pans and anything you can get down there. Pack it tight. We don't want that gold and silver spillin' out on the ground. That's our pay. That pass is only a mile long, and stay to the side of the river. That will brin' them right where we want them."

I got up in the wagon with Jose and got everything out, and we started packing it tight. The next morning, four men with three rifles got in the back of the wagon. I passed out four boxes of ammunition for each man. The anticipation was so great that no one wanted to eat. Jose spoke up.

"We make it through this one, and I'll fix you a big supper with all the trimmings, and some pies and cookies also."

Dawn was upon us. We got the cattle moving slow as usual. Jose was in front and over toward the river. We were lined up on each side of the cattle. I was watching the foothills to the right of us. That's when I spotted Geronimo and his six chiefs. They were sitting up high, looking very confident against this little bunch of men. Geronimo responded by sending five chiefs and their braves for the wagon. The last chief was ordered to go toward the back of us to cut us off. I pointed Sam to the last group that headed to our rear. I held up ten fingers. He peeled off with Josh and signaled for eight men to follow. As this happened, the bulk of the Indians were in front of us heading for the wagon. I raised my hand.

"Get them movin', boys."

Everyone started yelling and shooting in the air. At the same time, the men raised the canvas on the wagon and let loose with a volley of fire and didn't stop. The cattle started running and couldn't stop. The firing from the wagon knocked four Indians off their horses every time they fired. Jose had the wagon at full speed. He was halfway through the pass.

The Indians had a bigger problem—how to stay alive. They turned around, and 1,700 head of cattle and fifty horses and ten men with rifles were coming at them. Now that the cattle were running, we could focus on the Indians. The dust from the cattle was so bad the Indians had a hard time seeing us to shoot. They were just shooting through the dust, but there were so many of them that we just fired and had a better chance of hitting someone. The cattle were running through the Indians now. I saw some Indian ponies rear up on their hind legs and knock the braves into the dirt, and the cattle ran over them. The Indians' ponies weren't used to the cattle like our horses were, I looked ahead and saw Jose was at the far end of the pass. The four men were out of the wagon, with one knee on the ground, firing at the Indians trying to escape the cattle's deadly hooves. I turned around and saw Sam and Josh with their eight men off their horses among the boulders, firing at the group of Indians trying to catch up to us and the cattle with little progress, for our men were cutting them up pretty good. I looked around me, and then over to the right side, one of our men fell off his horse. I turned Blacky and worked my way through the cattle over to Ron. I put my arm out, and he grabbed it and swung up in back of me. I took him to the boulders.

"Stay here and fire at them."

We were moving at a fast speed. I looked back and saw the pass was littered with bodies. The shooting from behind was slowing. Sam's boys were picking off the few Indians that were left. Sam and his men had mounted up and were chasing those few toward us. I looked and saw three headdresses in the dirt and knew that they were among the dead or dying. I saw Geronimo wave his hand, and what was left of his band were heading up into the foothills. There couldn't be more than forty left.

All the men were mounted up, and we were heading to stop the cattle. They were already out of the pass. Some had stopped on the riverside to get some water. Some were among the foothills. I sent men to round those up. Jose had the wagon on the move. The main part of the herd had slowed and were milling around as though they were waiting for us to catch up to them. Sam and Josh and their men came up with some fifty head. The horses! I sent ten men to find where the horses had gone. We moved on down the trail. I went around to see if anyone was hurt. Ron came in with Sam.

"Ron, ride with Jose till the boys get back with the horses. Sam, how does it look back there? How many we lose?"

"I counted twenty head. How about the men?"

"Just some cuts and bruises and one head wound. He should be all right in a few days in the wagon."

"We were sure lucky. When I saw that bunch, I had my doubts."

"Let's get down the trail a ways, and we'll stop for the day and get things together. Sam, put three men on our back trail in case they try again."

"I don't think so. They took quite a beating."

"I'm thinkin' that too, but why take a chance?"

Pa came riding up with some cattle and horses.

"Where you been, Pa?"

"Back yonder on the battlefield. Found these over on the other side of the river. Took some doin' to get them to come along."

Sam said, "We might have lost twenty head."

"I counted twenty-five and five horses. They're already in the book. We can't bury all the dead Indians."

"They will come back and take care of that. They will bring back some women to butcher the cows also."

"I'm sendin' three men back to butcher two steers for us. Jose can make that feast for us tonight."

The men came in with about forty horses. We camped about three miles away from the pass. The men came back with the butchered steers, and we had a feast. We weren't celebrating. The meat had to be eaten or just left to lie there and rot in the hot sun. We were alive; only a few men were hurt, but not badly. None had died, and that we were very thankful for.

The next morning, our camp was nearly back to normal. The men on our back trail came in and ate. They reported that the Indians had come back and carried off their dead and the woman had butchered the steers and carried off the meat, even the dead horses. I sent two more men out on our back trail just to make sure they didn't come back. I wasn't sure that was the last we would see of Geronimo. We were back on the trail moving northwest to Riverton. We had 1,675 steers now and 40 horses. Five were killed in the battle, and five couldn't be found after. The cattle had become content with the river and grass nearby. Jose had all his pots and pans out of the bottom of the wagon. The rifles and what was left of the ammunition were stored back in their place under the wagon floor. The gold and silver were still in its place. I would have to try to buy more ammunition in Riverton. We had lost three rifles, but I think we have enough. The first day out of South Pass went well. We turned north and left Sweet Water River behind. Sam said the peak to the west was Grantland and there was Mount Arter to the northwest of where we were. I'm glad we didn't have to contend with those two. We came to Beaver Creek. The cattle watered there, but we didn't cross. We would follow it until right below Riverton. We would come to the Big Horn River. Then Riverton was across where the Wind and Big Horn Rivers met.

The next day, we crossed paths with a cavalry patrol with a second lieutenant in charge. The second lieutenant said, "I'm Second Lieutenant Hayman."

"I'm Buck Taylor."

"Where you heading?"

"To Riverton up on the Big Horn. How is it up ahead?"

"It's good except the Big Horn is riding high north of Anaphoe. With this many cattle, cross south of Anaphoe and go to the Wind River."

"Only four hundred are goin' to Riverton. The rest are headin' north to East Thermopolis."

"We're out of Fort Washakie. Be careful up that way. We had reports of Geronimo up there. We're heading that way."

"We just had a run-in with Geronimo in South Pass."

"Why do you think it was Geronimo?"

"He had about two hundred braves and six war chiefs with him. He was on a tall hill and was directin' the battle. My wife's father, Dancing Bear, told me what to look for."

"Dancing Bear is very peaceful. But how are you and your men still alive? How many did you lose?"

"We lost twenty-five head of cattle and five of our horse stock. His braves and ponies didn't know how to react to seventeen-hundred head of cattle and fifty horse stampede comin' at them full speed."

"I don't believe that. How many did they lose?"

"About one hundred and sixty, and three war chiefs. I know cause of the war bonnets we found on the ground."

"That's amazing! Thank you. We been looking for him for three months. We're heading that way."

"Good luck, Lieutenant."

"Pa, tomorrow Sam and me are goin' to check out what the lieutenant said. Just head up this creek till you hit Big Horn River, then turn north. We'll try to make it back before you turn north. I'll try to sell some horses."

"Josh will be here to guide me. We'll do fine. Sell all the horses you can. We don't want to drive them all the way back to Durango."

"That's for sure."

That afternoon, the five horses that we couldn't find came in from the south. With the cavalry behind us, I let the men that had been on our back trail return to their duty with the cattle.

The cattle were about two and a half days away from Riverton. Sam and me left that morning. We made it to Arapahoe by noon. We went to eat in the diner. We sat down, and the girl took our order. No beef, of course.

"Did you come here, Sam, when you were up here?"

"No, we ate in Riverton so there was no need."

The girl brought out our food, and I asked her, "Is the owner here today?"

"Sure, he's here every day. And me too. I'm his wife."

"Could I speak to you both?"

"Roy, over here. This man wants to talk."

Roy, came over to our table. "Yes, sir, what can I do for you?"

"We're headin' north to Riverton. Our cattle are about two days behind us. We're deliverin' four hundred head to the mine headquarters up there. I was wondering if you could use some beef. We have an extra seventy-five head. I noticed you don't have any beef on your menu."

"I don't know. This is a small town, and it's just me and my wife."

"It might increase your business. You ever hear of the town of Miner, Colorado? The diner there bought ten head and the next mornin' she woke us up to buy more 'cause she butchered three and they were gone in one afternoon and evenin'. She had to hire more people, and she could charge more for the beef dinners 'cause it's hard to get up here."

"Sounds good. What you think, Lilly?"

"Depends on the price."

"I like that. A real businesswoman. I know your delicious biscuits would go good with gravy over the top of our beef, and we'll deliver them. You need a place to keep them till you need them. We'll deliver them tomorrow for fifty dollars a head."

"How about thirty-five dollars and we'll take ten? We have a place to keep them on the outside of town."

"I'll tell you what, you're a nice young couple. You can have ten for forty if you have cash."

He looked at her, and she shook her head yes.

"Well, with that shake of your head, I guess that's a deal."

"Yes, sir."

"By the way, I'm Buck Taylor, and this is Sam. He'll be deliverin' them. I bet you made those wonderful biscuits."

"I make everything."

"Then I know you'll cook up some wonderful meals with that beef and charge more and make more profits."

"I know I will."

Sam said, "Too bad I have to keep going on to Riverton after I deliver them. I would sure like to taste them."

We left and headed on to Riverton. We rode in about three in the afternoon.

"The mining office is down by the sheriff's office."

"Did you sell any to the diner?"

"They said they would think about it. I quoted them $45, so you'll know. Mr. Carter is the owner of the mine. Jeff Dugan is the owner of the diner. Mark Turner is the sheriff."

We stopped in front of the mining office. Out of the corner of my eye, I saw a man walking toward us. I turned toward the man. It was Mark the sheriff. Sam turned, and then Mark said, "Why, Sam, I thought we had a couple of strangers in town. Now I know we have only one."

"Mark, this is my boss, Buck Taylor."

He shook hands with Sam and then with me.

"You got those cattle with you?"

I said, "Yes, sir. Just goin' inside to let Mr. Carter know we're here. By the way, you know anyone that might want to buy some fine horses? Sam didn't know we were bringin' horses with us."

"Mr. Stone next to my office. He might need some. He runs the stage line in these here parts."

"Thanks Mark, I'll go see him when we get done in here."

We went inside the mining office. Mr. Carter turned, and Sam shook his hand.

"Hello, Sam, you back already."

"Mr. Carter, this is my boss, Silver Buck Taylor."

"This is the silver king down in Colorado."

"Sam, what did you tell him?"

"No, Buck, I read it in the *Denver Express*. Comes in on the stage once a week. I knew when I read the article we had more in common than cattle. Let's go to the diner across the street and talk and have some coffee."

"Fine. I'm interested to hear more."

Sam said, "Silver, it wasn't me. I didn't say anything to no newspaper."

We went in the diner and had a seat. Mr. Carter ordered a meal, no beef. I ordered coffee and a piece of pie. Sam said, "I know that pie is delicious. Who baked it?"

"Why, Jeff's wife."

"Is Jeff here? If he is, would you ask him if I could speak to him when he gets time?"

"You going to deliver the cattle tomorrow."

"Probably in the afternoon. When we left, they were on the Beaver Creek headin' toward Arapahoe. Sam will deliver ten heads to the diner there, and me and the men will come on this way."

"Sounds good. I'll have the money ready for you."

The girl brought the food, and we were eating when I said, "I can't wait to hear how that article got in the Denver paper."

"The reporter said he was in Durango looking for a story. He said an old man with a beard ... his name was Foster. Here's the article. You can keep that one. I have another one in the office. He said you cleaned out Durango single-handed 'cause you were the fastest gun to come out of Texas. Now you were the silver king and a cattle baron."

"You hear that, Sam? I think I'll kill him when we get back."

"You don't know him. Those things aren't true."

"I know him. He's one of my partners. He puts more into it than there is. He stretches the truth. There are lots of people that helped me. He was one of them, and here is another. He calls me his boss. Really, he's my partner. I don't want to be known as a fast gun. That just brings trouble our way."

I tucked the article in my pocket.

"You heard of the Delta Gang?" Sam said.

"Sam … "Why, yes, I have."

"Well, he rounded them up."

"Sam, we all did that."

"It was your plan, and it was you and your pa that got the leaders."

"Mr. Carter, if you would keep this under your hat."

"I don't know. Lots of people take that paper. I think it's already out. Sorry."

"It's not your fault. Anyway, I didn't find the silver mine. My great-grandfather did. He was killed, and Foster and me found it after Jeb was killed. I captured the man that had him killed, and he was hanged in Denver. Anyways, that was long ago."

Jeff came over.

"Jeff, this is Silver Buck. He's bringing the cattle tomorrow."

"Sam said you were goin' to let us know if you wanted any beef."

Mr. Carter said. "I'm sorry. I need to get back to the office. The pasture is at the other end of town. Jeff, if you buy any, you can keep them in our pasture. I'll see you, Silver, and you, Sam."

"I don't know. Forty five dollars is a lot to pay."

"I'll tell you, look at your place. You're busy. With beef, you can charge more. The cattle are in a pasture, so you don't have to feed them. The girl said your wife baked this pie. Something this good, I know she can do wonders with beef. You'll have men from all around bringing their family for supper."

This woman walked over. "I'm his wife, and I heard you talking about my pie."

"What you think, dear? Should we buy?"

"Maybe at forty a head."

"I'll sell them at forty if you take twenty heads. That's $800 cash. I know you will double your money. You may wish you had bought more. You may be able to buy from Mr. Carter, but he's paying forth-five dollars."

"Let's do it."

I shook her hand and then his. We said our good-byes and then headed to the stage office. We went in, and there behind a desk was a man. Looked to be a big man. When he got up, I had to look up, and I'm over six feet.

"I'm Buck Taylor. I'm here in town to deliver some 420 head of cattle to Mr. Carter and Jeff at the diner, and Mark said to talk to you, Mr. Stone."

"I don't have any use for cattle."

"I know, but we have forty- five fine horses with us. Mark said you might want to do some business with us."

His eyes lit up, and his expression changed.

"That's different. Would you care to come in and sit awhile?"

"Sure thing."

"You know, this is the only stage line for a hundred miles none north of here."

"I didn't know, that's many miles. I bet you use up horses fast."

"We're losing some business to the railroad."

"That's way south of here, and the cost is more. That's why we headed up here to sell the cattle. We could get more than shipping them back east. Maybe later they'll get rails down our way and they'll cost less. You think you might be interested?"

"Depends on the price and how good they are. Those out west of here are trying to get an arm and leg out of me. I refused to deal with them. How much you want?'

"Depends on how many. Not an arm and leg. They are top notch. They may need to be broken to harness."

"At least thirty."

"I'd let you have them for $700 each."

"You may not want an arm and leg, but that's still highway robbery. I was thinking along the lines of $500 each."

"Why not get this over. I'll go down $100, and you come up $100. That's $600 each."

"I tell you what, that sounds good."

"That's $18,000 cash tomorrow."

"Sure."

Stone started laughing. "You know, I would have paid the $700. West of here, they wanted $1,000. I like haggling with you."

"I guess you know I would have taken the $500."

We both laughed out loud. "Good doin' business with you, Mr. Stone."

"Just call me John. There's a corral down by the stable. Just put them in there."

"We will. See you tomorrow in the afternoon."

We left town and headed south.

"We took too long, Sam"

"You sold $18,000 worth of horses and twenty more cattle, and I think you made some friends for the future."

"I do too. I like those people, and we didn't have any trouble from the article in the newspaper. That Foster."

"You know, Silver, I think it's just an old man living out his past. I know meeting you at the end of his life means everything to him. He wouldn't do anything to hurt you and your family or us on purpose."

"I know. I love the old buzzard. Let's get riding. I got a feelin' they will be waitin' for us at the head of the Beaver and the Bighorn."

We got to Arapahoe and were going down main when Roy stopped us and said, "An old man came in. He said he was your father Ross and Josh was with him. I told him we bought ten head and him and Josh brought them in. We butchered one, and it was gone in two hours once the word got around. I saw you and wanted to thank you. If you come back, bring me twenty more. Not now, but next year."

"Will do. I told you."

"Sam, let's get to the drive. I know my pa. He don't like to wait. That's why he took the cattle to them."

We were across the river and in camp in ten minutes.

"Where you been, son?'

"Got held up makin' friends and sellin' horses."

"How many? How much?"

"Thirty head at $600 each. That's $18,000."

"Well, I'll be. I guess you do have to spend some time to make that much."

"I'm goin' to need ten men tomorrow."

"That's fine. We only have 1,250 head of cattle and fifteen horses."

Josh said, "East Thermopolis is next. We'll mosey up that a ways. It's only forty-five miles, about four and a half days. By the time you deliver these four hundred, you and Sam should get to the next town."

"You think you can make it without Sam and me?"

"Josh and me do pretty good together. We just have to look out for madmen and more Indians."

"Pa, take a look at this."

I took the article out of my pocket and passed it to Pa. He read it and passed it around the campfire where most of the men had gathered.

"What got into Foster?"

The men were saying, "Silver, you made the front page."

"You don't know?"

"What, Silver?"

"Tell them, Pa."

"Foster just put a target on Buck and the rest of us."

"How?"

"Any gun hand that reads this will be lookin' to make his mark. If Buck won't fight, he can kill one of us to make him mad enough to fight."

"Hopefully, the other towns we're in won't see this till we're gone."

"This means the men that go to town need to be extra cautious."

"If asked, just say you're with a cattle drive. Don't say my name."

"Sure thing, boss."

The next morning, Sam picked ten men to round up the cattle and horses. I got the contract from Pa.

"Pa, we'll see you in East Thermopolis. If we're not there, let the cattle water and graze. Maybe it will fatten them up a little. Keep the people happy."

"You be careful."

We headed across the river once again, and within two hours, we were running them in the pasture of the mine. We could always tell 'cause it was always new fence wire. The horses were delivered to the stable.

"Sam and me will take a while, so here's twenty for drinks in the saloon."

"Thanks, boss."

I saw the sheriff as we rode up to the stage office.

"Mark."

"Yes, sir.

"I just want to thank you for sendin' us to Mr. Stone. Here's five dollars, have a couple of drinks on me."

"No need, just pointed you in the right direction,"

"Go ahead. Oh, there are my ten men in the saloon. Let me know if there's any trouble. I told them to stay clear of any. But you know how some men get with drinkin'."

I looked at Sam.

"Why you looking at me, Buck? I'm here with you."

"I'll keep an eye on them. It's the middle of the day, not much going on. I'll enjoy those drinks. Thank you."

We walked into the stage office, and Mr. Stone came up to the counter.

"I saw you talking to Mark. Anything wrong?"

"No, just like to keep the sheriff in the towns we are in informed about my men in the saloon havin' some drinks before we head to East Thermopolis."

"Got your cash right here. If you come up this way again, bring up some more horses. I hope the railroad don't run us out of business. You know, your men might enjoy East Thermopolis. Spend a little time there. They have a hot springs there that will do wonders for the body. Try it."

"Thanks, Mr. Stone, for the business and the tip."

We walked out to go to the mining office.

"Sam, why don't you go get a few drinks with the boys. I won't be long, and I'll send the men back to the drive, and we'll head to the next town."

"You sure, Silver? You have all that money. You think that's wise?"

"Go along, Sam. I'll be all right."

I walked into the mining office.

"Hello, Mr. Carter. We put your cattle in the pasture out west. I didn't know if you wanted to have someone count the cattle. We also put the twenty head for the diner."

We made arrangements. "I'm getting free lunch until the cattle are gone. No need to count them. I'm pretty good at knowing people by talking to them. Here's your $18,000. I went to the bank when I saw you talking to the sheriff. You know, it will be nice to have some nice beef."

"Thanks. I better get to the diner and get the boys out of the saloon before they get into trouble. So long."

I headed into the diner. I saw Jeff and went over. He was leaning on the counter.

"Hello, Buck. I have your money right here. I saw you, and I sent a man to get a steer, and we'll have beef on the menu by supper. You want to have something for the trail."

"No, but thank you. I have to get my men out of the saloon and get to the next town."

As I walked in the saloon, I saw the men at three tables. I got a beer and went to sit down. There were three bottles on the table half full, and three more were empty.

"Looks like you had your fill. When I get done with my beer, we're hittin' the trail."

"Buck, I just got started."

"Sam, I know you. One of those empty bottles is yours."

The men nodded their heads yes.

"Our next delivery is in East Thermopolis. They told me that they have a hot springs there. The way up here, y'all been workin' hard. I'm goin' to let everyone go in. They say it does miracles for the body. Now let's get out of here. Come on, Sam."

We mounted up. I told the boys to head north across the river and catch up with the drive. Sam and me are heading for East Thermopolis. It was forty miles, so I was going to make it tonight if possible. Dusk was coming fast.

I asked Sam, "Did you notice some dust arisen on our back trail?"

"Can't say I have."

"Let's stop at this next creek. The horses need some rest. We'll see what happens."

We stopped to let the horses water. Blacky threw back his head and neighed little.

"There's someone out there. Let's be ready. You all right, Sam?"

"I sure am, boss. That wind in my face sobered me up."

A rider came up to the creek.

"Sam, step back and keep an eye peeled in back of us. I'll take care of this one. Have your gun drawn and ready."

Sam stepped back about four feet. The stranger stepped out of his saddle and let his horse water at the creek. He said, "Where you headin'?'

"Up the trail a ways."

"I just came from Riverton. Didn't I see you there with a bunch of cowboys?"

"Could be."

"I think I saw you in the minin' office with your money belt off."

"Watch it, Sam."

The stranger started to draw his gun. Mine was out, and in that split second, before my bullet could hit him, I could see the fear in his eyes. That's when I heard another shot. I turned and saw a man was lying dead beside Sam's feet.

"Is that all, Sam?"

"Looks that way. Didn't hear anything else out there."

"Let's get them tied across their horses and get into town."

We crossed the river and headed up Main Street. It had already been dark for two hours.

"Over there, Sam."

We went inside the sheriff's office. A man was behind a desk with a star pinned to his chest.

"What can I do for you, fellers? I was just gettin' ready to lock up for the night and go home to supper. I hope you didn't brin' me any business."

"I'm sorry, but I'm afraid we might have, unless your undertaker isn't at supper."

"I best take a look."

We went outside, and he lifted up each of their heads. Then he turned and headed back inside.

"I know them two."

As he looked through his Wanted posters, he asked, "What happened?"

"I'm Buck Taylor, and this is Sam. We were comin' up from Riverton in front of our cattle, and these two stopped and tried to hold us up. They didn't."

"I see. Sounds 'bout right. Here you go. Wanted dead or alive. Part of the Delta Gang. Say, aren't you the one that got the leader down in Oak Creek? We got a telegraph about it. Guess you miss some. Why, Sam, with all the commotion, I didn't catch it was you. Sorry."

"That's all right. I was with someone else when I was here before."

I said, "We did get most of them, but four got away. I didn't think any would give us any more trouble. Looks like I was wrong."

"You say cattle. Mr. John's been talkin' about you for a week. He'll be glad you're here. I'm glad you didn't bring them in alive. I might have missed my supper. My wife don't like it when I'm late. Would you take those two over to the undertakers for me? I'll wire for approval tomorrow."

"Sure, we'll take them. Approval for what?"

"You got some bad ones. The reward is a $1,000 on each. I better get, or my wife will have my hide. By the way, Buck, I'm Eugene Baylor. See you tomorrow. Got to run."

The undertaker was there working on someone for burial the next day. I told him the sheriff said to bring them to him. I guessed he could sell their horses, saddles, and guns to pay for their burial. We took our horses to the stable, and then we went to the hotel and got two rooms.

Sam said, "We staying the night?"

"Looks that way. No girls in your room. We have to be up early and get to the minin' office. Then back to the herd."

"Yes, Silver. We're alone, I'll call you Silver."

"Let's go eat and sell some more beef."

We walked into the diner and took a seat. A girl brought us menus.

"Silver, is you always business?"

"I want to be finished with this drive and get back to Red Bird and the kids."

"I think I understand. Maybe if Ann comes back with me, I'll really know better how you feel."

"You been thinkin' 'bout what I said?"

"Some."

We ordered, and I asked if I could speak to the owner.

"I'm the owner."

Then Sam said, "Been here long. I didn't see you in here a month and a half ago."

"I've only been here about a month, but business is good. Why?"

I spoke up. "I noticed there's no beef on your menu."

"Not many cattle around these parts. I hear Mr. Johns has some coming in."

"Yes, that's why we're here. The cattle should be here day after tomorrow."

Our food came, and we began eating.

"I was wonderin' if you would want any cattle. You could charge more for beef. This is very good."

"I don't have a place for them."

"Mr. Johns does, and most places we been, the minin' companies have been lettin' the diner keep theirs in with the companies."

"What's the price?"

"I know you're new. We been getting $45 or $50 a head, and one place, $40. I say my lowest is $40 a head."

"That's the lowest. I could only buy ten at that price."

"Then that's a deal. You might talk to Mr. Johns. One place offered the mine owner free dinners till the steers were gone. If you want to."

She left, heading to the back of the diner.

"Sam, tomorrow I'm goin' to wire Red Bird. I'll have Bill take it to her."

"You do miss her."

"I truly do."

After sleeping on the ground for two months, it was hard getting to sleep. I finally did get to sleep, and then morning come too soon. I knocked on Sam's door, and he came to open it.

"Who is it?" He sounded as though he hadn't slept all night.

"It's me, open the door. Get dressed, it's time to go."

He opened the door to let me in. There on the table was a bottle.

"Sam, come on. Now I know why you don't want to get up."

"I know. Couldn't sleep last night, so I went and got something to drink. I know I got carried away. Shoot me."

"I feel like it."

I went down and paid for the room. Sam finally came down, and we went to breakfast. The same girl came over.

"I'm sorry I didn't tell you my name last night. I was tired last night. Worked all day. It's Joan Tyler. What can I get you?"

"This here is Sam, and I'm Buck Taylor. We'll take eggs and bacon, some coffee, and a lot for him. We'll be in maybe tomorrow with the cattle."

"Mr. Johns came in after you left. We made a deal, so you can run mine in with his. I'll get your food."

We ate and then went to the mining office. The man behind the desk was wearing a suit and tie and horn-rimmed glasses. He turned around when we walked in.

"Sam, good to see you. Joan told me you two were in."

"Mr. Johns, this is Buck Taylor, my boss."

We shook hands. "Good to meet you, Mr. Johns. We came in after dark last night, so we stayed at the hotel. We just came in to let you know we'll bring the cattle in tomorrow. I don't know what time. My pa has been running ahead of me lately."

"I'll go to the bank early, and I'll have your money ready. I don't like to keep a lot here."

"I know. We brought two in last night. Tried to rob us on the trail."

"We'll see you tomorrow."

We left and went to the sheriff's.

He said, "Glad you came in. I got the OK to pay you. Take this to the bank. You can collect there. I'm sorry about last night. But you know, wives some times."

"I know I have some cowboys that may come in town with the cattle. I'm hopin' they will go to the hot springs with my pa and me. I think some will go to the saloon. They been warned not to make trouble, but you know cowboys. Let me know if you have any trouble. We'll be back tomorrow with the cattle."

We collected the reward money from the bank and then went to the stable.

"Here, Sam, you got one of those men."

"No, Silver, you keep it for me in your money belt. If I have it, you know where it would go. I'll get it when we get back to Durango."

"Let's get back to the drive. They should be here soon."

We saddled the horses. I paid the man in the stable, and then we headed out of town south. We came to the chuck wagon in about thirty minutes. Jose was cooking dinner.

"Where's the cattle, Jose?"

"I need time to cook. They are an hour back."

"You hungry, Sam?"

"Sure am."

"If it's all right with you, we'll eat now and wait. They made it this far without us."

"That's good, senor."

"Me too. Let's have some grub."

We had just finished eating when Pa came riding in. He saw Sam and me.

"Josh, I'm goin' to sit and eat. Tell the men to let them settle down north of here."

"Yes, sir."

Pa asked, "How far to town? Everything all right?"

"It's about an hour drivin' cattle, and everything's fine, Pa. Sit and eat."

"Shouldn't we keep them movin'? Daylight a-wastin'."

"The cattle will be delivered tomorrow. Pa, I have some plans for you and me and some of the boys this afternoon. Pa, put some of this money in your money belt."

"What he talkin' about, Sam?"

"I been with him four days, and I don't know."

The men came in and were getting their food. I got up and started. "Men, I'm goin' to give you a choice. There is a hot springs north of here by the town. I'm takin' Pa and whoever wants to go. The choice is, if you don't go, you stay here with the cattle."

"We'll go, we'll go."

"Wait, let me finish. If you stay here, you will go with me tomorrow and go to the saloon. Let me tell you, the springs will make your body feel good, and the saloon won't. It's your choice. You decide, we leave in an hour."

"I can't go. The cattle."

"Pa, I've seen how long you take to get up in the mornin'. You need it, you're goin'. Jose, you're goin' too. You haven't had any time off since we started."

"But supper."

"No argument. You're goin'. If we don't get back in time to cook, they can eat jerky."

"Si, senor. Thank you."

The men decided. Ten of the younger ones stayed, and the others came with us. I told them to keep their guard up and their guns handy. There were signs pointing the way to the springs. It took us forty-five minutes to get there. Even Sam came. I told him, "No saloon tomorrow." He said that was fine. When we got there, we saw they had boardwalks leading to the pools. You could see the water bubble up and steam rising off the water.

"Get your clothes off and get in and relax."

"Silver, isn't it too hot? Look at it."

Sam spoke up. "I was here before. It's warm, real warm, but it's not too hot. It feels great."

Sam got in first, and everyone followed.

"Come on in, Silver. You too, Ross. It feels great. Just have to get used to the warmth."

We sat there up to our heads, and it did feel good. So good.

"I could stay in here forever."

Sam said, "They told me it's like this even in the winter, when the snow is five feet deep."

Pete said, "How they keep the snow off the water?"

Everyone laughed.

"Dummy, the heat melts the snow."

"What you say now, Pa?"

"Can Tim and Jim put one like this at the ranch?"

All of us laughed again.

"You can say one good thing about livin' round here."

"Ain't many can say they got something like this."

"Let them others have that saloon. I'd take this anytime."

"We better get out before we shrivel up and too weak to get back on our horse."

"Oh, Silver, just ten more minutes."

"All right, but that's all."

I threw the men's clothes in the water with them after I washed Pa's and my clothes and hung them to dry. Then I said, "Make use of those ten minutes."

"Silver, what you do that for?'

"Your clothes are more dirty than you are. Throw me your clean clothes, and you can stay in there till they dry."

"All right, that's a boy, Silver."

"Pa, your clothes are dry."

"It's cold when you get out. But warms when you get your clothes back on."

"Boys, get out. You can find your own clothes over on the trees in the sun." I turned to Jose.

"How you like it Jose?"

"They not believe me at the ranch, but it is a little of heaven on earth."

"Well said."

Everyone made it back in their own clothes. We headed back to camp. We were halfway back to camp when a rider came up fast.

"Silver, Ross, three men came in fast and got away with all the horses. Five went after them, and they sent me after you. The others stayed with the cattle with rifles across their saddles."

"Which way they head?"

"To the northeast."

I plotted our next move. "Pa, you take the men and protect the herd. Sam, let's go after them."

9

"Sam, we'll head southeast from here. We're bound to cut their trail."

"We still have three hours of daylight."

Blacky was at full gallop, and Sam's bay was right on our tail. It was twenty minutes before we cut their trail. They had turned north.

"Look, Sam, our boys are right on their trail."

It was another twenty minutes, and we saw dust a-flying. Another ten minutes, we were up to our men. We took out our rifles and began firing at them.

"Try not to hit the horses."

We kept it up. One fell off his horse.

"One of you stop and get him, dead or alive."

We were still flying at full speed. I knew our horses were tired, but we were almost upon them. We kept firing six shots at a time. Finally, another hit the dirt. One of our men dropped off to pick him up.

I yelled and pointed. "You two, head to the left and the other two to the right. Try to slow the horses."

I saw the last man give it up and head east. I headed right behind him. I got my rope and looped it out and whirled it around my head a few times and then flung it. It was on him. I wrapped the rope around the horn of my saddle. Blacky knew what to do then. He slowed down, and the man flew off his saddle and his horse kept going.

"Looks like you have to walk, mister. Let's get goin'."

About twenty minutes, Sam came up.

"We're wondering what's keeping you. There was only one man."

"His horse didn't like him much. Took off east."

"I'll be, Silver, can't have no fun. Somebody has to spoil it. Look at our clean clothes. Looks like we have to go back to the springs. By the way, those other two, they're dead."

"Should have shot this one, but I didn't have a horse to put him on."

Sam got off and tied him up and got him on his horse and jumped up behind him.

"They get the horses."

"Yep, half was back to camp by now."

The horse thrive spoke.

"You Silver Buck?"

"Yes."

"I told them other two not to try to get the horses. I thought they were yours."

"You should have listened to your own advice and lit out for another country."

When we returned to camp, Pa and the men were there. The dead men were laid out on the ground until the next day. The live one I tied to the wheel of the wagon.

"Get the horses?"

"Sure did, plus these other three. Two didn't make it. Goin' to take them to the sheriff. The other two we took in were wanted."

"What other two?"

"They followed us from Riverton. They saw me put money in my money belt. They tried and lost. They went to the undertakers after the sheriff identified them."

"Looks like we're cleaning up this place with this cattle drive."

"I'm only sorry they're spoilin' our fun." I let the men know.

"Men, I'm goin' to be sendin' a telegram back home. By in the mornin', you write a short message, and I'll have it sent to Bill. He'll make sure they get to your families. Jose has some writin' paper. Jose, make me a list of things you might need. This will be the last time till we get to Montana at the end of the drive."

The men drifted off to write their messages home. I had to write to Red Bird. It has always been easy for me to write or say what my feelings were about Red Bird. But I had to make it short and sweet.

To Bill Gills:

We are all well. We buried twenty outlaws that tried to get our money and horses. Tell John the Delta Gang has been broken up. Geronimo is alive, but we killed about 170 of his braves and three chiefs and the cavalry is on his trail. Don't let Red Bird read this if she can read yet.

We have delivered all but 800 of the cattle and fifteen horses. I am sending messages for the men's families. Have someone deliver them, please. We should be home in at least one and a half months.

Your friend and partner,

Buck Taylor

To Red Bird Taylor:

We are near the end of the drive. We should be home in a moon and a half. I miss you very much. It's been hard, but it's something a man has to do to take care of his family. Tell the children how much I miss them. When we get back, we can go somewhere together. I love you very much. Deep in my heart, we will always be together.

Love you, honey.

Your husband,
Buck Taylor

In the morning, we rounded up 410 head of cattle and headed for town. Pa and the men headed to Worland, which was only thirty-five miles away. We drove the cattle into East Thermopolis down Main Street.

People lined the street to put this picture in their mind forever. Sam and I dropped back as the men led the cattle in the pasture. We stopped at the sheriff's office.

"Hello, Eugene. We brought you and the undertaker some more business. Here's one. The other two are out there for the undertakers."

"I'll get this one locked up, then take a look at the other two. What happened?"

"My pa and some of the men and me went to visit your hot springs. 'Bout halfway back, one of my men from the herd came and told us that three men stole our fifteen horses. We took chase after them and caught up with them. This one headed in another direction. I caught up and roped him. His horse left him a foot. The two out there didn't want to give up."

Eugene went out and had a look and went back in.

"Sam, take those two. You know where. Keep our horse and take this list to the general store and tie it to our horses. I'll be at the telegraph office or the minin' office or the diner."

"Will do."

I went back in and talked to Eugene.

"Looks like your cattle drive is bringing the outlaws out of the woods. They are wanted, but for less. Only $300 each, and I can write a note for the bank to pay you. I know you and can trust you. You need to sign this paper as to what happened for the trial. I know you have to get moving north."

"Thank you, Eugene. My men will be in the saloon for a while."

I left and I saw the men coming in from the pasture.

"Here's fifty dollars for the saloon. I'll be back in a few hours, and we'll head back."

I went to the telegraph office and sent the telegrams off. When I came out, there was Sam.

"Got everything he wanted."

"Go on to the saloon and have some drinks with the men. I think we pretty well cleaned out the outlaws up here."

"You need us, come a-running."

I walked in to the bank. The teller saw me. People were coming in and out as I walked up to the teller.

"Are you catching all the bad men in the country?"

"I hope that's all. I've had enough of them."

He paid me the $900, and I walked out to an overcast sky. I hope it doesn't rain or, worse, snow. I walked in to the mining office, leaving Blacky and our supply horse.

"Have some more trouble? I saw you talking to Eugene."

"Just a little horses' thieves. Not much to deal with."

"That's good. You might think that all we have up here is outlaws."

I laughed. "The thought did cross my mind."

He laughed. "Here's your $ 18,000. You know those men weren't very bright. This would be a bigger bundle to go after."

As I put the money in my money belt, I said, "As you said, they're not very bright. Good doin' business with you, Mr. Johns. See you later."

I went over to the diner and sat down to order. Joan came over with a big plate and set it down in front of me. It had a big steak on it with mashed potatoes with gravy and peas and carrots.

"Soon as I saw your men going toward the pasture with the cattle, I sent a man to butcher a steer. Everyone is coming in. It's great, thank you. Here's your money, and this is on the house."

"Thank you, Joan. It's been a long drive. I have met lots of nice people. You are one of the best, and I will fully enjoy this meal."

"How far you going?"

"Up to Worland, and then Billings, and then back home to Durango."

"That's a long way. I bet you can't wait to get back."

"We already been gone two months, and I can't wait to see my wife and children. I really miss them."

"I know. I would miss my husband if he was gone that long. I better get back. Thanks again."

I ate a good meal and left for the saloon. We needed to catch up to the drive. I tied the horses outside. When I went in there, my men were laughing and enjoying themselves. I hated to break it up, but we had to get this drive over with. Sam came over.

"Come over and sit and have a beer."

I sat, and Sam brought a beer from the bar.

"Here you go, Buck."

"Y'all better drink those bottles up 'cause we got to get goin'. You know the boss when there's cattle to be moved."

The men were finishing up when a boy came running in; he was not much older than BJ.

"Silver Buck, Silver Buck."

"Over here, son."

Every eye in the place turned to me. He handed me a telegram. I handed him a silver dollar.

"I thought I missed you. I've been all over town. Thank you. I never got a sliver dollar before. Thank you again, Mr. Silver."

I put the telegram in my pocket. "Let's go, boys. We need to catch up to the drive before night falls."

Then a young man came over. "I've been watching you. I never saw you around here. Now I know why. You that fast draw from Colorado."

"Son, you need to go sleep it off. You'll feel better in the mornin'."

No one in the place moved because the young man was loud and getting louder. My men were up and looking around for men who might back him up, but there was no one.

"We're leaving, and we don't want any trouble."

"Well, you got trouble."

The bartender said, "Johnny, leave the man alone. If he's Silver Buck, you don't want to mess with him."

Everyone backed away.

"Now, son, go home and sleep it off."

He drew, and my hat was off and hit his gun down. It went off and the bullet went into the board of the floor. Then I gave him an upper cut on the chin. His gun went flying, and he hit the floor hard on his back.

One of my men picked up his gun and handed it to the bartender, who said, "Thanks, mister. He just drank too much. I'm sorry."

The sheriff walked in, and the bartender spoke up.

"Eugene, he could have killed Johnny and been in the right."

"Thanks, Buck. I owe you one. I'll put him in jail until in the mornin'."

"You don't owe me. I don't kill for the pleasure."

"Yes, I do. He's my son. We're goin' to have a long talk before I let him out."

"I'm glad I didn't have to draw. Bye, Eugene. Come on, boys, let's get back to the cattle."

I looked around at my men, and everyone looked stone sober. "Pete, brin' that horse with the supplies on it."

"Yes, sir, Silver. I don't ever want anything like that to happen to me."

"Me too, Pete."

We made it to camp just after dark. I yelled, "It's us, Pa, don't shoot."

"You have fun, boys?"

"We did till this boy tried to pull down on Silver. I'm glad Silver just knocked him out. He was the sheriff's son."

"I got all the telegrams sent off. Jose, here's your supplies. Let's get in the wagon for a minute. Get the things off the boards. Here, put all this under there. It's gettin' too heavy. I felt off balance when that kid drew on me. I don't want that to happen if a bad man does that."

"You was lucky, senor. It was good you didn't have to shoot him."

"Yes, it was lucky."

I went and sat down by Pa. "I got a telegram back. I haven't opened it yet."

I started reading it to Pa. Bill says,

> Don't worry, the mine and ranch are being well looked after. The vein of silver is still going south and north. Red Bird wanted me to send this right back before you left town and she said yes she can read and write better now and knows arithmetic also. Jenny says she is so smart. Your mother is well. The kids are growing like weeds. I don't know about Foster. He's taking a bath every

two days. And bought new clothes. Believe it or not, he had the barber cut his hair and trim his beard. The whole town was looking through the window. I don't know how Juanita did it. Carolyn is up early every day taking care of her mother. Red Bird says she's waiting for Josh. Lizzie is sitting up in bed taking her meals. Red Bird says she loves you very much and can't wait for you to get home.

Your friend and partner,

Bill Gills

I called Josh over and showed him the telegram. He read it, and a big smile broke out on his face as he read the last part.

"I can hardly wait."

"Have you decided on what we discussed?"

"I think if she still wants me when we get back and it is all right with her and her mother, if she is talking, I'll do it. I don't know how I'll pay you back, but I will. You can count on that. I still want to work for you."

"That's fine."

Pa said, "I'm glad everyone is all right. I was too, Pa. Except Foster, he must be sick."

We three laughed out loud.

Sam came over. "All right, what's so funny?"

I handed the telegram to him, and he read it.

"Foster, is he sick?"

We all laughed again.

The next morning, we were all moving north together again—at least until the next day when Sam and I would go into Worland to make arrangements for the cattle. We had too many men now that we had only eight hundred steers and fifteen horses. It seemed to work out fine. No one was going to be overworked now.

"Sam, we'll go to town tomorrow. We need to sell the horses. Any place you know of?"

"Not offhand. Maybe the stable would know of someone."

"What's the mine owner's name?"

"Jack Tome. The sheriff is Larry Jones."

In the morning, we headed out of camp, with the contract, for the last time. Josh stayed on point with Pa. Six men were with the horses. The rest were surrounding the cattle. Traveling along the river had been good. Water when they wanted and grass was plentiful. The cattle were well fattened up. We rode down Main Street before nine in the morning and walked in to the sheriff's office. He shook Sam's hand.

"How you doing Sam?"

"Fine. This is Buck Taylor, my boss."

"Good to meet you, Mr. Jones."

"Call me Larry."

"Larry, I like to come in and talk to the sheriff before someone reports some strangers are in town."

"That's good. I wish everyone would do that, especially the bad men. It would make my life easier."

"We're headin' to see Mr. Tome and then try to sell some horses."

"You have his cattle. He's been tellin' me about it. Seems he made a deal with the diner. Be nice to have some beef to eat. All we been gettin' is chicken or pork. Thanks for stoppin' by."

We rode down to the end of Main Street and walked in.

"Mr. Tome, I'm Buck Taylor.

You know Sam here."

He shook both our hands.

"Good to see you. I was just thinking. I hoped you would make it before winter comes in."

"I just hope we can make it home before the first snow flies."

"You see that mountain over yonder? That snow on top is getting lower every week. That's how we tell when we might get snow."

"On our way to Billings, we'll have to keep our eyes on the top of the mountains. Your cattle will be here tomorrow. I'd like to come in and meet the people before the cattle come in. Get the lay of the land."

"The pasture is out back here. The gate is over yonder."

"We better get to the stable and try to sell some horses."

"You have horses?"

"Yes, sir, we have fifteen left."

"You may not have to go any farther. I might be interested. How much?"

"We came all the way from Durango, Colorado. I've been seein' that horses are needed in these parts. We started with somewhere over a hundred or so. I think a thousand dollars apiece would be a good place to start."

"It would be, but I'm thinking of reselling them around here, and I would need to make a little profit. I would pay $700 for each."

"If you bought all fifteen, I would let them go for $850."

"I was set to go up to $750. I may buy ten at that price."

"I tell you what, for ten, I'll go down $50 if you come up $50. That will be $800."

He smiled and shook my hand. "Eight hundred dollars it is. What a great buy! So that's $18,000 for the cattle and $8,000 for the horses."

"A total of $26,000."

"Will you take gold?"

"Sure will. I'll collect tomorrow when we deliver them. We better get back to the herd. We'll see you tomorrow."

"You remember to watch the top of the mountains. I hope you have coats." We headed out of town. I waved to the sheriff. Then I rode Blacky over to him.

"We're bringin' four hundred cattle and ten horses in tomorrow. Is it all right to come down Main Street? The pasture is behind the minin' office."

"That will be fine. Give the people something different to look at and talk about."

"Sam, we better get to the herd. They might be close."

"I been thinking that myself," Sam said as we rode out of town.

It was less than two hours when we saw Pa and Josh. "How far we have to go?"

"We took two hours, so with the cattle, will be about three and a half. Before dark."

Josh said, "Tomorrow, when Silver delivers the cattle, we'll head north. Then about noon, we'll cross the river and head northwest through Bear Tooth Pass. That's about seventy miles."

I said, "We need to make it through that pass before it rains or snows. Coming back with the wagon will be bad enough, but with the cattle, we might never make it."

Sam spoke. "In Billings, the old-timer was saying to go east and it would be easy to go back. It's rolling prairie."

"Why didn't we come up that way?"

"You'll see why. It's about seventy miles from the prairie to the towns where we were going. This way, we went just about straight north."

"Pa, see that snow on top of those mountains? Mr. Tomes in town said that the snow is gettin' farther down the slope. So keep an eye on the mountains. Have you noticed the chill in the air at night?"

"I've got my blanket out. It's middle of September. Should it be gettin' cold this early."

"I guess we got kind of a late start. Up here snow might start early."

Pa said, "My worry is that pass. You know those passes we came through. One, we could barely fit through. The other, we had a war with the Indians. I tend not to care for passes."

"Don't worry, Ross. This pass has no rivers. I don't know about Indians. Could be either way."

The next morning, at breakfast, the men were asking, "We're down to 405 head of stock. What are we going to do?"

"I'm glad you asked. Two or three could scout northwest and find good crossin' in the rivers and creeks. See if they are runnin' high. Two could go west and two on our back trail. What Pa or Josh think's best?"

Sam picked ten men to take the cattle and horses into town.

"I'm sorry, but no saloon this time. We need to get back and move the cattle a little harder. That pass is ten days away, and Billings is another three or four. We can't get caught in the snow with these cattle. It's goin' to be hard enough to get back with the wagon."

The men cut out the cattle and horses, and we started for town. Pa and the last of the herd headed north.

"Silver, I think when we head home, I'll take some money and go visit Ann in Oak Creek. I may try to get her to come back with me."

"There might be room for another diner."

"She was talking about a women's place to sell all kinds of women doodads. Women seem to never have too much to buy."

We were on Main Street, and the people were coming out of the buildings to watch us going by. It was short-lived. The cattle and horses were in the pasture. Mr. Tomes was out by the fence watching us.

"Buck, those are mighty fine animals. I can tell I can get $1,100 for each horse."

"You know, Mr. Tomes, I can tell you now $800 is the most I've gotten since we left Durango."

We both laughed.

"Come in, I have your money."

"Good doin' business with you. Let me know if you need cattle next year. We'll start earlier. I'm in Durango."

We mounted and rode out of town as the people waved to us for the last time.

We crossed the Big Horn River and headed northwest. It was an hour before we caught up to the drive. It was close to dark. All the outriders were back in camp.

I called Jose to the wagon. "Jose, would you help me put this gold in its place?"

"Si, I will."

After that, all the men sat around the campfire a-talking.

"Sure seems quiet around here. We have a short hundred miles to go."

"You've forgotten the trip back home."

"No, but we won't be herding no bunch of stupid cows."

"We'll have a wagon."

"You noticed how cold it's getting. I'm gettin' out my coat tomorrow." That night, it got cold, and there was lightning in the sky. It was off to the west. It seemed to go south of us. The next morning, the sky was starry; and when the sun came out, it was bright. The air had a new freshness in it. The cattle seemed to notice the new freshness and were moving faster. The boys had been pushing them some. By the end of the second day, we had made it now on to twelve miles. The third day, we were riding along when Sam came over.

"You know, when we reach Lovell, there are five or six rivers that have to be crossed—the Shoshone River and four or five creeks. Then we'll be close to Montana. That a while yet."

"We don't know what's goin' on up in the mountains. That rain we had may have been a lot more up there. The snow seems to be gettin' lower on mountainside."

"I'm just glad it's clear and sunny now."

"We might make it to Lovell in five days Sam."

"The cattle keep moving like this, we will. Then a day through the pass and three or four to Billings."

The fourth day came, and we were still moving them at an increased pace. Some of the men rode alongside Jose to keep him company because it could be boring with only four hundred cattle and twenty-five men. The men in front of us would come in at night. We had begun rotating men on the night riders every three hours. We kept our coats on all day. The wind had begun blowing out of the north again. This time it was about a forty-miles-per-hour wind. I was sure it wasn't freezing yet. If it snowed, it would melt, leaving mud in its place. That night, Sam sat down to eat.

"Silver, I know if we make it past the Shoshone River and the creeks, we'll make it."

"Why you say that?"

"Past that point, there is a thin layer of dirt and rock underneath. Might be muddy, but the cattle and wagon won't sink and get stuck."

The sixth day was colder, but there was sunshine. It warmed up as the day went along. The scouts came in and told us. "It's just open spaces with mountains in the back ground."

"Like a picture."

"Yeah!"

We turned north toward Lovell. It was three days away.

"Pa, Sam and me leavin' in the mornin'! Sam says at Lovell there is one river and four or five creeks. I want to see for myself. They're one after another. I just want to make sure they're not swollen out of their banks. If they are, we need to find another way around."

"We'll just keep them headin' north."

We left in the morning, taking enough food for three days. Jose came up.

"Senor, be careful. It does not look good ahead."

"I need to find a way to get this wagon across five rivers in a row."

Our coats were already on, and we had our slickers in our saddlebags. We rode and rode. That night we camped among the boulders. They blocked some of the cold wind off our horses and us. We built a small fire for food and coffee and some warmth. We could see lighting and hear thunder to our east. As long as it stayed to our east, we were all right.

"Next time, we are goin' to start a month earlier. We might miss this."

"What, miss all the fireworks in the sky?"

"Yes, that's just what I mean. I just hope they don't have a stampede while we're gone. I worry about my pa."

"Don't worry. Josh will take care of him. I don't know if you noticed, but they have become close friends like us."

"Yes, I've seen that. I think if I didn't take you with me so much, you and Pa would be close."

"It's good he's teaching Josh lots of things he can use later."

We ate and rode off to find a way across the rivers. We were riding hard. It was dark as we set up camp about a mile from the river. We staked the horses in a nice green field. They needed the rest all night as much as we did. All night I could hear the roar of the river. It made me very uncomfortable. In the morning, while we were eating, I asked, "You hear that? I could hear it all night. Is it as bad as it sounds?"

"It wasn't as bad as I heard last night."

We rode the short distance to the river. It looked as bad as it sounded last night. The water was rolling fast. It might carry half the herd away before we crossed it. As I looked, I could see four smaller creeks. It was the Shoshone River that was going to be hell to cross.

"We need to find a place to cross. You go upriver, and I'll go down. Meet back here in two hours."

I headed down river. The forest was thick this way. I could see roots of huge trees jetting out into the river. Some places, whole trees had fallen across the river to the other bank. It made a natural bridge. Not wide enough for cattle, so we would still have to go through the water. I rode on for an hour. Then I came to it. The trees thinned out, and the river came and spread out into five smaller creeks. It was like fingers of a hand on an arm. They were full, but I thought they could be crossed. I rode Blacky into the water. It came up to his belly. The other four were about the same. We could even get the wagon across. The gold, silver, paper money, rifles, and ammunition would have to be moved up higher in the wagon. I don't think it would reach the food. We could put some of the fallen logs inside the wagon to raise things up about a foot to keep everything dry. If it was too heavy, we had ropes and horses to tie to the wagon to get her across. I came out of my thought. I had to go back to meet Sam. I rode back, and there was Sam cooking some food. It smelled really good and made my hunger come upon me.

"Sam, you find anything?"

"No, just about the same as here. You find a place? I thought you were lost."

"I found a spot. We might have to find a way in there, but there's an open area once you make it through the thick trees. We'll pack up after we eat, and I'll show you."

We rode into the thick forest. Then after an hour, we came to the clearing and five creeks. I rode Blacky across three of the creeks, and it came up to his belly. The cattle might have to swim. See those dead trees? We can cut them to fit inside the wagon and get things up a foot out of the reach of the water. We'll tie ropes to the wagon. With the team and five more horses, we should pull the wagon across. We sure have enough men to get the job done."

"Now we need to find a way in here. Let's head south to the end of this clearing. Once we're out of here, we can find how far we have to turn the cattle and wagon to get in here."

We rode on for a while and came to the end of the clearing.

"Here's the end. It looks like a small valley. We'll ride west to intersect where we were."

"There it is, Silver. I recognize this place. Over there is where we came in."

"Let's get back to the cattle drive and explain to Josh and Pa."

The sky cleared up, and the feel of fall was in the air. The cold north wind had turned into a nice breeze. If this would hold out and let us make it across this part. It was just before nightfall when we reached the cattle. We explained to them, "We should be there tomorrow. We'll bed them down, and the next day, we'll get a fresh start. It might take all day to get everything across."

"You think they'll make it?"

"They may have to swim, but with all the men we have, it's a good chance we won't lose any."

"Jose, tomorrow when we get to the river, we have to cut four trees and place them in the bottom of the wagon. I'll help you tomorrow once we bed down the cattle. We will get things out of the bottom, and our things will be three feet higher than the bottom of the wagon."

We left early. It was still dark when the herd started moving. Sam was on point with Pa and Josh. He had to lead them to the new crossing. I was back with Jose, explaining in more detail what we were going to do. As we came closer, Sam led us toward a more eastern direction. We bedded down the herd in the clearing about a half mile from the five creeks.

"Pa, Josh, Sam, Pete, and Carlos, let's go down to the river. I want you to see first hand what we're up against. Pete, you and Carlos rope those logs and pull them to Jose. Then come back and get the last two. Then help Jose cut them to fit inside the wagon."

Pete and Carlos already had the first logs roped and were heading back as we rode to the bank of the Shoshone River.

"What do you think, Pa?"

"How deep is it?"

"About belly deep to Blacky."

"I see there are five different creeks to cross. They look like rivers now. Wasn't there any better place?"

"No, this is the calmest place. West of here, I was worried that the cattle and horses would be swept away with the current."

"It was moving fast, Ross, when Josh and me came through here. It had been calm, but not now."

My pa moved into the creeks and then in and out of each creek. I knew him. He had to see for himself. He would come back and sit in the middle of the creek on his horse for a while. Then he would move on. When he came out, he said, "Looks good. Not too deep and not much pull on the horses or cattle."

"Then let's get back and get ready for a run at this."

When we rode up, Carlos and Pete already had the logs cut to size. Jose was trying to get the logs in the wagon. I got off Blacky.

"Here, Jose, let me help you. You have everything taken care of."

"Si, senor, over here."

We got in the wagon. I could see he had the ammunition and rifles wrapped in some canvas, then the food in another, and the money in a third. It took some time, but all the logs were in place. I had two more logs cut. They were longer than the wagon. They were tied, one to each side, to the wagon. I hoped if the wagon went down too much, the logs would keep it afloat. We were ready for tomorrow as much as we could be. The morning came with uncertainty as to what would happen.

"When they go across, keep them movin' till they're through all five creeks. I'm goin' to help on this side. Jose, you stay here till the end. Wait for us to come to get you. Jose, when you get to the other side, I'll already have some men start a big fire. With the cold, we need to get everyone dried out fast."

"Si, I will wait. It will be good to already have a fire started."

10

"Move them in and get them wet."

They headed in with Pa and Josh on point. Eleven men were on each side. If one side needed some extra help, men from the other side would help. The horses just walked across. Two men stayed with them. The cattle had to swim across the first three creeks, and the next two, they could walk across. They were halfway across when one of the steers stepped in a hole and fell over. This spooked a horse, and he reared up and surprised the cowboy, who ended up in the creek. The other hands were laughing and saying, "He needed a bath anyway."

The cowboy got back on his horse and got a rope around the horns of the steer that fell over and pulled him upright, and then he continued on. Everyone was fine. The herd was finally coming up the bank of the other side. The men were herding the last of the cattle through. They were all across.

"Seven of you stay and settle the cattle, and three get enough wood and start a big fire, and all of you take turns with the cattle and horses and you get dried out completely, even your socks and boots. We don't need anyone getting sick or freezing. The rest of you, let's go get the chuck wagon if you want to eat tonight."

Jose was waiting on the bank of the other side.

"What kept you, boys? I saw one of you had time to go swimming. Now if you want to eat tonight, you better get me across."

"You four get a loop around the horses. You four loop around the logs on the side. The others, just be ready to help when you're needed. Jose, when you get them goin', don't stop till the other side."

Jose took them in the water. All the men were pulling their ropes tight around their saddle horns. The wagon wheels were three-quarters of the way up to the top. The team was all right, but the wagon was tipping one way and then the other. The water was up to the boys, and the wagon was floating like a ship on the high seas. I saw Jose take a quick look in the back. I went over and looked in the back of the wagon. The logs inside were floating, but all the goods were nice and dry on top all tied down. The men kept pulling the team with their ropes. Jose had his reins out making them go forward. Then the four with their loops around the logs kept them tight and pulling. So all nine men were working together to get the wagon across. The wagon finally righted itself when the wheels hit the bottom of the creek bed. There were only two more creeks to be crossed. Jose didn't let up. He was relentless on the horses, and they kept moving. The last of the creeks came and went. Everyone was on dry land. The men had moved the stock on for two hours and set up camp and got a fire started. Jose got supper going. The men who had come with the herd were all dried out. Everyone was tired of dry jerky. We didn't have time to stop for dinner. By the time supper was ready, everyone was dried out.

"Jose, you sure kept that team movin'."

"Si, had to. I felt it going from side to side and floating. I just had to. I can't swim."

Everyone laughed.

"It's not funny."

"Jose, you had eight ropes around that wagon. One of us would have saved you. I sure don't want to eat Sam's cooking."

They laughed again. Now that it was over, we were all in a better mood.

"Jose, you can get the logs off the sides. But leave the ones inside there for a couple of days before we store everything down below. We don't want damp rifles or ammunition."

"Si, I understand."

We moved on in the morning. The days were a little warmer now. The nights did turn down right cold.

"Sam, let's go check out the pass before night."

"I'm ready."

"Pa, stop for the night on this side of the pass. Sam and me are goin' to check it out. No sense in gettin' careless this close to the end."

"Be careful, son. We haven't had very good luck with the passes."

The cattle were moving, and Sam and I were on the move to the pass.

"How far are we now?"

"After the pass, about five days. See, that mountains up ahead the pass is in between those two. That one on the right, it will take a half day to go around it."

"There's no way over it?"

"That would take longer. Let's go through the pass. There's a creek, but it didn't look like trouble at all."

We rode through the pass and crisscrossed the pass and went as far as we could on horseback. Then we walked up to a ledge I saw from below. I sat down to look out over the pass for a while. You could see nearly from one end to the other.

"Have a seat, Sam."

"What you looking for?"

"Just lookin' to see if anything's movin'. You know, I think I'll get up here when the herd heads in here. You can see far. Maybe see if trouble's a-comin' at us."

"We're coming into the Crow Indians area, from here to Billings. From what I heard, they are at peace right now. You might see a scout out here. Might look if we are passing through or staying."

"Like I would if someone unknown came across my ranch."

"I never thought about it that way."

"I've had enough look-see. Let's get back. We'll come through in the mornin'."

We worked our way down the mountain around the boulders to our horses and headed out of the pass. It was early when we got back to camp. They had already bedded down the cattle. Jose had cooked dinner. Everyone was eating their fill of Jose's cooking. Sam and I got a plate full and a cup of coffee. We sat down around the campfire.

"Silver, if you come on another drive, I sure hope Jose is with us. I think his food is better than the diner's in the towns we ate at," Pete said.

Pa asked, "How's the pass, Buck?"

"It looks good. Has a creek. Plenty of room, and I found a spot I can see nearly the whole pass. The men can keep an eye on me. I will let you know if any trouble is comin' your way. Sam told me this is Crow country, so we need to keep our eyes open. If you see a few Indians, they may be watchin' us. So don't shoot unless they attack us. You know what that sounds like?"

The next morning, the herd was heading through the pass. I went up to the ledge to keep an eye on the surrounding country. There was a hint of coolness in the air left over from the night. The snow had receded back toward the mountaintop. The pass was green from the fall rain. I could see the animals coming out this early to drink from the cold water of the creek or eat from the leafy plants along the creek. I could see the cattle below. As I scanned the other side of the pass toward the end where we were heading, I saw two Indians. They weren't wearing any headdress, so they weren't Chief's direction other Indians. I looked in both sides and up and down. Those were the only ones. They must be scouts. I headed down to Blacky to go on point with Pa, Josh, and Sam. As I came closer, I could see the two Indians coming down. I saw Tom, who knew some signs. I told him to come with me.

"Pa, see over to the left."

"I saw them, been watchin' them."

"Tom said they're Crow, all right."

"Can you talk to them?"

"I'll try."

They rode up to within six feet of us. We had moved to the left of the herd. The cattle went by with Josh on point.

"Ask what they want."

"I speak English some. What you doing here? This, my country. I am Chief Thunder Horse.

"We go to Billings, a town northwest of here to sell cattle."

"You have lot cattle. I know this town, lot white people."

"White man in town has bought these cattle. They are not like Crow. They do not hunt for food. They have to buy."

"I no want trouble with white man."

"My name is Buck Taylor. I no want trouble with Chief Thunder Horse or his people."

"Buck Taylor know Crow?"

"Just that this is your home. We are to leave cattle in town and go back to our home in Colorado."

"You say you leave cattle. You have horses also?"

"Not many left. Three are sold also."

"Then I take two horses for you go through Crow country. If stopped by others, say you pay Chief Thunder Horse."

"That's fair. Tom, go get two horses."

Tom brought the two horses. I looked over at Pa.

"Me go now. You travel safe now in this country."

Then they were gone.

"At least this fellow wanted to bargain, not kill us like Geronimo."

"I'm just glad we got off that cheap."

The herd was now out of the pass. We turned northwest to miss the Pryor Mountains. When we camped that night, we were still in the shadow of the mountain.

'Silver, the mine owner is Mr. Ottis, and the sheriff is Henry Garland."

"Do they have a telegraph in this town we're goin' to?"

"They do have one, Ross."

"I'm goin' to telegraph your mother, son. Let her know we're all right."

"Josh, you hear me, when Sam and me go to town, you watch over my pa."

"Sure thing, Silver."

"This has taken too long, and it is too much for him. But we need him on this drive."

The second day out of the pass, we were still heading northwest. There were some clouds brewing north of us. It woke all of us up. A storm, more lightning than thunder. The herd was milling around, not wanting to settle down. I told Sam and three more men to get out there, and I went myself.

"Sam, let's sing to them. Come on, boys, sing real softly. We can't lose them this close."

Sam started singing, and the rest of us went along with him. This went on for three hours. Finally, the cattle settled down as the lightning moved to the southeast. We changed shifts on the herd, and we went to bed.

We woke up to a cold north wind. It was cloudy, but it hadn't rained last night. This morning, however, it looked like it was going to pour buckets. We moved out, and as the sun rose, I could see the snow line had moved down the mountain. I rode to the point. I had to yell over the blowing north wind.

"Pa, look, the snow line has come down the mountain."

"I saw that. I noticed all the men have their coats on and collars up. Too bad we have to head north. This wind is bad."

"By tomorrow, we should turn the cattle northeast around the mountain."

"That will help some. I've noticed that there is a thin layer of dirt over the rock. If it does rain or snow, this should help."

"Sam said it's like this till we reach Billings."

"Are you all right?"

"Sure thing, son."

That afternoon, we had a few showers. When we went to bed, it was getting colder. By the morning, there was a thin coat of snow on the ground. I knew it was below freezing.

"Get up, boys, and eat fast. We have to get these cattle movin' before they freeze. Not to mention us freezin'."

Josh and the men were heading out. They would turn around the mountain today, and we would be heading northeast. Then I looked around and saw Pa was still in his bedroll. This wasn't like him. I went over and shook him.

"Pa, you need to get up. It's freezin'!"

"Buck, it's you?"

"Are you all right? It's freezin', and it snowed a little."

"Yes, I'm all right now. I guess the cold hit me."

He was up, and we ate a hot breakfast and some hot coffee. The day went on with it warmer. The snow had melted. It was a little muddy, but we didn't sink too far down. It seemed to get a little warmer as night fell. We drove the herd an hour past sunset. The mud wasn't as bad because the sun had come out and helped dry it up. The wind had died down. As the day wore on, Pa looked back to normal. He was yelling out orders. But I was worried about him at night.

"Jose, do you have an extra blanket or two?"

"Si, senor. Is your father all right?"

"I believe so. I think it was the cold last night. Tonight I'm goin' to put these over him."

"Is good you take care of your father."

"Here, Pa, two more blankets. It's goin' to get colder tonight."

"I don't need more blankets. This one fine."

"I don't want to find you like you were this mornin'. If I have to, I'll get Sam and Josh, and we'll tie you up in them."

"All right, it might be a little warmer."

In the morning, I didn't have to wake Pa. He was up and had already eaten and was saddling up.

"How did you sleep with those blankets?"

"Like a piece of toast. I had to turn over to keep from fryin'."

"I tell you, I was worried about you. But you look fine now."

"I know you were. Thanks for takin' care of your old man."

"I have to. You're the only one I got. Anyway, Mother would kill me if anything happen to you."

"Let's get them up and movin'. Daylight a-burnin'."

It was still dark, but that's my Pa. Back to his old self.

"Sam, get ready to go to town. Get the three horses rounded up. We're takin' them with us. We'll sell them before the cattle come in."

"Are we coming back tonight?"

"No, we'll be back in two days. I need to talk to Josh."

"Josh, Sam, and me won't be back tonight. Take care of Pa. Make sure he has those two extra blankets. If he don't want them, tell him you and the boys will tie him in them. We'll probably be gone a second night."

We rode out. The mud was gone, and the sun was out, and the temperature was up to about freezing for the first time in two days. We were slower this time with three extra horses. Sam had tied one to my saddle and two to his. It was faster than trying to herd them in. We stopped for the night. We had tied the horses close by in some nice tall grass. "Silver, it's cold. Maybe we should have brought those extra blankets."

"It feels like you're right. Tomorrow we'll stay in the hotel. It won't take us as long to get back. Hopefully, we won't have the extra horses, and the herd will be closer."

"Silver, I have a feeling inside, maybe 'cause we have the horses with us. I'm going to sleep over here by the bush."

"You'll freeze."

"No, that's better than being dead. Just wear your gun tonight."

I was woken up by Blacky making a bunch of noises. I threw off my blanket just as a man came walking into camp with his horse behind him. The horse looked all worn out. I was up on my feet in two seconds. I looked over and saw Sam was gone. I knew he was out there somewhere.

"I was trying to make it to town. It was farther than I believed it was. I saw your fire and thought I'd ride in."

"There's some coffee on the fire. You know you could get shot walkin' in a camp like that at night."

"I know, I'm sorry. I saw those four horses over there. They looked fine for these parts. You think you might sell one?"

"Maybe. How much you givin'?"

"Three hundred."

I laughed. "It would take $1,500 to buy one."

"What you say if I took it anyway? I got a partner out there. He got you covered by now."

I heard a shot ring through the dead of the night.

"I have a partner too, and that was his gun. Now what?"

It was below freezing, but I could see a cold sweat break out on his forehead.

He pulled for his gun. Mine was out already. My slug hit him square in the chest. Sam came in with the other one over his horse.

"Leave them till mornin'. It's too cold now. Tie up the horses and bring your bedroll closer to the fire."

In the morning, we decided to take them into town. The ground was mostly rock, so we couldn't dig, and it was a cold north wind. Two extra horses loaded with bodies slowed us down. We made it to town about noon.

We rode up to the sheriff's office, and as we walked in, Sam said, "His name is Henry Garland."

"Sheriff Garland, I'm Buck Taylor, and I think you know Sam here."

"That I do. Hello, Sam."

He shook both our hands.

"I came in to let you know the cattle are two days behind us. We brought three horses in to sell today, and last night, two fellows tried to steal them. They're outside, they didn't get them."

"Well, I'll be."

He walked out the door and lifted up the head of both and then walked back into his office.

"You got them, all right. I'm glad you did. It's just too cold out there to go lookin' for them. I guess those are their horses they're tied to. No wonder they wanted yours. Theirs are broken down. We might get enough to put them in the ground."

"You have a doc in town? Do you know where we can sell our three horses?"

"We have a doc, two doors down. The stable might help you with the sale of the horses. The man there is Gene."

"Where's your undertaker? We'll take them over for you."

"Thanks, Buck. It's over across the street. If I find they're wanted, I'll let you know."

We left for the undertaker's and then to the doc's. The sign said "Dr. Wills." We went in, and a middle-aged man come out of the back.

"May I help you, gents? You don't look hurt."

"No, I came in to find out something. We are up here from Durango, Colorado, on a cattle drive. The other night, when the temperature dropped so low and fast, and when my Pa didn't get up, I went over to him. He was slow to get up, and for a few seconds, he seemed not to know me or where we were. He said it was the cold."

"It sounds like it was just that. The fast-dropping temperature can cause the body temperature to drop below what it should be. It makes you not think straight and slows down your reactions. I take from your age he must be over fifty."

"He's fifty-seven. He didn't like it, but the next night, I covered him with three blankets. He's been back to normal ever since."

"You may have saved his life. Where is he?"

"About two days out."

"When he gets here, bring him in. I want to check him out. It may have been the cold. It's best to make sure. You have a long trip back, and if you can't get him to come in, just keep him warm. If you have a covered space that he can sleep under, that would keep the dampness off him."

"Thanks, Doc. What I owe you?"

"The advice is free. But try hard to get him in."

We went to the stable with our horses.

"Gene, you in here?"

"Over here trying to stay warm. It's been downright cold for this early. What can I do for you?"

"The sheriff said you might know someone lookin' for some good horse flesh."

"You can put your two in those stalls over there while I look over these three. Unsaddle them, if you don't mind, and there's hay and oats already in the stalls."

"What you think, Gene, you know someone?"

"Yes, I do. Me! How much?"

"$2,000 apiece"

"Are they broken to saddle?"

"Some, not much."

"$2,000, not broken You might as well come in here and rob me."

"Come on, Gene. I've seen the horses around here. How much?"

"$2,000 for both."

"Come on, Gene, who is robbin' who now? You know any farmers around here? They could be broke to plow."

"You wouldn't. These are too nice. I'll pay $1,300."

"No, $1,700."

"I like you. You really know how to haggle. If you go down $200, I'll go up $200. That's $1,500 apiece."

"Cash, right?"

"Right."

We shook hands, and he led them into the stalls.

"You want to walk over to the bank with me? I don't keep that much on hand."

"Sure, Sam. I'll be a minute. You want to go eat? I'll catch up."

"Sure, I'll be waiting."

Gene and I walked in to the bank. He handed me $4,500, and I gave him the bill of sale. Then I caught up with Sam.

"It seems funny. We don't have any cattle to sell here at the diner."

"What you think, Sam? I'm goin' to have Doc check Pa. I was thinkin' to let the boys have two full days here before headin' back."

"Twenty-some cowhands in one place. You better ask the sheriff. How about, Jose? Shouldn't we stock up the wagon before heading back?"

"We need to go to the general store. Maybe we can put the wagon in back and give Jose two nights in a hotel."

"That sounds good. We'll have to rotate guards."

We got done eating, then went to the general store. I explained to Mr. Kylar, "My cook, Jose, should be in to get supplies for our trip back to Durango. You think it would be all right if we put the chuck wagon in the back for two days? We'll keep guards around. It will be a big order. We have twenty-five men to feed. I'll pay cash."

"That sure will be all right. I heard you were coming. I didn't think I would get much out of it."

"Mr. Kylar, I think the chuck wagon is nearly empty. I hope we don't run you too low."

"Don't worry about that. Take what you need. I have a shipment coming in before the snow flies."

"Jose will be here in a couple of days. I'll be around town if you need me, or you could talk to Sam here."

"Sam, we better get rooms. I can take care of the rest, why don't you go to the saloon? It might warm your bones. I'll be there after a while. You need money?"

"I think I have enough, and you're right. It just might warm my bones. See you later. The mine owner is Mr. Ottis."

I went to the hotel.

"I need two rooms for tonight."

"Yes, sign in. That will be ten dollars. Five for each room."

"I'll pay now. We're leavin' early. We have a cattle herd comin' in. I have twenty-five men plus my pa, our cook, and me. Can you put us all up for two nights? That will be day after tomorrow."

"Let me see. I don't have that many rooms. But I can have fourteen ready. That will be two to a room."

"You have a bath?"

"No, we stopped that when the bathhouse opened up down the street. It's clean, and they have hot water, and it includes a shave and a haircut. Run by a woman, name of Jan. It's only a dollar."

"Sounds good. Can you have those rooms ready in two days?"

"You can count on it."

I walked into the mining office, and Mr. Ottis grabbed my hand and shook it before I got a word out.

"Hello, Mr. Taylor. The sheriff was by with the news of your arrival."

"Glad to meet you, Mr. Ottis. I had a few other things to take care of."

"I know. I'm just excited about the cattle getting here. It's been cold early. I was worried you wouldn't make it."

"Believe me, I was too. This is our last delivery, and we're headin' home. Between the outlaws, Indians, and storms, we only lost twenty-seven heads of cattle and seven horses."

"You're the ones. I thought it might be. I wasn't for sure."

"What?"

"It's been all over the telegraph wire. It said cowboys from a cattle drive cut up Geronimo's braves. The cavalry caught up to them, and they surrendered. This was just a week ago. You are heroes."

"We have been on trail. We were just tryin' to stay alive."

"Meet me at the diner about six and I'll buy you dinner."

"Sam's with me."

"I'll buy for him too. He was with you."

"The cattle will be here in two days. Where's the pasture?"

"It's south of town to the east. Drive them that way, you'll see it."

"Thank you, Mr. Ottis. I'll see you at six. I better catch up to Sam."

I went to the sheriff's office and told him about the men coming in.

"We'll be stayin' in the hotel. You know it's the end of the trail. They know not to cause any trouble. But you know men better than I do. If they cause any trouble, you let me know. I'll put a stop to it."

"I would say no, but I know who you are. You and your men are welcome."

"Who, I am?"

"Yes, you cleaned out the Delta Gang, and you broke up Geronimo. That's the only way the cavalry caught up to them, and those two you brought in were wanted for a total of $1,500. You're cleanin' up with the reward money."

"Let's keep the Delta Gang to ourselves. Too many gun hands out there, and I'm not lookin' for any trouble. Thanks. I have to meet Sam."

"Here's your $1,500."

I met Sam at the saloon.

"First, we are meetin' Mr. Ottis at six at the diner. He's buyin'."

"How come?"

"They know it was us that broke up Geronimo. The cavalry captured him and what was left of his braves. They think we're heroes. We don't need any trouble."

"Right now, let's go eat. It's almost six."

Mr. Ottis was at a table; we went over to join him. "Hello, Mr. Ottis."

"Well, Sam, good to see you and Buck."

We ordered our supper, and I was hoping he would forget about our talk before.

"How did you do it?"

"Mostly, the cattle handled it."

"What!"

"Yeah, we stampeded the herd into the Indians, and they didn't know how to handle the cattle. They attacked us. That's where we lost twenty-five steers."

"You mean these cattle I bought were in the Battle of South Pass?"

"That's about it, Mr. Ottis, but Buck here did come up with the plan," Sam said.

"Well, I'll be. They won't cost any more, will they?"

"No, Mr. Ottis, it's still $20,000."

Then Buck told Mr. Ottis, "Thanks for dinner Mr. Ottis. We'll see you in two days. We're leavin' early in the mornin'. Thank you again."

It was already dark when we walked over to the hotel. We headed up to our rooms.

"Sam, if you can't sleep, don't let it lure you to the saloon. Come wake me up."

He laughed and went in his room.

We were up by five, saddled our horses, and went in to eat. We ordered and were waiting for our meal.

"Do you really like Ann back in Oak Creek?

"Sure, I do. She's pretty and can cook like a dream. What's not to like? Silver, I've been with lots of women, mostly saloon gals. Ann is the first woman to ever turn my head more than once. I think about her all the time. Do you think everyone in Durango will take to her?"

"The question is, do you love her? If you do, then it doesn't matter what anyone else thinks. You have to be sure. The rest of your life is a long time. You better make sure she feels the same. Look at Red Bird. She was so brave comin' into the white man's world not knowin' if anyone would like her. All we knew was we loved each other. That's all that counts."

"I joke a lot, but I do have real love for Ann. Thanks, Buck. You are a real friend."

We ate and then rode out of town. It was a short ride. We came to the herd about sundown. The excitement was in the air. We had one more full day. It was a long way back to Durango, but it was a sure thing it would take a lot less time without the cattle and horses. We still had the wagon to deal with. We had to take it back because most of our money was gold and silver. I was sure at least three-fourths of the men would go back with us. Most had come up from Texas with my parents. Some were married and had their roots around Durango. Dad looked fine, but I still wanted Doc to check him out.

"Josh, has Pa had any more trouble?"

"No, it has warmed up some. After he was asleep, I would cover him with the extra blankets. He knew but never said anything."

"Are you ready, Pa, for the end of the drive?"

"I am, but I love the cattle drive even with all the trouble we had. I'm sad 'cause I know this will be my last drive. That trouble I had the other mornin' told me that this will be the last."

"We have one more river to cross into Billings. We'll camp on this side of the river tomorrow and cross the river early the next mornin'."

We went to our bedrolls and the night riders went out. Everyone was up early and eating, and then drifted out to get the cattle moving. We moved along all day. Pa came riding into camp. Jose had set up camp about half a mile from the river and a mile from Billings.

"Josh, bed them down. They seem content with some summer grass left over and water close by. You going to make a speech tonight."

"I think I should after supper."

All the men were in camp eating supper, so I got up and made a speech.

"Boys, Pa and me want to thank you for all the hard work you did. We had a few tense times, and we're very thankful no one got killed. Tomorrow we're headin' into Billings. Everyone is goin' to have a room at the hotel. They only had fourteen. That means two men to a room. The sheriff is fine with everyone at the saloon if no trouble. You know about that. I would like to know how many are goin' back with us to Durango. If you are goin' back, you can get some money now, and we'll put the rest in your account in Durango when we get back. Jose is goin' to park the chuck wagon outside the pasture gate. You can get what you want out. I'll have the total each one will get when I collect from the mine. I know y'all will be gettin' over $1,000, and you don't want to spend it all here. You are goin' to have two days in town, and then we head back home a different way."

Everyone was yelling and clapping. They were talking among themselves. How I missed Red Bird and our big bed at home.

11

It had turned cold during the night. The cattle were moving into the Yellowstone River. The cold and the river made it hard on everyone. We all got across the river, and the cattle were in the pasture by ten in the morning. The men gathered around the wagon.

"Before you draw some money out, I want to say you don't need money for eatin', hotel, or the saloon. I'm payin' for that and the stable bill. The wagon will be behind the general store. If you want to keep things in there, you can. Jose, I want you to drive in back of the general store and go inside and get everything you need for the trip home. We'll have four guards at the wagon in four hours at a time. There's a bathhouse in town. You get a bath, shave, and haircut. I'll pay for that."

"Silver, what you doin', tryin' to treat us like kings?"

"I think you deserve it, and y'all need a bath."

Everyone laughed and lined up to draw money. Most took out only $100. All were going back with us except Sam. He was going to spend time with Ann in Oak Creek.

We all went into town. Most of the horses had to go in the corral.

"Gene, we're goin' to be here two days. I have a team of four horses comin' in. They all need hay and oats. I'll pay you now. How much will that be?"

He counted all the horses. Then he looked up from his figurin' paper. "I'd say $120."

"What happened to the three I sold you?"

"Oh, I sold them that afternoon for $2,000 each."

"That's great. Fast turnover. It's nice to do business with a man who knows how to make a profit. Let me know if I owe you any more. I'll be around town."

"Don't worry, it won't be any more with the profit I made. If you come up this way again, bring more than three horses."

I paid him and headed to the general store while the boys went to the bathhouse.

"Tell Jan you're with the cattle drive and Buck Taylor will be in later to get a bath and settle the bill."

I walked into the general store. There was Jose getting things and piling them up. Mr. Kylar was writing it all down. Just like home.

"Mr. Kylar, you think we can pile this up in your back room till the night before we leave? Put on three cases of ammunition on that list if you have it."

"Sure thing, Buck."

Jose and I put everything in the back room by the door while Mr. Kylar added everything up.

"How much?"

"I'd say $140."

I paid him, and then Jose and I went to eat.

"Jose, we'll eat and then go to the bathhouse. On the drive, I don't spend much time with you. I need to talk to you."

The girl came to take our order.

"Could I speak to the owner?"

The owner came over, a heavyset woman with long black hair. "May I help you?"

"Yes, ma'am, I'm Buck Taylor. I'm running the cattle drive. I have twenty-five more men. They need to be fed for two days. This is my cook. He's got two days off. If it's all right, I'll settle up with you the night before we leave. Just keep a tab. You can ask Mr. Ottis or the sheriff about me."

"No need. You and your men are all the buzz around here. I was hoping to get some business. I'll keep track and will have the total that last night,"

While we were eating, I told Jose, "Pa and I decided when you made that false bottom in the wagon, you should get paid for that, and you didn't get much time off. You'll have to cook all the way back. Don't tell the other men. They might not understand how much you do for them."

"I did it 'cause it is my job. I like cooking."

"You'll get your regular pay, $50 a month. You get $450 for the bounty and $700 bonus and $200 for the bottom in the wagon. That comes to $1,550 total."

"I no understand. That too much for what I did."

"Not to us. You earned it. We are grateful. You also have a room at the hotel."

"Thank you, Senor Silver. That is much money."

"Do you want some now?"

"Maybe $50, senor Buck, I buy my sister something nice."

"Jose, let me, and we'll go take a bath."

"Si, that would be nice."

We walked to the bathhouse. As we walked in, I could feel the warmth in the air.

"Jan!"

"That's me."

"I'm Buck Taylor. This is my cook, take good care of him. He's the most important person on the drive. He feeds us. Have my men been here?"

"Sure have. Some are still here. Mr. Cliffton from the saloon sent over some of his girls. They're still in there taking a bath with your men and a bottle."

"Should I tell them to get out?"

"No, I'm used to it. The girls' fee you'll have to discuss with Mr. Cliffton. Now, if you and your cook will set over here, me and my girl will give you a haircut and a shave."

We got our shave and haircut. Jan said, "Better use this bath on this side. We'll bring some hot water."

"For an extra fifty cents, we'll wash and dry your clothes over the fire. It won't take us long. Just take your time."

"Do that. Jose, at least we'll be clean all over."

"Senor Buck, it sure beats the cold river."

"That it does, Jose. That it does."

We could hear them in the next room.

"You had your turn with her. Now it's mine."

I got up and wrapped a towel around me. I opened the door, and there were two of my men in the tubs and naked women on their laps moving up and down. The third man was sitting on the bench. I said, "Don't you think you had enough fun in here?"

"Buck, I haven't had my turn yet."

"There're more girls at the saloon, Ben."

The girls were laughing and riding the men's lap. When I got back in our tub, there was hot water, and our clothes were hanging over the stove.

"Better get in before it gets cold."

I climbed in, and in came more hot water.

"Senor, this is nearly as good as the hot springs."

"Yes, it is. Won't it be nice to get home?"

Jan said, "Thank you for breaking that up. Wash your hair and bathe, and we'll be in with another bucket of hot water to rinse."

They poured the hot water over us. We got out and got dressed. When we went, I could hear that my men were gone.

"How much do I owe you?"

"Let me see. Twenty-two men, plus you two, and some had their clothes washed. I won't charge you for the two girls. They used the same tub and water as your men. That's twenty-seven dollars."

"Here's fifty in case we want another bath before we leave. So, Jose, how you like that bath?"

"It was like heaven, senor."

"You heard him, like heaven. It was delightful. I'm sorry about my men. They've been on the trail for three months. Just blowin' off a little steam. Here's another twenty for the trouble."

"No trouble, just men. You don't seem the same as them. The older man that came in, he must be your father. I can tell. Thank you, Buck. Come back before you leave."

"Jose, I don't even know if you drink."

"Si, a little."

"I'm buyin'. Let's go have a beer."

When we walked in, I could see the place was packed. There were men playing cards, more at the bar and more around the tables. I spotted Sam.

"Hello, Sam. Mind if we sat down?"

"Sure, I don't mind."

"I sure thought I'd see you with two girls on your lap or in the bath with a girl like the other two."

The girl came and we order two beers.

I said, "You look different with clothes on. Could I speak to Mr. Cliffton please? Tell him Buck Taylor would like to speak to him."

"I'll see if he's busy. I enjoyed your men in the bath. Most fun I've had in a long time."

The girl then brought our beer.

"He's a little busy, but he'll be here in a little bit."

"Thanks. Here is five for you."

"Thanks, Mr. Taylor. If I can be of service to you, let me know. My boss said to make ourselves available to you or your men."

Mr. Cliffton came over and sat down. "Sorry it took a while, but your men are keeping us pretty busy."

"Complainin'." I laughed.

"No, sir, sure not."

"I guess my men told you I would settle with you."

"Sam here told me."

"You want me to give you money now, then I'll pay you the rest the night before we leave. I'll give you three hundred."

"That's fine. Sam said to let you know if they cause any trouble."

"Yes, you kick them out and tell me. I'll take care of them. Here's $300."

"Thanks, Buck. I better get back now."

"Sam, where's Pa and Josh?"

"Josh is over there, not really drinking much. Just being with the boys. Your dad had a beer and headed for the hotel. I think he's tired."

"I know he is. It will be good for him to be out of the cold for two nights. I'm goin' to make sure he sees the doc in the mornin'. I may need you two to help me."

"Si, I will help if need be."

"I'm a little beat myself. Jose, you can stay, have a few drinks."

"Si, I think I will."

"Oh, Sam, I know you're not goin' to be very popular, but we need four men to guard the wagon—two men now and two men at two o'clock in the mornin'. Tell them a different four tomorrow night and four the last night and four during the day also."

"I'll take care of it, Buck."

"I'll see you tomorrow. We don't have to get up too early. I'm sure most of the men won't."

I left and went down the dusty street into the hotel. Pa was lying on the bed.

"How does it feel after two and a half months on the ground at night?"

"It's better than the ground, but not as great as the one at home."

"You feelin' all right?"

"Sure. Just tired. I'm not like I was twenty years ago, or I would be down the street with the boys."

"You want to go eat?"

"No, I'll just stay here and rest."

I left the hotel and walked down the street. Then it dawned on me. I needed to collect for the cattle before it got too late. I could see a little light coming from the mining office. I walked in and saw Mr. Ottis at his desk. He got up and shook my hand.

"Mr. Ottis, I'm sorry I'm so late. I had so much to take care of for the men."

"I see that Jan took care of you. All that dust is gone from your clothes. She does a fine job. A widow, you know. I rode down to take a look at the cattle. Fine. Very fine. They will feed my men all winter and then some."

"I'm glad you did. Most don't. I'm glad you think of your men to care that they get good beef. Without our good men, we would have nothing."

"I want to hear about the outlaws and Indians. It gets boring here all day. I like adventure. Here, I'll pay you, and then you tell me the story."

He paid me in two sacks of gold. I was glad the general store was down the street. I went into my story about the outlaws and then the Indians and the bad men in between. I took my time and made sure that I told him every detail that I had stored up in my mind. As I told the story, the details came back so real. When I left the office, he looked content and happy. Here I was, in the middle of the street with two bags of heavy gold. I made it to the back of the general store and up in the wagon. I moved everything around and got the gold in place. Then the food and pots and pans arranged. As I started to turn around, I heard a click. I put up my hands. As I turned, I said, "Don't shoot."

"Silver, it's you. We just came around the corner and saw someone in the wagon."

"I'm just glad it's you. I got caught off guard."

"This will be the only watch you'll have to stand while we're in town."

"That's all right. We don't drink much. I hope those young studs done drink all your money up. I want to get paid." They laughed.

"Me too, boys."

"I'm goin' around and see if Mr. Kylar is still here. I'll help you load."

Mr. Kylar was there. He opened the back, and we loaded everything on top of the money. It would stay like that until we got back to Durango. I had gotten more ammunition. I put it in the corner. I hoped if anyone broke in, they could take that and think that was all there was. I went across the street to the diner. I saw Jose.

"You had the same idea I had."

"Can't take much of that drinking. But I like to eat things I haven't cooked. See how other people cook. You understand?"

"I think I do. Did you get your room all right?"

"Si, I bunk with Carlos. He and me understand each other."

"We got all the food loaded in the wagon. I put two men on guard."

"I would have helped."

"I know, but you deserve a rest."

"Thank, you senor."

We ate, and then I headed for the hotel. I wanted to see more of the town. It had been a long day. We still had two more days to see the town. When I opened the door of the room, I found Pa already asleep, so I got in bed. I was tired, and sleep came fast. The next thing I knew, my eyes were open. I could see sunlight coming. I looked around and saw Pa was out of bed and gone. I washed my face in the water bowl on the dresser and got dressed and was out the door. On the way to breakfast, I looked at my pocket watch. It was eight o'clock. There was Pa sitting with Sam, Josh, and Jose. I sat down and ordered breakfast.

Sam said, "There you are. I guess you got enough beauty sleep."

"Pa, you should have waked me."

"What for? There's nothin' to do except relax. Everything's done," Jose' said.

"You got the wagon loaded, and Sam got the guards posted. I figured you needed the rest."

"I guess I did. I was asleep when my head hit the bed."

I ate and drank my coffee. I said to Pa, "Come on, Pa, we're goin' to see the doc."

"What you talkin' about?"

"We need to have the doc check you out. That trouble you had on the trail. I've been worried about you ever sense."

"I told you it was the cold and bein' tired."

"Don't give me any trouble. We have a long way home. It might get cold like that again. I just want to make sure, and I promised Mom I would watch over you."

"Like I'm a baby."

"No, you know you've slowed down. You're not young anymore. I want to keep you around long as I can. It won't take that long. Then I will be happy."

"You know I can still beat you to the draw. All right, let's go now before I change my mind."

"I know you can beat me to the draw. You proved it on the trail with the outlaws. Sam, Josh, and Jose, we'll see you later. Make sure the men are stayin' out of trouble."

"Right now, they're asleep. The saloon's not open." He laughed

We walked up the steps to the front porch of the doc's house. The sign out front said "Dr. Kimble." We went in and sat down. The doc came out of the back room.

"Hello, Mr. Taylor."

"This is my father, Ross Taylor."

He shook our hands.

"I hear you had a little trouble on the trail. Both of you, come back to the examination room and tell me about it. Get up here, Ross."

"He's about the first one up, and that morning, he was still in his bedroll. I shook him, and he was slow to respond. Then he didn't seem to know me or where he was for five or ten seconds."

"Ross, do you remember any of that?"

"It was cold, way below freezin'. I remember Buck wakin' me, and it took me a while to respond. I've been fine ever since. I told Buck it was the cold and I was tired from the trail."

"I'm about your age, and I know our bodies change as we get older. They can't take things like when we were young. Let me check you a little."

As I sat there and watched, the doc made Pa take his shirt off. Then he listened to Pa's heart. He looked in his ears, nose, and mouth. He said he was listening to Pa's lungs from the back. He asked Pa to take off his boots and socks to check his feet and legs. The hands and arms were next. The doc looked through Pa's hair. Then he said, "You can get dressed. I can't find anything wrong. Everything looks normal. He may be right. It may have been the cold."

"Son, I told you."

"Wait a minute, Ross. Buck was right to bring you in. It could have been bad. We don't know."

"Pa, at least I feel better now."

"We are coming into the cold season. It would be good if you slept out of the dampness—all the more so if it gets cold like that again. Do you have a place like that?"

"We have our chuck wagon. It has canvas over the top and closes on both ends. When we get home, he has a house with a big fireplace."

"That sounds fine. The trouble is, when we get older and it gets cold, our body temperature can drop when it's that cold. That can be deadly. If Buck wouldn't have woke you up when he did, you might be dead right now. Ross, I know what I'm going to say you won't like. If you want to live a long while, you shouldn't go on another cattle drive. Save it for the younger men. You can do the day-to-day running of the cattle ranch. You'll be inside at night. You're all right. It's just your body changing, and you have to change with it. If it happens again on the trail and you're near a town, get him to a doctor."

"Thank you, Doc."

I paid the doc, and we left to check on the horses. I stopped and got an apple for Blacky. We talked to Gene, and he said. "They are all eating good. I brushed them out."

They did look good. The rest had done them good. I cut up the apple and fed it to Blacky. We left to go eat at the diner. Some of the men were there. I thought most had missed breakfast. If I knew them, they would be at the saloon after they ate.

"You want to get with me to the general store to check on the wagon?"

"No, son, I think my bones are tired. I'm goin' to our room and rest up for the long trip home. Son, please don't tell any of the men what the doc said. Sam, Josh, and Jose are fine, but not the rest."

"I won't, Pa."

I went behind the general store and saw two of our men there. "How's things goin', boys, any trouble?"

"No, Silver, it's been quiet."

"I'll stay here, and you two go eat. After you eat find your replacements and send them over later, you go have a good time."

"Thanks, Silver. We'll have a drink for you."

After they left, I got up inside and looked around. Everything looked the same. As I turned to get down, there was a gun pointed at my face. This time it wasn't my men.

"What you want? This is my wagon. If you know what's good for you, you'd leave."

"I'm the one with a gun in your face. I want your money belt."

"Sorry, mister. I don't have a money belt. You can feel if you want."

"What you do with it? You had all those cattle. Where is it?"

"I put it in the bank, and when I get to Durango, they send it to me."

"That's a lie."

"Why would I lie? You have the gun in my face. That man behind will shoot you."

As he turned to look, I jumped him, and we landed on the ground. His gun went flying out of his hand. I got up, and as he rose up, I hit him under the chin, and he was down in the dirt. He tried to pick up his gun while he was down on the ground, but I stepped on his hand. I took his gun and pointed it in his face and said,

"You want to go to the sheriff's office peacefully, or should I give your gun back and you can try your luck?"

He got up holding his smacked hand and headed out of the alley. Two of my men came up.

"What happened?"

"This one here thought he could get our stuff. You two go on watch at the wagon."

He opened the door to the sheriff's office, and I shoved him in. He landed on the floor in front of the sheriff's desk. "Well, what do we got here? Johnny, what you doing?"

"You know him, Sheriff?"

"Sure do. Johnny just hangs around tryin' to get handouts."

"He tried to get a handout from me with this gun." I tossed his gun on the desk.

"Sheriff, I just got so hungry and wanted some money to eat."

"I know this man, Johnny. If you had asked, he would have fed you for a week. Now you're goin' to eat as a guest of the state for a long time. Sorry, Buck, this happened. You know, Johnny, you're lucky to be alive. This is the man that got Bart Scott and broke up the Delta Gang."

He put him in jail, and I walked out onto the street. I turned and went to the saloon. This was the first time I felt that I needed a drink. I sat down by Sam and Josh.

"I need a beer."

Sam waved his finger in the air, and the girl brought a beer over. I drank down half.

"What's going on, Buck? I never seen you drink down half a beer at once."

"Someone just tried to rob me, at the wagon. He's in jail."

"Where were the men?"

"I let them go to supper, and that's when it happened."

"I hope we make it out of this town."

Mr. Chiffon came over and sat down.

'Haven't seen you in here much, Buck."

"I've been busy, and I just drink a beer once in a while. I'll be in tomorrow night to settle up. We'll be leavin' the mornin' after that."

"I hate to see you go."

"I bet you do." I laughed. I was getting back to normal.

"I better get back. See you tomorrow night, Buck."

"Sam, are the men havin' a good time in this town?"

"They sure are. I see them drinking and with women, and they've been gambling. Some have won big, some have lost. Most have broken even. They've all had fun doing everything, even some fun in the bathhouse. I'll just say the girls in the saloon are very accommodating and leave it at that. Josh and me have kept an eye on things, and there has not been any major trouble."

"I want them to enjoy 'cause it's goin' to be a long way back home and not much work. We have to have out riders to protect what's in the wagon. Sam and you, Josh, I want you both to know how thankful Pa and me are for you two's help before and on this drive. All the contracts were valid.

All but one were good men. That one, I didn't like the way he treated his men and the land. He'll probably try to sell the meat to his men."

"I know that one I wish we hadn't gone to."

"Anyway, Sam and you, Josh, are goin' to get a bigger bonus. I have the figures here. Sam, five months' pay $375, the reward $1,440, and a bonus of $1,000 equals $2,815, minus $100 you took out for, here is $2715. Josh, yours is a little less. It's because of the reward. It's $2,000."

Sam said, "Buck, I never thought. I don't know what to say. I gave you so many headaches with my drinking and the women in my room."

Then Josh said, "That's a lot of money. I never expected that. I thank you. I know it will help Carolyn and me. I'm not going to spend any."

"Why, Sam, you paid for the drinkin' the next day, but you were always there when we needed you. The women, I don't know what you paid." I laughed.

"I really can't pay you two enough for your loyalty to us. I thank you."

"Thanks, Buck."

"Sam, you know what you have at the bank at home. I wouldn't tell Ann about the money. See if she wants you first and not the money. You know Durango has really been growin'. We might could use another diner, or there might be some other type of business that she would like. Once you got back, you could back her with the money. I would do it if you got married."

"I don't know about that last part. It's all up in the air right now."

"Well, boys, you two have fun. I'm going to the hotel and call it a night."

Pa was resting in the room when I walked in.

"You look like you're gettin' enough rest."

"I've been thinkin' about what the doc said. I am gettin' older, and I think we should talk to Sam. You know he did one hell of a job up here. Make him the foreman of the ranch when he gets back from Job's Crossing. I think that woman will settle him down. I haven't seen him drinkin' that much, and no women I know of. I'll be there at the ranch most of the time to advise him if he needs help. I know your mother would want to do some travelin'. You know me, I like the ranch, but I'll do it for her. She has stood by me all these years."

"I'm goin' to add $10,000 to your and Mother's account. If you need more, just ask. I want to see both of you happy."

"Thanks, son. I think I'll try to get some sleep."

"Me too. I must be gettin' soft 'cause that trail 'bout did me in."

When we woke up, it was already daylight. Pa was just putting on his boots. "You goin' to breakfast?"

"Yeah, you want to join me?"

"Sure. You go ahead. I'll see if Sam and Josh are up. We'll meet you at the diner."

I put my clothes on and thought, *I'm goin' to take another bath and have a shave before today's over.* Knocking on their door, I heard Josh say, "Come in." They were both in bed.

"Come on, get out of bed. Pa and me want to talk to you both,"

"Silver, it's just too early."

"It's about your two's future. We'll be in the diner."

"All right, we'll be over there. Josh, I know he going to want us to sell cattle at the North Pole to Santa Claus."

Pa and I ordered breakfast, and in came Sam and Josh dragging in. They ordered, and I started, "Sam, I know we talked about you becomin' foreman when Pa retires. You take your time with Ann. Make sure she's the one. When you get back, you'll be the new foreman. Pa will be there to help you over the rough spots, and I'll be there. You and me have been through a lot together, and I hope a lot more in the future."

"Ross, Silver, I don't know if I can handle it. I'll sure give it a try with your help."

"Josh, I know you want to start a ranch with Carolyn, and I'll help you. That will take a long while. So until then, you can do both. Start buildin' a ranch and work for me as Sam's assistant. What you learn, you can put to use on your ranch. We have seen what a good job you two have done on this job."

"You think I can handle both? I want to, but I don't know if I can."

"You're young. I know if you work hard and don't give up, you will have a good ranch. You can do it, and Carolyn will be so proud of you."

"I say yes."

"Good. You both will see your pay raised. I'll talk to you later. Pa, anything to add?"

"Just what Buck has said. You both did a fine job, and I look forward to helpin' you two grow into your new job. I worked with y'all, and I know you can handle it. Josh, I know when you marry that gal, she is a strong girl. She will help you on your ranch. I hope you're thinkin' about a horse ranch. You saw what the horses brought. We only had a hundred horses, and let's see, we got $41,000 for them. We got them off the range, so that's 100% profit. We'll talk later. There will be plenty of spare time goin' home."

"Now you two go have some fun. We leave in the mornin'. I want to get home."

They left looking more awake now after the shock we gave them.

"You think we did good?"

"Yes, I do. Sam is your partner in your mine. We can trust both of them. I know by spendin' time on the trail with them."

"What you mean my mine? It's our mine. Jeb found it. Every time we get a shipment in, part goes in your account."

"I guess your mother knows about that."

The rest of the day went by. I got my bath and shave. I paid her some extra. I went and paid Gene at the stable. I settled up with the diner and gave her extra in case some men wanted to eat later. I got the bill paid to Mr. Kylar at the general store. I got the men together and told them, "We're pulling out at seven. So don't have too much fun on your last night, or you might pay for it tomorrow. Ask Sam." Everyone laughed.

"Jose, in the mornin' get the team hooked up and meet us at the pasture."

That night, Pa, Sam, Josh, and I went to the saloon and had a beer. Mr. Cliffton came over.

"Do I owe you anything?"

"Just two hundred more."

I paid him. Then said, "Can you bring all your girls and the bartenders over?"

After about ten minutes, they were all around our table. There were eight girls and two bartenders.

"I want to thank y'all for takin' care of my men, and some of you girls went all out."

I passed a hundred-dollar bill to each and an extra two hundred to Mr. Cliffton. They all said thanks. The girls gave me a kiss on the cheek.

We were having another beer when the sheriff came in and sat down with us along with Mr. Ottis.

"We just came by to thank you for all you did for our town. The business will help us make it through the winter," Mr. Ottis said.

The sheriff spoke up. "I want to say your men are the best we ever had that shows what kind of boss they have. Thanks for all the wanted men you brought to jail. Thank you. Come back anytime."

Pa stayed with the boys, and I went to the hotel and paid the bill. I wrote a quick note and went and sent it to Red Bird. I told her we were leaving for home and hoped to be back in a month and a half if the weather didn't turn really bad. I went to bed and heard Pa come in an hour later, and then I was off to sleep.

12

The morning came fast. The diner crew had their hands full. All twenty-seven of us were in there. Jose came over and said he was going to hitch up the horses and head to the pasture. I told Carlos to help him and to go with him. I would have his horse brought to him at the pasture. I told Carlos to tell the night guards to come eat breakfast.

Little by little, the men started drifting out to go to the stable.

"Sam, would you have two of the men saddle Blacky and Pa's horse."

"Sure thing, Silver."

Jose just passed the diner on the way out of town to the pasture. We headed to the stable and rode down the street and out of town.

Everyone was at the pasture.

"Jose, you checked the wagon?"

"Si, senor. Everything is where we put it."

"Sam, Josh head us home."

I hoped that without cattle and horses, it would be an easy trip home. Just out of town, we had to cross the Yellowstone River again. The wagon was pretty well loaded, but with twenty-five men, it was easy to get across. Sam was leading us to the southeast away from the way we came in. Sam rode over.

"Silver, for about fifty miles, we'll be in the main Crow Indian area. They're peaceful now. They might keep an eye on us. I hope that's all. We don't have the cattle to back us up."

"I'm goin' to put two men on our back trail in case someone has an idea to follow us from town. You never know. You and me ride in front a mile or two."

We headed out more east than south.

"That mountain to the west is the same one we went around before heading into Billings. It was to our east. We're heading down past Sheridan little to our east. Over this way, it's more rolling grassland. This is going to be a lot easier."

"If it's easier, why didn't we bring the cattle this way?"

"Every time we made a delivery, we would have to drive them fifty to seventy-five miles west, sometimes more, to go around the mountain to get to the mines. We should get to the Big horn River tonight. There it is."

"That looks deep. We better find a place for the wagon."

"Over this way, there it is, the marking. I've been over here."

"If we make this, it will be about forty miles."

"Tomorrow night, we might be a little north of Sheridan."

We rode back in time for dinner. This time, everyone was around the fire.

"Pa, we should make the next river by nightfall."

"This is a good track. Looks like a lot of wagons come this way."

"They must. The river is even marked for the wagon to cross."

The riders came in from our back trail.

"There are six riders come up on us soon. They're ridin' hard."

"We'll wait here awhile."

"Jose, when you're packed up head out. Josh, take ten men with you and lead Jose."

He packed up fast, and they were gone. The men rode in.

"Howdy, fellows. Have some coffee?"

"Sure, get down and have a cup."

"Where you headin'?"

"Colorado."

"That's a far piece."

"Where you headin'?"

"We're not sure yet. Depends on what happens here."

"Mister, you'd be stupid to draw down on fifteen men. My pa and me would kill four of you before you could draw your guns."

"We'll be ridin' on. There will be another place and time."

They rode out, and we packed up the coffeepot and left to catch up with the wagon. We made it to the Big Horn River by nightfall. I posted four men, two every four hours. We couldn't take a chance with $225,000 in the wagon. I called the men together.

"We have the final figures for the drive. Each man will receive $1,170, minus what you took out in town. That includes the bounty money. Mr. Gills will deposit that in your account at the bank once he does his count of the money. That's why we have to protect this wagon."

There were yells and hollering with hats off and in the air all around the camp. It was a small celebration. I called Pete over.

"Pete, you'll get a thousand dollars more than that for the bounty on the one you got."

"Thank you."

"Sam, I forgot you'll get $2,000 more than I told you for the two you got." The night went by without any trouble. The next morning, we had a little trouble as we went across the river, but we tied ropes from five men and they help put the wagon across. It was the same routine two men on our back and Sam and me about a mile ahead. That afternoon we saw some Crow scouts on top of a hill overlooking the trail.

Sam said, "They're keepin' an eye on us all right."

"First we've seen."

"That's probably 'cause they didn't want us to. Now we're going out of their territory. They know we're just passing through. You know, around here somewhere is where Cluster and his men were killed by these same Crows." "That's a soberin' thought. I'm glad to be leaving with everything we came in with."

We came within sight of Sheridan. We were going around the town. The men had enough of towns for a while. We turned around and saw that to the north were big black clouds.

"Look what's coming. I hope they pick up the pace."

"That looks bad."

We got back. They had sped up. I said, "Jose, keep goin' as far and fast as we can before that hits. We don't want to get bogged down if it rains."

The wind was blowing harder now from the south. This was late September. I hoped it was too early for a blizzard. We would just have to run ahead of it as much as we could. We made it to where Sam and me had been early.

"Keep goin' on, past the town."

The road was better close to town, so we could go farther. We passed the town about five miles before it hit. There was some rain. And then the cold hit. All the men had their coats out as we stopped. We got the saddles off and the horse staked out close by. The rain was only light. We found the driest wood we could, and Jose built a large fire. He cooked, and we stood around the fire. When supper was gone I took Jose in the wagon.

"Doc said Pa shouldn't spend the night out in the cold and now with the light rain. You think we can make room for him to sleep."

"Si, Senor Silver, we will do it. Then get him out of his clothes. I have these two blankets still. He'll be nice and warm."

I called, "Pa, come up here. Take off those wet clothes and get under these blankets. You know what the doc said."

"The rain has stopped."

"It's getting' colder. Jose will dry your clothes over the fire and then you can get back in them."

"All right, I guess you're right."

"Si, Senor Ross, we need you. You stay warm and dry. We saw what happen before. I had a uncle that died out in the cold. You listen to your son. He does what's right."

"Yes, Jose."

The next morning, Pa was up with Jose. We were on the trail to Casper. The road was a little muddy in places. The creek was still normal. The wagon took the creek with ease. We kept up the same routine day after day. The days had warmed up but stayed cloudy. Pa slept in the wagon. It made me feel good to see him back to his old self. We were two days from Casper when in rode ten men. Six we already met.

"You here to try your luck again?"

"We brought help."

"So did I. But this time, nobody walks away. And you're first."

My men spread out. His men were still on horseback.

"These are all gun hands."

"We aren't, but odds are in our favor. Men, if one man steps out of his saddle, shoot him. I'm tired of low lives like you."

"You said there was only fifteen. Now I count twenty-seven. I want no part of this."

"Mister, if I was you, I wouldn't turn that horse, or you'll be dead. You became part of it when you listened to this one. I'm tired of havin' to look out for men like you. Pa, you have your four picked out. I got my four."

"I got my four, son. I feel real good. Been a long while since I had this much fun, since we wiped out the Delta Gang, and there were a lot more of them. Boys, you can have the rest."

That's when they all pulled down on us. I got the three in front, and I heard Pa's gun go off equal to mine. That made six dead, and when the smoke cleared, the other four were dead on the ground.

"Ross, you and Silver didn't leave enough for us."

"Sorry, Sam, next time."

"That's all right, you can have them."

I walked over to the leader as he was lying in the dirt face-up with blood running out of his mouth.

"He called you Silver."

"That's me, Silver Buck."

His head fell to the side, and he was dead.

"Get them tied across their horses, and we'll take them to Casper. They might be wanted."

Then Sam spoke up. "You know, Silver, seems they would run out of bad men up this way. We plum cleaned them out."

"Jose, Casper is the last town to get supplies. So let's go to town, boys. This might be the last drink you get till home."

In two days, we rode up Main Street of Casper.

Boys, head to the saloon. You have two hours. Pa, would you go with Jose and get supplies. Josh, you and Sam come with me and bring the dead men."

"We rode to the sheriff's office and walked in.

"Sheriff, I'm Buck Taylor. My men and me are headin' back home to Durango. We were attacked about two days north of here. We have been on a cattle drive to Montana. We have all ten men dead outside."

"These men attacked you. Why would they attack you for no reason?"

"They had reason. They followed us from our last delivery in Billings. They knew what we were carryin' 'cause they followed us from there. My men are at your saloon, and my pa and the cook are at your general store gettin' supplies."

"Let me take a look."

We walk out and he looked at each body.

"Well, I'll be. These are real bad men. I've been looking for these four for months. They were all shot in the front."

"They pulled down on us. I warned them, but they wouldn't listen. Six of them came into camp but saw they had no chance. They came back with the other four. They were outnumbered, but I think they thought us as cowpunchers and not good with our guns. As you can see, they were wrong."

We waited while he went through the Wanted posters. He pulled out one, then two, three, and four.

"Here's four, and here's two more I hadn't seen before. I'll take them to the undertakers. He can sell their horses and things to pay for their burials. Here's a voucher. You can take it to the bank. You must be the cattle outfit that cleaned out the Delta Gang."

"That was a few months ago. Now, Sam you and Josh help the sheriff take these bodies to the undertakers."

"Will do, Silver."

"I heard about you. No wonder these fellows didn't have a chance. They didn't know whom they were dealing with. What you doing herding cattle when you a silver mine?"

"I came from Texas and love the cattle business. Except when they try to take what is ours."

I went out in the street and headed to the bank with Blacky's reins in my hand. Then I went to the general store, and as I went inside, I saw

Sam go in the saloon, and Josh was coming my way. I waited for him. I wanted to talk to him.

"I've been wantin' to talk to you alone. It's hard on the trail. Josh, you're goin' to get an extra $300 bonus 'cause of your help up here with Sam. We couldn't do it without the help of you two. Also your help with Pa when he needs it."

"You didn't have to do that. I enjoy working with Sam and Ross. I look up to them and you. I want to be a good man and father one day."

"You keep workin' like you do, and you will be. Now let's get Jose and Pa before they buy out the store."

I patted him on the back as we went in the store.

I paid, and we loaded everything in the wagon. As I looked up and down the street, all I could see were our horses. Pa, Jose, and Josh headed out of town, and I went to round up the men.

"Men, we need to hit the trail. The wagon is already gone."

"Buck, I just got here."

"Sam, you'll have plenty of time to drink in Oak Creek, among other things."

"All right, let's mount up. Next stop, Oak Creek."

We had turned south toward Medicine Bow. It was three days away. The trail wasn't too bad, but not as well traveled as the one to Casper. The weather had turned for the better. The days were warmer, but the nights were still on the cold side. Pa slept in the wagon at night and was full of energy during the day. Two men rode our back trail. Sam and I were out in front about a mile. Jose made everyone happy with his meals, and sometimes cookies or pies. We bypassed Medicine Bow on the third day. Sam turned us to the southwest. Sam said we had to go around Medicine Bow Mountains. We would go between two mountain ranges. The North Platte River went in between the two ranges. We traveled the east side of the river until we came to a spot that looked like it was passable. Sam and I rode our horses into the river. It was so cold that it could be felt through my pant-covered legs. It was up to Black's belly. We were halfway across. I kept going until I was across.

"Sam, go back and lead them to this spot."

"We'll be back."

The men and the wagon came rolling up.

"Sam, tie the ropes to the horses on the wagon and bring the ropes across. Men, tie your ropes to the back of the wagon and get in the river and pull with us."

Jose had disappeared for a while and then was back.

"Jose, ready?"

"Si, senor. Everything is ready in the back."

"Drive them in, Jose. Everyone, pull."

Jose drove the team in the river. The wheels disappeared under the water. It was a rock bottom if only the wheels didn't get caught in between two large rocks at the bottom of the river. We were pulling on the ropes wrapped around our saddle horns. The wagon came to a stop about three-quarters of the way across. The men pulled, and Jose got the team moving slowly, but they were moving. The team came out on the west side of the river. We got all the ropes off and headed on south.

"We'll go on until sundown. With these cold nights, the horses need to dry before we stop for the night."

The mountains were on both sides of us. It was sheer rock going up a few thousand feet above us. It was like dusk going through the mountains, but we could see our way until it was sundown. Then we stopped. The horses were dry, and our pants were dry, but the feet were something different. Jose built a fire. I saw everyone pulling off their boots and putting them by the fire along with their socks, the ones that had them. I sat by the fire, letting it warm my feet. The horses were staked out on some grass that was still a little green, close by the camp.

"Sam, when you leavin' us for Oak Creek?"

"About one and a half days. Josh will have no trouble leading you home. I'll be back with or without Ann. That's up to her."

"How you feel about that, Josh?"

"That's fine. I watch and listen. There is only one larger river, the Colorado. There are a lot of minor rivers and creeks. We'll be all right. Sam, about how far is it home?"

"Around 240 miles, but it takes time to go across rivers and around mountains and through passes. At the rate we been moving, it should take another twelve days or less. Right, Josh?"

"I think so. And about two days after Sam leaves, we'll be on the same trail you came up on."

"Men, I would let you ride on home, but we need to guard this wagon. All your pay is in there. And your job's also is in there, 'cause the ranch won't keep goin' unless we can make it on our own. The silver mine won't last forever. I hope you understand."

"We don't mind, boss. You let us have a great time at the end of the trail. I'm just sorry I couldn't bring a couple of those gals home. That bathhouse was real nice."

Everyone was laughing at Frank.

"I heard and saw what was goin' on in that bathhouse. I'm glad you and Pete didn't get in trouble."

"Me too, Silver, but it would have been worth it. Never done that before. It would have been nice to have those girls in that there hot springs."

The men laughed even harder.

"We better get in our bedrolls before y'all bust a gut laughin'. We need to get an early start, so we can get home before we get snowed in up here without the girls in the saloon in Durango."

"Silver, if I had a wife that looked like yours, I wouldn't have even come on this drive."

The roar went up in the air and through the night.

"Why you think I want to get home so fast?"

Another roar went up, and then we finally went to bed.

Everyone was up early and eating breakfast. With Jose packed up, we rolled on. The trail was easy going for now, but I knew that could change over the next rise. I kept an eye to the north and west for any weather changes that might come our way. We covered a lot of miles this day. The next day, Sam would be heading west to see Ann.

The next morning, I told Sam to pack up enough food for the trip and take some extra ammunition. Then Sam stopped, and I stopped beside him. Jose in the wagon and all the men said good-bye and moved on past.

"Be careful out there. Might still be some of those outlaws around."

"Sure will. If Ann says she will come with me, I might take longer. Packing up her stuff then have a wagon to drive home. If she says no, then I'll be home sooner. Don't worry too much."

I laughed out loud, and he rode off west. I caught up with the men, and we rode on until sundown. That night, I called the rancher over.

"Mat, Dru, Tom, and Will, I need to talk to you over here."

"What's going on, Silver?"

"I just wanted to tell you the last ten men that attacked us were wanted dead or alive. That will increase your reward to $600 for each of you, and I'm goin' to pay you what my men make—$50 a month and the bonus. That will be $175. A total of $1,500."

"You already paid us for the cattle. That's all we expected."

"I don't see it that way. You helped bring down the outlaws. The Indians could have killed you, and you worked just as hard as my men. This will give you a head start on next winter. We did make all we were hopin' for. And you have been away from your families same as us. Maybe we will do it again next year."

"Thank you, Silver. That's all we can say."

"That's enough for me."

The next morning, Josh and I left to scout ahead of us.

"Tomorrow we'll have to cross the Colorado River by a town called Gypsum, then a river called Roaring. You don't want to see why they call it that. We'll go across El Jebel."

"Why do they call it Roaring?"

"When we get closer, I'll take you to see it. You won't believe your eyes. You must have come up a little west of it, or you would have heard it."

The days had warmed again. I took off my coat as we road into camp after dark.

"Tomorrow we go across two rivers, then turn south into Durango."

"I know I'll be glad to get home and see your ma."

"Me too, Pa. I can't wait to see Red Bird and the children. Just a few more days and we'll be home. Josh and I will stay with you tomorrow till we cross both rivers. We'll camp on the other side of the Roaring River.

"Why they call it that?"

"You can come with us. Josh is goin' to show me when we pass by there." The next morning, we were on the trail again. About noon, we camped and ate on the north side of the river. Josh and I ate and took our horses in the river. It wasn't too bad. It came up halfway between Blacky's knees and his belly. We tied ropes to the team just to make sure we had no major trouble. The wagon came across without a hitch. We made good time. We pulled up to the next river by El Jebel. The river was rough. This time we tied ropes all around the wagon and the team. Pa and I crossed the river with our ropes tied off to our saddle horn, and the men were in the river and Jose on the wagon.

We pulled, and they pulled, and Jose got the team wet and was to the middle when a big log flowing down the river hit a horse and knocked Slim in the river. The log went on by. Slim caught a wagon wheel and pulled himself up in the wagon. His horse came out on our side of the river unhurt. The wagon came on across out the river. Slim got down and got on his horse and gathered up his rope.

"What, you takin' a bath so early, you just had one up the road in that nice bathhouse." We all laughed.

"It's not funny. I lost my hat."

Next morning, Jose led our little band of men south. Josh took Pa and me to see how the Roaring River got its name. We came closer, and the noise was unbelievable. We came to the edge of a cliff, and the sight was unreal. The water was like the ocean, with waves churning every which way and went around a boulder in the middle of the river. Then two or three places, the water dropped five to ten feet. There were whole trees torn up by their roots in the river. I tried to shout over the noise.

"No wonder they didn't build the town down this far."

"Nothing could get across that," Pa said.

"As beautiful as this is, we have to catch up to the men."

We caught up and headed out in the lead. That night we camped right past a little bump in the trail called Marble. The next morning, we were in a really dense part of the forest. Some places, the wagon just squeezed through. I remembered this on our way up. The cattle had a slow time. This night we camped north of Soap Creek. I saw why they called it that. It looked like soap was all in the creek foaming up, with no waves. The next morning, we went on, turning a little to the southwest after we crossed Soap Creek. We had to head a little more to the west to make it around Sheep Mountain. We made a turn south after getting around Sheep Mountain. It would be south until we hit Durango. It had been a long three and a half months.

"Josh, have you decided what to do yet?"

"It depends on what Carolyn says. She might have changed her mind. I been gone nearly five months."

"It won't be long now. I figure about three days or so."

"Just about right. I've been out this far when I was young. That's about how long it took. Should be to Ridgway by dark. Think we will have any more trouble?"

"I sure hope not."

We pulled down the street of Ridgway. There wasn't much there, just a general store to keep the surrounding area supplied with goods. We had enough food. They also had a stable and a saloon. We passed on through and camped just south of town.

"Silver, can we go in for a couple of drinks?"

"Sure you can, but we're pullin' out early if you're not here. You know the way home."

Only ten men left for town. The rest sat around talking about what they were going to do when they got home. They woke me up when they came in, but I went right back to sleep.

We left early as usual. The men that went to town didn't look at all happy. We passed Ouray about noon and then stopped for dinner. We moved out to Silverton. We went on around the town and camped.

"Pa, can I have a sheet of paper out of your book and a pencil? I need to write down what everyone's pay is so Bill will know what to put in each man's account. Are you and Josh goin' to stay with me till we reach town?" "Sure, son. It's my last trail drive. I have to finish it all the way to the ranch."

"Me too," Josh said.

"How about you, Jose?"

"Si, Senor, I'll cook for you."

We moved out. That night, we camped ten miles from town. I knew we couldn't make it by dark, so I had Jose stop before dark.

"Men gather around. Josh, Pa, Jose, and me are staying here tonight and pull into Durango tomorrow, but we only need ten men tonight to guard the wagon. So the other ten can go on in tonight. Here's my hat. I just put twenty stones in it. Jose marked ten. Whoever gets the ones that are marked goes to town. That's fair, and no hard feelings."

"Sounds fair."

I held my hat in the air, and they all picked. Every time a marked one was picked, a yell went out.

"Manuel, would you tell Bill that we are comin' tomorrow? When you go to the ranch, tell Red Bird and Foster."

The ten men took off to town. We were up and headin' into town before sunup.

13

As we took the wagon up Main Street, I noticed several new buildings. They were in different stages of development. One was made of brick and about half finished, and it was three stories high. One of the new buildings had a sign. It said Durango Saddle Shop. Underneath it said ANY TYPE OF LEATHER WORK. Pulling in front of our office, I noticed people were coming out in the street and were greeting us.

"Boys, you can get. The cattle drive is officially over. Have a drink on me, and head to the ranch and rest. We're home."

Some took off their hats and hit the horse on the rump and yelled out loud. The rest headed down the road that led to the ranch. I could see it was a well-used road by now. We were off our horses. I turned around, and there was Bill standing in front of me. He grabbed my hand and shook it hard with a big smile on his face. He had changed a little. He seemed manlier. I was smiling as he patted me on the back.

"Good to have all of you back. It seems so long."

"It's good to see you, Bill, and it's great to get back, and it was too long. How's Red Bird and the children?"

"And Molly," Pa broke in.

"Everyone's fine. Foster should be bringing them in. The children are in school."

"Bill, we need to unload the wagon here or at the bank. Some needs to go to the assayer office. It's gold and silver bars, and some raw ore also. I thought if we left it here, you could get it to where it needs to be and get the final tally."

"Sure, bring it in. It's in the chuck wagon."

"Yes, that was Jose's idea. He built a hideaway underneath the food stuff and pots and pans."

Pa, Jose, Josh, and I started unloading everything. Then Pa and I went inside and took off our money belts and laid them on Bill's desk.

Pa said, "Bill, here's my tabs on the amount and a breakdown of horses and cattle. We sold everything, would have sold the wagon, but we needed something to carry the gold and silver in." He laughed.

It took a while to bring it all in. It was more than I had realized.

"Bill, here's the breakdown on what each man receives in pay and bonus and reward money. Have it put in each man's account."

"Reward money? What happened out there?"

"Jose, tell him what happened, then go to the ranch and go see Juanita. Pa, Josh, I see our women comin'. Let's go, it's been a long ride."

By the time I was out the office door, Red Bird had jumped out of the wagon while it was still moving. She was in my arms, kissing and hugging me until I thought I would break.

"I'm so happy you are home. I have been worried about you for so long."

"I'm here, and here I'll stay. I love you so very much, honey."

"And I love you, Buck Taylor. I've been so lonely without you. But you do need a bath."

"I know. Now I can bathe every night with you beside me."

"That may not be proper to take a bath together."

"What! What has Jenny been teaching you?"

"I am just funning with you. I can hardly wait. It will be a dream come true. My lonely nights will be gone. Our spot down by the river has been waiting for us."

"How is Carolyn? She looks good and steady. And her mother?"

"She is all right on the outside, but on the inside, it still hurts. Her mother should be better, but Carolyn does too much for her."

"Look at Pa and mother, so close without sayin' much."

"I can see where you get your deep love for me."

By now, Foster had gotten down off the wagon and came over. He shook my hand, and I grabbed him and hugged him.

"Buck, what will people think?"

"I don't care. I missed you, you old buzzard. There were a few times when we could have used you. With the mountains, snow, and the Indians and the outlaws."

"Tell me'se later. I'se late gettin' the store open."

"What! Foster?"

He walked away, and I watched as he went in the saddle shop.

"What's that all about?"

"He got bored and took some of his money and built a new building and opened a shop. His biggest customer is Silver Buck Ranch. He told me that this had been his dream since he was young. Let him have his dream. I know the men can repair their own saddles and ropes. Bill said we could afford it. He won't be around forever, and we both love him, and he loves that shop."

"It's all right with me. I always knew you were smart. We have a lot of work for him now that we're back. Some of the saddles are so bad they barely made it. Now, Jose, take the chuck wagon home and go see your sister. Everyone, get in the wagon we're headin' home. Bill, I'll see you tomorrow."

I tied Blacky and Pa's horse to the back of the wagon and headed for the ranch, with Josh riding beside the wagon where Carolyn sat. Red Bird sat beside me with her arms around my waist and her head on my shoulder.

"When will the children be home?"

They go to Foster's shop, and when he closes up, he brings them home. We have the wagon, so we better go get them today. Give you more time to see the changes in the town and see Jenny."

"You two have become good friends?"

"Oh yes, she has taught me so much that I didn't know. I see now that Dancing Bear is so smart to be friends with the white men."

"It will be so good to sleep in our bed."

"Is that all?"

"You know better."

We went through the gate, and I could see the house over the next rise. We rode up to the barn. Red Bird untied Blacky and Pa's horse, and I got them both unsaddled. Red Bird just stood there watching me.

"Jose, I'll unhitch the team and let them loose in the pasture with Blacky. You go see how your sister is."

"Si, senor, I might get her to let me take a bath in her bathtub."

"I understand. That's where I'm headin' too, is to our tub. I'll help you unload the wagon tomorrow. Look, Red Bird."

We looked, and there were Josh and Carolyn walking up to the house as I finished up unhitching the teams from the wagons. As we walked up to the porch, we could hear Carolyn.

"Ma, you remember Josh, don't you? He's come back with Buck from the cattle drive."

"I think I do. He called on you when your father was alive."

"Yes, oh yes, Mama."

"Buck, that is the first time she has admitted that her husband is dead. This is a good sign. She will get well faster now. Wait and see."

We walked in, and Carolyn said, "Mother, this is Buck."

"Hello, Lizzie. It seems like I've know you a long time."

"You're the one my husband used to talk about. He wanted our ranch to be as nice as yours one day. I'm sorry he didn't get to see it."

"Maybe you'll get to see it one day. Bill Gills, my lawyer, will make sure that no one takes your ranch away from you."

"Thank you. I heard that a man was trying to buy it."

"I'll see about that. Now I'm goin' up and take a bath."

Josh said, "I'm sorry I just came in your house like this, Silver."

"Josh, after what we've been through, you're always welcome. You're like family."

"Thanks, Silver. I better get to the bunkhouse and get a bath. Carolyn, maybe we can sit on the front porch and talk tonight."

"Yes, Carolyn. Josh, please, come to supper." "Yes, ma'am, I surely would like that."

Josh left, and Red Bird and I went to the kitchen.

"Manuel!"

"Si, senor. Why, Senor Silver, so glad you're back. It's been a long while. How Jose work out?'

"He was great. He's up at Foster's house talkin' to Juanita. Before supper, you might go talk to him. He'll be takin' over your duties at the bunkhouse tomorrow. He can tell you what all went on. Now come on, Red Bird, I've got to take that bath, and you can wash my back."

When we climbed the staircase, I realized how much I missed this house. Red Bird ran my bath as I undressed. I went and jumped in the tub. I looked up, and Red Bird was standing there naked. She got in the tub with me.

"You didn't think you take a bath without me."

"No, dear."

We washed each other's bodies and dried each other off and got in our nice, soft big bed and made love for the first time in three and a half months. It was like heaven.

The afternoon went by fast. I told Mom what happened to Pa and what the doc said, and she said, "He won't be cold at night anymore long as I'm alive. This was his last drive."

"Yes, he admitted that to me out on the trail."

Red Bird and I went to town early. I wanted to talk to Bill. We went to the mining office, or Bill's office; both were in the same building.

"Bill, I couldn't wait till tomorrow."

"I don't have the final numbers yet. The numbers from the ore haven't come in."

"That's all right, I came in 'cause Lizzie told me that someone tried to buy her place. You know, I want to help them restart their ranch. It looks like Josh may help them."

"I know, Buck. The man has been trying to buy up land around here. He even tried to buy yours and the mine. I just let Carolyn know. I told Red Bird. She said no. That was it."

I looked at Red Bird, and she said, "Buck, we were a little busy getting to know each other again. I forgot."

"He tried to buy Foster's share. He said no. I sent a letter to Tim and Jim to let them know about it. I told them if they ever wanted to sell their shares, you would buy them. Your first day back, I knew you had some catching up to do. I didn't want to put a damper on your homecoming. I was going to explain everything tomorrow."

"I'm sorry I got so upset with you."

"I know. We're old friends, and I remember what you said a long time ago. If I got like Walters, you'd come looking for me." I laughed.

"You told Bill that? He told me about Walters."

"Hon, it was a joke."

Bill said, "Buck, I've seen how fast you are with that gun. I would never take a wrong turn." He laughed.

"I feel a little better now. You just don't know what we went through on that trail. We'll talk tomorrow. We have to pick up the children and Foster. See you tomorrow."

"I'll have the details and the final tabs."

We went to the school and waited for Song Bird and BJ. I said, "How have Jenny and Bill been?"

"She talks to me when she gives me a lesson. They go out to dinner and are friendly, but she doesn't understand why he doesn't ask her to marry him. He only kissed her once in all these months."

"You mind if I go in and talk to her? I'll get the children, and you take them and wait for me at Foster's. I won't be long."

Then here they came. Song Bird jumped in my arms. BJ shook my hand.

"Hello, Pa, I'm glad you're back."

"I am too, Song Bird, and you're gettin' so big I won't be able to pick you up much longer and look at you, son, you've grown four inches. I think you're taller than your mother. Do you like school now?"

"I am taller than Ma. And I like school lots. Ms. Trumble makes it fun to learn."

"Your ma's in the wagon. BJ, you drive your ma and sister over to Foster's and wait for me. I won't be long. I need to talk to Ms. Trumble."

I walked in to the school. All the children had gone. Jenny turned around.

"Hello, Buck, I'm glad you're back. Red Bird has missed you so much."

"I want to talk to you. Red Bird has told me about your problem with Bill. She said you love him. Now he told me before I left that you were so beautiful that you couldn't like him."

"Buck, I feel like I know you so well from what Red Bird has told me about you that I can talk to you openly. I think he is so handsome and smart, but I'm getting mad."

"I want to light a fire under him. I want your permission to tell him how you feel. I'll say Red Bird told me. I won't be lying 'cause she did. He won't know I talked to you."

"All right, Buck. I feel I can trust you. If you think it will help. There is a new man in town. He's been coming around, but I don't like him much."

"I've heard some things he is trying to do. I'll find out tomorrow from Bill. I don't mean to tell you what to do, but I would stay away from him. Give me a chance to get Bill movin' in the right direction."

"I will, Buck. Good to have you back."

I left and went to Foster's.

I walked in to Foster's shop. I looked around at saddles and bridles. He had all the tools for repairs behind the counter.

"Foster, I've known you for twelve years, and you never told me this is what you wanted to do."

"I'se forgot. When I'se was young, I'se came out here wantin' to do this. Then I'se didn't have any money. People were findin' a metal around here, so I'se went lookin'. After a while, it just got lost in my'se mind somewhere."

"Do you like it?"

"Sure do, and I'se makin' a little money at it."

"I was tellin' Red Bird that our saddles and bridles are in bad shape from the cattle drive. I'm goin' to have a couple of men go through our things and brin' them in town if you're up to it. Give the cost to Bill."

"I'se sure up to it. Thanks, Silver, for helpin' an old man."

"Nonsense. If you can do it, that will give my men more time for other things. So we're helpin' each other. Now y'all ready to go home?"

"Sure am. In the mornin', I'se can go through you'se tack room. Save you'se men some more time."

"Sounds good. Come on, y'all, let's get home. That sounds so good. Home."

After supper, Red Bird and I were sitting on the front porch. It had turned warmer when Josh and Carolyn came out and sat in the swing down on the other end of the porch,

"Listen, Red Bird, to what they're sayin'."

"Buck Taylor, you shouldn't be listening."

"Shh, listen."

"I love you, Carolyn. I want to marry you and help you and your mother get your ranch going again. On the drive, Silver and me were talking, and the prices he was getting for his horses were from $600 to a $1,000 apiece. He said he would help us get started by building a nice house for you and your mother, and a barn, and help us find some wild horses."

"That's nice. Silver is a nice and kind man."

"We could pay him out of our first sale of horses. I could work here too."

"Josh, this is your first day back. I know. I have the feeling down deep inside, but we need to get used to each other again. I want you to be sure after what I went through, and Doc says I may not be able to have any babies."

"That doesn't matter."

"I love you too, but it does matter. I don't want you to be sorry five years down the trail. Let's take our time and make sure."

"All right, but maybe you would let Silver build a house for you and your mother and start the ranch back."

"Maybe, but let me think on that."

"All right."

"Buck, that's one smart girl."

"Sounds that way to me. Why don't we leave them alone and go put the children in bed and have our own party?"

What all didn't happen this morning, it happened tonight. Now I remembered what I missed on the cattle drive. We were laughing there in bed, seeing if I had any more unanswered questions.

"You want to go to town with me in the mornin'?"

"You talk man talk all day. Jenney will be out for my lesson."

"I'll be up early. Foster might need some help loadin' the wagon. I just have one more question."

I turned out the light and kissed her. Her body responded to my kiss. The question was answered.

In the morning, I went to the barn. There was Foster, throwing things in the wagon.

"Need some help, Foster?"

"I'se sure could use some. Your men sure let their things get in bad shape."

"We were on the trail. I didn't want to lose any time." I was saddling Blacky.

"Buck, look at Blacky's saddle. You'se had this since I'se know you'se. A rich man like you'se."

"All right, Foster, I'll come in today and get a new saddle."

"That's the way I'se like to hears you'se talk. Here come the children. Let's get to town."

I tied Blacky to the back and helped Song Bird in the wagon, and BJ jumped in the back, and we were off to town. We let the children off at school. I waved to Jenny and tipped my hat.

At Foster's shop, I helped unload the tack. "What made you think of this shop?"

"After you'se left, Juanita and me finished fixin' up the house. We'se were sittin' there. She was sewing, and I'se thought about this. I'se told her, and she said I'se should try it and see if I'se liked it. Now you'se tell me'se about the outlaws and Indians."

I told him the whole story while I picked out a new saddle—black, of course."

"Sounds like you'se had a time of it."

"I'm just glad to be back home in one piece."

"I'se get to workin' on your new saddle and the other leatherworks."

"I don't get the saddle now?"

"No, Buck, these are just samples. I'se make a custom-made saddle just for you'se."

"All right. I just didn't know you had this in you."

"Ask Bill. I'se made one for him and a seat for his buggy."

"I will. I need to get over there to talk to him. He does my books for the cattle drive."

"He does my'se books for my'se shop here."

I walked out of there in real amazement. I just didn't know he had that in him. I went in my and Bill's office. I shook his hand.

"Glad to see you, Buck. I have the final figures on the drive."

"Good, but before we start on that, I want to ask you about Foster. I mean, how's he doin'? I just am surprised. He said he made a saddle and seat for your buggy."

"He did, and they're great. The saddle fits my horse great, and Jenny loves the seat in the buggy. It's so soft. He's making a little money. He's slowly making back what he put in the business. He had the building built, a real businessman. I saw the wagon unloaded. That should bring in a good amount."

"The work needed doin' from the cattle drive, and he reminded me that I'd had that saddle since he's known me. So I had him make me one. He's one of my best friends, and I just don't want to see him lose all his money."

"He owns the building, and this town is growing, thanks to you. I see his business growing. What he needs is a helper to learn his trade. He won't be around forever. He needs someone to leave it to. I thought of BJ or some young man around town."

"I'll watch BJ and see if he has any interest around Foster's shop. If he does, I can see if Foster would like to train him if BJ wants to. Now speakin' of the town growin', I saw that big brick buildin' when we came into town yesterday."

"That's the new bank. The young man that I trained to take my place talked Mr. Windslow into it. I agreed that was a small town bank. This new bank will take this town into the next century. It will have three tellers. The money you bring into this town has caused this growth."

"I just work hard at bringin' what's good to my family and friends."

"That's in the future. I have the final tabs on the cattle drive. Tell Ross that he keeps a fine set of books down to the last penny. The ore brought in more than you had down. You made a total of $252,552. That's a quarter of a million dollars. You still have more cattle than you started with. You brought in enough, as we paid for the ranch and the house and your dad's and Foster's houses and outbuildings, and all the work around the ranch, including the fencing, the ponds, and canals. It also paid for supplies, and the men's pay for the past ten years. All that was paid by the mining operations. Which is still coming in. If you paid, had to pay all that out of the drive's money, you would have $25,000 left. I put it in the ranch account. I need to know if you want to leave it there or transfer it to the mining account."

"Does it matter one way or another?"

"No, not really. You own both. You pay the partners their share when every shipment comes in. I thought I'd let you decide. It just keeps the books balanced. In other words, you would be paying the mining company back for all the ranch company took out. The mining company has plenty of money."

I guess leave it for now. You know where all the money goes?"

"Yes, I do. There's no way the ranch will deplete the mine's income as long as it keeps producing."

"There's another thing I want to talk to you about as a friend."

"Yes."

"You and Jenny, I think you two belong together. I know it's not money. You're well off from the mine. So what is it? She goes out with you when asked. Right?"

"Yes. I don't know. I love her. I know that. How could she feel the same?"

"Let me help you. Jenny talks to Red Bird when she gives her lessons. Jenny says she loves you and can't wait for you to ask her to marry you. She said you only kissed her once. She said that new man has been askin' her out. But she don't like him. She loves you. Don't tell her I told you. I'll have both of them mad at me. She also said you were so smart and handsome. I don't know. I don't see it." I laughed out loud.

"Oh, Buck, she really said that?"

"Yes, I tell you, better get on track, if you really love her. Your life will be complete. Now remember, don't say I told you."

"I won't. Will you come with me to the general store?"

"For what?"

"To pick out a ring. We're going out to dinner tonight, I'll ask her, and will you be my best man?"

"Let's go. I'll be honored. You two pick out a date. I'm sure everyone in town will be there. Before we go, I have to ask about the new man in town."

"His name is Larry Young. He seems nice."

"Like Dan Walters."

"I know. He's been buying up small ranches out east of town. I think he's trying to put together a bigger ranch with a lot of little ones. Look over here on the map. I pinned the ranches he's bought."

"What's these two down the middle? It splits it in two."

"That belongs to Lizzie and Carolyn. I've been keeping an eye on him. You might talk to John about him. This is all I know."

"How big is Lizzie and Carolyn's part?"

"When her husband bought, he bought two pieces. They're 650 acres in all. They are right down the middle."

"I'm goin' to talk to Lizzie and Carolyn tonight. If they say yes, I'll get Tim or Jim started building a house for them. Take it out of the minin' account. Josh wants to marry her, but she's not ready yet. Now let's go buy a ring."

We went to the general store.

Ed said, "Good to see you, Silver. It's good to have you back, and it's good to have your old partner as one of us businessmen."

"He seems to enjoy what he's doin' now. The way the town's growin', you're goin' to have to build a bigger store."

"It's looking that way. More people, more things they need. I've been thinking about it, but I have been putting it off long as I can. Try to save up money to pay cash, and I am nearly there. "Now, what can I do for you?"

"It's him."

"What is it, Bill?"

"Ed, you have to promise. I wouldn't want it getting around until after tonight."

"What, Bill? I promise."

"I want to see your engagement rings."

"Finally. Here they are."

"If she says yes and it doesn't fit ..."

"Sure, bring her in, and we'll find one that fits. Don't be so nervous, Bill. We all went through this. Right, Silver?"

"You said it, Ed."

"Here's one. What you think, Buck?"

"That looks good to me."

"It's my most expensive. Judging from her fingers, I would say this size. This should do the trick."

"How you know who it's for? That's it, then. I'll take it. You do have a box for it?"

"Yes, here's the box, and I'm not blind. I've seen the way Jenny looks at you and you at her. You were the only one that was blind. Now, that will be $60."

"See you later, Ed."

"Good luck."

We walked out. I started to the sheriff's office.

"Wait, Buck, will you and Red Bird be there? We'll eat at the hotel. It's more fancy for this night."

"Don't you want to be alone?"

"I might not do it if I'm alone."

"All right, we'll be there at eight o'clock. And don't be so nervous."

"Yes, thank you."

I was laughing as I walked in to the sheriff's office.

"Been hopin' I'd see you. It's been all over the wires about you gettin' the Delta Gang. Not to mention Geronimo. That was some doin'."

"Yeah, we were lucky. Geronimo just wasn't used to 3,000 head of cattle runnin' after him. The cattle and horses got about 170 of his braves."

"So that's how you did it."

"That and the good Lord."

"Amen to that."

"I came in to see if you know anything about this new feller Larry Young. He tried to buy my ranch and mine while I was gone. I just like to know something about whom I'm dealing with. We don't want another Walters and you know how things tend to repeat itself.

"No, we don't. When he started buyin' up ranches over east, I did some checkin'. He's not wanted. But we know that doesn't mean much. Other than that, I don't know. He has some bad-lookin' men workin' for him. They look like gun hands."

"Is there any people still in town that he bought land from? Maybe he had his men persuade them to sell."

"There is one family. I saw their wagon around back of the hotel. I talked to them, and they didn't act like anything was wrong. Maybe it was the badge. I don't know."

"I'll talk to them tomorrow. Tonight we have a special dinner to attend at the hotel. I need to get home and tell Red Bird."

"What's the special dinner about?"

"It's a secret, but if you won't tell anyone ..."

"I keep secrets all the time."

"All right. Bill Gills is goin' to ask Ms. Trumble to marry him."

"It's about time. I've seen them together. They make a good couple. We need more people like them, and you and Red Bird, and your parents come to this town."

"I better get now. I have to tell the wife. I'll see you later, John. Remember, secret."

I got Blacky and headed for the ranch. I turned Blacky and Lagger loose in the pasture. I looked in the barn and saw there were no wagons.

Foster took it to his shop every day with the children. I knew I need to order a nice buggy for special occasions like this. I decided I would do it tomorrow, and then I went inside the house.

"Hello, Manuel. You seen Red Bird?"

"Si, upstairs with Carolyn and Lizzie."

"We need to talk one day. Right now, I have some important news for the women. You know women?"

"Si, senor."

I ran up the stairs and looked in our room and the children's rooms. No Red Bird.

"Red Bird, where are you?"

"In here, Buck. What is it?"

"I have some news from town Red Bird and I'm glad you two are doin' good, so I need to talk to you about the new man in town, his name is Larry Young. Your husband was very smart. He bought two sections down the middle of all the other land. It has a big lake in the middle that's fed by a stream that goes through your land. This man needs your land. He's bought everyone's around yours. I don't know for sure yet, but I think he has some gun hands that are forcin' people to sell. You are here, so he can't get to you. There's too many witnesses here. I don't know if you want to stay or not. If you don't, I want to buy your land to force his hand. If you want to stay, and I hope you do, I want to help you. I'll build a nice house, and Josh and me talked about a horse ranch. Up north, we were gettin' $800 to $1,500 apiece. Down here, you can buy a good horse for $300 to $400. Carolyn, I know you need your time about marryin' your young Josh. On the drive, you are about all he talked about. He really loves you. But right now, my men and me could get wild horses to start a ranch. It's changin' fast. Later, you might not be able to get free horses. I know Josh could be your foreman and live on the ranch in the room I would have built next to the barn. I would help you take your stock to market. So you won't think I'm givin' you all this, you can pay me out of your sale of your stock. We had 100 horses and made $42,000. There is good money to be made. I know this is a lot to think about, but this Larry

Young won't wait forever. He might try to romance you, Carolyn, with money. So don't be fooled. Josh is a good, upstandin' man. He could make something of your place. Let me know, and I'll get Tim or Jim started on your house and barn soon. They'll get rid of your entire burned house. You'll never know it was there. If you want it that way."

"Thanks, Buck. You really think he will forget and not hold what I went through against me in the future?"

"I do. Go ask my pa. He rode with Josh the whole drive. He knows what kind of man he is. He's a man of his word, and I know I would ride trail with him anytime."

"Mother, I know it would be painful to go back. But I have a feeling Pa would want us to. Buck is giving us a big start. I know you're a strong woman, or you wouldn't have come out here with Pa, so let's do it. And I'm going to marry Josh if he still wants me. No room in the barn for my man. He'll live in the big house with us."

"Red Bird, your people must be very special. The way you and Buck's mother have taken care of us this many months, and you, Buck, for letting us stay in your beautiful home. I do mean a home, with all the love inside. The way you want to help us, I don't understand, except you're a good man. We need to be on our own. So I say let's do it."

"All right, I'll send a letter to Jim at the mine. It's getting colder, so I don't know how much they can get done before spring. Depends on the snowfall. Now, Red Bird, we have been invited to dinner at the hotel by Bill, and Jenny will be there. I know that you have a lesson after school. You can tell her we are goin' to join them for dinner that Bill invited us to eat with them. Don't tell her that Bill bought her a ring. I was with him. Let it be a surprise. I'm goin' to be his best man."

"You talked him into it? I'm so happy for her. I will not tell. Will be hard. I get ready for my lesson."

Foster brought the children home, and I went to the barn and talked to Foster and kept the children from being underfoot. When Red Bird took her lesson, Jenny rode up in her buggy and went inside.

"BJ, I haven't been around. How are you doin' in school?"

"I like it more than I thought I would. I like arithmetic and history. I'm doing well in those. English and reading, I'm not doing great, but I'm doing all right."

"He's in love with Wanda, a new girl in school," his sister said.

"Song Bird, I'll get you."

"All right, you two, stop it now."

"How are you doin', Song Bird?"

"I'm doing great. Ms. Trumble says I'm one of her best pupils."

"I see Ms. Trumble is leavin', so get to the house and change your school clothes."

"Aha, Pa."

"Go now. We'll go riding when you're out of school Friday."

"Foster, you look like a well-to-do man. You cut your hair and trimmed your beard. It makes you look distinguished."

"That's Juanita's idea. You'se know she's got me'se takin' a bath three or four times a week. She says I'se shouldn't smell, bein' a businessman like I'se am."

"She's right."

"That's not the bad part. She comes in to make sure I'se clean. Me'se a grown man, treats me'se like a child. Makes me change clothes too."

"Sounds like a wife."

"I'se better get home to eat, or she'll get mad."

I looked in the chuck wagon. I forgot I was going to help Jose unload this mess. I started unloading and taking the supplies into the kitchen.

"Senor, let me help you. I haven't had time. It's like out on the trail. I never have time. But I have a better stove and oven here."

We got all the foodstuff put away, and the pots and pans. I said, "How about the rifles and ammunition?"

"See here? I built a place for them since we been back."

We unloaded the rifles and got them stored away.

"Jose, you amaze me at what you do."

"I am glad I please you."

"You do. Now I got to get to the house."

Red Bird was waiting inside.

"Where you been, Buck? We have to get ready. I already took a bath. Now you get in there."

"You come in with me."

"Buck, we don't have time for that now. Tonight is important to Jenny. You know, except for you and your parents, she has become my best friend. Like you and Foster."

"All right, you won. I'm goin' to take a bath alone."

"Poor baby, I'll make it up to you later."

I got dressed, and then out came my most-beautiful wife, all decked out in some new clothes.

"You like my new clothes? Jenny helped me pick them out while you were gone. They are for dress-up times like this. They too tight, but for friend I wear tonight."

"You have one of those things underneath."

"No, she could not make me go that far."

"That I'm glad about. Now we better get goin'."

"Ma, you're so beautiful. And, Pa, you're so handsome."

Red Bird said, "Thank you, children. You mind Manuel and eat all your supper."

"We will, Ma."

I got the wagon hitched up, and we were on our way to town. Maybe by Bill and Jenny's wedding, we would have our new buggy. I would surprise Red Bird.

14

We pulled up to the hotel. As we entered the dining room, all eyes turned our way. Bill and Jenny were already seated. We walked to their table. Bill got up, and I seated Red Bird.

Jenny said, "How beautiful you look tonight. And, Silver, you're so dressed up. What's the occasion?"

"I have to wear these new clothes somewhere. Jenny, you're so radiant tonight."

"Buck, how you like all the big words Red Bird has learned? She learns well."

"I knew she would. She's beautiful and smart. I always knew that. She's goin' to know more than me. Bill, what's wrong? You haven't said two words tonight," I said.

"I'm not all here. I told Jenny how beautiful she was when I picked her up. She'll always be beautiful to me."

"That's kind of you to say, Bill," Jenny said.

We ordered supper and drinks. While we were waiting, a man came over to the table.

"Hello, Bill. Hello, Jenny. How are you tonight?"

"You can call me Ms. Trumble, I thank you."

"Now, Jenny, that's no way to be."

"You heard the lady, Mr. Young."

"Bill, I told you to call me Larry."

I said, "Mr. Young, I think you better leave before you get in more trouble."

"And who may you be?"

"I'm someone you don't want to mess with."

"Buck, let me handle this."

"So you're Buck Taylor?"

Bill said, "We are trying to have a nice, peaceful dinner with our ladies. If you would leave now."

"I'm going to leave, but I'll see you later," Young said, looking at me.

"You can count on it."

We ate with no further interruptions.

"I'm sorry for that man. It's my fault. He just keeps on coming around. No matter what I say."

Bill said, "Jenny, I know one way to stop it."

"How, Bill?"

"I love you very much. I hope you love me. I asked Red Bird and Buck here because I think they're our best friends."

"They are, I agree."

He took the box out of his pocket and opened it and was on one knee.

"Jenny, will you do me the honor of becoming my wife?"

A tear of joy came in her eye as she said, "Bill, I do love you. I will become your wife."

He placed the ring on her finger and kissed her in public. The whole place was clapping, except Young. He left.

"Oh, Bill, I'm so happy. I'm just mad that that man nearly spoiled it."

"Don't be. I think that's what dragged the words out of me."

We all laughed, and Jenny kissed him. "I like that."

"Get used to it. You're going to get plenty after we get married."

I said, "Bill, you watch that man. I don't know what he'll do now."

"You too, Buck. I saw the look in his eyes. He hates you 'cause he can't buy what you have."

"And you just asked the woman he wants to marry you."

Red Bird said, "We're here to enjoy the night."

"All right, when are you two gettin' married?"

"Bill, I want to get married soon as possible. I still want to teach."

"I wouldn't stop you from doing that. I know how much you love it. Is three weeks to soon? On a Saturday."

"That sounds good to me. We have to see if Reverend Goodbody can marry us on ... today is October fifth, Saturday would be October eighth—that would be October twenty-ninth. How's that sound?"

"Red Bird, you have become my best friend since I came here. Would you be my maid of honor?"

"I will, Jenny. But you have to tell me what that is."

"Don't worry, it's just my best friend. I'll tell you more later. We better get home now. I have school in the morning. I'm so excited I probably won't sleep a wink."

As the women walked out, I pulled Bill to the side. "I think you should learn to shoot."

"Buck, you know I wasn't always a lawyer or a bank teller. I know how to shoot. I'm just not a fast draw."

"I'm worried about that Young. You better get a gun to wear under your coat, to protect you and Jenny."

"I have a shoulder holster and a .45. I'll start practicing."

"That makes me feel better."

We walked out and left for home. I let Red Bird off in front of the house and then took the wagon to the barn. I lit a lantern and got the team unhitched and put them in the stalls. As I blew out the lantern, I heard a shot ring out. I reached for my gun, but it was in the house. The lanterns began to come on in the bunkhouse. About then, there was another shot in the barn, and I was on the ground. Men were coming out of the bunkhouse with their pistols and rifles.

I yelled, "Be careful, boys. I don't know where it came from."

"That you, Silver?"

"Yeah, it's me. Toss me a gun."

I crawled forward until I was out of the barn. The men were all round me. They had lanterns with them.

"Spread out and look around. Be careful."

"Over here, two shell casings."

"They must be gone. Y'all head back to bed. We'll look around better tomorrow for more. Thanks, boys."

"You tell us, and we'll saddle up and go after them."

"Thanks. Go back to bed. I'll be all right, Josh."

"Yes, sir. You talk to Carolyn tomorrow after work. I think she has a surprise for you."

"What is it?"

"You talk to her. Good night."

I walked up to the house, and Red Bird and Manuel were on the side porch facing the barn. Manuel had a shotgun with him.

"What was it, Buck?" she asked.

"Nothin', hon. Let's go to bed."

"Buck, I know it was something. Did someone shoot at you?"

"All right, they did."

Manuel spoke up. "Senor, just before you came up, a man was here. He wanted to talk to Carolyn or Lizzie. I told him they were asleep. He said to wake them up, it was important. It was about their ranch. I had my shotgun pointing right at him. I said 'Leave, or my shotgun might go off.' He left mad. I kept my shotgun on him until I could not see him. I do not know where he went."

"What did he look like?"

"He was tall and had blond hair and a grin on his face. Even when he was mad."

Red Bird said, "That's the man at the hotel. You better tell the sheriff and warn Bill tomorrow, first thing."

"I will tomorrow. Let's all go to bed. Thank you, Manuel. You did the right thing. Good night."

The next morning, we ate breakfast and went out. Red Bird came out with us.

"Foster, you have your shotgun with you?"

"Right here. Why?"

"I got shot at last night when we came back from town."

"Thought I'se heard something."

Red Bird said, "Buck, I know it's the man from last night."

"We have to prove it to the sheriff that it was him."

"It is hard for me to understand white man's law."

"Sometimes it is for me too. Keep an eye open, Foster."

"I'se will. The children will be all right. I'se with you'se, Red Bird. Sometimes I'se don't understand the law."

Foster left for town, and Red Bird and I walked over to where the men were looking.

"All we found are these horse tracks and boot prints."

I looked close at both sets of prints. Trying to put them in my mind. There was a large cut in the left heel of the boot.

Pa came over. "Find anything? I heard about it when I came down this mornin'."

Buck said, "Just this. See that large cut in the heel of the boot? Red Bird, I'm goin' to town and talk to Bill first. Be on the lookout. Tell Manuel to keep that shotgun handy."

"I will. You be careful."

"I got my guns on today."

I said bye to Pa, who was already rounding up the men to go to work. Then I kissed Red Bird and was off to town on Blacky.

I rode up to the office and heard shooting. I jumped off Blacky and ran inside. Bill wasn't there. I heard more gunfire. I noticed the back door was open. I ran to the door, and there was Bill, shooting at a target nailed to the lean-to out back. I had my gun drawn since I entered the office. I put it up.

"Bill!"

"Buck, I thought I'd practice some."

"Let me see that rig you have."

He opened his coat, and there was a shoulder holster and a .45. I drew and fired five shots into the target.

"I'll never be that fast."

"Not with that rig. Don't tell anyone how fast I am. I want the new men in town to just guess how fast I am. Gives me an advantage. But you keep on, and you'll get faster."

The sheriff came out of the back door of the office with his gun drawn. He saw us and put his gun away.

"What you two doin'?"

I smiled. "Just gettin' some practice."

"I suggest you do that on your ranch. You too, Bill."

"John, my ranch is gettin' downright dangerous."

"What you say?"

"Red Bird and me left Bill and Jenny after their engagement dinner."

"Well, I'll be. Congratulations, Bill. She'll make a fine wife."

"Now, John, can I finish?"

"Sure, go ahead."

"Anyway, I dropped Red Bird off in front of the house and went to the barn to put up the wagon and team. Someone shot two times at me. Woke up everyone. We found these shells, but didn't see anyone. Manuel said Young had just left the ranch, mad. Manuel had a shotgun on him. He demanded to see Carolyn and Lizzie about their ranch."

Bill said, raising his coat, "That's why I'm wearing this and practicing. We had a little run-in with him at dinner last night. He left mad at Buck."

I wondered about Young.

"Come inside. Since Young tried to buy Buck's ranch and mine, I've been keeping track of land he has bought. See here? Lizzie's ranch is in the middle and has the only water nearby."

"She's not selling. Here's a letter I'm sendin' to Jim on the ore wagon for him or Tim to come to town and build a ranch house on her land. She and Carolyn okayed it yesterday. Carolyn is goin' to marry Josh, and they're goin' to start a horse ranch. Up north, horse flesh is worth a lot of money."

"I don't know what to say."

"I know you don't have any real proof. I think we went through this with Walters ten years ago. I'm goin' to see him today to tell him to stay away from my ranch and not to cross Lizzie's ranch and stay away from the lake and creek on her ranch. I'll post guards if I have to. The Indians took enough from those two women. If one of his men draws on me, they're dead."

"All right, Silver, I can see you're mad. I believe you. Just take it easy."

The sheriff left, and I handed the letter to Bill.

"Send this to the mine. I'm goin' to talk to the people at the hotel that he bought land from. Then to the general store. And I'm orderin' a buggy for Red Bird and me to use. Like for your weddin' or church. Then to see Young."

"I'm going with you, Buck."

"You can go see the people that are leavin', and to buy our buggy, I want it to be a surprise for Red Bird. I don't think it's a good idea for you to go to Young's with me. There might be gun play."

"I know, but Jenny is going to be my wife, and I need to let him know that I'm not afraid of him, or he will keep bothering her after we're married."

"All right, Bill, but follow my lead. Now let's go talk to those people."

As the hotel came into view, I could see a covered wagon on the side and the people were around the outside. We rode up.

"Are you the people that Mr. Young bought land from?"

"Yes, we are. Are you the police?"

"No, I'm just lookin' for information on how Mr. Young conducted his business with you."

"How does it matter to you?"

"I'm Buck Taylor, and this is Bill Gills. I was out of town on a cattle drive. When I returned this week, I learned Mr. Young had tried to buy my land, and I just want to make sure he is not treatin' people wrongly. I was shot at last night in my barn. I don't like people that take advantage of others."

"That's the way it started. A shot here, a shot there. Close by where you are without hitting you. Then they will come, the bad ones, run off your stock and poison your water tanks. Then he comes up and offers you way less than your land is worth. He has these two men with him that look mean with guns on their hips like yours."

"Mine is only to protect me and my family. Not to harm others. Why didn't you tell this to the sheriff?"

"This is not done where we come from. The police are for the rich only. His men said they would kill my wife and children if I went to the sheriff. So we move on to California. Maybe it will be better there. I told you this because I heard what a good man you are."

"I just wish I had got here sooner to help all the people that lost their land. This is not how people are around here."

"I know, but we have to be leaving now."

They rolled out of town down the road leading west.

"Bill, I'm too mad to go to see Young. I need to calm down. Let's go buy that buggy."

"Let's go. I don't feel too calm myself."

We walked in to the general store. Ed asked, "How'd it go last night, Bill? Did she turn you down?" He laughed.

"No, Ed, she didn't. We're getting married three weeks from Saturday, October twenty-ninth. You and your family are invited."

"We'll sure be there."

"I'm throwin' them a party at the ranch, and the whole town's invited. If it rains or snows, we'll have a barn dance or in the house."

"Now that sounds good. About time this town has a real big party."

"Buck, we haven't even talked about that."

"I know, what else makes sense for my good friend and partner and his wife? I am the best man. We'll let the women figure the party out. They're good at that. Now, Ed, we came in to buy a new buggy for my family. I'm tired of goin' in the wagon everywhere."

"Right. Here is the catalog. They make some in Denver now."

"Do they build them for six or more?"

"Let me see. There's only three. There is one for four, one for six, and here's one for eight. I hadn't even seen that one."

"What you think, Bill?"

"You have you and Red Bird and the children, that's four. Your mother and father, and don't forget Foster. He's like your family."

"Yes, he is. Ed, order me two, one for four and one for eight, so that way, we'll have one for the children and us and the other for the whole family. Do you know when they'd be in?"

"Let me see, it should say here somewhere. No one has ordered one except Bill. That's a while back, and it's a two-seater. Here, it says they have the two- and four-seaters on hand. Should be a week or ten days. The eight-seater should take two weeks. If everything goes right, should be here before the wedding. I'll order it, and it will be in tomorrow's mail. That's a total of $1,600."

"Maybe you can telegraph them and they can let you know sooner by telegraph, and I'll pay for the telegram. Give the bill to my business manager."

"I'll bring you the money first thing in the morning."

"I'll get that telegram off this afternoon. Tomorrow will be fine for the money. If we luck out, they might have an eight-seater ready."

"That would be great. Now I'm in a better mood. Let's go, Bill. We have some other business east of town."

We went to the east. I knew where Lizzie and Carolyn's land was, so I headed to it. I wanted to see for myself the lay of the land. It was about five months ago that I was out here and had to bury her husband and her son. I had not looked around much for we had other things to do. We found the burned-out homestead. The overgrown graves were there as a reminder of what happened here. I would have the bodies moved to a nicer place with nice headstones and a white picket fence, with room enough for the whole family in the future.

"This is their place. That is their family. You can see why I am so determined not to let anything happen to their land. They have already paid the price."

"Is this where they were killed?"

"We found her husband over there, tied to the corral gate, full of arrows. Her boy was over there in the burned-out house. Let's ride down that way. The lake should be to the north."

"There it is, Buck, over there. Let's follow this creek to the east. Look, Bill, over there, it's an underground spring. It comes up on their land.

No wonder her husband bought two sections of land. He knew the land and what water meant to this area. This will make a fine horse ranch."

"I can see that. No wonder Young wants it so bad."

Blacky and Bill's horse were drinking out of the creek.

"This creek and the lake are why Young hasn't poisoned this. It's too important to the whole area. I'm goin' to have Tim remove all the burned things from up there and put the house and barn down here somewhere. He knows about these kinds of things. Now let's get to Young's. When we get there, keep your hand inside your coat on your gun. You can draw faster, and no matter what he says, stay on your horse. They could plug us when gettin' off our horses. So stay on."

We rode on east. I was guessing, but Lizzie's land looked to be six hundred acres. I could tell because we were now on improved land. As we rode up, I said,

"Look to the right and left of the porch. There's a man at each end. While we're talkin' to him, keep an eye on the man on the right."

As we rode up to the yard, I looked toward the barn and around the whole area. These two seemed to be the only ones around. As we reached the porch, one of the men yelled out, "Boss, there's two fellows out here."

Young came out and at once put a grin on his face. "Well, I'll be. Buck, Bill. What you two doing out this far? Step down and come sit on the porch out of the cold wind."

"No, thanks. We were just out lookin' over Lizzie's ranch for her. Heard you were down to my ranch last night."

"Yes, I just wanted to talk to Lizzie about selling her land. She's living with you. I don't see what good it is to her all burned down like that."

"She had it bad. Her husband and son were killed by Apaches. She's just gettin' better after five months. She told me yesterday she wasn't goin' to sell it, and next summer, she'll be living on it. So you just stay away from her and her ranch."

"You're not being very friendly."

"Don't give me that. I talked to some people that told us what happened to them by your men. You better tell them to stay away from their guns, or you'll be the first one dead."

"Boys, stay away from your guns."

"I can beat him, boss."

"Maybe, maybe not. Now's not the time."

"Mr. Young, I just want to tell you to stay away from Ms. Trumble."

"That's up to her, not you."

"She's already told you several times to leave her alone."

I could see he was trying to hide that he was getting mad. Everything he wanted, we were telling him to stay away from.

I said, "You might be used to gettin' everything you want, but not in this town. Your trouble was you waited till I got back. Now you don't have a chance of doin' what you wanted. I will have men posted at Lizzie's ranch. The sheriff needs proof. I don't. Anything happens to her water or my men get hurt, I'll come lookin' for you, and I won't stop till I find you. Just ask the Delta Gang or Geronimo, if you can find any of their men alive to tell about it. So you better pack up and leave, or we can have a showdown right now."

"You have men to back you up. I have these two."

"My men are at the ranch. I'm right here with Bill, my partner. If anything happens to him or Jenny, you better run, and that won't be far or fast enough. I think you should pack up and leave."

"I have this ranch."

"I don't see any cattle or men except these two want-to-bes."

"Come on, boss, let's take them now."

"No, boys, you got a coward for a boss when he might get hurt. He don't mind you get hurt. Bill, let's back out. You don't want to give cowards your back."

I could see Young was fluming. We backed out of the yard and then turned and headed for Durango.

"I'm glad I'm on your side. I've never seen you that mad."

"I just get angry when men try to take something for nothin'. I want you and Jenny to be very careful. Carry that gun with you at all times, and buy Jenny a shotgun today and teach her to load and shoot it and keep it by her bed at night. I still don't trust him. He was mad, but he thought he might die. He does things at night 'cause he's a coward."

As soon as we reached town, we went to the general store. Bill said, "Ed, I need a shotgun with a short barrel, if possible. So it can be used in a small space."

"Like this, Bill? This is an eight-inch barrel and a .20 gauge. Some people were coming through and needed to trade this for food. He had it made for his wife when they headed west. Here are two boxes of shells. That comes with it. You may have to have someone make more. I've tried to get some and am having a hard time finding this size."

"This is all right, isn't it, Buck?"

"Less gauge means less kick. Let's take it over to the school. I want to see her protected at all times."

"Red Bird doesn't have a gun."

"Manuel is around the house with his shotgun, and there are thirty-five cowboys around the ranch. I worry about Jenny 'cause she's by herself. Except when you're with her."

"I think we should tell Foster about this. I wouldn't put it past Young to hurt your children or Foster coming to town or going home."

We went to Foster's shop and explained things to him.

"Goin' or comin' to town, don't trust anyone comin' up on you. I'll put a rifle under the canvas in back of the wagon for BJ. He's handy with a rifle in a tight fix, and Song Bird can get under the canvas."

"I'se don't think he'se be that stupid."

"I don't know, Foster. When Buck got done with him and then I let him know about Jenny, he was steaming."

"I'se keep an open eye and tell BJ to be on the lookout."

Bill said, "All right, Buck, let's get to the school."

We arrived at the school just as they were letting out. I told BJ and Song Bird to go home with Uncle Foster; he would explain to them. Bill and I walked in to the school with the shotgun and explained things to Jenny.

She said, "Bill, Buck, I've been shooting since I was five. My dad believed in a girl protecting herself. I like this. It's handy with this short barrel. Come out back, I'll show you."

"See that branch on that lower part of the tree? The one with two forks, and now watch the fork part."

She loaded shells and aimed and pulled the trigger. The fork disappeared.

"Buck, remind me not to make this woman mad at me after we get married."

We all had to laugh.

"I'll bring this to school. I'll keep it close but out of sight. I wouldn't want to scare the children."

"If you do have any trouble here, BJ is a fine shot, if you need some help. I'll see you two later. I better get to the ranch and warn everyone."

As I left town, I saw Foster and the children going down the trail to the ranch. I caught up, and I noticed the wagon was full of our tack.

"Foster, you're already done with all this?"

"Sure is. I'se don't mess around. All but you'se saddle, but that will take some time. I want it to be just right for Blacky and you'se."

I grabbed one bridle and looked it over and yanked on it. 'That's a fine piece of work. Now I'm lookin' forward to that saddle. BJ, you know a Mr. Young?"

"Yes, sir. He comes to see Ms. Trumble one time at school."

"If he comes again, or any strange man, you stand up with Ms. Trumble and send one of the girls to get the sheriff. Ms. Trumble will tell you what to do. Song Bird, you tell all girls to get in the back room. Let the boys handle it. All right?"

"Yes, Pa. What's the matter, Pa?"

"Nothin' right now. Just want you to know what to do in case of trouble. Don't worry."

We rode up to the barn. I helped Foster unload the wagon. Dad came over and looked at a saddle and some of the bridles.

"Damn, Foster, that's fine work. Buck was tellin' me about your saddle shop, but I had my doubts. But this is fine workmanship."

"Thanks, Ross. It does me'se good to hear that from a rancher like you'se."

"You know me. I wouldn't praise something that wasn't done right. I appreciate good work when it's done."

"What are you doin' in so early?"

"The weather is turnin' colder, and I remembered what the doc said. There's not much to do around here. I may have to let those ten men we hired for the drive go."

"Children, go on up to the house. I need to talk to Grandpa."

I started telling Pa about all the trouble the small ranchers and farmers had and what I planned for Lizzie's ranch.

"I know it's gettin' colder, and maybe snow anytime, but I'm puttin' nothin' past that man. That lake and creek is too important to that area to maybe be poisoned. Those ten men we can post at Lizzie's lake at her ranch and our tanks out on the range at night for sure. I hate to have to do this, but I think it should be done till this comes to a head."

"I'll let them choose to stay and do night patrol at night here or around the clock at Lizzie's ranch. They can be rotated all day at least two men at all times. I'll let them choose one-way or another. I'll be up at the house if you need me."

We finished unloading the tack, and I hurried to the house to talk to Red Bird and Manuel. Lizzie and Carolyn would have to be told also.

Josh came up to the house that night. He and Carolyn and Lizzie talked. They called Red Bird and me in. We sat down hand in hand, and they started talking.

"I said I would marry Josh. He knows about what the doc said about I may not be able to have children. He's all right with that. I do love him, and after we talked to Mother, she said, yes, it is all right with her. Right, Ma?"

"Yes, dear, he is young, but I do believe he is a good man. I can see it in his eyes he does love you."

"Silver, Ross told me before I came up here of the trouble you think Lizzie will have at her ranch until the house is built. I want to be one of the men that guards the water supply."

"Red Bird, you have done so much for my mother and me. Josh and me want to marry soon. Could we live here until the house is built? We'll pay you and Buck back one day for everything."

"Lizzie, I know that you are right. I see it in their eyes also. Buck, you always said we would fill this house."

We all laughed. Josh and Carolyn were sitting there holding on to each other.

"Thank you, Red Bird. And you, Buck, I don't know what to say. I never thought Mother and I would be happy again."

"With as much love as I see between you two, I don't care what the doc says. Lizzie, till the grandchildren come, you'll really be happy. I know that. Now, Bill and Jenny are getting' married in three weeks from this Saturday, October 29. I'll ask Bill and Jenny, but I think they'll say yes."

"What, honey?"

"We'll have a double weddin', and we're havin' a party at the ranch after the weddin'—a barn dance if the weather turns bad. Sorry, honey, I just thought about it in town. I told Bill."

"That's a lot of planning, Buck, for three weeks."

"I know it is."

"That is all right. I'm sure Manuel and Jose, and maybe Juanita. And you, Lizzie, if you feel up to it, will help with the cooking. What do you say?"

"We're speechless, but all right to both a wedding and a party, if it's all right with Bill and Jenny," Carolyn and Josh said.

Then I said, "We can invite the whole town. I'm sure the women will help. They came to our weddin' way up in the mountains. It was in Red Bird's father's village. We had a double weddin'. Tell them, Red Bird."

"My father, Dancing Bear, and the preacher from town married us."

Josh said, "I didn't know that."

"Yes, my father is good man. He knows we were in love."

The children were at the top of the stairs.

"We didn't know Grandpa married you."

We all let out a laugh. Manuel came running in. "What's wrong, senor?"

"Nothing, Manuel. Just be ready in three weeks. We're having a wedding party here. We'll get Jose and Juanita to help us. Carolyn, we'll have to go to town and get you a wedding dress. I'm sure Jenny will help us. She has her mother's."

"Ma, Ms. Trumble is getting married too."

"Yes, to Mr. Gills. She'll be Mrs. Gills as soon as they're married." Everyone went to bed happy. Except I didn't know what trouble Young would cause these two fine couples.

15

The next morning, everyone was down for breakfast. I got the wagon ready, and we left early. They wanted to talk to Jenny before school started. I stopped at the school.

"Buck, we're going to talk to Jenny. Then we're going to the general store."

"What's going on, Buck?"

"Josh and Carolyn are getting' married. They went to ask Jenny if it's all right to get married on the same day. Then we're goin' to have a big party at the ranch. Can I have a peek at my new saddle?"

"No, sir. Not till it's done."

"OK, Foster. I'll go see Bill."

I walked into the office. Bill looked up. He didn't look very happy.

"What's the matter? Gettin' nervous already?"

"No, not yet. Yesterday after you left, four men, hard-looking, came into town. John saw them, and they went in the saloon. They were in there ten minutes. They came out and headed east."

"You think they're goin' to Young's place?"

"I know they are. I followed them, not close. They didn't see me."

"Bill, I told you to be careful."

"I know, but I just had to know. I came and let John know. I passed Lizzie's place on the way back, and two of your men were just getting there. You know, I think Young is up to no good."

"Here I came with some happy news, and you hit me with this. I know you need to practice drawin' that gun from under your coat as fast as you can."

"I will. I set up a target behind my house, and I practiced until dark yesterday. I'm determined to be able to protect Jenny against anyone, like you have Red Bird. I'm sorry, Buck. What's the happy news?"

"Josh and Carolyn are getting' married, and Red Bird, Lizzie, and Carolyn are talkin' to Jenny right now to see if it's all right for them to get married with you two. A double weddin', and we'll have a big party at the ranch after. If it's too cold, we'll have a barn dance."

"That sounds great. You said Lizzie came in, she was so bad?"

"When I came back from the drive and talked to Carolyn about the ranch, I guess she heard us. The next day, she got up and ate with us. She's a little weak, but I can see her gettin' stronger already. Bill, also, if we have to go one on one with his men, take off your jacket. You'll be faster, and Young will be surprised. He was thinkin' you are just a pencil pusher. No offense."

"None taken. That might work in our favor, and that's how I've been practicing."

"Good. You check Jenny every day."

"I'm going to pick her up every morning and see her home in the afternoon. I may even bring her out to your ranch to give Red Bird her lesson. What you think about, Red Bird?"

"I've noticed a change in her speech and her manner. Now if Jenny can teach Foster, that would be a miracle." We both laughed.

"What's Mr. Windslow goin' to do with the old bank buildin'? When is he movin' to the new buildin'?"

"He's moving in about two weeks. I think he's going to sell it. When I see him, I'll ask. Why do you ask?"

"I don't know, just that Sam has this gal up the country apiece. She has a diner and is a really good cook. Her pies are out of this world. Sam was thinkin' about marryin' her and bringin' her here. He went to get to know her better. We already have a diner. It was just a thought. I didn't tell you, but he's goin' to be my new ranch foreman and Josh his assistant when he gets back at $150 a month and Josh at $75. Pa had a little trouble on the drive. Doc in Billings said he needs to stay out of the damp cold and take it easy. Ma wanted that for a while. He's still goin' to help when he's needed. I still want to pay him the same."

"That's too bad. I'll make sure about the pay when Sam gets back. I have been wondering where you left him."

"I'll see you later. I better see what the women are up to."

The general store was right next to Foster's. I went in and looked around. "Have you seen my wife, Ed?"

"I did. They picked out a wedding dress. I put it on your account. But before they had left, a man came in, big and mean-looking. He started with Carolyn about how she could be a friend with an Indian Squaw after what those savages did to her. Then he told Lizzie, 'They killed your husband and son.' Buck, I tried to stop him, but he pushed me aside."

"Where did they go? And him, did you see where he went?"

"They went to Foster's. He went in the saloon. Carolyn gave him hell. She told him Red Bird was a better person than he would ever be. He pushed her into Red Bird and Lizzie. Then they left crying. Not Red Bird. She went up to him and hit him across the face. He's got a big red mark across his right cheek."

"Thanks, Ed. Would you have someone tell John?"

"I did already."

I left and went to Foster's. There they were; the two women were crying. I looked at Red Bird, and she came to me. I could tell she was mad. John was there. Foster was trying to calm Lizzie and Carolyn down.

"Lizzie, Carolyn, you don't take any mine to what he said. We all love you very much and he's just doin' this to get at me. John, you comin' with me."

"Buck, you can't go. That's just what he wants."

"I have to go. He can't get away with pushin' women around. You know I'll stand up with you."

"I know that, but we have to be careful."

"Come on, John. I don't want to use my gun unless I have to."

"We'll put him in jail and put him on trial for assault."

"If he gives us any trouble, I might have to start where Red Bird left off. He has a red mark on his right cheek where Red Bird hit him."

Red Bird said, "Buck, be careful."

We left and went to the saloon. I looked over the bat-winged doors of the saloon. Three men were at the bar. The others in the place were just men from around town.

"John, I think those three at the bar are the ones we're after. When we see the one with the red mark on his face, I'll take care of him. You get the drop on the other two."

"I know you're mad. I'll let you handle it."

We walked right up to the back of the three. I said, "Which one of you likes to hit women?"

The one on my side started to turn. I saw the red mark on his face. John saw it too and pulled his gun on the other two.

"No squaw is a woman. I'll treat her like any Indian."

By the time he had turned around and finished his sentence, I hit him square in the face. Blood flew everywhere. Before he could recover, I hit him in the belly. This put his back against the bar. I grabbed his shirtfront and threw him across the floor. At a glance, I saw John had pulled the other two men's guns out of their holsters. The one on the floor grabbed for his gun. I stepped on his hand and picked up his gun and put it in my belt. I pulled him up to his feet and pushed him out the door into the dusty street. He landed on his face in the dirt. John followed me out with a gun in the other two's backs.

"You two get out of town and tell your boss Silver Buck is comin' his way. I warned him."

The two got on their horses and rode out of town as fast as they could. As John was taking the beaten third man to jail, and as I picked up my hat off the dusty ground, we heard a shot. I looked toward the school. All the children were running out of the school.

"John, get him in jail and hurry back. I'll see what happened."

"I'll be right back."

I turned toward the school and saw two men running out carrying a little girl with black hair. They mounted their horses and started heading out of town. That's when I saw BJ running out of the school with the shotgun. He raised it and fired. The man in the rear slumped down. They were gone east out of town. Bill came running up behind me. That's when Jenny came out of the school. She and BJ came running to us.

Bill said, "What happened, Jenny?"

Blood was running down her face. By now, Red Bird and everyone else were out on the street. Red Bird went to Jenny. Bill already had his handkerchief out, trying to get the blood off her face.

"Three men came in the school. I told them they would have to leave. Two hung back. One came at me so fast I didn't have time to grab the shotgun. He hit me in the face, and as I was falling, I managed to grab the shotgun. As I hit the floor, I aimed and pulled the trigger and there was a surprised look on the man's face as the blast hit him in the chest. He's dead on the floor of the school. The others grabbed Song Bird and ran out. BJ took the shotgun out of my hands and ran after them."

"Pa, I hit one, but the other one got away with Song Bird."

"BJ, I'm proud of you. You did good."

John came riding up.

"I saw most of what happened, and I heard enough. I'll get a deputy to get the dead man out of the school, and I'll catch up."

"Buck, you have to get her back."

Red Bird was crying and yelling. This was the first time I'd ever seen her show this kind of emotion. Then I thought, *"Blacky, he's at the ranch.*

"I'll bring her back to you, I promise. Blacky is at the ranch."

One of the cowboys that came out of the saloon said, "Silver, I saw everything. Take my horse."

"Thanks. Red Bird, take Jenny to Doc's. Bill, you ready?"

He took off his suit coat. His .45 was exposed, and I took off my heavy coat and handed them to Foster. We were up in the saddle and out of town. It was cold, but Bill and I were so mad that we couldn't feel it. Our bones were hot with anger.

I pulled up and sat a minute.

"What you waiting for?"

"We need to calm down. We can't go in all angry. Anger will take away our readiness. Take your loop off your trigger. A small thing like that will get you killed.

We need to wait for John a while."

John rode up to us. "What you waitin' for, Silver?"

"You, and to calm down."

"Y'all ready? Let's go."

We rode up into the yard. They came out on the porch.

"Young, your men are all under arrest."

"You heard him, Young. You sent your men to hurt women and children."

"Yes, I have one child in my house." He laughed.

"Song Bird, you all right?" I called out.

"Yes, Pa."

"Honey, get down on the floor, now! And Young, you overplayed your hand. I told you what would happen if you cause any trouble."

"We'll do it your way, Silver."

"Young, your trouble was you waited until I got back from the cattle drive. Now it's too late."

"Boss, you said he would back down if we got his daughter."

"Shut up. He hasn't drawn yet, has he?"

"Just waitin' for you, Young. I thought it would be nice if I let you get your gun out before I kill you. Bill, you take the one on your right. John, you take the one on your left. I'll take Young and the other one in the middle. Boys, we brought a shovel, we'll bury you right here."

John said, "I'll give you one last chance, or like Silver said, we'll bury you right here."

They pulled their guns, and I looked, and Bill had shot his man. I drew as the others started to come up with theirs. John put one through his target's heart. I fired twice. One I hit in the head, and Young I got in the chest.

I walked over to Young. He said, "I didn't count on you."

"You should have listened."

Bill walked over and looked down at him. "I took you for a nobody."

"This is what you get when you mess with other men's women."

He rolled over and died on the spot.

"Song Bird, you can come out now."

"They were bad men. Is Ms. Trumble and BJ all right?"

I hugged her tight. "Yes, honey, they are fine. Bill, you want to look around for a shovel."

We buried them in front of the house and then headed for Durango.

"Let's stop by Lizzie's and tell Josh they can go home. Bill, you did great. John, I never knew you were that fast."

"How you think I grew so old?" We laughed.

I stopped by and told Josh what happened in town, and he rode in with us. We rode down the street of Durango with Song Bird in front of me. Foster was out in front of his saddle shop. He went to the door and yelled inside, and all the women and BJ came out. Red Bird ran to the horse, took Song Bird off the saddle, and hugged and kissed her, and Red Bird was crying. Then she reached for my neck as I got off. I told the cowboy thanks for the use of his horse.

Red Bird said, "You two are all right? I was so worried."

"We're fine. The others aren't. We won't have to worry about them anymore."

"Mama, those were bad men."

"Yes, they were, dear."

Bill went to Jenny. "You all right, dear?"

"Yes, Doc said my face would heal in a week or two. I was so worried about you."

"I'm good, now that I know you're all right."

"Jenny, you have a good man here. He'll stand up for you anytime."

"Buck, I knew that all along."

John said, "I better get and check on my prisoner."

Josh was with Carolyn.

"Josh, that man said some horrible things about Ma and me and Red Bird. I don't know if we should get married if people think like that."

Red Bird spoke up. "All people do not think like that. Some people say Indians are animals, but that man in jail is more of an animal. We all love you and Josh. You two are our friends. Please marry him."

"Carolyn, I love you very much, and I rode with Silver, Ross, and Sam. I know they are truly our friends. I will always defend you against what anyone says or does to you."

"What do you think, Ma?"

"I lost a husband and a son. Now I'm looking forward to having another son." Then Carolyn turned to Josh.

"I will love you, and Ma will love you. I will marry you. I have a beautiful dress to wear."

Bill and Jenny walked toward her house. We all loaded up in the wagon, and Josh rode beside us, still looking love-struck at Carolyn. We got back to the ranch, and I told Pa to take everyone off guard duty. The danger was over. We all had happier times to look forward to.

At the end of the week, Tim and Jim both came riding into town on the mining wagon. They had rented horses and came out to the ranch.

"What are you both doin' here?"

"You have two houses to build. You need both of us."

"Who's takin' care of the mine?"

"Thomas. He was one of the first to sign on years ago. He knows a lot about the mine. Where you want the new foreman's house?"

"You know better than I do. But near the bunkhouse and the barn. We need to take a ride out east of town where the other will be."

"Let's go. The weather's not going to get any warmer soon. Silver, next spring we need Foster up at the mine for a while. If we can talk him into it."

"What's wrong?"

"The vein is producing less now than it was. We need him to see if he can spot any sign that might lead to another vein. You might remind him that the ore gets less, his bank account goes down. That should light a fire under him."

"Maybe I'll come up with him. Be good to see the men and mine again where all this began. Would y'all hitch up the wagon? I'm goin' to get

Carolyn and Lizzie to go. Would you try to locate Josh? I want his input. He's goin' to marry Carolyn in two weeks."

I went to the house.

"Red Bird, would you help me to get Carolyn and Lizzie to go to their ranch? Tim and Jim are here to start on their house. We need their input."

Red Bird brought the women down.

"Tim and Jim are here to start on your house. They need your thoughts on everything. Josh is comin'. Red Bird, you come too."

Red Bird said, "I know it is hard, but you need to face your fears about the ranch. By next spring, you will be living there."

"You're right. We have discussed this. We're ready, right, Ma?"

"Yes, it's been long enough."

We loaded up in the wagon, and we went east to their new ranch. I pulled up to the old burned-out ranch house. As we helped them down, I saw a tear form in their eyes. Their husband, son, father, and brother were buried on this land.

"Lizzie, where would you like the new house? Tim and Jim can guide you."

"My husband wanted it where it is now. I always wanted it with a front porch facing the little lake down below there and the barn somewhere behind the house."

"That sounds good. I'll get rid of all the burned-out buildings."

"Tim, if you find anything in the burned ruins that is good, would you save them for us to be put in the house?"

"I sure will, ma'am. You can count on it."

"Buck, do you know where they're buried?"

"I buried them over here. It was the hardest thing I ever have done." We walked a ways.

"You buried them. I didn't know that. I thank you very much."

"We didn't have a lot of time. So I thought if we could move them to a nice spot and make it large enough for future family members. I would like to put a headstone statin' that he was the one that started this ranch and fought and died to keep it. So that future generations will know this land was fought for."

"I would like that. And he would too. Carolyn, do you and Josh like what was talked about the house today?"

"Yes, but we think it should be more of the size of Ross and Molly's house, but with four bedrooms and two stories. I know Doc said I may not be able to have children, but with God's help, I may. A nice kitchen like Red Bird has. I like indoor plumbing."

We all laughed.

"It is better than going out behind a bush like I did in my father's village."

This got another laugh.

"I don't know, honey, I like the pond where we met. I was takin' a bath in the pond when Foster brought this beautiful Red Bird to meet me for the first time. I was embarrassed."

"I did not mind. My mother thought he was part Indian because he always was turning red."

This brought the biggest laugh. Even Lizzie laughed. It was good to see.

Then Carolyn said, "Josh, you know we have a lake out front."

"Now you are going to embarrass me."

"Tomorrow we'll plot out the house and the barn and a bunkhouse."

It was two weeks until the weddin', so the next day, I stopped in to see Ed about the buggies.

"I've been wanting to see you, Silver. The buggies should be here early next week. They telegrammed me that they had an eight-seater that had been special-ordered and then the man backed out. They said it was all fancied up but they would give it to you at a lower price. I said yes, since it was the lower price and you wanted it fast."

"Thanks, Ed. That sounds good."

I saw the progress on Sam's house. It was the second week in October. It was still mild for this time of year in Durango. I rode Blacky out to see the progress on Lizzie's ranch. They had all the old buildings put in one pile and burning. The new house was staked out, also the barn and the bunkhouse. I had brought out two pine coffins a few days ago in the wagon. I now dug up the skeletons and placed them in the coffins. I made a graveyard about thirty feet by thirty feet and dug two six-foot holes. I lowered them into the ground.

When I got back to town, I would order two headstones and some white picket fence and some white paint. When spring set in, I would put the fence in place on top of the knoll overlooking the ranch house and lake. It would be very peaceful. This made me think I should make a family cemetery. My mother and father weren't getting any younger, and Foster was old as my great-grandfather Jeb would have been. Foster was now one of my family. I could have Jeb moved from the Durango cemetery. That was fitting since he was the first of our family in Colorado. I would have to ask Red Bird if her family could be buried here. I didn't know their traditions or customs. It would be nice. I thought I better get back home then. It was getting late. I got in town early enough to order the headstones. They read,

John Starder
Fought and died

For this land
Born 1850 – Died 1882

Ben Starder
Fought and died

For this land
Born 1870 – Died 1882

I would get it all finished and then bring Lizzie and Carolyn to see it. Get the preacher to say a few words over the graves.

When I returned home, I went into the house and took Red Bird in my arms and kissed her. The children came over, and I hugged them and kissed them on the cheek.

"What's wrong, Pa?"

"Buck, you all right?"

"I am now. I just dug up Lizzie's husband's and son's remains and reburied them. It just made me sad, and I thought how lucky I am to have you three."

Red Bird told the children, "Your father is just sentimental. Buck, can we eat supper now?"

"Yes, dear. I am hungry. I missed dinner."

The next morning, I rode Blacky out with Red Bird on Lagger. I was always going to find Red Bird another horse. She had become parcel to Lagger from the beginning of our marriage. We were out to see how the men were doing now the winter was getting closer. I knew Pa would have them working at the right assignment, but it was nice to get out and take a look at the workings of the ranch. I also liked to make sure Pa was all right in this cold. It was too cold to go to our favorite spot on the river to take a bath and, more important, to enjoy each other as we always had.

Most of the men were gathering in hay and getting it in the barn before the snow flew. We had gotten behind because of the cattle drive. Pa was there supervising the men. We rode on to the ponds where men were clearing out the water plants that grew in the summer. The rest of the men were out riding along the river to make sure the cattle hadn't wondered across.

Red Bird and I got back from our tour of the ranch. We were in the barn unsaddling the horses. I put them in the pasture. They loved the pasture, so they could be free to run all they wanted. Afterward, I cut up two apples and gave them to Blacky and Lagger. I now kept a bag of apples in the barn. They liked oats, but they loved apples. We were walking to the house when I stopped and kissed Red Bird. We heard someone, and as we turned, there was Ma.

"What are you two up to? After all these years, you still look so much in love."

Red Bird spoke. "Mother, we are, and I saw it in your eyes when Father came home."

"You see too much, Red Bird. But you are right. I still have that feeling. When are we going to plan the party for the wedding?"

"I know. Tomorrow morning. The children and Buck are going for a ride. We'll get Lizzie and Carolyn and Manuel. I'll let Jose and Juanita know also. That way, we'll have four ovens baking pies and cakes. Buck, you can go to town today and tell Jenny. You can tell Mrs. Windslow and Mrs. Themes about the meeting tomorrow morning. I know they will want to come. This will be the biggest party Durango has seen since you and Father came up from Texas. I'll get Manuel to bake some pies and cakes for tomorrow."

"Son, with Red Bird in charge, this will be some doings. You know Josh asked your father to be his best man?"

"Jenny asked me to be her maid of honor, and Lizzie is going to be Carolyn's maid of honor."

We heard some noise coming over the rise leading to the gate of the ranch, and saw two heavily loaded wagons coming. The man in the lead wagon was standing up yelling. I couldn't make out what he was saying. The second wagon had a woman in the driver's seat. Then as they got closer, I could hear him.

"Silver, it's me, your new foreman."

I called out, "Red Bird, Mother, it's Sam and Ann."

Mother said, "Now your father can get some real rest."

Ann had a man's shirt and pants on. On top of her head, she had a large hat pulled down. I started waving at them, and Ann waved back. They pulled up by the barn. Then Sam jumped off the seat and shook my hand.

"I see you're still in one piece, partner."

"I see you have a new partner."

He ran over and helped Ann down off the seat of the wagon.

"Ann, you know Buck. This is his wife, Red Bird, and his mother, Molly. This is my bride-to-be, Ann Cummings."

They all shook hands.

"I'm sorry I look a sight. I tried to get Sam to take me to the hotel and bathe and change. He wouldn't have it."

Red Bird said, "Shame on you, Sam. Never mind, men. Ann, you can use my bath in my room. I'll help you. Mother, I'll see you later. You two get the wagons in the barn and get the teams fed."

"I have to tell Ross that Sam's back when he comes in."

"Red Bird, I need to get some clothes out of the wagon. Buck, I can see why you didn't go to the saloon much. Red Bird, you're so beautiful."

"Ann, once we get you out of Sam's clothes and into a bath, you'll be beautiful."

"She sure is, Red Bird," Sam said.

Ann got a suitcase out of the wagon, and the two women went to the house. Sam and I got on the wagons and pulled them in the barn. We got the horse unhitched and fed.

"What's all you got in here?"

"Ann's furniture and clothes. Everything she owns. She sold the diner with all the equipment."

"Sam, let's leave the wagons loaded, except for what you two might need. Your house won't be ready till spring. It depends on the weather. Come on, I'll take you down there. It's in between Pa's and Foster's houses."

"A house for us?"

"You didn't think I'd have you two sleep in the bunkhouse, did you? It's about the size of Foster's."

We walked down the road leading to Foster's house. After we passed Pa's, we could see the new house.

"I just thought that I would build a house in town so Ann would be close to her shop. You are too much to believe."

"You can still have a house in town. I just thought it would be closer to your job."

"This will be good. It looks as if Ann and Red Bird will get along fine."

"Ann might want to be at the party meetin' tomorrow. I'm sure Red Bird will ask her."

"What's the party for?"

"That's right, you haven't been here to know. Bill and Jenny the schoolteacher, and Josh and Carolyn are getting' married on the twenty-ninth of this month."

"Things sure have changed in four months."

"You haven't seen the biggest change of all. You have to come in to town later. I'll show you. You won't believe your eyes. What kind of shop is Ann wantin' to have?"

"She always wanted a dress shop. But she has another one in mind also."

"What, Sam?"

"Her father was a gunsmith. They never had a son. He taught her everything there is to know about guns. The second wagon is filled with her father's equipment. She would like to open both and have someone run the dress shop for her. She was tired of the diner. She had to get up so early and stay late."

"A lady gunsmith. I have another idea. I'll show you when we go to town."

"I'm sure Red Bird will ask Ann when you plan on getting married."

"We haven't set a date."

"What you think about the twenty-ninth?"

"What?"

"Yeah, we'll have a triple marriage ceremony."

"I don't! This is moving fast."

"Ann can stay in our other bedroom and you in the bunkhouse."

"Silver, you know we already sleep together."

"I know, but she's new in town, and you know how women in town can be. You wouldn't want them getting the wrong impression of her and not buy her dresses. They could even stop their husbands from havin' her fixin' their guns."

"You make sense. I wouldn't want her and the town getting off on the wrong foot."

"Let's get back to the house and see if the women are done."

Red Bird and Ann were sitting in the front room. "Where you two been?"

"Just talkin'. I took Sam down and showed him your new house they're startin'. He was tellin' me about the shops you want to start."

"What you think?"

"I think they're both a good idea."

Red Bird said, "I told her we have to go to the general store for dresses, and he only has a few. There's no place to try them on. The women have to order them if they want a fancy dress."

Ann said, "Red Bird told me about the wedding in two weeks."

"Silver told me too. What you think?"

"It's all right with me if it's good with you. I know I love you, Sam, and that won't change the longer we wait. Red Bird was saying that we shouldn't sleep together until the wedding. The women might not buy my dresses."

"Silver told me the same thing. I know I love you, so the sooner the better. I don't want to sleep too long without you by my side, and those cowboys snore in the bunkhouse."

"Same old Sam with the jokes. But I know how you feel, Sam. When Buck was gone, I felt a part of me was missing. It was worst at night. Well, I better go tell Manuel about tomorrow. There's going to be quite a few of us if Buck remembers to tell the women in town today. Ann, you can wear your best dress, and some of your best customers will be here. I know them. They'll ask where you got it. I just hope you can make some of my favorite Mexican dresses."

"I sure can, Red Bird. Very colorful and cool in the summer."

Sam said, "Buck, she sure has changed since you brought her from Dancing Bear's village."

I called to Red Bird, "Honey, Sam and me are headin' for town. I got two surprises for him. You want to come, Ann? One of the surprises is for you."

"Thank you, Buck. I'm tired from the trip. You can show me later."

"All right, you better get some rest. The next two weeks are goin' to be hectic on everyone."

We stopped by the bank.

"See this buildin'?"

"It's the bank."

"Not for long. See that brick buildin' behind the bank?"

"Yes."

"That's the new bank, and Bill thinks that Mr. Windslow is goin' to sell this buildin'."

"So!"

"Look, Sam, two big windows in front for displays. Place a wall down the middle with a door in the wall, you have two stores."

"I've been on the trail too long. Now I see what you mean. Ann's two stores could be right next to each other. But that's a lot of money."

"Sam, look around, how this town is growin'. You and Ann would own part of Durango for the future. We can talk to Bill later. Right now, I have a bigger surprise."

"What could that be? That one knocked me for a loop."

"Wait. You'll faint on the floor."

We rode down a ways and got off and tied our horses.

"This is new. A saddle shop."

"He repaired all the saddles and brittles from the cattle drive, and he's makin' me a new saddle for Blacky."

We walked in, and Foster had his back to us with his apron around his neck and tied around his waist in back.

"You got my saddle ready yet, you old buzzard."

"I'se told you'se, Buck, it would take a while."

He turned, and Sam's mouth was wide open, and I thought he was going to fall onto the floor.

"Sam, how you'se be doin'?"

I said, "Sam, you can shut your mouth and get up off the floor now."

"Foster, I wouldn't believe it if I hadn't seen it with my own eyes."

"Let me see my saddle."

"I'se told you'se, Buck, not till I'se done."

"All right!"

"Foster, what made you think of this?"

"When I'se be young, this is what I'se wanted to do, but no money. Now I'se have money. This town is growin'. All I'se need is a young man to train for when I'se gone. BJ seems to watch me. I'se would like to train him if he wants after school and on Saturday. I'se knows you'se want him to learn ranchin', but this is a trade he can have also."

"We'll see if he wants to later. Sam, see what I mean? Invest in this town while it's small. Your money can run out. The mine won't last forever. This town I can see growin', and I want to see my friends well off."

"All right, we'll talk to Bill. Then to Ann."

"Who's Ann?"

"My wife-to-be on the twenty-ninth. She wants to start two shops here. I met her on the drive."

"This town is growin'. Three weddin's and all the children that will come from these three."

"We better go before Bill leaves the office. I'll brin' Ann and Sam to see your house, if that's all right?"

"Sure, I'se tell Juanita."

We went out into the street. I saw the general store.

"Come on in, Sam."

"Hello, Buck. Why, Sam, good to see you. It's been what, six or seven months? I thought you got lost on the trail."

They shook hands.

"Ed, Red Bird sent me in to let your wife know she's havin' a meetin' tomorrow mornin' about the party after the weddings. She thought your wife and Mrs. Windslow would want to be there 'cause it's goin' to be the biggest event in Durango's history."

"I'll tell her. I'm sure she'll want to be there."

"It's goin' to be even bigger. Sam's getting' married at the same time. They can meet his bride to me there, and she is goin' to open a fancy dress shop here in town."

"Now I know she'll come."

"We need to see Bill."

As we walked out, I saw Mr. Windslow. "Mr. Windslow, I'm glad I caught you. Would you tell your wife that Red Bird is havin' a meetin' tomorrow mornin' about the party after the weddin's? She thought your wife might want to be there and meet Sam's bride- to-be, Ann is openin' a fancy dress shop here in town."

"Well, Sam, somebody finally roped you. No more saloon girls."

"Now, Mr. Windslow, that might be kept under your hat, if you know what I mean."

"I understand. I'll tell her."

"By the way, when are you goin' to move into your new buildin'? What are you doin' with the old buildin'?"

"We move into the new place November 1. I'm selling the old building."

"How much?"

"Five thousand dollars. You interested?"

"I may know someone."

"That's wonderful. I better get home. I'll tell my wife."

We walked into Bill's office. He looked up.

"Buck, Sam, good to see you. You did a fine job for the ranch. Good to have you back. Buck said you might be bringin' a fine businesswoman with you?"

"I did. Her name's Ann. If you don't mind, we're getting married at the same time as you and Josh are."

"What did you say? I heard you, but I thought I wasn't hearing you right."

"You heard right."

"That's great. We'll have a real humdinger of a party."

"Bill, would you tell Jenny that Red Bird is havin' a meetin' tomorrow mornin' about the party? She can meet Ann there."

"I'll tell her tonight at supper at the hotel. We can dine in comfort now that Young and his men are out of the way."

"Bill, don't you have Sam's statement from the bank?"

"Right here. I've been holding on to them until you got back."

Sam opened up the statement and looked closely at the top. As he went down, there were all the deposits for the last year. He looked at the bottom where the final total was. I thought he was going to fall out of the chair.

"This can't be right. It says I have $232,542 in the bank."

"That is right. I know. I do the books for the mine and the ranch."

"Sam, every time a shipment comes in, Bill deposits your share in your account. You haven't spent hardly anything out of it for ten years. You've been living off your pay at the ranch. This is good. You talk to Ann tonight. After you get hitched, you can buy the old bank buildin' for Ann's two shops."

"What business does she want to start?"

I spoke up. "She wants a dress shop for one and a gun shop for two. She's a gunsmith. Her father taught her. Never had a son."

"A lady gunsmith and a seamstress—what a combination. Get the wife and husband at the same time. You were right. She has the smarts. You said the bank building."

"I talked to Mr. Windslow. He said they're movin' into the new bank buildin' November 1. He is sellin' the old buildin' for $5,000. If they place a wall down the middle and a door between the two shops, the husbands won't mind his wife stayin' as long as she wants and spendin' more money at the dress shop as long as he can buy at the gun shop."

"I don't believe they're selling it that cheap. Sam, you can get her started off right. That's chicken feed out of what you have."

Sam still wasn't thinking. All he would say was, "$232,542—that is a lot."

"Sam, snap out of it."

"Buck, when he comes out of this spell, have him bring Ann in, and I'll talk to her. She might be the brain in the family. I'll get with Mr. Windslow, and if Sam gets straight, We'll get a good deal."

"I'll get him back to Ann. maybe she can get him straight. I'll tell her if he can't."

"Here's his statement."

We left and got to the ranch, and Sam finally came out of it as we walked in to the house. I kissed Red Bird. She had learned the meaning of money from her lessons from Jenny. Sam handed Ann his statement.

"Here, Ann, look at this. I still have a hard time believing it."

She opened the statement and looked at it. Her mouth dropped open. "Sam, you said you had some money to help me get started. I never dreamed it was anything close to this."

"Ann, don't get like Sam. He couldn't talk for twenty minutes. He still doesn't seem fully right. The bank is movin' to a new buildin'. Bill is a lawyer, and my business manager and partner like Sam is. We want you to look at the old bank buildin'. They are sellin' it for $5,000. They're not movin' out till after the wedding. Myself, I think it would be a fine buildin' for both businesses. As you can see, that wouldn't be much out of what he has. But it would go a long ways for your business."

"In Job's Crossing, I never made more than $10,000 a year, and that was a good living."

The next morning, I woke to find Red Bird was not beside me. I went to Lizzie's room and knocked. No response. The same with Ann's room. And then it hit me: the smell of pies. Then it came to me. I got the children up and going.

"Pa, why are you getting us up so early?"

"Ma's havin' her meetin' about the party. We have to get out of the house. I want you to help me. BJ, go to the barn and hitch up the team."

Song Bird said, "Pa, we get to go to the party."

"Sure. Almost everyone in town will be at the party."

"Don't we get to eat?"

"On the way out, we'll stop by the kitchen. I'm sure Manuel has something for us."

BJ was gone, and Song Bird and I went down to the kitchen, and all the women were there. We got some breakfast.

"Buck, taste this. Ann made a pie for us. It's delicious."

"It is. I ate her apple pie at her diner. Now you know the real reason Sam's marryin' her."

All the women laughed. I gave Red Bird a kiss and a hug. She gave Song Bird a piece of pie and kissed her. We left for town. I saw Sam with Pa heading out to the range. I let BJ drive the wagon.

"BJ, head to the stonecutter's in town."

We picked up the two headstones and the picket fence, white paint, and a gate from Ed's. I wanted to see if BJ could find his way.

"Go out to Lizzie's and Carolyn's ranch. That's where we stopped to get Josh early this week."

"I know, Pa. Song Bird told me."

"Who are these for?"

"One's for Lizzie's husband, and the other's for her son. That would be Carolyn's father and brother. The Indians killed them."

"Grandpa killed them?"

"No, Song Bird. Dancing Bear is a good man and at peace. These were bad Indians. Dancing Bear didn't like them."

We came to the place where the two were buried.

"Pull the back of the wagon close to the graves."

"Right there, pa."

"Just right, BJ. I'm proud of you."

We dug down a ways and got the headstones set in the right place. I remembered which side I placed each man's remains. BJ pulled the wagon out. We started digging the holes for the fence. I was going to wait, but I thought with the wedding coming up and the house going up, it would be better before the snow fell. Tim came over from the house construction.

"I saw you over here, and I wondered who they were. Mighty young, weren't they."

"Yeah, they died before their time. Josh is gettin' married to his daughter."

"Here, let me help you. These will make it easier."

The holes were dug; the posts were in place. Next the fence went up. Then Tim put the gate in place. I put the children to painting the fence. Tim took me down to the house.

"I want to have it enclosed and the roof on before the first snow. Who knows when that may happen."

"It looks a good size."

"It has a great room, a big kitchen. We put two water closets inside—one in the big bedroom like yours, and the other in between the other three bedrooms. There are four bedrooms like Carolyn wanted upstairs. The barn and the bunkhouse will be over there."

"After the three couples get married, we are havin' a big party at the ranch. You have to come to the church to see Sam get hitched the twenty-ninth

"Sam married. I'll be there."

"He showed up at the ranch yesterday with Ann. He met her on the cattle drive. He's goin' to be ranch foreman. My pa is goin' to be taken it easy."

"Pa, we're done."

"Well, Tim, we better head back to the ranch. Red Bird had a party meetin'. It must be over by now."

"BJ, take us home."

All the women were more excited now that the meeting was over. It seemed the word spread, and more women came from town. Red Bird said that even two of the girls came that Sam had been friendly with. Some didn't like it, but Red Bird invited them in. They wanted to meet Ann, the woman who got Sam to settle down. They told Red Bird that this was the biggest event that had ever happened in Durango since Silver came to town with all that silver. They weren't going to miss it.

Ed sent out word that the buggies were going to be in a week early. I knew we were going to have to train up to six horses for the buggies. But for now, I would use the four I used for the wagon. On Monday, I got Josh to come to town with me. We took four horses with us. Ed said all the riggings came with the buggies. They were behind the store.

"Josh no one knows about this. This big one is goin' to take you six from the church to the ranch. Red Bird and the children and me will take the brides to the church in this. Don't say anything. Let the girls be surprised."

"Silver, you're full of surprises. I don't know what we'd do without you. This is so fancy. The girls are going to love it."

Josh and I pulled up to the barn. Everyone came out and had a look-see. I told Red Bird what I had planned. We just had to get Jenny out to the ranch that morning. We took everyone for rides around the house and barn areas. Song Bird thought of them as big toys to play with. Finally, everyone got a ride. We had to make room in the barn.

The next morning, Josh and I started training four horses to pull the buggies. We worked four whole days at it. By Wednesday, I felt good about them. It was downright cold. We had decided to have the party in the house. We had a large fireplace to keep everybody warm. It was close to the kitchen, so the food wouldn't get cold.

It was Sunday, and we got ready for church. Josh and BJ hitched up the buggy. After church, I asked the preacher to follow us out to Lizzie's ranch. We pulled up to the cemetery on the knoll. We got down, and Lizzie and Carolyn looked around.

"You did this, Buck?"

"The children and me. Tim helped also. He's the one that's building your home."

"Carolyn, look at what it says," Lizzie said.

"I wanted you future generations to know who fought for this land. I made enough room for generations to come."

Lizzie said, "I want all of you to know how much you mean to us. We were a great burden on you. Red Bird and Molly, you made us whole again. Buck, you rescued us from our captors, and, Josh, you stood by Carolyn. I will be proud to have you for my son."

We all went by and hugged her and Carolyn. Then the preacher said words over the two buried here. I said thanks to the preacher and handed him fifty dollars. Then we went down to the house.

"It's so big. John would have liked it. He always wanted me to have a large house."

We went back to the ranch. We had a wedding and a party to get ready for in six days. Red Bird told Jenny at her lesson that Jenny was going to come to the ranch Saturday morning and Josh and Sam was going to town that morning.

"Why, Red Bird?"

"Bring your wedding dress. All the brides are getting ready out here, and the men in town are at Bill's house. You know they can't see you, and Buck has a surprise for everyone."

16

It was Saturday morning. Red Bird and I were up early. When we went to the kitchen, Manuel, Jose, Juanita, and Ann were there. There were bake goods stacked up on the table and the counter.

"What are all of you doing in here so early? It's still dark. Ann, you're getting married today. Why are you here?"

"I came in last night. They looked like they could use some help."

"Senora Red Bird, I told her she should not. She insisted on helping. She is a great cook, and she bakes like a dream. Senor Sam is a lucky man."

Ann said, "Thank you, Manuel."

"You mean you have been up all night?"

Juanita said, "It had to be done. I just came over here. I've baked at our house all night. On the way over, I saw a light was on at your parents' house. Molly said she was up all night baking. Senor Silver, if you could go to my house and Molly's house with the wagon and bring everything over here. We'll just about be done."

"Buck, stop and get Josh and Sam heading into town. I'll get BJ up to go get Jenny and bring her out here in the small buggy. Ann, you need to go get some rest. I'll wake you in three or four hours."

"I'm all right. I'm used to staying up like this."

"This is your wedding day. You don't need to look like you've been up all night. You listen to me, I am yours and Jenny's mother, for today."

"Yes, Ma. I'll go."

"Now, Buck, get out of here. You have another buggy to decorate. I'm going to get BJ up. Hitch the buggy for him."

I had the buggy ready for BJ and took the wagon down to Foster's house and knocked and walked in. "Foster, I'm here to get the food." I walked in the kitchen, and there he was, eating a piece of cake. "Foster, that's for the party."

"I'se can't help it. I'se be hungry."

"Juanita said your breakfast is in the oven."

"Oh, sorry."

"You help me load everything. Keep that for yourself. Come on."

"Let me get in my pants."

We loaded everything in the wagon.

"Foster, our best friends are getting married today. Take a bath. The boys and me don't want to have to come down here and throw you in that bathtub like we threw you in the pond before my wedding."

"I'se don't mine a bath anymore. I'se take one every two days. Juanita sees to it."

"Fine, Foster. Wear that new suit you have. I'll see you later today. The big buggy is goin' to be for the brides. Red Bird and me are takin' them to the church. My parents are takin' the children and Lizzie in the small buggy. If you don't mind to take Juanita, Jose, and Manuel and whoever else won't to go with you in the wagon. The men can ride their horses."

"All right, I will. I'se don't mind."

I got all the food from my parents' house and told Sam to get Josh and get to Bill's house in town. "And don't forget your suits."

Song Bird came out and helped me get everything in the kitchen. It was nice and sunny outside, but cold. The wind was blowing from the north. I'm glad we moved the party into the house. It looked as though it was going to be well below freezing by tonight.

"Silver, I'm missing one cake. Where is it?"

"I left it at Foster's. Guess what happened?"

"What?"

"He ate two pieces. He didn't see the breakfast in the oven."

"That man, I'm going to kill him. I left him a note. Sometimes I feel like his mama."

Red Bird said, "You sound like a wife." Everyone laughed.

"Red Bird, if you need me, I'll be in the barn takin' care of the buggy."

"You better take your clothes to your parents'. We girls are going to need both tubs and rooms. I'll send BJ down there with his clothes. You men get ready down there."

"Yes, Mama."

Everyone laughed.

"Manuel, you can stay. You have your own room and tub. We may need some help later."

"Si, senora. I'll get ready, then stay busy in here until you need me."

I left before she thought of anything else. Just imagine that a short eleven years ago she was a shy young Indian princess coming into the white man's world. I still loved her, and her body still moved me.

BJ came back with Jenny. He drove up to the front of the house and helped Jenny down and helped her with her wedding dress into the house. It looked as though we had done a good job with him. He was turning into quite a young man.

I saw Sam and Josh leave for town. I had taken their horses down to my parents. I was going to send the three couples to Denver for a wedding present, but this time of year, the weather was unknown. We wouldn't want them in a snowstorm out in nowhere. Too bad the train hadn't made it this way, yet this was one time they could be useful. I booked their rooms at the hotel for them to spend their honeymoon.

BJ came up to the barn in the buggy. "Pa, I like driving that new buggy. What are you doing?"

"Just decoratin' the buggy the brides are goin' to ride to the weddin' in. You take your clothes to Grandma's?"

"I did. Why did Ma run me out of the house? She told me I had to take a bath."

"She ran you out 'cause all the women have to get ready. You're gettin' too old to see women half dressed. No place for a man until they're ready for the church. Now help me with this, son."

"Let's go see if Grandpa's gettin' ready. We can't all take a bath at the same time."

"Mean you going to take a bath too?"

"Yes, son, even me. If I don't, your mother would have my hide pinned to the wall."

"Monday, what will I call Ms. Trumble?"

"After the wedding, she'll be Mrs. Gills. You call her that. I'm sure she'll let all the children know."

"He'll still be Mr. Gills, won't he?"

"Yes, son. I don't know why or when it started, but the women take the men's last name. Carolyn will be Mrs. Thorton, and Ann will be Mrs. Ganger. They keep their first name."

"That's enough questions. Let's get ready. We're goin' to have a real fine party. Now, how does that look son?"

"It looks all right."

"Never mind. The women will love it if the wind doesn't blow it all apart on the way to the church."

"Pa, you ready?" I said when we went to my parents' house.

"I just got out of the bath."

"BJ, I'll heat up some water. You get in that tub and wash good and wash your hair. You're a young man. Girls don't like their men dirty at a weddin' or a real fancy party."

"Oh, Pa."

"Go ahead."

He took a bath. I checked him close 'cause I knew his mother would. Then it was my turn. After the bath, I got dressed in my real nice suit.

"Come on, BJ, let's go get the teams hitched up. Pa come on up to the barn when you're ready,"

We got all the horses hooked up, and we waited. Foster came down with Manuel, Jose, and Juanita, and they were all decked out. Then Pa came out of the house.

Pa said, "They're not ready yet?"

"When I left, Red Bird said she would send Song Bird when they were ready to go," Juanita said.

"Why didn't you stay and get ready with the women?"

She pointed to Foster. "I had to make sure he took a bath and put on his nice new suit."

"Foster, I have to say, you never looked better."

"I'se feel funny in these dress-up clothes. I'se goin' to change before the party."

We laughed at Foster.

We saw Song Bird come running down the side porch steps after only a few minutes, looking all dolled up, pretty as a picture.

"Pa, Ma said to come to the front of the house. They'll come down the front steps in a few minutes. Wait until you see them. They're so beautiful, even the ones not getting married."

We all laughed.

"Thanks, honey. You are so beautiful too. Now, you and BJ ride in back of the four-seat buggy. Pa, you drive them. Mother will ride with you. Red Bird and I will take the brides and Lizzie in the eight-seat buggy. Foster, you pull up behind Pa with everyone else."

"All right."

We pulled up to the front steps of the house. I got down to help the brides and others into the buggies. Pa and BJ got down to help. The doors swung open, and the brides came out. First came Carolyn, with her mother behind her. Then came Jenny, with Ma behind her. And then Ann, with Red Bird and Song Bird behind her. Then Manuel came out and closed the doors. To me, my darling Red Bird was the most gorgeous of them all. She had on a beautiful light-blue dress that fit her body like a glove, down to the ruffles around the bottom to about a foot up. This was the dress that Jenny had helped her pick out. It took three weeks to come in from St. Louis. When I picked it up, I was told by Red Bird not to look at it, as it was a surprise. I'd say the brides were also very beautiful. This was going to be some occasion for Durango. I took my wife's hand.

"Buck, you did all this."

"Me and BJ. I'm just glad the wind has died down. May I say the wait was well worth it? We men are so lucky to have such beautiful women to be our wives."

I had sent word to the grooms what time to be inside the church before we arrived. We helped all the women up, and they got their dresses arranged; and the parade of buggies and a wagon headed down the road for town. The brides had decided that Carolyn's mother would give her away, and Pa would give Ann away, and I would give Jenny away. We came over the rise overlooking the town with a clear view of the church. There were people all around the front of the church waiting to get a glimpse of the brides, even in this cold. Buggies, wagons, and horses lined the street and all around the church. I hadn't seen this many people since we left on the cattle drive. We stopped in front. There were men all in front to help the brides down. You could hear,

"They're so beautiful, and three of them. There's Lizzie. It's good to see her looking so strong."

"Buck, Sam, Bill, and Josh are already inside. They all look scared to death. Even more than when those Indians came up the country. I never seen Sam look like that."

"That's just the beginnin' of marriage. That will wear off soon enough."

When we entered the church, there was a wall so the brides and us three that were to give them away waited behind that wall until we heard the music. The rest of our party was escorted to the front row for family members. I looked around the wall, and I saw all heads were turned to watch for the brides. My wife was so beautiful.

The music started. Carolyn and Lizzie went first. Pa and Ann second, then Jenny and me last. As we walked down the aisle, I whispered to Jenny, "Look at Bill. He looks so nervous."

"That won't last long."

We all stopped in front of the preacher. He said, "I've never married three couples at once. So when I ask a question, wait until I ask all three. Then answer, 'We do' instead of 'I do.' Now who gives these brides away?"

"We do."

Then we stepped back, and the grooms joined their brides. Lizzie and Pa sat down between Red Bird and Mother. I stepped up to the right of the couples, for I was the best man for all three.

"We are gathered here to join the three men and these three women in the bonds of holy matrimony. If there is anyone here that knows why these three couples should not be joined in holy wedlock, let them speak now or forever hold their peace. Join right hands and repeat after me. Will you, Carolyn, Ann, and Jenny take Josh, Sam, and Bill as your lawful wedded husbands to honor and obey until death do you part?"

"We do."

"Now, Josh, Sam, and Bill do you take Carolyn, Ann, and Jenny as your lawful wedded wives to honor and obey until death do you part?"

"We do."

Some of the cowboys outside yelled. "That's a boy, Sam."

There was a small giggle in the church.

"Now after that, who has the rings?"

"I do," I said.

I pulled the rings out of my pocket, and I let the grooms get their ring.

"Place the rings on their left hand, and, Buck, do you also have the men rings?"

"Yes, sir."

The brides took the rings and placed them on their groom's left hand.

"Now, by the power vested in me, by God and the state of Colorado, I now pronounce you husband and wife. Now you may kiss your own wife."

There was a small laugh through the church. They kissed their wives and then turned and faced the crowd. All in the church clapped and shook the men's hands and kissed the three brides on the cheeks. Red Bird came up and joined me by my side. She was crying.

"What's wrong, honey?"

"It was so beautiful, as much as ours."

I hugged her and kissed her. Then hugged and kisses the brides and shook hands with the grooms. They had all become our best friends.

I asked the preacher, "You're comin' to the party at the ranch?"

"I wouldn't miss it."

The married couples went down the aisle to the outside of the church and stopped at the gate and turned their backs to the unmarried women and threw their bouquets over their heads. Juanita caught one and looked over at Foster. I don't know what that was all about, but he better watch Jose. The couples got in the fancy, decorated buggy, and Red Bird and I drove them to the party at the ranch.

As we rode to the ranch, I said, "Did you see Juanita catch the bouquet? Did you see the look she gave Foster?"

"I know. I saw that."

"What went on while we were gone?"

"I don't know. I knew they had become close. He did trim his hair and beard, and Juanita said he takes three or four baths a week."

Then Bill said, "Buck, what a buggy. I thought you order a plain one. I had no idea you planned this."

We pulled up in front of the house. We ran inside for it was getting colder and darker.

Red Bird said, "Girls, let's go up and change out of your beautiful wedding dresses before all the town folks get here."

I went to the kitchen and saw everything was put out. I said, "Manuel, Jose, and Juanita, all of you have worked hard enough on this party. Everyone can serve themselves tonight. You are all part of our family. I want you to enjoy yourselves. No workin'. You hear me. Now go have some fun. Red Bird, the children and me will help clean up tomorrow. Tonight's for fun."

"Si, senor. Thank you."

The townspeople started to arrive. More food arrived with the people. The house was packed with people and food. When most of the people had arrived, the brides came down.

"Everyone, the food is in the kitchen. Make your way back there and help yourself. Get as much as you want."

Johnny from town brought his fiddle and was playing some old tunes. The new husbands and wives were dancing the first dance. Then everyone was dancing. I asked Red Bird to dance, and she came into my arms, and we were dancing around the floor.

"You been learning more than schoolwork while I was gone."

"I was never allowed to dance in the village, being the chief's daughter. When Jenny said women could dance, I had always wanted to so I had her teach me to surprise you."

"You did! What a lovely dancer you are, and I loved your dress today. I could tell you did not have on anything underneath."

"Buck, behave."

We danced and danced. I danced with all the brides, and Red Bird danced with the grooms. I looked over and saw BJ was dancing with the young ladies from school. Song Bird was dancing with the boys. Then Sam brought out his guitar, and he and Johnny played some more old tunes. The food was going. I saw Manuel and Jose sneak into the kitchen and bring out some more food and drink. The punch bowl was nearly overflowing. As the night wore on, I got up to make a toast to the couples.

"I want to thank y'all for comin'. You can stay as long as you want. But before it gets too late, I just want to make a toast to the newlyweds. Everyone, get a drink. You three couples have become Red Bird's and my closest friends, and our lives are fuller for it. I hope and pray that you will be as happy as I have been since I found and married my lovely wife, Red Bird."

Everyone raised their glass and drank. It was along about midnight that people started to leave and say good night to the newlyweds. Lizzie came over and said good night to Carolyn.

"Buck, good night. I want to thank you and Red Bird for all you've done for my daughter. For the past six months, I never thought I could be this happy again. It's been a long week and has really tired me out. So good night."

"You six ready to go to your honeymoon lodge?"

"What do you mean, Buck?

"Red Bird and me told them the story of our honeymoon lodge."

Pa said the men would take the wagon and buggy to the barn after taking him and ma home, and Foster and Juanita to their house.

Then Red Bird said, "Buck, you take them to the hotel. I am tired. I'll put the children to bed. I'll be waiting for you in our bed."

I smiled. "Looks like I'm goin' to have another honeymoon tonight."

They laughed.

"Oh Buck, good night. You enjoy yourselves. And, Sam, don't come to work for a week."

She kissed them all good night and then headed upstairs.

"Good night, Red Bird. Thanks for everything."

Everyone loaded up in the buggy. It was so windy now that almost all the decorations were blown away. As we rode on the road to town, it started to rain lightly. I was glad it had a strong canopy on it. We made it to the hotel without getting too wet. They rushed into the hotel. The men were carrying the women's suitcases. I turned and headed home.

I was about halfway home when light snows began. It was becoming even heavier now. The road in front of me was turning white. I'm just glad I put the more experienced team on this buggy. The ranch gate was now in sight. The wheels were sliding from one side of the road to the other as I pulled up to the barn. A light in the bunkhouse came on, and a few seconds later, the door opened as I got down to open the barn door. It was Jose.

"Senor, I was not in bed yet. I heard the horses. It sounded as if they were afraid."

"The snow is buildin' up on the road. We were slidin' up and down the slope."

We got them in the barn and got some hay and dried off the horses and put their blankets on them. We did the same to Blacky and Lagger and Foster's old mule.

'Thank you, Jose. Now get back to bed. I'll see if I can make it to the house. Don't get up too early. The men won't be."

"After I feed the men tomorrow, I'll come help with the mess. I had great fun tonight."

After plugging through the icy snow, I made it up to the porch. Finally, I was home. It was nice and cozy in the house with the big fireplace ablaze. A blaze. What is that raging so high for? Then I saw a blanket on top of the bearskin rug. I pulled back the blanket and on top of the bearskin was Red Bird, completely naked.

"What are you doin'? The children and Lizzie, and how about Manuel?"

"All asleep. I felt something inside. The wedding reminded me of our wedding night. So get out of your clothes and come make me warm inside. My wild Indian blood is rising."

"Yes, dear, I'll rise to the occasion."

'You better."

We rolled into each other's arms for the rest of the night.

"Ma, Pa, what, you sleeping down here?"

I woke up. It was Song Bird!

"We sat down here in front of the fireplace and fell asleep. You know where your ma keeps her robe?"

"Yes, Pa."

"Would you go up and get it? Ma might be cold. The fire went out?"

She ran up the stairs. I jumped up and got my pants and shirt on.

"Red Bird, wake up, dear. Song Bird's awake."

She opened her eyes just as Song Bird came running down with Red Bird's robe.

"Here, Ma. Pa said you might be cold."

"Thank you, honey. That was sweet of you."

We were up and starting to pick up the blanket when Manuel came in from the kitchen. He looked around and turned and headed into the kitchen. He was laughing.

"We'll be down to help you after we take a bath."

Si, senora. I understand."

"Song Bird, would you please help Manuel until me and pa get back."

"Yes, Ma. That was fun last night."

"More than you know, honey."

When we came down, the children were eating and Lizzie was eating. All six of us were cleaning; it still took us four or five hours.

"Red Bird, did you notice all the gifts by the front door?"

"The townspeople brought them for the couples. It says whom they're for. They'll get them when they come out here."

"Did you see it snowed last night? I almost didn't make it home."

"I'm glad you did. You think it will stay on the ground long?"

"The wind stopped. I don't know how cold it is."

"The children have a week off from school for Bill and Jenny's honeymoon. I hope all three couples enjoy theirs as much as we did."

"Sam already knows what Ann's all about. Buck, don't tell anyone that, not even Jenny. I want her business to go over well. Some people might hold that against her."

The snow stayed around another two days. It turned clear and mild afterward. The work on the two houses resumed. I had been in town, and the bank was in the process of moving. I went to the hotel just to see whom I could see. They were in the dining room all together. I didn't know if I should intrude or not when Bill and Sam waved me over.

"Hello, Buck. How you like that snow?"

"I didn't. I nearly didn't get back home when I brought y'all to town."

"Was it that bad? We didn't seem to notice."

Jenny smiled and poked Bill in the side. The other two women laughed a little.

"After I got in the house, it didn't matter to me either. Sam, I know you and Ann have other things on your mind right now. The bank is moving today and tomorrow. If you can take some time and show Ann the old bank buildin', and, Ann, you can see if that will work for your business. The price is right. I better get home. Red Bird will be mad if she knew I was botherin' you. Her people believe that the couple do not speak to anyone for a week."

No bother, Buck. We'll take a look before headin' to the ranch."

"Carolyn, you and Josh all right? Red Bird was worried about you two."

"I know she was. Tell her I'm fine. Josh is everything I thought a man should be."

Josh had a smile on his face.

"After a week, I'll tell her, or she'll know I bothered you. I know she'll be happy. Your mother is fine. She helped us clean up the house after that wing-ding of a party."

I left and went to the ranch. Dad was in the barn.

"What's goin' on around the ranch?"

"After that snow, I had the men checkin' the cattle and the grass. I wanted to see when we needed to start fillin' up the hay mangers for the cattle. I had them checkin' the ponds to make sure they were not frozen over and to break the ice if they were. They need water. The rivers are flowin'. So they should be all right 'til we get a continuous hard freeze. Hopefully, that won't come till January."

I walked up to check on how Sam's house was coming along. I saw Jim.

"Looks pretty good. Got it closed in. How's Lizzie's house?"

"Tim told me it is about the same as this. The snow put us behind some. I hope it will dry out so we can get the roof fully on and get them painted. Those two things will protect it if the winter gets really bad."

"You know, Jim, I think if the mine peter's out. You and Tim could make a livin' puttin' up homes around here. There are more people in and around Durango. They will need homes one day."

"We've talked about investing our profit in the mine. Buy some land outside of town and put up eight or ten homes and sell them for a profit to people that work in town."

"Sounds like you'll use your money for the good. I'm goin' to get to the house. Keep up the good work."

While I was up here, I went to Foster's house. I knocked, and Juanita came to the door.

"Come in, Silver. John is in town at his work."

"John, is it?"

"Yes, since I got it out of him what his first name is."

"Red Bird and me wanted to thank you for all your help with the party and weddin'."

"This was a good wedding and party. I had a good time, and helping was a pleasure. I enjoyed it."

"We noticed that you caught the weddin' bouquet and looked over at Foster. Red Bird and me were wonderin' if something is goin' on. You are old enough to make up your own mind. I did promise Jose that nothin' would happen to you."

"We have just become close. That is all. Please do not tell Jose. He may not understand."

"I love him like I would have my great-grandfather Jeb. He is my best friend. Red Bird has known him since she was a little girl. We just wouldn't want to see either of you hurt."

"Right now, I do love him, but like you do, not like a woman does."

"I won't worry. You are as smart as my wife. I better go home."

"I'll see you, Silver. Come back."

The next day, the children would return to school. Mrs. Gills would be their teacher. The house was quiet. Manuel was cooking supper. He said the party and the wedding had worn out everyone. Lizzie was tired the most. The children were taking a nap. I went to our room to find Red Bird lying down asleep. I was tired, Manuel was right, so I took off my boots and lay down beside Red Bird. I didn't wake until Red Bird woke me for supper. We ate and were all back in bed by nightfall.

The next morning, I tied Blacky to the wagon. We dropped the children at school. I said hello to Jenny. I called her Mrs. Gills. She smiled at that. We parked the wagon in front of Foster's, and I went in to see Bill.

"Hello, you old married man. That woman tamed you yet?"

"Hello Buck. Now I know how you feel for Red Bird. I'm glad you came in. I waited until after the wedding. I wanted to talk to you about how you make your money for the ranch."

"What could that be?"

"The railroad. I know we talked about it. The prices back east were low. It made more sense to drive them yourself. But while you were gone, the price has kept rising until it's about $45 a head. I figured the price of your labor and being away that long. It would now be cheaper to go by rail. You would have to drive them to Grand Junction, but there and back would be only three or four weeks. You could do it three or four times a year. Keep money coming in all year. The cattle buyers would buy them there. You would get your money then. Of course, if prices dropped back down, you could drive them again."

"That sounds good, if the market holds up."

"I talk to Josh and Carolyn. They could ship them up to near where you were and get near what you got for your horses. They could drive their horses and your cattle together to Grand Junction. I also talked to Sam and Ann. She saw the bank building and said it would work well with that wall and a door in the middle and some dressing rooms to try on clothes. They will pay for two of Tim's men to do it. It shouldn't take more than a day or two. I'm going to talk to Mr. Windslow today and make a deal."

"Bill, when did you have time to get to know Jenny on your honeymoon?"

"Believe me, Buck, I did. I never knew a woman could be so wonderful."

"They do have their charms."

"I can't believe, first, Foster has made a complete change, and now we are going to have a lady gunsmith."

"I came in to talk to you about something. You made me forget. I'll remember what it was by the time I get home. See you later."

"Sam came over to Foster's.

"Foster, mind if I hitch a ride to the ranch?"

I said, "That gal already kicked you out?"

"No, Silver, I'm goin' to get that four-seater and come get my bride and take her home. Carolyn and Josh too."

"Sure, hop in."

The children jumped in, and we saw Jenny go in Bill's office. When we got to the ranch, Sam hitched the team up and headed to town. When they came back, Sam dropped Carolyn and Josh off in front of the house and him and Ann headed for the barn. It was time to begin their new life. Josh and Carolyn came to the door and knocked. I went out front.

"Son, come on in. You live here, for a while. Just walk in. It will save us a lot of steps."

"Yes, Silver."

Lizzie came down and hugged Carolyn and Josh.

"Red Bird helped me fix up the room next to mine for you."

"Thank you, Mother, and, Red Bird."

"Buck told me you enjoyed your honeymoon."

"Yes, Red Bird, it went real good. I think Josh was happy."

"Yes, I am, and it will last forever."

"You are all here. If you don't mind, I'm goin' to ask Bill to look into buyin' some of Young's land for you. If it's for sale. Horses need lots of land."

"If you don't think we're getting in too deep to you."

"I know you will make a go of it. I just know it. We'll just fence around it so the horses won't wonder off. They go farther than cattle do. Bill told you about the railroad. It will be easy to get them to market. You won't have to leave this pretty one for long."

"Oh, Buck, you're embarrassing me."

"You're right. She's downright beautiful."

"You men, I tell you."

The next morning, I rode to town to talk to Bill. He was at his office.

"Bill, I remembered what I was goin' to ask you yesterday. I want you to try to find out what is goin' to happen to Young's land and see if you can buy it for Lizzie and Carolyn, and now Josh. If you can pay for it out of my account but put it in their names."

"I've looked a little but haven't found anything yet. Tell Sam and Ann that the building is theirs. Have them come in and sign the papers. Then they can start on the work and move in."

The children saw me as I came out of the office. Song Bird came running to me, and I picked her up, and then BJ was beside me.

"Song Bird, you are getting big. Pretty soon, I won't be able to pick you up. Come on, I'm goin' to, Foster."

We walked in Foster's shop.

"BJ, Foster told me you were interested in learnin' the leather business."

"I sure am, Pa."

"Foster, you heard him."

"So you'se want to learn what I'se do?" "Sure would, Uncle John."

"Well, let's see. When can you'se work?"

"Right now."

"How about after school for an hour? Till we go home. Then on Saturday all day."

"Really! That would be great."

"Don't you'se want to know how much I'se pay and what you do?"

"Yes, sir."

"Well, to start, you'se would have to sweep out the store and out front. We have to keep it clean. Then just watch me'se and see how I'se get done. Then later, you'se can help the customers. Then one day, when I think you have learned, I'll let you work on some small piece that needs work. I'se pay you twenty-five cents for after school and $2.00 on Saturday. That's $3.25 a week. I'll pay you on Saturday after work. How's that, Buck? You'se the expert on wages? What you'se think?"

"Sounds fair to me for his first job."

"When you learn more, I'll pay you more."

"Pa, I want to work," Song Bird said.

"I don't know. This is heavy work for a little girl. I know. You can ask Mrs. Ganger. I don't know if she'll have work, but you can ask."

17

I put Song Bird in front of me on Blacky. BJ had stayed to start his new career. We rode up to the barn, and Sam came up while we were unsaddling Blacky.

"Sam, can Mrs. Ganger hire me?" Song Bird asked.

"Song Bird, go on up to the house. You can ask her later. Right now I need to talk to Sam."

"Yes, Pa."

"I'll ask her soon, Song Bird."

"Thank you, Sam."

She ran off to the house to tell her mother for sure.

"Bill has the papers for you and Ann to sign. The buildin' is yours. You can get Tim to send over two men to get started on the inside. How you feel, Mr. Property Owner?"

"I told her it's happened so fast. I was a lone cowboy and mine owner, and now I'm married and a property owner. It's unreal."

"And you have your position here. Let Pa know when you're ready to take over, and Josh will be your assistant."

"We'll go in today. I'll talk to Ann about Song Bird."

"She just thought about workin' 'cause BJ started trainin' with Foster today. She don't need to. It's just a little girl's whim. If she does, I'll pay Ann what she pays Song Bird. I'm sure she'll grow tired of it soon."

"We'll see. Now I better go tell Ann."

The next week, after the papers had been signed, Red Bird and I, and Sam and Ann, and even Song Bird, took the two wagons into Ann's new business. One was called "Ganger Dress Shop, and under that, it said "Made by hand and made to order." The other said "Ganger's Gun Shop," and under that, "Guns and rifles sold and repairs of all kinds, special designs made. They both said, "Owner: Ann and Sam Ganger." We unloaded both wagons except one, which was half filled with furniture for the house. She had so many guns and rifles and ammunition that I was very surprised. There were some that I had never seen.

"My dad made some of them. But I made most of what I have. These dresses I made, and some came from Paris and London."

Song Bird was sweeping out the stores. Ann had given her a job after school for an hour. She said when Song Bird was a little older, she would show her how she made the dresses. She had always hoped to have shops like these. She had kept everything she had made.

Thanksgiving, we had a big celebration. It was hard for many of the town's people to come for it had snowed three inches. We took the wagon and made ruts in the snow all the way to town. Some made it. Most didn't. We still had a good old time with singing and dancing and eating. Mr. Windslow and his wife made it, and John and his wife and children, and Ed and his wife. Bill and Jenny stayed the night. The next morning, they went back to town with Ann and Foster, with the children behind them. It was Ann's first day to open. She knew it would be slow with the snow on the ground. She hoped with Christmas a month away, she would have some business. People had been coming around after we had unloaded the wagons. Sure enough, two weeks before Christmas, her business picked up. Men were getting dresses for their wives and daughters, and Ann had a policy that if they didn't fix the dress, the women could bring them back to get fitted right. Then next door the mothers would bring in their sons to pick out some type of firearms for the father. She was very happy.

Just before Christmas, Red Bird started getting sick every morning. Then she would be all right. I took her to see the doc. We walked in the office, and there was Bill sitting, looking all worried.

"Bill, what are you doing here? You sick?"

"No, Jenny's been sick, and I'm worried about her. She's never sick as long as I've known her. Why are you and Red Bird here?"

"Same reason. She's been sick."

"I know what it is, but Buck does not believe me."

"You know the doc said you couldn't have any more."

"Is Jenny sick in the morning?"

"Yes, how did you know?"

"I'm sick in the morning. I know I will have a baby in seven and a half months. You remember that night of the wedding? The bearskin rug in front of the fireplace. I felt it then."

"Red Bird, I don't know."

The door opened, and the doc and Jenny came out, and Jenny had a big smile on her face. "Bill, nothing's wrong with her that about seven and a half months won't cure."

"We're going to be parents," Jenny said.

Bill fell down in the chair with his mouth wide open. I shut his mouth and shook his hand. "Get a hold of yourself, Bill."

"A daddy. Red Bird said, but—"

That was all he could get out.

"What's this, Red Bird?"

"I told Bill I was going to have a baby, and so were you."

"You don't mean ..."

"Doc, this couldn't be. You said she couldn't have any more."

"I've been wrong before. The good Lord gives us what he thinks we should have. Come on in, Red Bird."

"Bill, I'm going to wait to see about Red Bird."

"Daddy, bearskin."

"Bill, snap to."

"Buck, I don't know about him, smart as he is. "Bearskin! What did that mean?"

"A baby will do that to a man. I was like that when BJ came along. I'll let Red Bird tell you about the bearskin."

The door opened, and they came out.

"I told you, Buck Taylor. I know what I feel."

"You should listen to your wife. Seven and a half months. You two better not have them at the same time. She might need to stay in bed toward her time. She had a hard time with Song Bird."

"Red Bird, what did Bill mean? All he would say was bearskin."

"Night of the wedding, Buck took you three to town. He came back, and I was waiting for him on our bearskin in front of the fireplace. I knew then when it happened. You come to ranch on Christmas. You are part of our family."

"Thank you, Doc. I better get Bill home. He would be no good at the office in this condition."

As we four were leaving the doc's office, in walked Sam and Ann; and then Josh and Carolyn came in about five minutes later.

"You sick, Ann? You too, Carolyn?"

"Yes, in the morning."

"Me too, Doc."

"Good luck, Doc."

"I don't mind business, but all at once? Come on in, Ann. Carolyn, I'll be with you in a while. The good Lord does work miracles."

We found out later that Ann and Carolyn were having babies. Doc was beside himself. He said we should outlaw getting married on the same day.

Christmas Day was very special. I went to the bunkhouse in the morning and gave out bonuses and invited everyone to the house for Christmas dinner. Jose, Manuel, and Juanita got with the wives and made a big dinner. Lizzie had been beside herself when she found out about Carolyn, and a little concerned because of what happened, and she was only fifteen. But Doc had a talk with her, and now she was happy.

The winter was mild again this year. We had snow, but only one blizzard in early February that lasted only a day. It was a week after when I said, "Josh, I think we should get the boys together and go fence some of that ranch, and after that, we'll go round up some wild stock from the range."

"It's not much going on around here. Everything taken care of. A few men can stay and make sure the cattle can get water and have hay. I'm ready."

After the snow melted, we took ten men and picked up some fence and posts and gates at the general store and headed for Lizzie's ranch. It took us four days to complete. We left the corners where we could put more gates in easily in case Young's land became available. Then the gates could be left open or closed to grow grass for hay. Josh and I went to the house.

"Buck, it looks big, and that barn is huge."

"You need a barn that size for hay in the winter. Just like we do. You've seen the two big barns out on our range full of hay. Why, in the late summer, the men think they've become farmers. And the bunkhouse is goin' to be for ten men. You don't have to fill it unless you get Young's land. When you take them to market, you can hire more men like we did."

"That house, should it be that size?"

"You'll have four people livin' in it shortly after it's finished, Daddy."

"Isn't it great? I still can't believe it. After we got her to the doc's out of the Indians' hands, he said she might not be able to have any. I haven't told her what Doc had said back then."

"Well, look what he told us after Song Bird, and we're having another. I wouldn't tell her and just be glad that God saw fit to let her have children."

"I thank him every day, and pray to let her be all right."

"We better catch up to the boys and get back to town. I think we should talk to Bill about Young's land. I want you to hear what he has to say. You're goin' to represent Lizzie in most dealings."

The men went to the ranch. Josh and I went to the office.

"I'm glad to see you both. I have found out some things about Young's land.

"First, Bill, how's Jenny? Red Bird and Carolyn are fine."

"Sorry, I get carried away when I hear some exciting news. Jenny is doing well. Mrs. Jenson is taking over the school until Jenny has the baby. We don't know just how she can teach and take care of the baby. I know we'll figure it out."

"That's great! Now, Bill, what did you find out?"

"Where Young's house sits, he owned and paid taxes on. But the rest that he stole from the farmers and ranchers, he owned it but never paid taxes on any of it. There are no heirs to be found. I put notices in a lot of papers even back east, and no response."

Josh said, "What exactly does that mean to us?"

"He never put it together into a large piece of land. So each part has taxes due on it. We can pay the taxes, and the land is Lizzie's. If you don't think Lizzie would mind, Jenny and I would like to pay the taxes on one part closer to town because of our jobs. We would be neighbors, and our children can grow up together."

"You want to build a house away from town?"

"We decided it would be good."

Josh said, "I'm sure Lizzie would like that. Maybe Carolyn can take care of your baby with ours while you two are at work. Until they start school."

"Josh, you already have them in school. I'm getting to know women. We'll let them talk about that."

I said, "Bill, you are a fast learner." We all laughed.

"I think if we can get it, do it. If we don't, that will limit the size of the herd you can have. Someone will get it, and you won't be able to get it later. This way, you will know your neighbor."

"Josh, I know you are going to make most of the decisions about the ranch. I will have a paper drawn up that will do just that. It wouldn't let you sell any of the land. It would let you buy and sell horses and hire and fire men and what to pay them. I'm sure in a short time Lizzie will make Carolyn and you partners. But until then, this will protect her. She might already think of you two as partners. I'll have those papers ready also. I'll come out in a few days and explain it all to her and Carolyn."

"As long as you explain it to them."

"I will. This way, she knows you didn't marry Carolyn to get your hands on the ranch."

"Bill, go ahead and get all the land you can. Take it out of my account but put it in Lizzie's name. Get the part that you want. I talked to Foster, and he's headed for the mine soon as the weather stays nice. Probably when the first wagon comes in with ore. He'll see if he can find another vein in another direction. You know, we have taken more silver out of that mine than I ever thought we would."

Sam was going to take over the operation of the ranch from Pa April 1. Ann was doing well in both of her businesses and had started making clothes for women, having babies, and also baby clothes. She already had three buyers.

Bill came out and explained all the options Lizzie had. Lizzie chose to make Josh and Carolyn a half-and-half partner. She said she trusted those two with everything she had.

Soon as Sam took over for Dad, Mother talked Dad into going to St. Louis for three weeks. She told him that they had to leave soon so they would be back in time for the baby's arrival. I didn't think that Dad wanted to go, but it was something that Mother had always wanted to do. They had the money, so they left the morning of April 3 on the stage to Denver, then on the train to St. Louis.

Bill had been able to get all the land for Lizzie and his part also. It was ten thousand acres. Bill and Jenny's were three hundred acres. They were living in Bill's house now. Jenny had only been renting hers. They had talked to Tim to start on their house after the other two. That would be soon.

Ann's furniture wasn't enough to fill their new house. She, Carolyn, and, of course, Lizzie and Red Bird. Jenny just happened to be there also. It was clear to us men that the houses would have similar furnishings in them and Jenny's later on. They spent the whole day one Saturday at the general store. I felt sorry for Ed. I thought he was going to pull out the little hair he had left. They were asking him, "How long will it take to get this or that? What color it came in? Then came the baby things and furniture. The clothes they were buying from Ann. They were there all day. But finally, they had made up their minds and made an order. I could see Red Bird now, the difference in her from her simple life into the world of the white man. She had stayed the same in some ways, and others had changed. Some I liked, and some I did not. Even with the changes, she was still my young Indian princess that I had fallen in love with many years ago at the pond outside Dancing Bear's village. Sometimes I wish we could return to those days when life was hard but simpler. I always would love her so deeply.

The next day, Red Bird had me hitch up the team to the big buggy.

"After church, we will go to see the house on Lizzie's ranch. I want to see it. It won't be very long until it is done. I may not get to see it again until after the baby."

We rode out to the ranch after church. The barn was finished, and the bunkhouse. Everyone got out and went in the house. The doors were up, the windows in. The roof was in place. The kitchen and water closets were not complete. The stairs were in place, so we went up to the second floor. The four bedrooms were not done. There were three fireplaces. Two were in between the wall of the four bedrooms. The third was in the large bedroom with a water closet in it. The other water closet was in the middle for the other three bedrooms.

Jenny said, "Now I know we're going to have Tim do our house. I would like a big water closet with a big tub like Red Bird's in it. I don't like going to the outhouse."

Red Bird said, "Jenny should try going behind a bush like I did for seventeen years."

We all had to laugh. So she did remember some of the old days.

"Red Bird, how about takin' a bath in the pond?"

"That I did not mind after I met you there."

"She got in and washed my clothes with soap root."

"I like the soap I use now. It smells better."

"You two should write a book about how you met and fell in love and stayed in love. Two people came together from different worlds and made it last."

"Maybe, when Jenny teaches me to write better and we get old."

"Lizzie, I can see you and your children are going to have a very nice home."

"All thanks to Buck and Red Bird. I see this, and it is so hard to believe."

"Not me. I did nothing."

"We wouldn't be here without you and Molly taking care of us all those months. I don't know anyone else that would have taken us in, and Buck and Bill took up for our ranch. It wouldn't have been."

"Tim said both houses would be ready in a month. Josh, tomorrow we will get ten men and get the whole ranch fenced in with gates to be shut to let a pasture mature for hay. It's goin' to happen, Lizzie."

The next morning, we picked up more fence and four more gates and went to Lizzie's ranch. We worked hard all day. On the way back to our ranch, the men were complaining about being sore all over.

"I'm sore too, that's what we get for taking it easy all winter. I sure wish we had some of those hot springs. You better eat and get some rest. Tomorrow it will be the same."

We went out there for a week. It finally was all fenced in. The boys headed home, and Josh and I went to the house to check on the progress. Tim was there.

"It will be done in two weeks or sooner. Josh, the women might want to come out in about a week and start cleaning the saw dust and dirt we have tracked in. Sam's place will be ready next week before your parents get back."

"The furniture should be in by then. I'll get most of my men, and we'll get everything in both houses put in. Looks like you're movin' into your house soon. Tomorrow we'll take men and go up to the plateau where we got Dancing Bear's white stallion."

I asked Manuel and Foster to look after the women. We might be gone two weeks. We left the next day, and even Sam came along. We packed our saddlebags with food and pots and some pans. The wagon would just slow us down. Five men stayed at the ranch. We were going to have a holding pen until we had as many as could be had. Then we would bring them to Lizzie's ranch. I rode Blacky, and I had Josh ride Lagger. Both horses were getting up there in age. It took us three days to get there. We built a large pen in a canyon that was big enough for a thousand head. We had twenty men to drive them back.

The next morning, we split up into three groups. We would go in and out of canyons. Up and down the gullies. The stallion we had seen got away, but we got a hundred of his mares. That night, we just ate and sat by the fire.

"We need to get two or three stallions if we can get a thousand horses. I'm goin' to lend Blacky and Lagger to you for studs. I know they're fine horses. You can let me have their first folds."

"Sure, Buck. Anything you want. I never expected to get two hundred horses, much less a thousand. I will never forget this. I made sure that Sam is writing down what we'll owe you for all the men's help for this and the fencing."

The next two days, we got another 400 head and one stallion. He was raising cane, but the pen held. Another three days, and we managed to round up 300 head and 1 more stallion. It took two more days to round up 250 more head and 1 more stallion.

The next morning, we left for the ranch. I had two men on each stallion with ropes attacked to each. The mares would follow the stallions. The other men just kept them from wandering too far off. The only night on the trail, we tied the stallions with double ropes around three different trees to keep them separated. Once on the ranch, they should split up and make a section of the ranch their own. Josh and Sam and I with five others stayed up all night. It was late the next afternoon when we ran them in the fence. We put a stallion in each pasture and let the mares find their stallions. We then closed the gates so the stallions couldn't get at each other. We wouldn't want them to hurt or kill each other. Hopefully, the mares would keep them calm and they wouldn't try to jump the fence.

"Josh, you and me will come out here every day and see how there doin'. Maybe try openin' one gate after a few days and see what happens. It might take some time for them. They have plenty of grass and the creek and pond. I'm glad we put the fence down the middle of the lake."

I put three men to watch them that first night. We stopped by the general store. The furniture would be arriving in two days, and Bill had word my parents would be in tomorrow. I found out from Bill that the townswomen had gone out to Lizzie's ranch and cleaned it up from top to bottom.

"Buck, you know I took the papers out for Lizzie to sign, and she would have no part of one. She signed the other one that gave half of the ranch to Carolyn and Josh. She said, 'He's my son now, so they get half.' She wants a brand with a large *S* with a large *T* through it."

"I'll have the blacksmith make that up. It's goin' to be a while before those wild horses can be branded."

"How many did you round up?"

"Little over a thousand and three stallions. No tellin' how many are with foals. It's spring, you know. Speakin' of foals, I better get home and check on Red Bird. How's Jenny doin'?"

"She's good, real good. Red Bird is fine. Carolyn and Lizzie have been keeping a good watch on her. Won't let her do much of anything. I can't believe you got that many horses. It will take a while to brand them."

"I'll be in to pick up Mom and Dad in the mornin'."

When I arrived at the ranch, I found Josh and Sam with the help of two others. They were unloading the last of Ann's wagon into the house.

"Is it ready?"

"Sure is. The women cleaned it while we were gone. We have most of what we need until the furniture gets here."

"My folks should be here in the mornin', and the furniture the next day."

"They can have their house back."

"Sam, get what food you need from Mother's pantry. When you stock up, tell Ed to put it on the ranch bill. Did you stop and see Ann?"

"Sure did. She's fat and sassy." He laughed.

"I better see how mine's coming along."

After putting Blacky in the barn and giving him and Lagger an apple, I headed to the house. Red Bird met me halfway. She flew into my arms, and we kissed. I picked her up and carried her up the stairs into the house.

"You look good. Have you been takin' care of yourself? You still feel wonderful in my arms."

"I'm big and fat."

"And I love you. Have you been a good girl?"

"I have, but I'll be a better one tonight."

"Yes, I know you will."

The next morning, I took the children in the buggy to school. Then I went to wait for the stage. I didn't wait too long, and here it came down the street from the east. First thing I noticed was that Mother had on a new dress and a hat and looked younger.

"How's the ranch?"

"That's all he talked about. How's Sam doing?"

"Mother, you look younger. It must have done you good."

"It did. All the shops, and it was quite nice even if your father didn't enjoy it. How's my daughter doing carrying that new baby?"

"The doc says she's doin' well. Pa, I know how you and Josh got along on the drive. We just came in yesterday with a thousand horses for Lizzie and Carolyn and Josh's ranch. You know about horses, you can give him some pointers if you have the time. He could use the help. Sam and Ann moved into their house last night."

"Now let's get to the ranch. I want to see Red Bird, and then Ann and her house."

The next day, a rider came up to the ranch.

"Buck, Ed said to tell you that the furniture is in and ready to unload."

I rounded up fifteen men with Josh and Sam. Sam took five men and one wagon to our ranch, and Josh and I took ten men and two wagons to their ranch. We unloaded everything and put it where we thought it should go. Then here came Carolyn and Lizzie in the buggy.

"Josh, you should know Mother and me would want to be here."

"I was concerned about your condition."

"There's nothing wrong with me."

Lizzie said, "Carolyn, take it easy. He just loves you. He was thinking about the baby."

She started crying. "Josh, I'm sorry I snapped at you. Would you please help Mother and me down?"

"Don't worry, Josh. It's just her condition."

"I know, Ma."

She was directing men where to put everything, the dishes and pot and pans to the kitchen. Which bed went in what room? The baby's bed and clothes to their big bedroom. Some furniture went in the formal front room and the dining room. It all had its place, and Carolyn and her mother knew where that place was. We men just did the heavy work; the women would put all the smaller things where they went.

There was a commotion in front of the house. One of the men called out, "Josh, Buck, you better come out here."

There were three riders that we didn't know. They looked a little familiar.

"What can we do for you?"

"I'm not like my brother. I don't beat around the bush. What are you doing on my brother's ranch and in his house?"

"Who are you? And who is your bother?"

"I'm Sean Young, and these are my other two brothers, Jeff and Tom."

Josh said, "This is my mother's and my wife's and my land. You must be Larry Young's brothers. His place is a ways east. You'll find him buried there. He tried to steal all this land."

Lizzie and Carolyn came out onto the porch, with each holding a shotgun. I was right beside Josh.

"I was the one that killed your coward of a brother. He beat up on women and took my little daughter. The sheriff was with us."

"You and your pregnant bitch better get off this land."

"Mister, you don't talk to my wife like that. You had better draw before my wife blows you off your horse. We'll plant y'all beside your brother."

The silence was deadly. The seconds went by like hours. But then the silence was broken when the three brothers pulled their guns. Josh and I drew a split second after. Theirs were barely out when Josh and mine were out and level. As the flames came out of the ends of our guns, there were two blasts from the shotguns. Both women had pulled the triggers as our guns went off. Before the slugs entered their bodies, you could see the great surprise in their eyes that this could happen to them. The three men lay dead in the dirt.

Carolyn ran into Josh's arms and kissed him. Then Lizzie went to him.

"It's so good to have a son like you. Why can't people leave us to be happy? My husband and son died for this land, and not anyone is going to take it from us."

They were both crying.

"I'm so glad you and Buck are all right."

"Are you and Mother all right?"

"We are, now and forever."

Josh said, "How were they to know I took fast draw lessons from Ross and Buck on the cattle drive? Now I really feel I can protect you and this land. I will have no man call my wife a name like that."

I had three men take the bodies to Young's ranch and bury them beside their brother.

"Bring back the horses and put them in the pasture, and the guns and saddles."

"I don't want them," Josh said.

"Then take the saddles to Foster's and the guns to Ann's shop."

We finished up the house and went to the ranch after letting John know what had happened. By the end of May, Josh, Carolyn, and Lizzie had moved to their ranch. Dad would go over to their ranch and show and tell Josh all that he knew about ranching and horses. Dad enjoyed the time spent over there, and Josh soaked in all the knowledge like a sponge that was dry and now was wet.

By the end of June, Lizzie and Carolyn had gotten the house in order. They had a big party, and a lot of people from town came to see the new STARDER-THORTON RANCH and the big ranch house. The gifts were piled up beside the tables beside the front doors. Red Bird insisted on going against Doc's wishes.

I drove slowly all the way, and everything went well. Ann had trained one of the ladies in town to watch the dress shop and a man to sell the guns in her gun shop. School was out for the summer, so Jenny was supervising Tim and his men who were building their house closer to town.

All four mothers-to-be were at home now until the babies came. Red Bird was confined to the house. She was bigger than she was the other two times. She went up and down the stairs as little as possible.

On July 9, 1883, Red Bird couldn't get out of bed in the morning. "Buck, it is time. I hurt all night."

I sent Manuel to get Doc. By the time they returned, we had another beautiful little girl and a handsome baby boy. Doc checked them over, and everything was well with the two and Red Bird. Red Bird was beside herself and was crying tears of joy as Mother and Father came into the room. Mother saw the two, and tears started rolling down her face.

"What are you going to name these two youngsters?"

"Why, we agreed on Indian Summer Taylor and Robert Taylor."

BJ and Song Bird came in to see their new brother and sister.

"They're so tiny," Song Bird said.

Doc said, "That's because there's two of them, and they were three weeks early. Thank God. Three more to go."

That's when Doc left our little family.

It was five days later, on July 14, that Doc was called to Carolyn's bedside. She had a very hard time, and their son wasn't born for twenty hours. Carolyn was tired but well. The baby boy was strong and healthy for being two weeks early. Josh nearly fainted dead away, but he recovered fast. Lizzie was crying while looking at the baby. They named him Randall Thorton.

The doc said, "It is kind of you to wait this long after Red Bird. Now only two more."

The next one was on July 24. Doc was called back out to our ranch. It was Ann, and Sam was walking the floors. But before he wore a hole in them, they had a handsome baby boy. BJ and Song Bird came down to see the baby. It let everyone know he had arrived in this world with a very health cry.

"Sam, he sounds like you when you're singin'." Everyone laughed.

They named him David Wayne Ganger after Ann's father.

Doc left, saying, "Just one more. I still think they should outlaw getting married on the same day in the same town with only one poor old doc."

Everyone was laughing as he left.

Bill was beside himself. It was August 1, and still they waited. The next night, Doc was called once again. It was early morning, August 3, and the little girl was in a big hurry she arrived an hour after Doc arrived. They named her Molly Gills. My mother was elated over their choice of a name.

Doc just sat in the chair and said one word: "Finally!"

This was the summer of 1883, when the five babies were born to three mothers of the first triple wedding in Colorado and their best friend, Red Bird.

THE END

www.ingramcontent.com/pod-product-compliance
Lightning Source LLC
Chambersburg PA
CBHW030354310726
48979CB00001B/299

* 9 7 8 1 9 9 8 7 8 4 6 6 0 *